I0585075

John Ross Browne

The Land of Thor

John Ross Browne

The Land of Thor

ISBN/EAN: 9783742813800

Manufactured in Europe, USA, Canada, Australia, Japa

Cover: Foto ©Andreas Hilbeck / pixelio.de

Manufactured and distributed by brebook publishing software
(www.brebook.com)

John Ross Browne

The Land of Thor

THE
LAND OF THOR.

BY

J. ROSS BROWNE,

AUTHOR OF

"YUSEF," "CRUSOE'S ISLAND," "AN AMERICAN FAMILY IN
GERMANY," ETC.

Illustrated by the Author.

NEW YORK:

HARPER & BROTHERS, PUBLISHERS,

FRANKLIN SQUARE.

1870.

AN AMERICAN FAMILY IN GERMANY. Illustrated by the Author. 12mo, Cloth, $2 00.

THE LAND OF THOR. Illustrated by the Author. 12mo, Cloth, $2 00.

CRUSOE'S ISLAND: A Ramble in the Footsteps of Alexander Selkirk. With Sketches of Adventure in California and Washoe. Illustrations. 12mo, Cloth, $1 75.

YUSEF; or, The Journey of the Frangi. A Crusade in the East. With Illustrations. 12mo, Cloth, $1 75.

Published by HARPER & BROTHERS, New York.

Entered, according to Act of Congress, in the year one thousand eight hundred and sixty-seven, by HARPER & BROTHERS, in the Clerk's Office of the District Court of the Southern District of New York.

CONTENTS.

CONTENTS.

THE LAND OF THOR.

CHAPTER I.

IMPRESSIONS OF ST. PETERSBURG.

I LANDED at St. Petersburg with a knapsack on my back and a hundred dollars in my pocket. An extensive tour along the borders of the Arctic Circle was before me, and it was necessary I should husband my resources.

In my search for a cheap German gasthaus I walked nearly all over the city. My impressions were probably tinctured by the circumstances of my position, but it seemed to me I had never seen so strange a place.

The best streets of St. Petersburg resemble on an inferior scale the best parts of Paris, Berlin, and Vienna. Nothing in the architecture conveys any idea of national taste except the glittering cupolas of the churches, the showy colors of the houses, and the vast extent and ornamentation of the palaces. The general aspect of the city is that of immense level space. Built upon islands, cut up into various sections by the branches of the Neva, intersected by canals, destitute of eminent points of observation, the whole city has a scattered and incongruous effect—an incomprehensible remoteness about it, as if one might continually wander about without finding the centre. Some parts, of course, are better than others; some streets are indicative of wealth and luxury; but without a guide it is extremely difficult to determine whether there are not still finer buildings and quarters in the main part of the city—if you could only get at it. The eye wanders continually in search of heights and

LAWYERS AND SHIPWRIGHTS.

prominent objects. Even the Winter Palace, the Admiralty, and the Izaak Church lose much of their grandeur in the surrounding deserts of space from the absence of contrast with familiar and tangible objects. It is only by a careful examination in detail that one can become fully sensible of their extraordinary magnificence. Vast streets of almost interminable length, lined by insignificant two-story houses with green roofs and yellow walls;

RUSSIAN AND FINN.

vast open squares or ploschads; palaces, public buildings, and churches, dwindled down to mere toy-work in the deserts of space intervening; countless throngs of citizens and carriages scarcely bigger than ants to the eye; broad sheets of water, dotted with steamers, brigs, barks, wood-barges and row-boats, still infinitesimal in the distance; long rows of trees, forming a foliage to some of the principal promenades, with glimpses of gardens and shrubbery at remote intervals; canals and dismal green swamps—not all at one sweep of the eye, but visible from time to time in the course of an afternoon's ramble, are the most prominent characteristics of this wonderful city. A vague sense of loneliness impresses the traveler from a distant land—as if in his pilgrimage through foreign climes he had at length wandered into the midst of a strange and peculiar civilization—a boundless desert of wild-looking streets, a waste of colossal palaces, of gilded churches and glistening waters, all perpetually dwindling away before him in the infinity of space. He sees a people strange and unfamiliar in costume and expression; fierce, stern-looking officers, rigid in features, closely shaved, and dressed in glittering uniforms; grave, long-bearded priests, with square-topped black turbans, their flowing black drapery trailing in the dust; pale women richly and elegantly dressed, gliding unattended through mazes of the crowd; rough, half-savage serfs, in dirty pink shirts, loose trowsers, and big boots, bowing down before the shrines on the bridges and public places; the drosky drivers, with their long beards, small bell-shaped hats, long blue coats and fire-bucket boots, lying half asleep upon their rusty little vehicles awaiting a customer, or dashing away at a headlong pace over the rough cobble-paved streets, and so on of every class and kind. The traveler wanders about from place to place, gazing into the strange faces he meets, till the sense of loneliness becomes oppressive. An invisible but impassable barrier seems to stand between him and the moving multitude. He hears languages that fall without a meaning upon his ear; wonders at the soft inflections of the voices; vainly seeks some familiar look or word; thinks it strange that he alone should be cut off from all communion with the souls of men around him; and then wonders if they have souls like other people, and why

there is no kindred expression in their faces—no visible
consciousness of a common humanity. It is natural that
every stranger in a strange city should experience this
feeling to some extent, but I know of no place where it
seems so strikingly the case as in St. Petersburg. Accustomed as I was to strange cities and strange languages,
I never felt utterly lonely until I reached this great mart
of commerce and civilization. The costly luxury of the
palaces; the wild Tartaric glitter of the churches; the
tropical luxuriance of the gardens; the brilliant equipages of the nobility; the display of military power ; the
strange and restless throngs forever moving through
the haunts of business and pleasure; the uncouth costumes of the lower classes, and the wonderful commin-
gling of sumptuous elegance and barbarous filth, visible
in almost every thing, produced a singular feeling of mingled wonder and isolation—as if the solitary traveler
were the only person in the world who was not permitted to comprehend the spirit and import of the scene, or
take a part in the great drama of life in which all others
seemed to be engaged. I do not know if plain, practical men are generally so easily impressed by external objects, but I must confess that when I trudged along the
streets with my knapsack on my back, looking around in
every direction for a gasthaus; when I spoke to people
in my peculiar style of French and German, and received
unintelligible answers in Russian ; when I got lost among
palaces and grand military establishments, instead of
finding the gasthaus, and finally attracted the attention
of the surly-looking guards, who were stationed about
every where, by the anxious pertinacity with which I ex-
amined every building, a vague notion began to get possession of me that I was a sort of outlaw, and would
sooner or later be seized and dragged before the Czar for
daring to enter such a magnificent city in such an uncouth and unbecoming manner. When I cast my eyes
up at the sign-boards, and read about grand fabrications
and steam-companies, and walked along the quays of the

Neva, and saw wood enough piled up in big broad-bottom-
ed boats to satisfy the wants of myself and family for ten
thousand years; when I strolled into the Nevskoi, and jostled my way through crowds of nobles, officers, soldiers,
dandies, and commoners, stopping suddenly at every pic-
ture-shop, gazing dreamily into the gorgeous millinery
establishments, pondering thoughtfully over the glittering wares of the jewelers, lagging moodily by the grand
cafés, and snuffing reflectively the odors that came from
the grand restaurations—when all this occurred, and I
went down into a beer-cellar and made acquaintance with
a worthy German, and he asked me if I had any meerschaums to sell, the notion that I had no particular business in so costly and luxurious a place began to grow
stronger than ever. A kind of dread came over me that
the mighty spirit of Peter the Great would come riding
through the scorching hot air on a gale of snowflakes, at
the head of a bloody phalanx of Muscovites, and, rising
in his stirrups as he approached, would demand of me in
a voice of thunder, "Stranger, how much money have
you got?" to which I could only answer, "Sublime and
potent Czar, taking the average value of my Roaring
Grizzly, Dead Broke, Gone Case, and Sorrowful Countenance, and placing it against the present value of Russian securities, I consider it within the bounds of reason
to say that I hold about a million of rubles!" But if he
should insist upon an exhibit of ready cash—there was
the rub! It absolutely made me feel weak in the knees
to think of it. Indeed, a horrid suspicion seized me, after
I had crossed the bridge and begun to renew my search
for a cheap gasthaus on the Vasoli Ostron, that every fat,
neatly-shaved man I met, with small gray eyes, a polished hat on his head drawn a little over his brow, his lips
compressed, and his coat buttoned closely around his
body, was a rich banker, and that he was saying to himself as I passed, "That fellow with the slouched hat and
the knapsack is a suspicious character, to say the least
of him. It becomes my duty to warn the police of his

COOPER'S SHOP AND RESIDENCE

movements. I suspect him to be a Hungarian refu-
gee."

With some difficulty, I succeeded at length in finding
just such a place as I desired—clean and comfortable
enough, considering the circumstances, and not unusually fertile in vermin for a city like St. Petersburg, which
produces all kinds of troublesome insects spontaneously.
There was this advantage in my quarters, in addition to
their cheapness—that the proprietor and attendants spoke
several of the Christian languages, including German,
which, of all languages in the world, is the softest and
most euphonious to my ear — when I am away from
Frankfort. Besides, my room was very advantageously
arranged for a solitary traveler. Being about eight feet
square, with only one small window overlooking the back
yard, and effectually secured by iron fastenings, so that
nobody could open it, there was no possibility of thieves
getting in and robbing me when the door was shut and
locked on the inside. Its closeness presented an effectual barrier against the night air, which in these high
northern latitudes is considered extremely unwholesome
to sleep in. With the thermometer at 100 degrees Fahrenheit, the atmosphere, to be sure, was a little sweltering during the day, and somewhat thick by night, but
that was an additional advantage, inasmuch as it forced
the occupant to stay out most of the time and see a great
deal more of the town than he could possibly see in his
room.

Having deposited my knapsack and put my extra shirt
in the wash, you will now be kind enough to consider
me the shade of Virgil, ready to lead you, after the
fashion of Dante, through the infernal regions or any
where else within the bounds of justice, even through
St. Petersburg, where the climate in summer is hot
enough to satisfy almost any body. The sun shines
here, in June and July, for twenty hours a day, and
even then scarcely disappears beneath the horizon. I
never experienced such sweltering weather in any part

of the world except Aspinwall. One is fairly boiled with the heat, and might be wrung out like a wet rag. Properly speaking, the day commences for respectable people, and men of enterprising spirit — tourists, pleasure-seekers, gamblers, vagabonds, and the like—about nine or ten o'clock at night, and continues till about four or five o'clock the next morning. It is then St. Petersburg fairly turns out; then the beauty and fashion of the city unfold their wings and flit through the streets, or float in Russian gondolas upon the glistening waters of the Neva; then it is the little steamers skim about from island to island, freighted with a population just waked up to a realizing sense of the pleasures of existence; then is the atmosphere balmy, and the light wonderfully soft and richly tinted; then come the sweet witching hours, when

> "Shady nooks
> Patiently give up their quiet being."

None but the weary, labor-worn serf, who has toiled through the long day in the fierce rays of the sun, can sleep such nights as these. I call them nights, yet what a strange mistake. The sunshine still lingers in the heavens with a golden glow; the evening vanishes dreamily in the arms of the morning; there is nothing to mark the changes—all is soft, gradual, and illusory. A peculiar and almost supernatural light glistens upon the gilded domes of the churches; the glaring waters of the Neva are alive with gondolas; miniature steamers are flying through the winding channels of the islands; strains of music float upon the air; gay and festive throngs move along the promenades of the Nevskoi; gilded and glittering equipages pass over the bridges and disappear in the shadowy recesses of the islands. Whatever may be unseemly in life is covered by a rich and mystic drapery of twilight. The floating bath-houses of the Neva, with their variegated tressel-work and brilliant colors, resemble fairy palaces; and the plashing of the bathers falls upon the ear like the gambols

MERCHANT, PEDDLER, AND COACHMAN.

of water-spirits. Not far from the Izaak Bridge, the equestrian statue of Peter the Great stands out in bold relief on a pedestal of granite; the mighty Czar, casting an eagle look over the waters of the Neva, while his noble steed rears over the yawning precipice in front, crushing a serpent beneath his hoof. The spirit of Peter the Great still lives throughout Russia; but it is better understood in the merciless blasts of winter than in the soft glow of the summer nights.

Wander with me now, and let us take a look at the Winter Palace—the grandest pile, perhaps, ever built by human hands. Six thousand people occupy it during the long winter months, and well they may, for it is a city of palaces in itself. Fronting the Neva, it occupies a space of several acres, its massive walls richly decorated with ornamental designs, a forest of chimneys on top—the whole pile forming an immense oblong square so grand, so massive, so wonderfully rich and varied in its details, that the imagination is lost in a colossal wilderness of architectural beauties. Standing in the open plozchad, we may gaze at this magnificent pile for hours, and dream over it, and picture to our minds the scenes of splendor its inner walls have witnessed; the royal *fêtes* of the Czars; the courtly throngs that have filled its halls; the vast treasures expended in erecting it; the enslaved multitudes, now low in the dust, who have left this monument to speak of human pride, and the sweat and toil that pride must feed upon; and while we gaze and dream thus, a mellow light comes down from the firmament, and the mighty Czars, and their palaces, and armies, and navies, and worldly strifes, what are they in the presence of the everlasting Power? For "it is he that sitteth upon the circle of the earth, and the inhabitants thereof are as grasshoppers."

But these dreamings and these wanderings through this city of palaces would be endless. We may feast our eyes upon the Admiralty, the Winter Palace, the Marble Palace, the Senate-house, the palace of the Grand-duke

Michael, the Column of Alexander, the colleges, universities, imperial gardens and summer-houses, and, after all, we can only feel that they are built upon the necks of an enslaved people; that the mightiest Czars of Russia, in common with the poorest serfs, are but " as grasshoppers upon the earth."

The *istrovoschik* (sneeze and you have the word)—in plain English, the drosky drivers—are a notable feature in St. Petersburg. When I saw them for the first time on the quay of the Wassaly Ostrow, where the steamer from Stettin lands her passengers, the idea naturally impressed my mind that I had fallen among a brotherhood of Pilgrims or Druids. Nothing could be more unique than the incongruity of their costume and occupation. Every man looked like a priest; his long beard, his grave expression of countenance, his little black hat and flowing blue coat, gathered around the waist by means of a sash, his glazed boots reaching above the knees, his slow and measured motions, and the sublime indifference with which he regarded his customers, were singularly impressive. Even the filth and rustiness which formed the most prominent characteristics of the class contributed to the delusion that they might have sprung from a Druidical source, and gathered their dust of travel on the pilgrimage from remote ages down to the present period. It is really something novel, in the line of hackery, to see those sedate fellows sitting on their little droskys awaiting a customer. The force of competition, however, has of late years committed sad inroads upon their dignity, and now they are getting to be about as enterprising and pertinacious as any of their kindred in other parts of the world. The drosky is in itself a curiosity as a means of locomotion. Like the driver, it is generally dirty and dilapidated; but here the similitude ends; for, while the former is often high, his drosky is always low. The wheels are not bigger than those of an ordinary dog-cart, and the seat is only designed for one person, though on a pinch it can accommodate two.

ISTROVOSCHIKS.

Generally it consists of a plank covered with a cushion, extending lengthwise in the same direction as the horse, so that the rider sits astride of it as if riding on horseback; some, however, have been modernized so as to afford a more convenient seat in the usual way. Night and day these droskys are every where to be seen, sometimes drawn up by the sidewalk, the driver asleep, awaiting a customer, but more frequently rattling full tilt over the pavements (the roughest in the world) with a load, consisting, in nine cases out of ten, of a fat old gentleman in military uniform, a very ugly old lady with a lap-dog, or a very dashy young lady glittering with jewels, on her way, perhaps, to the Confiseur's or somewhere else. But in a city like St. Petersburg, where it is at least two or three miles from one place to another, every body with twenty kopecks in his pocket uses the drosky. It is the most convenient and economical mode of locomotion for all ordinary purposes, hence the number of them is very large. On some of the principal streets it is marvelous how they wind their way at such a rattling pace through the crowd. To a stranger unacquainted with localities, they are a great convenience. And here, you see, commences the gist of the story.

On a certain occasion I called a drosky-man and directed him to drive me to the United States Consulate. Having never been there myself, I depended solely upon the intelligence and enterprise of the istrovoschik. My knowledge of the Russian consisted of three words—the name of the street and *dratzall kopeck*, the latter being the stipulated fare of twenty kopecks. By an affirmative signal the driver gave me to understand that he fully comprehended my wishes, and, with a flourish of his whip, away we started. After driving me nearly all over the city of St. Petersburg—a pretty extensive city, as any body will find who undertakes to walk through it —this adroit and skillful whipster, who had never uttered a word from the time of starting, now deliberately drew up his drosky on the corner of a principal street and began a conversation. I repeated the name of the street in which the consulate was located, and *dratzall kopeck*. The driver gazed in my face with a grave and placid countenance, stroked his long beard, tucked the skirts of his long blue coat under him, and drove on again. After rattling over a series of the most frightful cobble-stone pavements ever designed as an improvement in a great city, through several new quarters, he again stopped and treated me to some more remarks in his native language. I answered as before, the name of the street. He shook his head with discouraging gravity. I then remarked *dratzall kopeck.* From the confused answer he made, which occupied at least ten minutes of his time, and of which I was unable to comprehend a single word, it was apparent that he was as ignorant of his own language as he was of the city. In this extremity he called another driver to his aid, who spoke just the words of English, "Gooda-morkig!" "Good-morning," said I. From this the conversation lapsed at once into remote depths of Russian. In despair I got out of the drosky and walked along the street, looking up at all the signs—the driver after me with his drosky, apparently watching to see that I did not make my escape. At length I espied a German name on a bakery sign. How familiar it looked in that desert of unintelligible Russian—like a favorite quotation in a page of metaphysics. I went in and spoke German—*vie gaetz?* You are aware, perhaps, that I excel in that language. I asked the way to the United States Consulate. The baker had probably forgotten his native tongue, if ever he knew it at all, for I could get nothing out of him but a shake of the head and *nicht furstay.* However, he had the goodness, seeing my perplexity, to put on his hat and undertake to find the consul's, which, by dint of inquiry, he at length ascertained to be about half a mile distant. We walked all the way, this good old baker and I, he refusing to ride because there was only room for one, and I not liking to do so and let him walk. The drosky-man followed in the rear, driving along very leisurely, and with great apparent comfort to himself. He leaned back in his seat with much gusto, and seemed rather amused than otherwise at our movements. At length we reached the consulate. It was about three hundred yards from my original point of departure. Any other man in existence than my istrovoschik would have sunk into the earth upon seeing me make this astounding discovery. I knew it by certain landmarks—a church and a garden. But he did not sink into the earth. He merely sat on his drosky as cool as a cucumber. I felt so grateful to the worthy baker, who was a fat old gentleman, and perspired freely after his walk, that I gave him thirty kopecks. The drosky-man claimed forty kopecks, just double his fare. I called in the services of an interpreter, and protested against this imposition. The interpreter and the drosky-man got into an animated dispute on the question, and must have gone clear back to the fundamental principles of droskyism, for they seemed likely never to come to an end. The weather was warm, and both kept constantly wiping their faces, and turning the whole subject over and over again, without the slightest probability of an equitable conclusion. At length my interpreter said, "Perhaps, sir, you had better pay it. The man says you kept him running about for over two hours; and since you have no proof to the contrary, it would only give you trouble to have him punished." This view accorded entirely with my own, and I cheerfully paid the forty kopecks; also ten kopecks drink-geld, and a small douceur of half a ruble (fifty kopecks) to the gentleman who had so kindly settled the difficulty for me. After many years' experience of travel, I am satisfied, as before stated, that a man may be born naturally honest, but can not long retain his integrity in the hack business. He must sooner or later take to swindling, otherwise he can never keep his horses fat, or make the profession respectable and remunerative. Such, at least, has been my experience of men in this line of business, not excepting the istrovoschik of St. Petersburg.

CHAPTER II.

A PLEASANT EXCURSION.

I HAD the good fortune, during my ramble, to meet with a couple of fellow-passengers from Stettin. One of them was a rough, weather-beaten man of middle age, with rather marked features, but not an unkindly expression. His mysterious conduct during the voyage had frequently attracted my attention. There was something curious about his motions, as if an invisible companion, to whom he was bound in some strange way, continually accompanied him. He drank enormous quantities of beer, and smoked from morning till night a tremendous meerschaum, which must have held at least a pint of tobacco. When not engaged in drinking beer and smoking, he usually walked rapidly up and down the decks, with his hands behind him and his head bent down, talking in a guttural voice to himself about "hemp." He slept—or rather lay down, for I don't think he ever slept—with his head close to mine on a bench in the cabin, and it was a continued source of trouble to me the way he puffed, and groaned, and talked about "hemp." Sometimes he was half the night arguing with himself about the various prices and qualities of this useful article, but I did not understand enough of his *blat deutsch* to gather the drift of the argument. All I could make out was "*Zweimal zwei macht vier*—(a puff) —*sechs und vierzig*—(a groan)—*acht und sechzig macht ein hundert*—(a snort)—*sieben tausend—acht tausend fünf und dreissig thaler*—(a sigh)—*schilling—kopeck —ruble—hemphf! Mein Gott! Zwei und dreissig tausend—hemphf—ruble*—(a terrible gritting of the teeth) —*sechs und fünfzig— Gott im Himmel!—Ich kann nicht schlafen!*" Here he would jump up and shout, "Kellner'

Kellner! *ein flask bier!—sechs und zechzig—zweimal acht und vierzig! Kellner, flask bier!—Liebe Gott— was ist das?—Nine und sechzig—flask bier! Kleich! Kleich!*" When the beer came he would drink off three bottles without stopping, then light his pipe, fill the cabin with smoke, and after he had done that go on deck to get the fresh air. I could hear him for hours walking up and down over my head, and thought I could occasionally detect the words "*Hemphf—ruble—thaler— fünfmal sechs und zwanzig—mein Gott!*" It was evident the man was laboring under some dreadful internal excitement about the price of hemp. What could it be? Was he going to hang himself? Did he contemplate buying some Russian hemp for that purpose especially? The mystery was heightened by the fact that he was frequently in close conversation with the young man whom I have already mentioned as my other fellow-passenger, and they both talked about nothing else but hemp. What in the name of sense were they going to do with hemp in Mechlenberg, their native country, where people were beheaded — unless they meant to hang themselves? The mystery troubled me so much that I finally made bold to ask the young man if his friend had committed any serious crime, and whether that was the reason he talked so much about hemp? These North Germans are a queer people. I don't think they ever suspect any body to be joking. They take the most outrageous proposition literally, and never seem to understand that there can be two meanings to any thing. As Sydney Smith says of the Scotch, it would take a surgical operation to get a joke well into their understanding. When I propounded this question to my young fellow-passenger—a very amiable and intelligent young man—he looked distressed and horror-stricken, and replied with great earnestness, "Oh no, he is a very respectable man. I am certain he never committed a crime in his life." "But," said I, "if he doesn't intend to hang somebody, why should he rave about hemp all night?"

"Oh, he is a rope-maker. He is going to Russia to buy a cargo of hemp, and he's afraid prices will go up unless he gets there soon. The head wind and chopping sea keep us back a good deal." "Yes, yes, I understand it all now. Suppose, my young friend, you and I go to work and help the steamer along a little? It would be doing a great service to the cause of hemp, and enable me to sleep besides." The Mechlenberger looked incredulous. "How are we to do it?" he asked at length. "Oh, nothing easier!" I answered. "Just put a couple of these handspikes in the lee scuppers—so! and hold her steady!" At this the Mechlenberger, who was a very genial and good-natured fellow, could scarcely help laughing, the absurdity of the idea struck him so forcibly. Seeing, however, that I looked perfectly in earnest, he was kind enough to explain the erroneous basis of my calculation, and accordingly entered into an elaborate mathematical demonstration to prove that what we gained by lifting we would lose by the additional pressure of our feet upon the decks! After this I was prepared to believe the story of the old Nuremberger, who, when about to set out on his travels, got on top of his trunk and took hold of each end for the purpose of carrying it to the post station. The question about the hemp was too good to be lost, and my young friend had too strong a business head not to perceive the delightful verdancy of my character. He accordingly took the earliest opportunity to mention it to his comrade, Herr Batz, the rope-maker, who never stopped laughing about the mistake I had made till we got to St. Petersburg. They were both very genial, pleasant fellows, and took a great fancy to the Herr American who thought Herr Batz was going to hang himself, and who had proposed to steady the steamer by means of a handspike. Such primitive simplicity was absolutely refreshing to them; and, since they enjoyed it, of course I did, and we were the best of friends.

On the present occasion, after we had passed the usual

compliments it was proposed that we should hire a boat, as the night was fine, and take a trip down to the Kamennoi Island. I was delighted to have two such agreeable companions, and readily acceded to the proposition. A young Russian in the hemp business accompanied us, and altogether we made a very lively and humorous party. I was sorry, however, to be prejudiced in the estimation of the Russian by having the hemp and handspike story repeated in my presence, but finally got over that, and changed the current of the conversation by asking if the Emperor Alexander would send me to Siberia in case I smoked a cigar in the boat? To which the Russian responded somewhat gravely that I could smoke as many cigars on the water as I pleased, although it was forbidden in the streets on account of the danger of fire; but that, in any event, I would merely have to pay a fine, as people were only sent to Siberia for capital crimes and political offenses.

We got a boat down near the Custom-house, at a point of the Vassoli Ostrou, called the Strelka, and were soon skimming along through a small branch of the Neva, toward the island of Krestofskoi. The water was literally alive with boats, all filled with gay parties of pleasure-seekers, some on their way to the different islands, some to the bath-houses which abound in every direction, and all apparently enjoying a delightful time of it. Passing to the right of the Petrofskoi Island, whose grass-covered shores slope down to the water like a green carpet outspread under the trees, we soon reached the Little Nevka, about three miles from our starting-point. We disembarked on the Krestofskoi Island, near the bridge which crosses from Petrofskoi. On the right is a beautiful palace belonging to some of the royal family, the gardens of which sweep down to the waters of the Nevka, and present a charming scene of floral luxuriance. Gondolas, richly carved and curiously shaped, lay moored near the stone steps; the trestled bowers were filled with gay parties; pleasant sounds of voices and

FISH PEDDLER.

music floated upon the air, and over all a soft twilight gave a mystic fascination to the scene. I thought of the terrible arctic winters that for six months in the year cast their cold death-pall over the scene of glowing and tropical luxuriance, and wondered how it could ever come to life again; how the shrubs could bloom, and the birds sing, and the soft air of the summer nights come back and linger where such dreary horrors were wont to desolate the earth.

The constant dread of infringing upon the police regulations; the extraordinary deference with which men in uniform are regarded; the circumspect behavior at public places; the nice and well-regulated mirthfulness, never overstepping the strict bounds of prudence, which I had so often noticed in the northern states of Germany, and which may in part be attributed to the naturally conservative and orderly character of the people, are not the prominent features of the population of St. Petersburg. It appeared to me that in this respect at least they are more like Americans than any people I had seen in Europe; they do pretty much as they please; follow such trades and occupations as they like best; become noisy and uproarious when it suits them; get drunk occasionally; fight now and then; lie about on the grass and under the trees when they feel tired; enjoy themselves to their heart's content at all the public places; and care nothing about the police as long as the police let them alone. I rather fancied there must be a natural democratic streak in these people, for they are certainly more free and easy in their manners, rougher in their dress, more independent in their general air, and a good deal dirtier than most of the people I had met with in the course of my travels. I do not mean to say that rowdyism and democracy are synonymous, but I consider it a good sign of innate manliness and a natural spirit of independence when men are not afraid to dress like vagabonds and behave a little extravagantly, if it suits their taste. It must be said, however, that the police regulations of St. Petersburg, without being onerous or vexatious, are quite as good as those of any large city in Europe. When men are deprived of their political liberties, the least that can be done for them is to let them

YOUNG PEASANTS.

enjoy as much muncipal freedom as may be consistent with public peace. I should never have suspected, from any thing I saw in the city or neighborhood of St. Petersburg, that I was within the limits of an absolute despotism. If one desires to satisfy himself on this point he must visit the interior.

I was led into this train of reflection partly by the

scenes I had witnessed during my rambles through the
city and on the way down the river, and partly by what
we now saw on the island of Krestofskoi. A bridge
unites this island with the Petrofskoi, and two other
bridges with the islands of Kamennoi and Elaghinskoi.
It was eleven o'clock at night, yet the twilight was so
rich and glowing that one might readily read a newspaper in any of the open spaces. The main avenues were
crowded with carriages of every conceivable description
—the grandly decorated coach of the noble, glittering
with armorial bearings and drawn by four richly-capari-
soned horses ; the barouche, easy and elegant, filled with
a gay company of foreigners ; the drosky, whirling along
at a rapid pace, with its solitary occupant ; the kareta,
plain, neat, and substantial, carrying on its ample seats
some worthy merchant and his family ; the nondescript
little vehicle, without top, bottom, or sides—nothing but
four small wheels and a cushioned seat perched on springs,
with an exquisite perched astride upon the street, driving a magnificent blood horse at the rate of 2.40 ; and
English boxes with stiff Englishmen in them ; and French
chaises with loose Frenchmen in them ; and a New York
buggy with a New York fancy man in it ; and hundreds
of fine horses with dashing Russian officers in uniform
mounted on them, and hundreds of other horses with
secretaries and various young sprigs of nobility struggling painfully to stay mounted on them ; and, in short,
every thing grand, fanciful, and entertaining in the way
of locomotion that the most fertile imagination can conceive. Don't do me the injustice, I pray you, to consider
me envious of the good fortune of others in being able
to ride when I had to walk, for it does me an amazing
deal of good to see people enjoy themselves. Nothing
pleases me better than to see a fat old lady, glittering all
over with fine silks and jewels, leaning back in her cushioned carriage, with her beloved little lapdog in her arms
—two elegant drivers, four prancing horses, and a splendid little postillion in front ; two stalwart footmen, in plush

breeches, behind, with variegated yellow backs like a pair
of wasps. Can any thing be more picturesque? It always makes me think of a large June-bug dragged about
by an accommodating crowd of fancy-colored flies! And
what can be more imposing than a Russian grandee?
See that terrific old gentleman, sitting all alone in a gorgeous carriage, large enough to carry himself and half
a dozen of his friends. Orders and disorders cover him
from head to foot. He is the exact picture of a ferocious
bullfrog, with a tremendous mustache and a horribly ma-
lignant expression of eye, and naturally enough expects
every body to get out of his way. That man must have
had greatness thrust upon him, for he never could have
achieved it by the brilliancy of his intellect. Doubtless
he spends much of his time at the springs, but they don't
seem to have purified his body, or subdued the natural
ferocity of his temper. His wife must have a pleasant
time. I wonder if he sleeps well, or enjoys Herzain's essays on Russian aristocracy? But make way, ye pedestrian rabble, for here comes a secretary of legation on
horseback—make way, or he will tumble off and inflict
some bodily injury upon you with the points of his wax-
ed mustache! I know he must be a secretary of legation by the enormous polished boots he wears over his
tight breeches, the dandy parting of his hair, the supercilious stupidity of his countenance, and the horrible tortures he suffers in trying to stick on the back of his
horse. Nobody else in the world could make such an
ass of himself by such frantic attempts to show off and
keep on at the same time. I'll bet my life he thinks he
is the most beautiful and accomplished gentleman ever
produced by a beneficent Creator. Well, it is a happy
thing for some of us that we don't see ourselves as others see us; if we did, my friends in the hemp business
and myself would fare badly. Beregrissa! Padi! Padi!
—have a care! make way, for here comes a cloud of dust,
and in that cloud of dust is a kibitka, drawn by three
wild horses, and in that kibitka, half sitting, half cling-

ing to the side, is an official courier. Crack goes the whip of the *yamtschick ;* the three fiery horses fly through the dust; the courier waves his hand to an officer on horseback, and with a whirl and a whisk they disappear. *Pashol!* I hope they won't break their necks before they get through.

Soon the main road branches out in various directions, and we strike off with the diverging streams of pedestrians, families of the middle and lower classes, young men of the town, gay young damsels with their beaux, burly tradesmen, tinkers, tailors, and hatters, waiters and apprentices, sailors and soldiers, until we find ourselves in the midst of a grand old forest. Open glades, pavilions, and tables are visible at intervals; but for the most part we are in a labyrinthian wilderness of trees, rich in foliage, and almost oppressive in their umbrageous density, while

> "Deep velvet verdure clothes the turf beneath,
> And trodden flowers their richest odors breathe."

Insects flit through the still atmosphere; the hum of human voices, softened by distance, falls soothingly upon the ear; and as we look, and listen, and loiter on our way, we wonder if this can be the dreamland of the arctic regions? Can there ever be snow-storms and scathing frosts in such a land of tropical luxuriance? Thus, as we lounge along in the mellow twilight amid the groves of Katrofskoi, what charming pictures of sylvan enjoyment are revealed to us at every turn! Rustic tables under the great wide-spreading trees are surrounded by family groups—old patriarchs, and their children, and great-grandchildren; the steaming urn of tea in the middle; the old people chatting and gossiping; the young people laughing merrily; the children tumbling about over the green sward. Passing on we come to a group of Mujiks lying camp-fashion on the grass, eating their black bread, drinking their vodka, and sleeping whenever they please—for this is their summer home, and this grass is their bed. Next we come to a group

DVORNICK AND POSTMAN.

of officers, their rich uniforms glittering in the soft twilight, their horses tied to the trees, or held at a little distance by some attendant soldiers. Dominoes, cards, Champagne, and cakes are scattered in tempting profusion upon the table, and if they are not enjoying their military career, it is not for want of congenial accompaniments and plenty of leisure. A little farther on we meet a jovial party of Germans seated under a tree, with a goodly supply of bread and sausages before them, singing in fine accord a song of their faderland. Next we hear the familiar strains of an organ, and soon come in sight of an Italian who is exhibiting an accomplished monkey to an enraptured crowd of children. The monk-

ey has been thoroughly trained in the school of adversi-
ty, and makes horrible grimaces at his cruel and cadaverous master, who in ferocious tones, and without the least
appearance of enjoying the sport, commands this miniature man to dance, fire a small gun, go through the
sword exercise, play on a small fiddle, smoke a cigar,
turn a somersault, bow to the company, and hold out his
hat for an unlimited number of kopecks. Herr Batz suggests that such a monkey as that might be taught to
spin ropes, and our younger Mechlenberger laughs, and
says he once read a story of a monkey that shaved a
cat, and then cut off his own or the cat's tail, he could
not remember which. This reminds the Russian of a
countess in Moscow who owned a beautiful little dog, to
which she was greatly attached. She required her serfs
to call it "My noble Prince," and had them well flogged
with the knout whenever they approached it without
bowing. One day a cat got hold of the noble Prince,
and gave him a good scratching. The countess, being
unable to soothe her afflicted poodle, caused the cat's
paws to be cut off, and served up on a plate for his unhappy highness to play with—after which the noble pug
was perfectly satisfied! Of course, we all laughed at
the Russian's story, but he assured us it was a well authenticated fact, and was generally regarded as a most
delicate *jeu d'esprit*. Not to be behindhand in the line
of cats and monkeys, I was obliged to tell an anecdote
of a Frenchman, who, on his arrival in Algiers, ordered a
ragout at one of the most fashionable restaurants. It
was duly served up, and pronounced excellent, though
rather strongly flavored. "Pray," said the Frenchman
to the *maître d'hotel*, "of what species of cat do you
make ragouts in Algiers?" "Pardon, monsieur," replied
the polite host, "we use nothing but monkeys in Africa!"
Disgusted at this colonial barbarism, the Frenchman immediately returned to Paris, where he remained forever
after, that he might enjoy his customary and more civilized dish of cat. Herr Batz had not before heard of

GLAZIER, PAINTER, CARPENTERS.

such a thing, neither had the young Mechlenberger, and they both agreed that cats must be a very disgusting article of food. The Russian, however, seemed to regard it as nothing uncommon, and gave us some very entertaining accounts of various curious dishes in the interior of Russia, to which cats were not a circumstance.

With such flimsy conversation as this we entertain ourselves till we reach a village of summer residences on the Kamennoi Island. Here we pause a while to enjoy the varied scenes of amusement that tempt the loiterer at every step; the tea-drinking parties out on the porticoes, the gambling saloons, the dancing pavilions, the cafés, the confectioneries, with their gay throngs of customers, their gaudy-colors, their music, and sounds of joy and revelry. A little farther on we come to a stand of carriages, and near by a gate and a large garden. For thirty kopecks apiece we procure tickets of admission. This is the Vauxhall of Kamennoi. We jostle in with the crowd, and soon find ourselves in front of an open theatre.

So passes away the time till the whistle of a little steamer warns us of an opportunity to get back to the city. Hurrying down to the wharf, we secure places on the stern-sheets of a screw-wheeled craft not much bigger than a good-sized yawl. It is crowded to overflowing—in front, on top of the machinery, in the rear, over the sides—not a square inch of space left for man or beast. The whistle blows again; the fiery little monster of an engine shivers and screams with excess of steam; the grim, black-looking engineer gives the irons a pull, and away we go at a rate of speed that threatens momentary destruction against some bridge or bath-house. It is now two o'clock A.M. The rays of the rising sun are already reflected upon the glowing waters of the Neva. Barges and row-boats are hurrying toward the city. Carriages are rolling along the shady avenues of the islands. Crowds are gathered at every pier and landing-place awaiting some conveyance homeward. Ladies are waving their handkerchiefs to the little steamer to stop, and gentlemen are flourishing their hats. The captain blows the whistle, and the engineer stops the boat with such a sudden reversion of our screw that we are pitched forward out of the seats. Some of the passengers clamber up at the landing-places, and others clamber down and take their places. The little engine sets up its terrific scream again; the hot steam hisses and fizzes all over the boat; involuntary thoughts of maimed limbs and scalded skins are palpably impressed upon every face; but the little steamer keeps on—she is used to it, like the eels, and never bursts up. Winding through the varied channels of the Neva, under bridges, through narrow passes, among wood-boats, row-boats, and shipping, we at length reach the landing on the Russian Quay, above the Admiralty. Here we disembark, well satisfied to be safely over all the enjoyments and hazards of the evening.

Evening, did I say? The morning sun is blazing out in all his glory! We have had no evening—no night. It has been all a wild, strange, glowing freak of fancy. The light of day has been upon us all the time. And now, should we go to bed, when the sun is shining over the city, glistening upon the domes of the churches, illuminating the windows of the palaces, awaking the drowsy sailors of the Neva? Shall we hide ourselves away in suffocating rooms when the morning breeze is floating in from the Gulf of Finland, bearing upon its wings the invigorating brine of ocean, or shall we,

> "Pleased to feel the air,
> Still wander in the luxury of light?"

CHAPTER III.

VIEWS ON THE MOSCOW RAILWAY.

THE St. Petersburg and Moscow Railroad has been in operation some eight or ten years, and has contributed much to the internal prosperity of the country. In the summer of 1862 it was extended as far as Vladimir, and now connects St. Petersburg with Nijni Novgorod, one of the most important points in the empire, where the great annual fair is held, where tea-merchants and others from all parts of Tartary and China meet to exchange the products of those countries with those of the merchants of Russia. During the present year (1862) it is expected that the line of railway connection will be completed from St. Petersburg to the Prussian frontier, and connect with the railroads of Prussia, so that within twelve months it will be practicable to travel by rail all the way from Marseilles or Bordeaux to Nijni Novgorod.

The Moscow and St. Petersburg Railway is something over four hundred miles in length, and consists of a double track, broad, well graded, and substantially constructed. The whole business of running the line, keeping the cars and track in repair, working the machine-shops, etc., embracing all the practical details of the operative department, is let out by contract to an American company, while the government supervises the financial department, and reserves to itself the municipal control.* It is a remarkable fact, characteristic of the Russians, that while they possess uncommon capacity to acquire all the details of engineering, and are by no means lacking in mechanical skill, they are utterly deficient in management and administrative capacity. Wasteful, improvident, and short-sighted, they can never do any thing without the aid of more sagacious and economical heads to keep them within the bounds of reason. Thus, at one time, when they undertook to run this line on their own account, although they started with an extraordinary surplus of material, they soon ran the cars off their wheels, forgetting to keep up a supply of new ones as they went along; ran the engines out of working order; kept nothing in repair; provided against no contingency; and were finally likely to break down entirely, when

* This contract terminated last year (1865).

they determined that it would be better to give this branch of the business out by contract. One great fault with them is, they labor under an idea that nothing can be done without an extraordinary number of officers, soldiers, policemen, and employés of every description— upon the principle, I suppose, that if two heads are better than one, the ignorance or inefficiency of a small number of employés can be remedied by having a very great number of the same kind. In other words, they seem to think that if five hundred men can not be industrious, skillful, and economical, five thousand trained in exactly the same schools, and with precisely the same propensities, must be ten times better. Even now there is not a station, and scarcely a foot of the railway from St. Petersburg to Moscow, that is not infested with an extraordinary surplus of useless men in uniform. At the great dépôts in each of these cities the traveler is fairly confused with the crowds of officers and employés through which he is obliged to make his way. Before he enters the doorways, liveried porters outside offer to take his baggage; then he passes by guards, who look at him carefully and let him go in; then he finds guards who show him where to find the ticket-office; when he arrives at the ticket-office, he finds a guard or two outside, and half a dozen clerks inside; then he buys his ticket, and an officer examines it as he goes into the wirthsaal; there he finds other officers stationed to preserve order; when the bell rings the doors are opened; numerous officers outside show him where to find the cars, and which car he must get into; and when he gets into a car he sits for a quarter of an hour, and sees officers going up and down outside all the time, and thinks to himself that people certainly can not be supposed to have very good eyes, ears, or understanding of their own in this country, since nobody is deemed capable of using them on his individual responsibility. I only wonder that they don't eat, drink, sleep, and travel for a man at once by proxy, and thereby save him the trouble of living or moving at all. In fact, I had some thought of asking one of these licensed gentlemen if the regulations could not be stretched a point so as to embrace the payment of my expenses; but it occurred to me that if I were relieved of that responsibility, they might undertake at the same time to write these letters for me, which would be likely to alter the tone and thereby destroy my individuality. But it must be admitted that good order, convenience, politeness, and comfort are the predominant characteristics of railway travel in Russia. The conductors usually speak French, German, and English, and are exceedingly attentive to the comfort of the passengers. The hours of starting and stopping are punctually observed—so punctually that you can calculate to the exact minute when you will arrive at any given point. Having no watch, I always knew the time by looking at my ticket. Between St. Petersburg and Moscow there are thirty-three stations, seven of which are the grand stations of Lubanskaia, Malovischerskaia, Okoulourskaia, Bologovskaia, Spirovskaia, Tver, and Klinskaia. The rest are small intermediate stations. At every seventy-five versts—about fifty miles—the cars stop twenty minutes, and refreshments may be had by paying a pretty heavy price for them. At the points above-named there are large and substantial edifices built by the company, containing various offices, spacious eating-saloons, ante-chambers, etc., and attached to which are extensive machine-shops, and various outbuildings required by the service. Occasionally towns may be seen in the vicinity of these stations, but for the most part they stand out desolate and alone in the dreary waste of country lying between the two great cities. At every twenty-five versts are sub-stations, where the cars stop for a few minutes. These are also large and very substantial edifices, but not distinguished for architectural beauty, like many of the stations in France and Germany. Usually the Russian station consists of an immense plain circular building, constructed of brick, with very thick walls, and a plain zinc roof, the outside painted red, the roof green; wings or flanges built of the same material extending along the track; a broad wooden esplanade in front, upon which the passengers can amuse themselves promenading, and a neat garden, with other accommodations, at one end. Some of the large stations are not only massive and of enormous extent, but present rather a striking and picturesque appearance as they are approached from the distance, standing as they do in the great deserts of space like solitary sentinels of civilization. The passengers rush out at every stopping-place just as they do in other parts of the world, some to stretch their limbs, others to replenish the waste that seems to be constantly going on in the stomachs of the traveling public. I don't know how it is, but it appears to me that people who travel by railway are always either tired, thirsty, or hungry. The voracity with which plates of soup, cutlets, sandwiches, salad, scalding hot tea, wine, beer, and brandy are swallowed down by these hungry and thirsty Russians, is quite as striking as any thing I ever saw done in the same line at Washoe. But it is not a feature confined to Russia. I notice the same thing every where all over the world; and what vexes me about it is that I never get tired myself, and rarely hungry or thirsty. Here, in midsummer, with a sweltering hot sun, and an atmosphere that would almost smother a salamander, were whole legions of officers, elegantly-dressed ladies, and a rabble of miscellaneous second and third class passengers like myself, puffing, blowing, eating, drinking, sweating, and toiling, as if their very existence depended upon keeping up the internal fires and blowing them off again. It is dreadful to see people so hard pushed to live. I really can't conjecture what sort of a commotion they will make when they come to die. A sandwich or two and a glass of tea lasted me all the way to Moscow—a journey of eighteen hours, and I never suffered from hunger, thirst, or fatigue the whole way.

If I had "gone in" like other people, I would certainly have been a dead man before I got half way; and yet, I think, two sandwiches more would have lasted me to the Ural Mountains. It continually bothers me to know how the human stomach can bear to be tormented in this frightful way. Per Baccho! I would as soon be shot in the hand with an escopette ball as drink the quantity of wine and eat the quantity of food that I have seen even women and children dispose of, as if it were mere pastime, on these railway journeys. I think it must be either this or the frost that accounts for the extraordinary prevalence of red noses in Russia, and it even occurred to me that the stations are painted a fiery red, so that when travelers come within range of the refracted color their noses may look pale by contrast, and thereby remind them that it is time to renew the caloric.

With the exception of the seventy-five versts between Moscow and Tver, I can not remember that I ever traveled over so desolate and uninteresting a stretch of country as that lying between St. Petersburg and Moscow. For a short distance out of St. Petersburg there are some few villas and farms to relieve the monotony of the gloomy pine forests; then the country opens out into immense undulating plains, marshy meadows, scrubby groves of young pine, without any apparent limit; here and there a bleak and solitary village of log huts; a herd of cattle in the meadows; a wretched, sterile-looking farm, with plowed fields, at remote intervals, and so on hour after hour, the scene offering but little variety the whole way to Tver. The villages are wholly destitute of picturesque effect. Such rude and miserable hovels as they are composed of could scarcely be found in the wildest frontier region of the United States. These cabins or hovels are built of logs, and are very low and small, generally consisting of only one or two rooms. I saw none that were whitewashed or painted, and nothing like order or regularity was perceptible about them, all seem-

ing to be huddled together as if they happened there by
accident, and were obliged to keep at close quarters in
order to avoid freezing during the terrible winters.
Some of them are not unlike the city of Eden in Martin
Chuzzlewit. The entire absence of every thing approaching taste, comfort, or rural beauty in the appearance of
these villages; the weird and desolate aspect of the boggy and grass-grown streets; the utter want of interest
in progress or improvement on the part of the peasantry
who inhabit them, are well calculated to produce a melancholy impression of the condition of these poor people.
How can it be otherwise, held in bondage as they have
been for centuries, subject to be taxed at the discretion
of their owners; the results of their labors wrested from
them; no advance made by the most enterprising and
intelligent of them without in some way subjecting them
to new burdens? Whatever may be the result of the
movement now made for their emancipation, it certainly
can not be more depressing than the existing system of
serfage. Looking back over the scenes of village life I
had witnessed in France and Germany—the neat vine-
covered cottages, the little flower-gardens, the orchards
and green lanes, the festive days, when the air resounded to the merry voices of laughing damsels and village
beaux—

> "The hawthorn bush, with seats beneath the shade,
>   For talking age and whispering lovers made"—

the joyous dancers out on the village green, the flaunting
banners and wreaths of flowers hung in rich profusion
over the cross-roads—with such scenes as these flitting
through my memory, I could well understand that there
is an absolute physical servitude to which men can be
reduced, that, in the progress of generations, must crush
down the human soul, and make life indeed a dreary
struggle. In the splendor of large cities, amid the glitter and magnificence of palaces and churches, the varied
paraphernalia of aristocracy and wealth, and all the ex-
citements, allurements, and novelties apparent to the su-

perficial eye, the real condition of the masses is not perceptible. They must be seen in the country—in their
far-off villages and homes throughout the broad land;
there you find no disguise to cover the horrible deformi-
ties of their bruised and crushed life; there you see the
full measure of their civilization. In the huts of these
poor people there is little or no comfort. Many of them
have neither beds nor chairs, and the occupants spend a
sort of camp life within doors, cooking their food like
Indians, and huddling round the earthern stove or fireplace in winter, where they lie down on the bare ground
and sleep in a mass, like a nest of animals, to keep each
other warm. Their clothing is of the coarsest material,
but reasonably good, and well suited to the climate. The
men are a much finer-looking race, physically, than their

HAY GATHERERS.

masters. I saw some serfs in Moscow who, in stature, strong athletic forms, and bold and manly features, would compare favorably with the best specimens of men in any country. It was almost incredible that such noble-looking fellows, with their blue, piercing eyes and manly air, should be reduced to such a state of abject servitude as to kiss the tails of their master's coats! Many of them had features as bold and forms as brawny as our own California miners; and more than once, when I saw them lounging about in their big boots, with their easy, reckless air, and looked at their weather-beaten faces and vigorous, sun-burnt beards, I could almost imagine that they were genuine Californians. But here the resemblance ceased. No sooner did an officer of high standing pass, than they manifested some abject sign of their degraded condition.

Some of the agricultural implements that one sees in this country would astonish a Californian. The plows are patterned very much after those that were used by Boaz and other large farmers in the days of the Patriarchs; the scythes are the exact originals of the old pictures in which Death is represented as mowing down mankind; the hoes, rakes, and shovels would be an ornament to any museum, but are entirely indescribable; and as for the wagons and harnesses—herein lies the superior genius of the Russians over all the races of earth, ancient or modern, for never were such wagons and such harnesses seen on any other part of the globe. To be accurate and methodical, each wagon has four wheels, and each wheel is roughly put together of rough wood, and then roughly bound up in an iron band about four inches wide, and thick in proportion. Logs of wood, skillfully hewed with broad-axes, answer for the axle-tree; and as they don't weigh over half a ton each, they are sometimes braced in the middle to keep them from breaking. Upon the top of this is a big basket, about the shape of a bath-tub, in which the load is carried. Sometimes the body is made of planks tied together with bullock's hide, or no body at all is used, as convenience may require. The wagon being thus completed, braced and thorough-braced with old ropes, iron bands, and leather straps, we come to the horses, which stand generally in front. The middle horse is favored with a pair of shafts of enormous durability and strength. He stands between these shafts, and is fastened in them by means of ropes; but, to prevent him from jumping out overhead, a wooden arch is out over him, which is the *chef-d'œuvre* of ornamentation. This is called the *duga*, and is the most prominent object to be seen about every wagon, drosky, and kibitka in Russia. I am not sure but a species of veneration is attached to it. Often it is highly decorated with gilding, painted figures, and every vagary of artistic genius, and must cost nearly as much as the entire wagon. Some of the *dugas* even carry saintly images upon them, so that the devout driver may perform his devotions as he drives through life. To suppose that a horse could pull a wagon in Russia without this wooden arch, the utility of which no human eye but that of a Russian can see, is to suppose an impossibility. Now, the shafts being spread out so as to give the horse plenty of room at each side, it becomes necessary, since they are rather loosely hung on at the but-ends, to keep them from swaying. How do you think this is done? Nothing easier. By running a rope from the end of each shaft to the projecting end of the fore axle, outside of the wheels. For this purpose the axle is made to project a foot beyond the wheels, and the only trouble about it is that two wagons on a narrow road often find it difficult to pass. It is very curious to see these primitive-looking objects lumbering about through the streets of Moscow and St. Petersburg. The horses are most commonly placed three abreast. In the ordinary kibitka or traveling wagon the outside horses are merely fastened by ropes, and strike out in any direction they please, the whip and a small rein serving to keep them within bounds. It is perfectly astonishing with what reckless and headlong speed these animals dash over the rough pavements. Just imagine the luxury of a warm day's journey in such a vehicle, which has neither springs nor backed seats—three fiery horses fastened to it, and each pulling, plunging, and pirouetting on his own account; a ferocious yamtschick cracking his whip and shrieking "Shivar! shivar!"—faster! faster!—the wagon rattling all over, plunging into ruts, jumping over stones, ripping its way through bogs and mud-banks; your bones shaken nearly out of their sockets; your vertebræ partially dislocated; your mouth filled with dust; your tongue swollen and parched; your eyes blinded with grit; your *yamtschick* reeling drunk with *vodka*, and bound to draw to the destined station—or some worse place; your confidence in men and horses shaken with your bones; your views of the future circumscribed by every turn of the road—oh! it is charming; it is the very climax of human enjoyment. Wouldn't you like to travel in Russia?

In addition to the villages which are scattered at frequent intervals along the route, the gilded dome of a church is occasionally seen in the distance, indicating the existence of a town; but one seldom catches more than a glimpse of the green-covered roofs of the houses, over the interminable patches of scrubby pine. It is not a country that presents such attractive features as to induce the mere tourist to get out and spend a few days rambling through it. In these dreary solitudes of marshes and pines, the inhabitants speak no other language than their own, and that not very well; but well or ill, it is all Greek—or rather Russian—to the majority of people from other countries.

But, as I said before, this habit of digression will be the death of me. Like a rocket, I start off splendidly, but explode and fall to pieces in every direction before I get half way on my journey. If the scintillations are varied and gayly colored, to be sure, the powder is not utterly lost; but the trouble of it is, if one keeps going off like rockets all the time, he will never get any where,

C

and in the end will leave nothing but smoke and darkness to the gaping multitude.

If my memory serves me, I was talking of the Emperor Alexander's convoy of private railway carriages—the most magnificent affair of the kind, perhaps, in existence. It was made purposely for his use, at a cost of more than a hundred thousand dollars, and presented to him by the American company, Winans and Company. Nothing so magnificent in decoration, and so admirably adapted to the convenience, comfort, and enjoyment of a royal party has ever been seen in Europe. The main carriage—for there are several in the suite—called, *par excellence*, the emperor's own, is eighty-five feet long, and something over the usual width. It rests upon two undivided sleepers of such elastic and well-grained wood that they would bear the entire weight of the carriage, without the necessity of a support in the middle, forming a single stretch or arch, from axle to axle, of about seventy feet. The springs, wheels, brakes, and various kinds of iron-work, are of the finest and most select material, and highly finished in every detail, combining strength and durability with artistic beauty. The interior of the main or imperial carriage is a masterpiece of sumptuous ornamentation. Here are the richest of carvings; the most gorgeous hangings of embroidered velvet; mirrors and pictures in profusion; carpets and rugs that seem coaxing the feet to linger upon them; tables, cushioned sofas, and luxurious arm-chairs; divans and lounges of rare designs, covered with the richest damask; exquisite Pompeian vases and brilliant chandeliers —all, in short, that ingenuity could devise and wealth procure to charm the senses, and render this a traveling palace worthy the imperial presence. Connected with the main saloon is the royal bedchamber, with adjoining bathing and dressing rooms, equally sumptuous in all their appointments. Besides which, there are smoking-rooms, private offices, magnificent chambers for the camarilla, the secretaries, and body-guard of the emperor.

The whole is admirably arranged for convenience and comfort; and it is said that the motion, when the convoy is under way, is so soft and dreamy that it is scarcely possible to feel a vibration, the effect being as if the cars were floating through the air, or drawn over tracks of down. Fully equal to this, yet more subdued and delicate in the drapery and coloring, are the apartments of the empress. Here it may truly be said is "the poetry of motion" realized—saloons fit for the angels that flit through them, of whom the chiefest ornament is the empress herself—the beautiful and beloved Maria Alexandrina, the charm of whose presence is felt like a pleasant glow of sunshine wherever she goes. Here are drawing-rooms, boudoirs, apartments for the beautiful maids of honor, reading-rooms, and even a dancing-saloon, from which it may well be inferred that the royal party enjoy themselves. If the emperor fails to make himself agreeable in this branch of his establishment, he deserves to be put out at the very first station. But he has the ladies at a disadvantage, which probably compels them to be very tolerant of his behavior; that is to say, he can detach their branch of the establishment from his own, and leave them on the road at any time he pleases by pulling a string; but I believe there is no instance yet on record of his having availed himself of this autocratic privilege. It is usually understood at the start whether the excursion is to be in partnership or alone. When the emperor goes out on a hunting expedition, he is accompanied by a select company of gentlemen, and of course is compelled to deprive himself of the pleasure of the more attractive and intoxicating society of ladies, which would be calculated to unsteady his nerves, and render him unfit for those terrific encounters with the bears of the forest upon which his fame as a hunter is chiefly founded.

CHAPTER IV.

MOSCOW.

WHAT the great Napoleon thought when he gazed for the first time across the broad valley that lay at his feet, and caught the first dazzling light that flashed from the walls and golden cupolas of the Kremlin—whether some shadowy sense of the wondrous beauties of the scene did not enter his soul—is more than I can say with certainty; but this much I know, that neither he nor his legions could have enjoyed the view from Sparrow Hill more than I did the first glimpse of the grand old city of the Czars as I stepped from the railroad dépôt, with my knapsack on my back, and stood, a solitary and bewildered waif, uncertain if it could all be real; for never yet had I, in the experience of many years' travel, seen such a magnificent sight, so wildly Tartaric, so strange, glowing, and incomprehensible. This was Moscow at last—the Moscow I had read of when a child—the Moscow I had so often seen burnt up in panoramas by an excited and patriotic populace—the Moscow ever flashing through memory in fitful gleams, half buried in smoke, and flames, and toppling ruins, now absolutely before me, a gorgeous reality in the bright noonday sun, with its countless churches, its domes and cupolas, and mighty Kremlin.

Stand with me, reader, on the first eminence, and let us take a bird's-eye view of the city, always keeping in mind that the Kremlin is the great nucleus from which it all radiates. What a vast, wavy ocean of golden cupolas and fancy-colored domes, green-roofed houses and tortuous streets circle around this magic pile! what a combination of wild, barbaric splendors! nothing within the sweep of vision that is not glowing and Oriental.

Never was a city so fashioned for scenic effects. From the banks of the Moskwa the Kremlin rears its glittering crest, surrounded by green-capped towers and frowning embattlements, its umbrageous gardens and massive white walls conspicuous over the vast sea of green-roofed houses, while high above all, grand and stern, like some grim old Czar of the North, rises the magnificent tower of Ivan Veliki. Within these walls stand the chief glories of Moscow—the palaces of the Emperor, the Cathedral of the Assumption, the House of the Holy Synod, the Treasury, the Arsenal, and the Czar Kolokol, the great king of bells. All these gorgeous edifices, and many more, crown the eminence which forms the sacred grounds, clustering in a magic maze of beauty around the tower of Ivan the Terrible. Beyond the walls are numerous open spaces occupied by booths and markets; then come the principal streets and buildings of the city, encircled by the inner boulevards; then the suburbs, around which wind the outer boulevards; then a vast tract of beautiful and undulating country, dotted with villas, lakes, convents, and public buildings, inclosed in the far distance by the great outer wall, which forms a circuit of twenty miles around the city. The Moskwa River enters near the Presnerski Lake, and, taking a circuitous route, washes the base of the Kremlin, and passes out near the convent of St. Daniel. If you undertake, however, to trace out any plan of the city from the confused maze of streets that lie outspread before you, it will be infinitely worse than an attempt to solve the mysteries of a woman's heart; for there is no apparent plan about it; the whole thing is an unintelligible web of accidents. There is no accounting for its irregularity, unless upon the principle that it became distorted in a perpetual struggle to keep within reach of the Kremlin.

It is sometimes rather amusing to compare one's preconceived ideas of a place with the reality. A city like Moscow is very difficult to recognize from any written description. From some cause wholly inexplicable, I had pictured to my mind a vast gathering of tall, massive houses, elaborately ornamented; long lines of narrow and gloomy streets; many great palaces, dingy with age; and a population composed chiefly of Russian nabobs and their retinues of serfs. The reality is almost exactly the reverse of all these preconceived ideas. The houses for the most part are low—not over one or two stories high—painted with gay and fanciful colors, chiefly yellow, red, or blue; the roofs of tin or zinc, and nearly all of a bright green, giving them a very lively effect in the sun; nothing grand or imposing about them in detail, and but little pretension to architectural beauty. Very nearly such houses may be seen every day on any of the four continents.

Still, every indication of life presents a very different aspect from any thing in our own country. The people have a slow, slouching, shabby appearance; and the traveler is forcibly reminded, by the strange costumes he meets at every turn—the thriftless and degenerate aspect of the laboring classes—the great lumbering wagons that roll over the stone-paved streets—the droskies rattling hither and thither with their grave, priest-like drivers and wild horses—the squads of filthy soldiers lounging idly at every corner—the markets and market-places, and all that gives interest to the scene, that he is in a foreign land—a wild land of fierce battles between the elements, and fiercer still between men—where civilization is ever struggling between Oriental barbarism and European profligacy.

The most interesting feature in the population of Moscow is their constant and extraordinary displays of religious enthusiasm. This seems to be confined to no class or sect, but is the prevailing characteristic. No less than three hundred churches are embraced within the limits of the city. Some writers estimate the number as high as five hundred; nor does the discrepancy show so much a want of accuracy as the difficulty of determining precisely what constitutes a distinct church. Many of these remarkable edifices are built in clusters, with a variety of domes and cupolas, with different names, and contain distinct places of worship—as in the Cathedral of St. Basil, for instance, which is distinguished by a vast number of variegated domes, and embraces within its limits at least five or six separate churches, each church being still farther subdivided into various chapels. Of the extraordinary architectural style of these edifices, their many-shaped and highly-colored domes, representing all the hues of the rainbow, the gilding so lavishly bestowed upon them, their wonderfully picturesque effect from every point of view, it would be impossible to convey any adequate idea without entering into a more elaborate description than I can at present attempt.

But it is not only in the numberless churches scattered throughout the city that the devotional spirit of the inhabitants is manifested. Moscow is the Mecca of Russia, where all are devotees. The external forms of religion are every where apparent—in the palaces, the barracks, the institutions of learning, the traktirs, the bath-houses—even in the drinking cellars and gambling-hells. Scarcely a bridge or corner of a street is without its shrine, its pictured saint and burning taper, before which every by-passer of high or low degree bows down and worships. It may be said with truth that one is never out of sight of devotees baring their heads and prostrating themselves before these sacred images. All distinctions of rank seem lost in this universal passion for prayer. The nobleman, in his gilded carriage with liveried servants, stops and pays the tribute of an uncovered head to some saintly image by the bridge or the roadside; the peasant, in his shaggy sheepskin capote, doffs his greasy cap, and, while devoutly crossing himself, utters a prayer; the soldier, grim and warlike, marches up in his rattling armor, grounds his musket, and forgets for the time his mission of blood; the tradesman, with his leather apron and labor-worn hands, lays down his tools and does homage to the shrine; the drosky-driver, noted for his petty villainies, checks his horse, and, standing up in his drosky, bows low and crosses himself before he crosses the street or the bridge; even my guide, the saturnine Dominico—and every body knows what guides are all over the world—halted at every corner, regardless of time, and uttered an elaborate form of adjurations for our mutual salvation.

Pictures of a devotional character are offered for sale in almost every booth, alley, and passage-way, where the most extraordinary daubs may be seen pinned up to the walls. Saints and dragons, fiery-nosed monsters, and snakes, and horrid creeping things, gilded and decorated in the most gaudy style, attract idle crowds from morning till night.

It is marvelous with what profound reverence the Russians will gaze at these extraordinary specimens of art. Often you see a hardened-looking ruffian—his face covered with beard and filth; his great, brawny form resembling that of a prize-fighter; his costume a ragged blouse, with loose trowsers thrust in his boots; such a wretch, in short, as you would select for an unmitigated ruffian if you were in want of a model for that character—take off his cap, and, with superstitious awe and an expression of profound humility, bow down before some picture of a dragon with seven heads or a chubby little baby of saintly parentage.

That these poor people are sincere in their devotion there can be no doubt. Their sincerity, indeed, is attested by the strongest proofs of self-sacrifice. A Russian will not hesitate to lie, rob, murder, or suffer starvation for the preservation of his religion. Bigoted though he may be, he is true to his faith and devoted to his forms of worship, whatever may be his short-comings in other respects. It is a part of his nature; it permeates his entire being. Hence no city in the world, perhaps —Jerusalem not excepted—presents so strange a spectacle of religious enthusiasm, genuine and universal, mingled with moral turpitude; monkish asceticism and utter abandonment to vice; self-sacrifice and loose indulgence. It may be said that this is not true religion —not even what these people profess. Perhaps not; but it is what they are accustomed to from infancy, and it certainly develops some of their best traits of character—charity to each other, earnestness, constancy, and self-sacrifice.

On the morning after my arrival in Moscow I witnessed from the window of my hotel a very impressive and melancholy spectacle—the departure of a gang of prisoners for Siberia. The number amounted to some two or three hundred. Every year similar trains are dispatched, yet the parting scene always attracts a sympathizing crowd. These poor creatures were chained in pairs, and guarded by a strong detachment of soldiers. Their appearance, as they stood in the street awaiting the order to march, was very sad. Most of them were miserably clad, and some scarcely clad at all. A degraded, forlorn set they were—filthy and ragged—their downcast features expressive of an utter absence of hope. Few of them seemed to have any friends or relatives in the crowd of by-standers; but in two or three instances I noticed some very touching scenes of separation— where wives came to bid good-by to their husbands, and children to their fathers. Nearly every body gave them something to help them on their way—a few kopecks, a loaf of bread, or some cast-off article of clothing. I saw a little child timidly approach the gang, and, dropping a small coin into the hand of one poor wretch, run back again into the crowd, weeping bitterly. These prisoners are condemned to exile for three, four, or five years —often for life. It requires from twelve to eighteen months of weary travel, all the way on foot, through barren wastes and inhospitable deserts, to enable them to reach their desolate place of exile. Many of them fall sick on the way from fatigue and privation—many

PRISONERS FOR SIBERIA.

die. Few ever live to return. In some instances the whole term of exile is served out on the journey to and from Siberia. On their arrival they are compelled to labor in the government mines or on the public works. Occasionally the most skillful and industrious are rewarded by appointments to positions of honor and trust, and become in the course of time leading men.

In contemplating the dreary journey of these poor creatures—a journey of some fifteen hundred or two thousand miles—I was insensibly reminded of that touching little story of filial affection, "Elizabeth of Siberia," a story drawn from nature, and known in all civilized languages.

Not long after the departure of the Siberian prisoners, I witnessed, in passing along one of the principal streets, a grand funeral procession. The burial of the dead is a picturesque and interesting ceremony in Moscow. A body of priests, dressed in black robes and wearing long beards, take the lead in the funeral cortége, bearing in their hands shrines and burning tapers. The hearse follows, drawn by four horses. Black plumes wave from the heads of the horses, and flowing black drapery covers their bodies and legs. Even their heads are draped in black, nothing being perceptible but their eyes. The coffin lies exposed on the top of the hearse, and is also similarly draped. This combination of sombre plumage and drapery has a singularly mournful appearance. Priests stand on steps attached to the hearse holding images of the Savior over the coffin; others follow in the rear, comforting the friends and relatives of the deceased. A wild, monotonous chant is sung from time to time by the chief mourners as the procession moves toward the burial-ground. The people cease their occupations in the streets through which the funeral passes, uncover their heads, and, bowing down before the images borne by the priests, utter prayers for the repose of the dead. The rich and the poor of both sexes stand upon the sidewalks and offer up their humble petitions.

The deep-tongued bells of the Kremlin ring out solemn peals, and the wild and mournful chant of the priests mingles with the grand knell of death that sweeps through the air. All is profoundly impressive: the procession of priests, with their burning tapers; the drapery of black on the horses; the coffin with its dead; the weeping mourners; the sepulchral chant; the sudden cessation of all the business of life, and the rapt attention of the multitude; the deep, grand, death-knell of the bells; the glitter of domes and cupolas on every side; the green-roofed sea of houses; the winding streets, and the costumes of the people—form a spectacle wonderfully wild, strange, and mournful. In every thing that comes within the sweep of the eye there is a mixed aspect of Tartaric barbarism and European civilization. Yet even the stranger from a far-distant clime, speaking another language, accustomed to other forms, must feel, in gazing upon such a scene, that death levels all distinctions of race—that our common mortality brings us nearer together. Every where we are pilgrims on the same journey. Wherever we sojourn among men,

> "The dead around us lie,
> And the death-bell tolls."

CHAPTER V.

TEA-DRINKING.

THE *traktirs*, or tea-houses, are prominent among the remarkable institutions of Russia. In Moscow they abound in every street, lane, and by-alley. That situated near the Katai Gorod is said to be the best. Though inferior to the ordinary cafés of Paris or Marseilles in extent and decoration, it is nevertheless pretty stylish in its way, and is interesting to strangers from the fact that it represents a prominent feature in Russian life—the drinking of *tchai*.

Who has not heard of Russian tea?—the tea that comes all the way across the steppes of Tartary and over the Ural Mountains?—the tea that never loses its flavor by admixture with the salt of the ocean, but is delivered over at the great fair of Nijni Novgorod as pure and fragrant as when it started? He who has never heard

TEA-SELLERS.

of Russian tea has heard nothing, and he who has never enjoyed a glass of it may have been highly favored in other respects, but I contend that he has nevertheless led a very benighted existence. All epicures in the delicate leaf unite in pronouncing it far superior to the nectar with which the gods of old were wont to quench their thirst. It is truly one of the luxuries of life—so soft;

so richly yet delicately flavored ; so bright, glowing, and transparent as it flashes through the crystal glasses ; nothing acrid, gross, or earthly about it—a heavenly compound that " cheers but not inebriates."

> "A balm for the sickness of care,
> A bliss for a bosom unbless'd."

Come with me, friend, and let us take a seat in the traktir. Every body here is a tea-drinker. Coffee is never good in Russia. Besides, it is gross and villainous stuff compared with the *tchai* of Moscow. At all hours of the day we find the saloons crowded with Russians, French, Germans, and the representatives of various other nations—all worshipers before the burnished shrine of *Tchai*. A little saint in the corner presides especially over this department. The devout Russians take off their hats and make a profound salam to this accommodating little patron, whose corpulent stomach and smiling countenance betoken an appreciation of all the good things of life. Now observe how these wonderful Russians—the strangest and most incomprehensible of beings—cool themselves this sweltering hot day. Each stalwart son of the North calls for a portion of *tchai*, not a tea-cupful or a glassful, but a genuine Russian portion—a tea-potful. The tea-pot is small, but the tea is strong enough to bear an unlimited amount of dilution ; and it is one of the glorious privileges of the tea-drinker in this country that he may have as much hot water as he pleases. Sugar is more sparingly supplied. The adept remedies this difficulty by placing a lump of sugar in his mouth and sipping his tea through it—a great improvement upon the custom said to exist in some parts of Holland, where a lump of sugar is hung by a string over the table and swung around from mouth to mouth, so that each guest may take a pull at it after swallowing his tea. A portion would be quite enough for a good-sized family in America. The Russian makes nothing of it. Filling and swilling hour after hour, he seldom rises before he gets through ten or fifteen tum-

blersful, and, if he happens to be thirsty, will double it—
enough, one would think, to founder a horse. But the
Russian stomach is constructed upon some physiological

MUJIKS AT TEA.

principles unknown to the rest of mankind—perhaps
lined with gutta-percha and riveted to a diaphragm of
sheet-iron. Grease and scalding-hot tea; *quass* and cab-

bage soup; raw cucumbers; cold fish; lumps of ice; decayed cheese and black bread, seem to have no other effect upon it than to provoke an appetite. In warm weather it is absolutely marvelous to see the quantities of fiery-hot liquids these people pour down their throats. Just cast your eye upon that bearded giant in the corner, with his hissing urn of tea before him, his *batvina* and his *shtshie!* What a spectacle of physical enjoyment! His throat is bare; his face a glowing carbuncle; his body a monstrous caldron, seething and dripping with overflowing juices. Shade of Hebe! how he swills the tea—how glass after glass of the steaming-hot liquid flows into his capacious maw, and diffuses itself over his entire person! It oozes from every pore of his skin; drops in globules from his forehead; smokes through his shirt; makes a piebald chart of seas and islands over his back; streams down and simmers in his boots! He is saturated with tea, inside and out—a living sponge overflowing at every pore. You might wring him out, and there would still be a heavy balance left in him.

These traktirs are the general places of meeting, where matters of business or pleasure are discussed; accounts settled and bargains made. Here the merchant, the broker, the banker, and the votary of pleasure meet in common. Here all the pursuits of human life are represented, and the best qualities of men drawn out with the drawing of the tea. Enmities are forgotten and friendships cemented in tea. In short, the traktir is an institution, and its influence extends through all the ramifications of society.

But it is in the gardens and various places of suburban resort that the universal passion for tea is displayed in its most pleasing and romantic phases. Surrounded by the beauties of nature, lovers make their avowals over the irrepressible tea-pot; the hearts of fair damsels are won in the intoxication of love and tea; quarrels between man and wife are made up, and children weaned

—I had almost said baptized—in tea. The traveler must see the families seated under the trees, with the burnished urn before them — the children romping about over the grass; joy beaming upon every face; the whole neighborhood a repetition of family groups and steaming urns, bound together by the mystic tie of sympathy, before he can fully appreciate the important part that tea performs in the great drama of Russian life.

CHAPTER VI.

THE PETERSKOI GARDENS.

This draws me insensibly toward the beautiful gardens of the Peterskoi—a favorite place of resort for the Moskovites, and famous for its chateau built by the Empress Elizabeth, in which Napoleon sought refuge during the burning of Moscow. It is here the rank and fashion of the city may be seen to the greatest advantage of a fine summer afternoon. In these gardens all that is brilliant, beautiful, and poetical in Russian life finds a congenial atmosphere.

I spent an evening at the Peterskoi which I shall long remember as one of the most interesting I ever spent at any place of popular amusement. The weather was charming—neither too warm nor too cold, but of that peculiarly soft and dreamy temperature which predisposes one for the enjoyment of music, flowers, the prattle of children, the fascinations of female loveliness, and the luxuries of idleness. In such an atmosphere no man of sentiment can rack his brain with troublesome problems. These witching hours, when the sun lingers dreamily on the horizon; when the long twilight weaves a web of purple and gold that covers the transition from night to morning; when nature, wearied of the dazzling glare of day, puts on her silver-spangled robes, and receives her worshipers with celestial smiles, are surely enough to soften the most stubborn heart. We must make love, sweet ladies, or die. There is no help for it. Resistance is an abstract impossibility. The best man in the world could not justly be censured for practicing a little with his eyes, when away from home, merely as I do, you know, to keep up the expression.

The gardens of the Peterskoi are still a dream to me. For a distance of three versts from the gate of St. Petersburg the road was thronged with carriages and droskies, and crowds of gayly-dressed citizens, all wending their way toward the scene of entertainment. The pressure for tickets at the porter's lodge was so great that it required considerable patience and good-humor to get through at all. Officers in dashing uniforms rode on spirited chargers up and down the long rows of vehicles, and with drawn swords made way for the foot-passengers. Guards in imperial livery, glittering from head to foot with embroidery, stood at the grand portals of the gate, and with many profound and elegant bows ushered in the company. Policeman with cocked hats and shining epaulets were stationed at intervals along the leading thoroughfares to preserve order.

The scene inside the gates was wonderfully imposing. Nothing could be more fanciful. In every aspect it presented some striking combination of natural and artificial beauties, admirably calculated to fascinate the imagination. I have a vague recollection of shady and undulating walks, winding over sweeping lawns dotted with masses of flowers and copses of shrubbery, and overhung by wide-spreading trees, sometimes gradually rising over gentle acclivities or points of rock overhung with moss and fern. Rustic cottages, half hidden by the luxuriant foliage, crowned each prominent eminence, and little byways branched off into cool, umbrageous recesses, where caves, glittering with sea-shells and illuminated stalactites, invited the wayfarer to linger a while and rest. Far down in deep glens land grottoes were retired nooks, where lovers, hidden from the busy throng, might mingle their vows to the harmony of falling waters ; where the very flowers seemed whispering love to each other, and the lights and shadows fell, by some intuitive sense of fitness, into the form of bridal wreaths. Marble statues representing the Graces, winged Mercuries and Cupids, are so cunningly displayed in relief against the green banks of foliage that they seem the natural inhabitants of the place. Snow-spirits, too, with outspread wings, hover in the air, as if to waft cooling zephyrs through the soft summer night. In the open spaces fountains dash their sparkling waters high into the moonlight, spreading a mystic spray over the sward. Through vistas of shrubbery gleam the bright waters of a lake, on the far side of which the embattled towers of a castle rise in bold relief over the intervening groups of trees.

On an elevated plateau, near the centre of the garden, stands a series of Asiatic temples and pagodas, in which the chief entertainments are held. The approaching avenues are illuminated with many-colored lights suspended from the branches of the trees, and wind under triumphal archways, festooned with flowers. The theatres present open fronts, and abound in all the tinsel of the stage, both inside and out. The grounds are crowded to their utmost capacity with the rank and fashion of the city, in all the glory of jeweled head-dresses and decorations of order. Festoons of variegated lights swing from the trees over the audience, and painted figures of dragons and genii are dimly seen in the background.

Attracted by sounds of applause at one of these theatres, I edged my way through the crowd, and succeeded, after many apologies, in securing a favorable position. Amid a motley gathering of Russians, Poles, Germans, and French—for here all nations and classes are represented—my ears were stunned by the clapping of hands and vociferous cries of *Bis! Bis!* The curtain was down, but in answer to the call for a repetition of the last scene it soon rose again, and afforded me an opportunity of witnessing a characteristic performance. A wild Mujik has the impudence to make love to the maid-servant

of his master, who appears to be rather a crusty old
gentleman, not disposed to favor matrimonial alliances
of that kind. Love gets the better of the lover's discretion, and he is surprised in the kitchen. The bull-dog is
let loose upon him; master and mistress and subordinate

RUSSIAN THEATRE.

members of the family rush after him, armed with sauce-pans, tongs, shovels, and broomsticks. The affrighted Mujik runs all round the stage bellowing fearfully; the bull-dog seizes him by the nether extremities and hangs on with the tenacity of a vice. Round and round they run, Mujik roaring for help, bull-dog swinging out hori-zontally. The audience applauds; the master flings down his broomstick and seizes the dog by the tail; the old woman seizes master by the skirts of his coat; and all three are dragged around the stage at a terrific rate, while the younger members of the family shower down miscellaneous blows with their sticks and cudgels, which always happen to fall on the old people, to the great satisfaction of the audience. Shouts, and shrieks, and clapping of hands but faintly express the popular appre-ciation of the joke. Finally the faithful maid, taking ad-vantage of the confusion, flings a bunch of fire-crackers at her oppressors and blows them up, and the Mujik, re-lieved of their weight, makes a brilliant dash through the door, carrying with him the tenacious bull-dog, which it is reasonable to suppose he subsequently takes to market and sells for a good price. The curtain falls, the music strikes up, and the whole performance is greeted with the most enthusiastic applause. Such are the entertain-ments that delight these humorous people—a little broad to be sure, but not deficient in grotesque spirit.

From the theatre I wandered to the pavilion of Zin-galee gipsies, where a band of these wild sons of Hagar were creating a perfect furor by the shrillness and dis-cord of their voices. Never was such terrific music in-flicted upon mortal ears. It went through and through you, quivering and vibrating like a rapier; but the com-mon classes of Russians delight in it above all earthly sounds. They deem it the very finest kind of music. It is only the dilettante who have visited Paris who profess to hold it in contempt.

Very soon surfeited with these piercing strains, I ram-bled away till I came upon a party of rope-dancers, and after seeing a dozen or so of stout fellows hang themselves by the chins, turn back somersaults in the air, and swing by one foot at a dizzy height from the ground, left them standing upon each other's heads to the depth of six or eight, and turned aside into a grotto to enjoy a few glasses of tea. Here were German girls singing and buffoons reciting humorous stories between the pauses, and thirsty Russians pouring down whole oceans of their favorite beverage.

Again I wandered forth through the leafy mazes of the garden. The gorgeous profusion of lights and glittering ornaments, the endless variety of colors, the novel and Asiatic appearance of the temples, the tropical luxuriance of the foliage, the gleaming white statuary, the gay company, the wild strains of music, all combined to form a scene of peculiar interest. High overhead, dimly visible through the tops of the trees, the sky wears an almost supernatural aspect during these long summer nights. A soft golden glow flushes upward from the horizon, and, lying outspread over the firmament, gives a spectral effect to the gentler and more delicate sheen of the moon; the stars seem to shrink back into the dim infinity, as if unable to contend with the grosser effulgence of the great orbs that rule the day and the night. Unconscious whether the day is waning into the night, or the night into the morning, the rapt spectator gazes and dreams till lost in the strange enchantment of the scene.

At a late hour a signal was given, and the company wandered down to the lake, along the shores of which rustic seats and divans, overshadowed by shrubbery, afforded the weary an opportunity of resting. Here we were to witness the crowning entertainment of the evening—a grand display of fire-works. A miniature steamboat, gayly decorated with flags, swept to and fro, carrying passengers to the different landing-places. Gondolas, with peaked prows and variegated canopies, lay floating upon the still water, that lovers might quench their flames in the contemplation of its crystal depths, or draw fresh inspiration from the blaze of artificial fires. Soon a wild outburst of music was heard; then from the opposite shore the whole heavens were lighted up with a flood of rockets, and the ears were stunned by their explosions. Down through the depths of ether came showers of colored balls, illuminating the waters of the lake with inverted streams of light scarcely less bright and glowing. Anon all was dark; then from out the darkness flashed whirling and seething fires, gradually assuming the grotesque forms of monsters and genii, till with a deafening explosion they were scattered to the winds. From the blackened mass of ruins stood forth illuminated statues of the imperial family, in all the paraphernalia of royalty, their crowns glittering with jewels, their robes of light resplendent with precious gems and tracery of gold. A murmur of admiration ran through the crowd. The imperial figures vanished as if by magic, and suddenly a stream of fire flashed from a mass of dark undefined objects on the opposite shore, and lo! the waters were covered with fiery swans, sailing majestically among the gondolas, their necks moving slowly as if inspired by life. Hither and thither they swept, propelled by streams of fire, till, wearied with their sport, they gradually lay motionless, yet glowing with an augmented brilliancy. While the eyes of all were fixed in amazement and admiration upon these beautiful swans, they exploded with a series of deafening reports, and were scattered in confused volumes of smoke. Out of the chaos swept innumerable hosts of whirling little monsters, whizzing and boring through the water like infernal spirits of the deep. These again burst with a rattle of explosions like an irregular fire of musketry, and shot high into the air in a perfect maze of scintillating stars of every imaginable color. When the shower of stars was over, and silence and darkness once more reigned, a magnificent barge, that might well have represented that of the Egyptian queen—its gay canopies resplendent with the

THE PETERSKOI GARDENS.

glow of many-colored lamps—swept out into the middle of the lake, and

> "Like a burnished throne
> Burn'd on the water."

And when the rowers had ceased, and the barge lay motionless, soft strains of music arose from its curtained recesses, swelling up gradually till the air was filled with the floods of rich, wild harmony, and the senses were ravished with their sweetness.

Was it a wild Oriental dream? Could it all be real—the glittering fires, the gayly-costumed crowds, the illuminated barge, the voluptuous strains of music? Might it not be some gorgeous freak of the emperor, such as the sultan in the Arabian Nights enjoyed at the expense of the poor traveler? Surely there could be nothing real like it since the days of the califs of Bagdad!

A single night's entertainment such as this must cost many thousand rubles. When it is considered that there are but few months in the year when such things can be enjoyed, some idea may be formed of the characteristic passion of the Russians for luxurious amusements. It is worthy of mention, too, that the decorations, the lamps, the actors and operators, the material of nearly every description, are imported from various parts of the world, and very little is contributed in any way by the native Russians, save the means by which these costly luxuries are obtained.

CHAPTER VII.

THE "LITTLE WATER."

On the fundamental principles of association the intelligent reader will at once comprehend how it came to pass that, of all the traits I discovered in the Russian people, none impressed me so favorably as their love of vodka, or native brandy, signifying the "little water." I admired their long and filthy beards and matted heads

D

of hair, because there was much in them to remind me
of my beloved Washoe; but in nothing did I experience
a greater fellowship with them than in their constitutional thirst for intoxicating liquors. It was absolutely
refreshing, after a year's travel over the Continent of
Europe, to come across a genuine lover of the "taran-
tula"—to meet at every corner of the street a great
bearded fellow staggering along blind drunk, or attempting to steady the town by hugging a post. Rarely had I enjoyed such a sight since my arrival in the Old
World. In Germany I had seen a few cases of stupe-
faction arising from overdoses of beer; in France the
red nose of the *bon vivant* is not uncommon; in England some muddled heads are to be found; and in Scotland there are temperance societies enough to give rise
to the suspicion that there is a cause for them; but, generally speaking, the sight of an intoxicated man is somewhat rare in the principal cities of the Continent. It
will, therefore, be conceded that there was something
very congenial in the spectacle that greeted me on the
very first day of my arrival in Moscow. A great giant
of a Mujik, with a ferocious beard and the general aspect
of a wild beast, came toward me with a heel and a lurch
to port that was very expressive of his condition. As he
staggered up and tried to balance himself, he blurted out
some unmeaning twaddle in his native language which I
took to be a species of greeting. His expression was
absolutely inspiring—the great blear eyes rolling foolishly in his head; his tongue lolling helplessly from his
mouth; his under jaw hanging down; his greasy cap
hung on one side on a tuft of dirty hair—all so familiar,
so characteristic of something I had seen before! Where
could it have been? What potent spell was there about
this fellow to attract me? In what was it that I, an
embassador from Washoe, a citizen of California, a resi-
dent of Oakland, could thus be drawn toward this hideous wretch? A word in your ear, reader. It was all
all the effect of association! The unbidden tears flow-

ed to my eyes as I caught a whiff of the fellow's
breath.　It was so like the free-lunch breaths of San
Francisco, and even suggested thoughts of the Legis-
lative Assembly in Sacramento.　Only think what a
genuine Californian must suffer in being a whole year
without a glass of whisky—nay, without as much as a
smell of it!　How delightful it is to see a brother human downright soggy drunk; drunk all over; drunk
in the eyes, in the mouth, in the small of his back, in his

VODKA.

knees, in his boots, clear down to his toes!　How one's
heart is drawn toward him by this common bond of human infirmity!　How it recalls the camp, the one-horse
mining town, the social gathering of the "boys" at
Dan's, or Jim's, or Jack's; and the clink of dimes and
glasses at the bar; how distances are annihilated and
time set back!　Of a verity, when I saw that man, with

reason dethroned and the garb of self-respect thrown aside, I was once again in my own beloved state!

> "What a beauty dwelt in each familiar face,
> What music hung on every voice!"

Since reading is not a very general accomplishment among the lower classes, a system of signs answers in some degree as a substitute. The irregularity of the streets would of itself present no very remarkable feature but for the wonderful variety of small shops and the oddity of the signs upon which their contents are pictured. What these symbols of trade lack in artistic style they make up in grotesque effects. Thus, the tobacco shops are ornamented outside with various highly-colored pictures, drawn by artists of the most florid genius, representing cigar-boxes, pipes, meerschaums, narghillas, bunches of cigars, snuff-boxes, plugs and twists of tobacco, and all that the most fastidious smoker, chewer, or snuffer can expect to find in any tobacco shop, besides a good many things that he never will find in any of these shops. Prominent among these symbolical displays is the counterfeit presentment of a jet-black Indian of African descent—his woolly head adorned with a crown of pearls and feathers; in his right hand an uplifted tomahawk, with which he is about to kill some invisible enemy; in his left a meerschaum, supposed to be the pipe of peace; a tobacco plantation in the background, and a group of warriors smoking profusely around a camp-fire, located under one of the tobacco plants; the whole having a very fine allegorical effect, fully understood, no doubt, by the artist, but very difficult to explain upon any known principle of art. The butchers' shops are equally prolific in external adornments. On the sign-boards you see every animal fit to be eaten, and many of questionable aspect, denuded of their skins and reduced to every conceivable degree of butchery; so that if you want a veal cutlet of any particular pattern, all you have to do is to select your pattern, and the cutlet will be chopped accordingly. The bakeries excel in their artistic displays. Here you have painted bread from black-moon down to double-knotted twist; cakes, biscuit, rolls, and crackers, and as many other varieties as the genius of the artist may be capable of suggesting. The bakers of Moscow are mostly French or German; .and it is a notable fact that the bread is quite equal to any made in France or Germany. The wine-stores, of which there are many, are decorated with pictures of bottles, and bas-reliefs of gilded grapes—a great improvement upon the ordinary grape produced by nature.

CHAPTER VIII.

THE MARKETS OF MOSCOW.

If there is nothing new under the sun, there are certainly a good many old things to interest a stranger in Moscow. A favorite resort of mine during my sojourn in that strange old city of the Czars was in the markets of the Katai Gorod. Those of the Riadi and Gostovini Dvor present the greatest attractions, perhaps, in the way of shops and merchandise; for there, by the aid of time, patience, and money, you can get any thing you want, from saints' armlets and devils down to candlesticks and cucumbers. Singing-birds, Kazan-work, and Siberian diamonds are its most attractive features. But if you have a passion for human oddities rather than curiosities of merchandise, you must visit the second-hand markets extending along the walls of the Katai Gorod, where you will find not only every conceivable variety of old clothes, clocks, cooking utensils, and rubbish of all sorts, but the queerest imaginable conglomeration of human beings from the far East to the far West. It would be a fruitless task to attempt a description of the motley assemblage. Pick out all the strangest, most ragged, most uncouth figures you ever saw in old pictures, from childhood up to the present day; select

OLD-CLOTHES' MARKET.

from every theatrical representation within the range of your experience the most monstrous and absurd caricatures upon humanity; bring to your aid all the masquerades and burlesque fancy-balls you ever visited, tumble them together in the great bag of your imagination, and pour them out over a vague wilderness of open spaces, dirty streets, high walls, and rickety little booths, and you have no idea at all of the queer old markets of the Katai Gorod. You will be just as much puzzled to make any thing of the scene as when you started, if not more so.

No mortal man can picture to another all these shaggy-faced Russians, booted up to the knees, their long, loose robes flaunting idly around their legs, their red sashes twisted around their waists; brawny fellows with a reckless, independent swagger about them, stalking like grim savages of the North through the crowd. Then there are the sallow and cadaverous Jew peddlers, covered all over with piles of ragged old clothes, and mountains of old hats and caps; and leathery-faced old women —witches of Endor—dealing out horrible mixtures of *quass* (the national drink); and dirty, dingy-looking soldiers, belonging to the imperial service, peddling off old boots and cast-off shirts; and Zingalee gipsies, dark, lean, and wiry, offering strings of beads and armlets for sale with shrill cries; and so on without limit.

Here you see the rich and the poor in all the extremes of affluence and poverty; the robust and the decrepit; the strong, the lame, and the blind; the noble, with his star and orders of office; the Mujik in his shaggy sheep-skin capote or tattered blouse; the Mongolian, the Persian, and the Caucasian; the Greek and the Turk; the Armenian and the Californian, all intent upon something, buying, selling, or looking on.

Being the only representative from the Golden State, I was anxious to offer some Washoe stock for sale— twenty or thirty feet in the Gone Case; but Dominico, my interpreter, informed me that these traders had never heard of Washoe, and were mostly involved in Russian securities—old breeches, boots, stockings, and the like. He did not think my "Gone Case" would bring an old hat; and as for my "Sorrowful Countenance" and "Ragged End," he was persuaded I could not dispose of my entire interest in them for a pint of grease.

I was very much taken with the soldiers who infested

these old markets. It was something new in military economy to see the representatives of an imperial army supporting themselves in this way; dark, lazy fellows in uniform, lounging about with old boots and suspenders hanging all over them, crying out the merits of their wares in stentorian voices, thus, as it were, patriotically relieving the national treasury of a small fraction of its burden. They have much the appearance, in the crowd, of raisins in a plum-pudding.

The peasant women, who flock in from the country with immense burdens of vegetables and other products of the farms, are a very striking, if not a very pleasing feature in the markets. Owing to the hard labor imposed upon them, they are exceedingly rough and brawny, and have a hard, dreary, and unfeminine expression of countenance, rather inconsistent with one's notions of the delicacy and tenderness of woman. Few of them are even passably well-looking. All the natural playfulness of the gentler sex seems to be crushed out of them; and while their manners are uncouth, their voices are the wildest and most unmusical that ever fell upon the ear from a feminine source. When dressed in their best attire they usually wear a profusion of red handkerchiefs about their heads and shoulders; and from an unpicturesque habit they have of making an upper waist immediately under their arms by a ligature of some sort, and tying their apron-strings about a foot below, they have the singular appearance of being double-waisted or three-story women. They carry their children on their backs, much after the fashion of Digger Indians, and suckle them through an opening in the second or middle story. Doubtless this is a convenient arrangement, but it presents the curious anomaly of a poor peasant living in a one-story house with a three-story wife. According to the prevailing style of architecture in well-wooded countries, these women ought to wear their hair shingled; but they generally tie it up in a knot behind, or cover it with a fancy-colored handkerchief, on the presumption, I suppose, that they look less barbarous in that way than they would with shingled heads. You may suspect me of story-telling, but upon my word I think three-story women are extravagant enough without adding another to them. I only hope their garrets contain a better quality of furniture than that which afflicts the male members of the Mujik community. No wonder those poor women have families of children like steps of stairs! It is said that their husbands are often very cruel to them, and think nothing of knocking them down and beating them; but even that does not surprise me. How can a man be expected to get along with a three-story wife unless he floors her occasionally?

Ragged little boys, prematurely arrested in their growth, you see too, in myriads—shovel-nosed and bare-legged urchins of hideously eccentric manners, carrying around big bottles of *sbiteen* (a kind of mead), which they are continually pouring out into glasses, to appease the chronic thirst with which the public seem to be afflicted; and groups of the natives gathered around a cucumber stand, devouring great piles of unwholesome-looking cucumbers, which skinny old women are dipping up out of wooden buckets. The voracity with which all classes stow away these vicious edibles in their stomachs is amazing, and suggests a melancholy train of reflections on the subject of cholera morbus. It was a continual matter of wonder to me how the lower classes of Russians survived the horrid messes with which they tortured their digestive apparatus. Only think of thousands of men dining every day on black bread, heavy enough for bullets, a pound or two of grease, and half a peck of raw cucumbers per man, and then expecting to live until next morning! And yet they do live, and grow fat, and generally die at a good old age, in case they are not killed in battle, or frozen up in the wilds of Siberia.

Outside the walls of the Katai Gorod, in an open square, or plaza, are rows of wooden booths, in which innumerable varieties of living stock are offered for sale—

geese, ducks, chickens, rabbits, pigeons, and birds of various sorts. I sometimes went down here and bargained for an hour or so over a fat goose or a Muscovy duck, not with any ultimate idea of purchasing it, but merely because it was offered to me at a reduced price. It was amusing, also, to study the manners and customs of the dealers, and enjoy their amazement when, after causing them so much loss of time, I would hand over five kopeks and walk off. Some of them, I verily believe, will long entertain serious doubts as to the sanity of the Californian public; for Dominico, my guide, always took particular pride in announcing that I was from that great country, and was the richest man in it, being, to the best of his knowledge, the only one who had money enough to spare to travel all the way to Moscow, merely for the fun of the thing.

I may as well mention, parenthetically, that Dominico was rather an original in his way. His father was an Italian and his mother a Russian. I believe he was born in Moscow. How he came to adopt the profession of guide I don't know, unless it was on account of some natural proclivity for an easy life. A grave, lean, saturnine man was Dominico—something of a cross between Machiavelli and Paganini. If he knew any thing about the wonders and curiosities of Moscow he kept it a profound secret. It was only by the most rigid inquiry and an adroit system of cross-examination that I could get any thing out of him, and then his information was vague and laconic, sometimes a little sarcastic, but never beyond what I knew myself. Yet he was polite, dignified, and gentlemanly—never refused to drink a glass of beer with me, and always knew the way to a traktir. To the public functionaries with whom we came in contact during the course of our rambles his air was grand and imposing; and on the subject of money he was sublimely nonchalant, caring no more for rubles than I did for kopeks. Once or twice he hinted to me that he was of noble blood, but laid no particular stress upon that, since it was his misfortune at present to be in rather reduced circumstances. Some time or other he would go to Italy and resume his proper position there. In justice to Dominico, I must add that he never neglected an opportunity of praying for me before any of the public shrines; and at the close of our acquaintance he let me off pretty easily, all things considered. Upon my explaining to him that a draft for five hundred thousand rubles, which ought to be on the way, had failed to reach me, owing, doubtless, to some irregularity in the mail service, or some sudden depression in my Washoe stocks, he merely shrugged his shoulders, took a pinch of snuff, and accepted with profound indifference a fee amounting to three times the value of his services.

I was particularly interested in the dog-market. The display of living dog-flesh here must be very tempting to one who has a taste for poodle soup or fricasseed pup. Dominico repudiated the idea that the Russians are addicted to this article of diet; but the very expression of his eye as he took up a fat little innocent, smoothed down its skin, squeezed its ribs, pinched its loins, and smelled it, satisfied me that a litter of pups would stand but a poor chance of ever arriving at maturity if they depended upon forbearance upon his part as a national virtue. The Chinese quarter of San Francisco affords some curious examples of the art of compounding sustenance for man out of odd materials—rats, snails, dried frogs, star-fish, polypi, and the like; but any person who wishes to indulge a morbid appetite for the most disgusting dishes ever devised by human ingenuity·must visit Moscow. I adhere to it that the dog-market supplies a large portion of the population with fancy meats. No other use could possibly be made of the numberless squads of fat, hairless dogs tied together and hawked about by the traders in this article of traffic. I saw one man—he had the teeth of an ogre and a fearfully carnivorous expression of eye—carry around a bunch of pups on each arm, and cry aloud something in his native tongue, which I am confident had reference to the tenderness and juiciness of their flesh. Dominico declared the man was only talking about the breed—that they were fine rat-dogs; but I know that was a miserable subterfuge. Such dogs never caught a rat in this world; and if they did, it must have been with a view to the manufacture of sausages.

CABINET-MAKERS.

A Russian peasant is not particular about the quality of his food, as may well be supposed from this general summary. Quantity is the main object. Grease of all kinds is his special luxury. The upper classes, who have plenty of money to spare, may buy fish from the Volga at its weight in gold, and mutton from Astrakan at fabulous prices; but give the Mujik his *batvina* (salt grease and honey boiled together), a loaf of black bread, and a peck of raw cucumbers, and he is happy. Judging by external appearances, very little grease seems to be wasted in the manufacture of soap. Indeed, I would not trust one of these Mujiks to carry a pound of soap any where for me, any more than I would a gallon of oil or a pound of candles. Once I saw a fellow grease his boots with a lump of dirty fat which he had picked up out of the gutter, but he took good care first to extract from it the richest part of its essence by sucking it, and then greasing his beard. The boots came last. In all probability he had just dined, or he would have pocketed his treasure for another occasion, instead of throwing the remnant, as he did, to the nearest cat.

In respect to the language, one might as well be dropped down in Timbuctoo as in a village or country town of Russia, for all the good the gift of speech would do him. It is not harsh, as might be supposed, yet wonderfully like an East India jungle when you attempt to penetrate it. I could make better headway through a boulder of solid quartz, or the title to my own house and lot in Oakland. Now I profess to be able to see as far into a mill-stone as most people, but I can't see in what respect the Russians behaved any worse than other people of the Tower of Babel, that they should be afflicted with a language which nobody can hope to understand before his beard becomes grizzled, and the top of his head entirely bald. Many of the better classes, to be sure, speak French and German; but even in the streets of Moscow I could seldom find any body who could discover a ray of meaning in my French or German, which is almost as plain as English.

Some people know what you want by instinct, whether they understand your language or not. Not so the Russians. Ask for a horse, and they will probably offer you a fat goose; inquire the way to your lodgings, and they are just as likely as not to show you the Foundling Hospital or a livery-stable; go into an old variety shop, and express a desire to purchase an Astrakan breast-pin for your sweet-heart, and the worthy trader hands you a pair of bellows or an old blunderbuss; cast your eye upon any old market-woman, and she divines at once that you are in search of a bunch of chickens or a bucket of raw cucumbers, and offers them to you at the lowest market-price; hint to a picture-dealer that you would like to have an authentic portrait of his imperial majesty, and he hands you a picture of the Iberian Mother, or St. George slaying the dragon, or the devil and all his imps; in short, you can get any thing that you don't want, and nothing that you do. If these people are utterly deficient in any one quality, it is a sense of fitness in things. They take the most inappropriate times for offering you the most inappropriate articles of human use that the imagination can possibly conceive. I was more than once solicited by the dealers in the markets of Moscow to carry with me a bunch of live dogs, or a couple of freshly-scalded pigs, and on one occasion was pressed very hard to take a brass skillet and a pair of tongs. What could these good people have supposed I wanted with articles of this kind on my travels? Is there any thing in my dress or the expression of my countenance —I leave it to all who know me—any thing in the mildness of my speech or the gravity of my manner, to indicate that I am suffering particularly for bunches of dogs or scalded pigs, brass skillets or pairs of tongs? Do I look like a man who labors under a chronic destitution of dogs, pigs, skillets, and tongs?

It is quite natural that the traveler who finds himself for the first time within the limits of a purely despotic government should look around him with some vague idea that he must see the effects strongly marked upon the external life of the people; that the restraints imposed upon popular liberty must be every where appar-

PIGS, PUPS, AND PANS.

ent. So far as any thing of this kind may exist in Moscow or St. Petersburg, it is a notable fact that there are few cities in the world where it is less visible, or where the people seem more unrestrained in the exercise of their popular freedom. Indeed, it struck me rather forcibly, after my experience in Vienna and Berlin, that the Russians enjoy quite as large a share of practical independence as most of their neighbors. I was particularly impressed by the bold and independent air of the middle classes, the politeness with which even the lower orders address each other, and the absence of those petty and vexatious restraints which prevail in some of the German states. The constant dread of infringing upon the police regulations; the extraordinary deference with which men in uniform are regarded; the circumspect behavior at public places; the nice and well-regulated mirthfulness, never overstepping the strict bounds of prudence, which I had so often noticed in the northern parts of Germany, and which may in part be attributed to the naturally orderly and conservative character of the people, are by no means prominent features in the principal cities of Russia.

Soldiers, indeed, there are in abundance every where throughout the dominions of the Czar, and the constant rattle of musketry and clang of arms show that the liberty of the people is not altogether without limit.

CHAPTER IX.

THE NOSE REGIMENT.

I saw nothing in the line of military service that interested me more than the Imperial Guard. Without vouching for the truth of the whole story connected with the history of this famous regiment, I give it as related to me by Dominico, merely stating as a fact within my own observation that there is no question whatever about the peculiarity of their features. It seems that the Emperor Nicholas, shortly before the Crimean War, discovered by some means that the best fighting men in his dominions belonged to a certain wild tribe from the north, distinguished for the extreme ugliness of their faces. The most remarkable feature was the nose, which stood straight out from the base of the forehead in the form of a triangle, presenting in front the appearance of

a double-barreled pistol. A stiff grizzly mustache underneath gave them a peculiarly ferocious expression, so
that brave men quailed, and women and children fled
from them in terror. The emperor gave orders that all
men in the ranks possessed of these frightful noses should
be brought before him. Finding, when they were mustered together, that there was not over one company, he
caused a general average of the noses to be taken, from
which he had a diagram carefully prepared and dissem-
inated throughout the empire, calling upon the military
commanders of the provinces to send him recruits corresponding with the prescribed formula.

In due time he was enabled to muster a thousand of
these ferocious barbarians, whom he caused to be carefully drilled and disciplined. He kept them in St. Petersburg under his own immediate supervision till some
time after the attack upon Sebastopol, when, finding the
fortunes of war likely to go against him, he sent them
down to the Crimea, with special instructions to the
commander-in-chief to rely upon them in any emergency. In compliance with the imperial order, they were
at once placed in the front ranks, and in a very few days
had occasion to display their fighting qualities. At the
very first onslaught of the enemy they stood their ground
manfully till the French troops had approached within
ten feet, when, with one accord, they took to their heels,
and never stopped running till they were entirely out of
sight. It was a disastrous day for the Russians. The
commander-in-chief was overwhelmed with shame and
mortification. A detachment of cavalry was dispatched
in pursuit of the fugitives, who were finally arrested in
their flight and brought back. "Cowards!" thundered
the enraged commander, as they stood drawn up before
him; "miserable poltroons! dastards! is this the way
you do honor to your imperial master? Am I to report
to his most potent majesty that, without striking one
blow in his defense, you ran like sheep? Wretches,
what have you to say for yourselves?"

IMPERIAL NOSEGAY.

"May it please your excellency," responded the men, firmly and with unblenched faces, "we ran away, it is true; but we are not cowards. On the contrary, sire, we are brave men, and fear neither man nor beast. But your excellency is aware that nature has gifted us with noses peculiarly open to unusual impressions. We have smelled all the smells known from the far North to the far South, from the stewed rats of Moscow to the carrion that lies mouldering upon the plains of the Crimea; but, if it please your highness, we never smelled Frenchmen before. There was an unearthly odor about them that filled our nostrils, and struck a mysterious terror into our souls."

"Fools!" roared the commander-in-chief, bursting with rage, "what you smelled was nothing more than garlic, to which these Frenchmen are addicted."

"Call it as you will," firmly responded the men with the noses, "it was too horrible to be endured. We are willing to die by the natural casualties of war, but not by unseen blasts of garlic, against which no human power can contend."

"Then," cried the commander, in tones of thunder, "I'll see that you die to-morrow by the natural casualties of war. You shall be put in the very front rank, and care shall be taken to have every man of you shot down the moment you undertake to run."

On the following day this rigorous order was carried into effect. The nose regiment was placed in front, and the battle opened with great spirit. The French troops swept down upon them like an avalanche. For an instant they looked behind, but, finding no hope of escape in that direction, each man of them suddenly grasped up a handful of mud, and, dashing it over his nostrils, shouted "Death to the garlic-eaters!" and rushed against the enemy with indescribable ferocity. Never before were such prodigies of valor performed on the field of battle. The French went down like stricken reeds before the ferocious onslaught of the Imperial Guard. Their dead bodies lay piled in heaps on the bloody field. The fortunes of the day were saved, and, panting and bleeding, the men of Noses stood triumphantly in the presence of their chief. In an ecstasy of pride and delight he complimented them upon their valor, and pronounced them the brightest nosegay in his imperial majesty's service, which name they have borne ever since.

CHAPTER X.

THE EMPEROR'S BEAR-HUNT.

THE present emperor, Alexander III., is more distinguished for his liberal views respecting the rights of his subjects than for his military proclivities. In private life he is much beloved, and is said to be a man of very genial social qualities. His predominating passion in this relation is a love of hunting. I have been told that he is especially great on bears. With all your experience of this manly pastime in America, I doubt if you can form any conception of the bear-hunts in which the Autocrat of all the Russias has distinguished himself. Any body with nerve enough can kill a grizzly, but it requires both nerve and money to kill bears of any kind in the genuine autocratic style. By an imperial ukase it has been ordered that when any of the peasants or serfs discover a bear within twenty versts of the Moscow and St. Petersburg Railway, they must make known the fact to the proprietor of the estate, whose duty it is to communicate official information of the discovery to the corresponding secretary of the Czar. With becoming humility the secretary announces the tidings to his royal master, who directs him to advise the distant party that his majesty is much pleased, and will avail himself of his earliest leisure to proceed to the scene of action. In the mean time the entire available force of the estate is set to work to watch the bear, and from three to five hundred men, armed with cudgels, tin pans, old kettles, drums, etc., are stationed in a circle around him. Dogs also are employed upon this important service. The advance trains, under the direction of the master hunter, having deposited their stores of wines, cordials, and provisions, and telegraphic communications being transmitted to head-quarters from time to time, it is at length privately announced that his imperial majesty has condescended to honor the place with his presence, and, should the saints not prove averse, will be there with his royal party at the hour and on the day specified in the imperial dispatch. The grand convoy is then put upon the track; dispatches are transmitted to all the stations; officers, soldiers, and guards are required to be in attendance to do honor to their sovereign master—privately, of course, as this is simply an unofficial affair which nobody is supposed to know any thing about. The emperor, having selected his chosen few—that is to say, half a dozen princes, a dozen dukes, a score or two of counts and barons—all fine fellows and genuine bloods—proceeds unostentatiously to the dépôt in his hunting-carriage (a simple little affair, manufactured at a cost of only forty thousand rubles or so), where he is astonished to see a large concourse of admiring subjects, gayly interspersed with soldiers, all accidentally gathered there to see him off. Now hats are removed, bows are made, suppressed murmurs of delight run through the crowd; the locomotive whizzes and fizzes with impatience; bells are rung, arms are grounded; the princes, dukes, and barons—jolly fellows as they are—laugh and joke just like common people; bells ring again and whistles blow; a signal is made, and the Autocrat of all the Russias is off on his bear-hunt!

In an hour, or two or three hours, as the case may be, the royal hunters arrive at the destined station. Should the public business be pressing, it is not improbable the emperor, availing himself of the conveniences provided for him by Winans and Co., in whose magnificent present of a railway carriage he travels, has in the mean time dispatched a fleet of vessels to Finland, ten or a dozen extra regiments of Cossacks to Warsaw, closed upon terms for a loan of fifty millions, banished various objectionable parties to the deserts of Siberia, and partaken of a game or two of whist with his camarilla.

But now the important affair of the day is at hand—

the bear—the terrible black bear, which every body is fully armed and equipped to kill, but which every body knows by instinct is going to be killed by the emperor, because of his majesty's superior skill and courage on trying occasions of this sort. What a blessing it is to possess such steadiness of nerve! I would not hesitate one moment to attack the most ferocious grizzly in existence if I felt half as much confidence in my ability to kill it. But the carriages are waiting; the horses are prancing; the hunters are blowing their bugles; the royal party are mounting on horseback or in their carriages, as best may suit their taste, and the signal is given! A salute is fired by the Guard, huzzas ring through the air, and the Czar of all the Russias is fairly off on his hunt. Trees fly by; desert patches of ground whirl from under; versts are as nothing to these spirited steeds and their spirited masters, and in an hour or so the grand scene of action is reached. Here couriers stand ready to conduct the imperial hunters into the very jaws of death. The noble proprietor himself, bare-headed, greets the royal pageant; the serfs bow down in Oriental fashion; the dashing young Czar touches his hunting-cap in military style and waves his hand gallantly to the ladies of the household, who are peeping at him from their carriages in the distance. Once more the bugle is sounded, and away they dash—knights, nobles, and all—the handsome and gallant Czar leading the way by several lengths. Soon the terrific cry is heard—"Halt! the bear! the bear! Halt!" Shut your eyes, reader, for you never can stand such a sight as that—a full-grown black bear, not two hundred yards off, in the middle of an open space, surrounded by five hundred men hidden behind trees and driving him back from every point where he attempts to escape. You don't see the men, but you hear them shouting and banging upon their pots, pans, and kettles. Now just open one eye and see the emperor dismount from his famous charger, and deliver the rein to a dozen domestics, deliberately cock his rifle, and fearlessly get behind the nearest tree within the range of the bear. By this time you perceive that Bruin is dancing a *pas seul* on his hind legs, utterly confounded with the noises around him. Shut your eyes again, for the emperor is taking his royal aim, and will presently crack away with his royal rifle. Hist! triggers are clicking around you in every direction, but you needn't be the least afraid, for, although the bear is covered by a reserve of forty rifles, not one of the hunters has nerve enough to shoot unless officially authorized or personally desirous of visiting the silver-mines of Siberia. Crack! thug! The smoke clears away. By Jove! his imperial majesty has done it cleverly; hit the brute plumb on the os frontis, or through the heart, it makes no difference which. Down drops Bruin, kicking and tearing up the earth at a dreadful rate; cheers rend the welkin; pots, pans, and kettles are banged. High above all rises the stern voice of the autocrat, calling for another rifle, which is immediately handed to him. Humanity requires that he should at once put an end to the poor animal's sufferings, and he does it with his accustomed skill.

Now the bear having kicked his last, an intrepid hunter charges up to the spot on horseback, whirls around it two or three times, carefully examines the body with an opera-glass, returns, and, approaching the royal presence with uncovered head, delivers himself according to this formula: "May it please your most gallant and imperial majesty, THE BEAR IS DEAD!" The emperor sometimes responds, "Is he?" but usually contents himself by waving his hand in an indifferent manner, puffing his cigar, and calling for his horse. Sixteen grooms immediately rush forward with his majesty's horse; and, being still young and vigorous, he mounts without difficulty, unaided except by Master of Stirrups. Next he draws an ivory-handled revolver—a present from Colt, of New York—and, dashing fearlessly upon the bear, fires six shots into the dead body; upon which he coolly dismounts, and pulling forth from the breast of his hunting-coat an Arkansas bowie-knife—a present from the poet Albert Pike, of Little Rock—plunges that dangerous weapon into the bowels of the dead bear; then rising to his full height, with a dark and stern countenance, he holds the blood-dripping blade high in the air, so that all may see it, and utters one wild stentorian and terrific shout, "Harasho! harasho!" signifying in English, "Good! very well!" The cry is caught up by the princes and nobles, who, with uncovered heads, now crowd around their gallant emperor, and waving their hats, likewise shout "Harasho! harasho!"—"Good! very well!" Then the five hundred peasants rush in with their tin pans, kettles, and drums, and amid the most amazing din catch up the inspiring strain, and deafen every ear with their wild shouts of "Harasho! harasho!"—"Good! very well!" Upon which the emperor, rapidly mounting, places a finger in each ear, and, still puffing his cigar, rides triumphantly away.

The bear is hastily gutted and dressed with flowers. When all is ready the royal party return to the railroad dépôt in a long procession, headed by his majesty, and brought up in the rear by the dead body of Bruin borne on poles by six-and-twenty powerful serfs. Refreshments in the mean time have been administered to every body of high and low degree, and by the time they reach the dépôt there are but two sober individuals in the entire procession—his royal majesty and the bear. Farther refreshments are administered all round during the journey back to St. Petersburg, and, notwithstanding he is rigidly prohibited by his physician from the use of stimulating beverages, it is supposed that a reaction has now taken place, which renders necessary a modification of the medical ukase. At all events, I am told the bear is sometimes the only really steady member of the party by the time the imperial pageant reaches the palace. When the usual ceremonies of congratulation are over, a merry dance winds up the evening. After this the company disperses to prayer and slumber, and thus ends the great bear-hunt of his majesty the Autocrat of all the Russias.

CHAPTER XI.

RUSSIAN HUMOR.

THE Russians have little or no humor, though they are not deficient in a certain grotesque savagery bordering on the humorous. There is something fearfully vicious in the royal freaks of fancy of which Russian history furnishes us so many examples. We read with a shudder of the facetious compliment paid to the Italian architect by Ivan the Terrible, who caused the poor man's eyes to be put out that he might never see to build another church so beautiful as that of St. Basil. We can not but smile at the grim humor of Peter the Great, who, upon seeing a crowd of men with wigs and gowns at Westminster Hall, and being informed that they were lawyers, observed that he had but two in his whole empire, and he believed he would hang one of them as soon as he got home. A still more striking though less ghastly freak of fancy was that perpetrated by the Empress Anne of Courland, who, on the occasion of the marriage of her favorite buffoon, Galitzin, caused a palace of ice to be built, with a bed of the same material, in which she compelled the happy pair to pass their wedding night. The Empress Catharine II., a Pomeranian by birth, but thoroughly Russian in her morals, possessed a more ardent temperament. What time she did not spend in gratifying her ambition by slaughtering men, she spent in loving them:

> "For, though she would widow all
> . Nations, she liked man as an individual."

She never dismissed an old admirer until she had secured several new ones, and generally consoled those who had served her by a present of twenty or thirty thousand serfs. On the death of Lanskoi, it is recorded of her that "she gave herself up to the most poignant grief, and remained three months without going out of her palace of Czarsko Selo," thus perpetrating a very curious practical satire upon the holiest of human affections. Her grenadier lover Potemkin, according to the character given of him by the Count Ségur, was little better than a gigantic and savage buffoon—licentious and superstitious, bold and timid by turns—sometimes desiring to be King of Poland, at others a bishop or a monk. Of him we read that "he put out an eye to free it from a blemish which diminished his beauty. Banished by his rival, he ran to meet death in battle, and returned with glory." Another pleasant little jest was that perpetrated by Suwarrow, who, after the bloody battle of Tourtourskaya, announced the result to his mistress in an epigram of two doggerel lines. This was the terrible warrior who used to sleep almost naked in a room of suffocating heat, and rush out to review his troops in a linen jacket, with the thermometer of Reaumur ten degrees below freezing point. Of the Emperor Paul, the son of Catharine, we read that he issued a ukase against the use of shoe-strings and round hats; caused all the watch-boxes, gates, and bridges throughout the empire to be painted in the most glaring and fantastic colors, and passed a considerable portion of his time riding on a wooden rocking-horse—a degenerate practice for a scion of the bold Catharine, who used to dress herself in men's clothes, and ride a-straddle on the back of a live horse to review her troops. Alexander I., in his ukase of September, 1827, perpetrated a very fine piece of Russian humor. The period of military service for serfs is fixed at twenty years in the Imperial Guard, and twenty-two in other branches of the service. It is stated in express terms that the moment a serf becomes enrolled in the ranks of the army he is free! But he must not desert, for if he does he becomes a slave again. This idea of freedom is really refreshing. Only twenty

or twenty-two years of the gentle restraints of Russian
military discipline to be enjoyed after becoming a free
agent! Then he may go off (at the age of fifty or sixty,
say), unless disease or gunpowder has carried him off
long before, to enjoy the sweets of hard labor in some
agreeable desert, or the position of a watchman on the
frontiers of Siberia, where the climate is probably considered salubrious.

These may be considered royal or princely vagaries,
in which great people are privileged to indulge; but I
think it will be found that the same capricious savagery
of humor—if I may so call it—prevails to some extent
among all classes of Russians. In some instances it can
scarcely be associated with any idea of mirthfulness, yet
in the love of strange, startling, and incongruous ideas
there is something bordering on the humorous. On
Recollection Monday, for example, the mass of the people go out into the grave-yards, and, spreading table-
cloths on the mounds that cover the dead bodies of
their relatives, drink quass and vodka to the health of
the deceased, saying, "Since the dead are unable to
drink, the living must drink for them!" Rather a grave
excuse, one must think, for intoxication.

In the museum of Peter the Great at St. Petersburg
stands the stuffed skin of his favorite servant—a gigantic
Holsteiner—one of the most ghastly of all the grotesque
and ghastly relics in that remarkable institution. It is
not a very agreeable subject for the pencil of an artist,
yet there is something so original in the idea of stuffing
a human being and putting him up for exhibition before
the public that I am constrained to introduce the following sketch of this strange spectacle.

In one of the arsenals is an eagle made of gun-flints,
with swords for wings, daggers for feathers, and the
mouths of cannons for eyes. A painting of the Strelitzes,
in another, represents heaven as containing the Russian
priests and all the faithful; while the other place—a region of fire and brimstone—contains Jews, Tartars, Germans, and negroes!

SKINNED AND STUFFED MAN.

The winter markets of Moscow and St. Petersburg present some of the most cadaverous specimens of the startling humor in which the Russians delight. Here you find frozen oxen, calves, sheep, rabbits, geese, ducks, and all manner of animals and birds, once animate with life, now stiff and stark in death. The oxen stand staring at you with their fixed eyes and gory carcasses; the calves are jumping or frisking in skinless innocence; the

FROZEN ANIMALS IN THE MARKET.

sheep ba-a at you with open mouths, or cast sheep's-eyes at the by-passers; the rabbits, having traveled hundreds of miles, are jumping, or running, or turning somersaults in frozen tableaux to keep themselves warm, and so on with every variety of flesh, fowl, and even fish. The butchers cut short these expressive practical witticisms by means of saws, as one might saw a block of wood; and the saw-dust, which is really frozen flesh and blood in a powdered state, is gathered up in baskets and carried away by the children and ragamuffins to be made into soup.

I can conceive of nothing humorous in these people which is not associated in some way with the cruel and the grotesque. They have many noble and generous traits, but lack delicacy of feeling. Where the range of the thermometer is from a hundred to a hundred and fifty degrees of Fahrenheit, their character must partake in some sort of the qualities of the climate—fierce, rigorous, and pitiless in its wintry aspect, and without the compensating and genial tenderness of spring; fitful and passionate as the scorching heats of summer, and dark, stormy, and dreary as the desolation of autumn.

I could not but marvel, as I sat in some of the common traktirs, at the extraordinary affection manifested by the Russians for cats. It appeared to me that the proprietors must keep a feline corps expressly for the amusement of their customers. At one of these places I saw at least forty cats, of various breeds, from the confines of Tartary to the city of Paris. They were up on the tables, on the benches, on the floor, under the benches, on the backs of the tea-drinkers, in their laps, in their arms—every where. I strongly suspected that they answered the purpose of waiters, and that the owner relied upon them to keep the plates clean. Possibly, too, they were made available as musicians. I have a notion the Russians entertain the same superstitious devotion to cats that the Banyans of India do to cows, and the French and Germans to nasty little poo-

MUJIK AND CATS.

dles. To see a great shaggy boor, his face dripping
with grease, his eyes swimming in vodka, sit all doubled
up, fondling and caressing these feline pets; holding
them in his hands; pressing their velvety fur to his
eyes, checks, even his lips; listening with delight to
their screams and squalls, is indeed a curious spectacle.

Now I have no unchristian feeling toward any of the

brute creation, but I don't affect cats. Nor can I say that I greatly enjoy their music. I heard the very best bands of tom-cats every night during my sojourn in Moscow, and consider them utterly deficient in style and execution. It belongs, I think, to the Music of Futurity, so much discussed by the critics of Europe during the past few years—a peculiar school of anti-melody that requires people yet to be born to appreciate it thoroughly. The discords may be very fine, and the passion very striking and tempestuous, but it is worse than thrown away on an uncultivated ear like mine.

CHAPTER XII.

A MYSTERIOUS ADVENTURE.

THE police of Moscow are not an attractive class of men, considering them in the light of guardians of the law. With a good deal of pomposity and laziness, they mingle much filth and rascality. The emperor may have great confidence in them, based upon some knowledge of their talents and virtues not shared by casual tourists; but if he would trust one of them with ten kopeks, or agree to place the life of any intimate personal friend in their keeping, in any of the dark alleys of Moscow, his faith in their integrity and humanity must be greater than mine. Indeed, upon casting around me in search of a parallel, I am not quite sure that I ever saw such a scurvy set of vagabonds employed to preserve the public peace in any other country, except, perhaps, in Spain. The guardians of the law in Cadiz and Seville are dark and forbidding enough in all conscience, and unscrupulous enough to turn a penny in any way not requiring the exercise of personal energy; and the police of Barcelona are not inferior in all that constitutes moral turpitude, but they can not surpass the Moscovites in filthiness of person or any of the essential attributes of villainy.

I have it upon good authority that they are the very

worst set of thieves in the place, and that they will not hesitate to unite with any midnight prowler for the purpose of robbing a stranger. True, they did not rob me, but the reason of that is obvious. I gave them to understand at the start that I was connected with the press. You seldom hear of a writer for newspapers being robbed; and if such a thing ever does happen, the amount taken is never large.

As a consequence of this proclivity for ill-gotten gains on the part of the guardians of the law, it is unsafe for a stranger to go through the less frequented streets of Moscow at night. Should he chance to be stopped by two or three footpads and call for help, he will doubtless wake up some drowsy guardian of the law, but the help will be all against him. Instances have been related to me of robberies in which the police were the most active assailants, the robbers merely standing by for their share of the plunder. Should the unfortunate victim knock down a footpad or two in self-defense, it is good ground for an arrest, and both robbers and policemen become witnesses against him. A man had better get involved in a question of title to his property before the courts of California than be arrested for assault and battery, and carried before any of the civil tribunals in Russia. There is no end of the law's delays in these institutions, and his only chance of justice is to get his case before the emperor, who is practically the Supreme Court of the empire. Otherwise the really aggrieved party must pay a fine for defending himself, and support the assaulted man, whose nose he may have battered, during an unlimited period at the hospital, together with physician's fees for all the real or imaginary injuries inflicted. I met with a young American who was followed by a stalwart ruffian one night in returning from one of the public gardens. The man dogged his footsteps for some time. At length, there being nobody near to render aid, the robber mustered courage enough to seize hold and attempt to intimidate his supposed victim by brandishing a knife.

He came from a country where they were not uncommon, and, besides, was an adept on the shoulder. With a sudden jerk he freed himself, and, hauling off a little, gave his assailant a note of hand that knocked him down. I am not versed in the classics of the ring, or I would make something out of this fight. The pad dropped like a stricken ox, his knife flying picturesquely through the silvery rays of the moon. Next moment he was on his feet again, the claret shining beautifully on his cheeks and beard. Throwing out his claws like a huge grizzly, he rushed in, gnashing his teeth and swearing horribly. This time our friend was fairly aroused, and the wretch promptly measured his length on the ground. Thinking he had scattered it on rather heavy, the American stooped down to see how matters stood, when the fellow grasped him by the coat and commenced shouting with all his might for the police — "Help! help! murder! murder!" There was no remedy but to silence him, which our friend dexterously accomplished by a blow on the os frontis. Hearing the approaching footsteps of the police, he then concluded it was best to make his escape, and accordingly took to his heels. Chase was given, but he was as good at running as he was at the noble art of self-defense, and soon distanced his pursuers. Fortunately, he reached his quarters without being recognized. This was all that saved him from arrest and imprisonment, or the payment of a fine for the assault.

A common practice, as I was informed, is to arrest a stranger for some alleged breach of the law, such as smoking a cigar in the streets, or using disrespectful language toward the constituted authorities. Not being accustomed to the intricacies of a Russian judiciary, it is difficult, when once the matter comes before a tribunal of justice, for a foreigner to rebut the testimony brought against him; and if he be in a hurry to get away, his only course is to bribe the parties interested in his detention. It would be unjust to say that this system prevails universally throughout Russia. There is a small

circle around the imperial presence said to be exempt
from corruption; and there may possibly be a few digni-
taries of the government, in remote parts of the empire,
who will not tell an untruth unless in their official correspondence, or steal except to make up what they consider due to them for public services; but the circle of
immaculate ones is very small, and commences very near
the Czar, and the other exceptions referred to are exceedingly rare. Thieving may be said to begin within
gunshot of the capital, and to attain its culminating ex-
cellences on the confines of Tartary. The difference is
only in degree between the higher and the lower grades
of officers. Hence, although it is quite possible to obtain full reparation for an injury before the Czar, through
the intervention of a consul or a minister, it is a vexatious and expensive mode of proceeding, and would only
result at last in the transportation of some miserable
wretch to the mines of Siberia. Of course no man with
a spark of feeling would like to see a poor fellow-crea-
ture go there. For my part, I would rather suffer any
amount of injustice than be the cause of sending a fel-
low-mortal on so long and dreary a journey.

The whole bearing of which you will presently discover. I am going to tell you a very singular adventure
that befell me in Moscow. Do not be impatient; it will
all come in due time. A few dashes of preliminary description will be necessary, by way of introduction, otherwise it would be impossible to comprehend the full
scope and purpose of my narrative. If you be of the
rougher mould, cherished reader, just cast yourself back
somewhere at your ease, take this most excellently printed book deftly between your fingers, with a good cigar
between your teeth; throw your legs over your desk, a
gunny-bag, a fence-rail, or the mantel-piece of the bar-
room, as the case may be; give me the benefit of your
friendship and confidence, and read away at your leisure.
But if you be one of those gentle beings placed upon
earth to diffuse joy and happiness over the desert of

life, I pray you consider me a serf at your imperial footstool; bend on me those tender eyes; and with the mingled respect and admiration due by all men to female loveliness, I shall proceed at once to tell you (confidentially of course)

A MYSTERIOUS ADVENTURE.

It so happened in Moscow that I fell in with a very pleasant and sociable party of Americans, several of whom were in the railway service, and therefore might reasonably be regarded as fast young gentlemen, though far be it from me to imply any thing injurious to their reputation.   Beyond an excessive passion for tea, acquired by long residence in Moscow, I do not know that a single one of them was at all dissipated. When I first called at the rooms of these lively countrymen, they immediately got out their tea-urns, and assured me that it would be impossible to comprehend any thing of Russian life till I had partaken freely of Russian tea, therefore I was obliged to drink five or six glasses by way of a beginning. Having freely discussed the affairs of the American nation at one room, we adjourned to another, where we had a fresh supply of tea; and then, after settling the rebellion to our common satisfaction, adjourned to another, and so on throughout the best part of the day. Sometimes we stopped in at a *traktir* and had a portion or two, dashed with a little Cognac, which my friends assured me would prevent it from having any injurious effect upon the nervous system. In this way, within a period of twelve hours, owing to the kindness and hospitality of these agreeable Americans, who insisted upon treating me to tea, in public and in private, at every turn of our rambles, I must have swallowed a gallon or two of this delicious beverage. The weather was exceedingly warm, but these experienced gentlemen insisted upon it that Russian tea was a sovereign antidote for warm weather, especially when dashed with Cognac, as it drove all the caloric out of the body through the pores of the skin. "Don't be afraid!" said they, encouragingly; "drink just as much as you please—it will cool you! See how the Russians drink it. Nothing else enables them to stand these fiery hot summers after their polar winters!" Well, I didn't feel exactly cool, with thirty or forty tumblers of boiling hot tea, dashed with Cognac, in my veins, but what was the use of remonstrating? They *lived* in Moscow —they *knew* better than I did what was good for strangers—so I kept on swallowing a little more, just to oblige them, till I verily believe, had any body stuck a pin in me, or had I undertaken to make a speech, I would have spouted Russian tea.

Why is it that the moment any body wants to render you a service, or manifest some token of friendship, he commences by striking at the very root of your digestive functions? Is it not exacting a little too much of human nature to require a man to consider himself a large sponge, in order that hospitality may be poured into him by the gallon? When a person of pliant and amiable disposition visits a set of good fellows, and they take some trouble to entertain him; when they think they are delighting him internally and externally—not to say infernally—with such tea as he never drank before, it is hard to refuse. The moral courage necessary for the peremptory rejection of such advances would make a hero. Thus it has ever been with me—I am the victim of misplaced hospitality. It has been the besetting trouble of my life. I remember once eating a Nantucket pudding to oblige a lady. It was made of corn-meal and molasses, with some diabolical compound in the way of sauce—possibly whale-oil and tar. I had just eaten a hearty dinner; but the lady insisted upon it that the pudding was a great dish in Nantucket, and I must try it. Well, I stuffed and gagged at it, out of pure politeness, till every morsel on the plate was gone, declaring all the time that it was perfectly delicious. The lady was charmed, and, in the face of every denial, instantly filled the plate again. What could I do but eat it? And after eating till I verily believe one half of me was composed of Nantucket pudding, and the other half of whale-oil and tar, what could I do but praise it again? The third attempt upon my life was made by this most excellent and hospitable lady; but I gave way, and had to beg off. Human nature could stand it no longer. The consequence was, I wounded her feelings. She regretted very much that I disliked Nantucket pudding, and I don't think ever quite forgave me for my prejudice against that article of diet, though her kindness laid me up sick for two weeks. Nor is this an isolated case. I might relate a thousand others in illustration of the melancholy fact that hospitality has been the bane of my life. When I think of all the sufferings I have endured out of mere politeness—though by no means accounted a polite person—tears of grief and indignation spring to my eyes. Old John Rogers at the stake never suffered such martyrdom. But there is an end of it! The *tchai* of Moscow finished all this sort of thing — so far, at least, as the male sex is concerned. I would still eat a coyote or a weasel to oblige a lady, but as to drinking two gallons of strong tea per day, dashed with Cognac to reduce its temperature, to oblige any man that ever wore a beard, I solemnly declare I'll die first. The thing is an imposition—an outrage. Every man has a right to my time, my purse, my real estate in Oakland, my coat, my boots, or my razor —nay, in a case of emergency, my tooth-brush—but no man has a right to deluge my diaphragm with slops, or make a ditch of Mundus of my stomach.

At the Peterskoi Gardens we had a little more tea, dashed with *vodka*, to keep out the night air. As soon as the fire-works were over we adjourned to the pavilion, and refreshed ourselves with a little more tea slightly impregnated with some more *vodka*. Now I don't know exactly what this vodka is made of, but I believe it is an extract of corn. In the Russian lan-

guage *vodu* is water, and *vodka* means "little water."
There certainly was very little in what we got, or the
tea must have been stronger than usual, for, notwithstanding these agreeable young gentlemen protested a

gallon of such stuff would not produce the slightest effect, it seemed to me — though there might have been
some delusion in the idea, arising from ignorance of
Russian customs — that my head went round like a

whirligig; and by the time I took my leave of these experienced young friends and retired to my room at the *Hotel de Venise*, it did likewise occur to me—though that too may have been a mere notion—that there was a hive of bees in each ear. Upon due consideration of all the facts, I thought it best to turn in, and resume any inquiries that might be necessary for the elucidation of these phenomena in the morning.

[Here, you perceive, I am gradually verging toward the adventure. The heroine of the romance has not yet made her appearance, but depend upon it she is getting ready. You should never hurry the female characters; besides, it is not proper, even if this were all fiction instead of sober truth, that the heroine should be brought upon the stage just as the hero is tumbling into bed.]

But to proceed. Sleep was effectually banished from my eyes, and no wonder. Who in the name of sense could sleep with forty tumblers of Russian tea—to say nothing of the dashes that were put in it—simmering through every nook and cranny of his body, and boiling over in his head? There I lay, twisting and tumbling, the pillow continually descending into the depths of infinity, but never getting any where—the bed rolling like a dismantled hulk upon a stormy sea—the room filled with steaming and hissing urns—a fearful thirst parching my throat, while myriads of horrid bearded Russians were torturing me with tumblers of boiling-hot tea dashed with *vodka*—thus I lay a perfect victim of tea. I could even see Chinamen with long queues picking tea-leaves off endless varieties of shrubs that grew upon the papered walls; and Kalmuck Tartars, with their long caravans, traversing the dreary steppes of Tartary laden with inexhaustible burdens of the precious leaf; and the great fair of Nijni Novorgod, with its booths, and tents, and countless boxes of tea, and busy throngs of traders and tea-merchants, all passing like a panorama before me, and all growing naturally out of an indefinite background of tea.

I can not distinctly remember how long I tossed about in this way, beset by all sorts of vagaries. Sometimes I fancied sleep had come, and that the whole matter was a ridiculous freak of fancy, including my visit to Moscow —that Russian tea was all a fiction, and *vodka* a mere nightmare; but with a nervous start I would find myself awake, the palpable reality of my extraordinary condition staring me in the face. Unable to endure such an anomalous frame of mind and body any longer, I at length resolved to go down and take an airing in the streets, believing, if any thing would have a beneficial effect, it would be the fresh air. Acting upon this idea, I hastily dressed myself and descended to the front door. The *Hotel de Venise* is situated in a central part of the city, at no great distance from the Kremlin. It stands back in a large open yard, with a very pretty garden to the right as you enter from the main street. The proprietor is a Russian, but the hotel is conducted in the French style, and, although not more conspicuous for cleanliness than other establishments of the same class in Moscow, it is nevertheless tolerably free from vermin. The fleas in it were certainly neither so lively nor so entertaining as I have found them at many of the Spanish ranches in California, and the bugs, I am sure, are nothing like so corpulent as some I have seen in Washington City. I throw this in gratis, as a sort of puff, in consideration of an understanding with the landlord, that if he would refrain from cheating me I would recommend his hotel to American travelers. It is very good of its kind, and no person fond of veal, as a standard dish, can suffer from hunger at this establishment so long as calves continue to be born any where in the neighborhood of Moscow.

The porter, a drowsy old fellow in livery, whose only business, so far as I could discover, was to bow to the guests as they passed in and out during the day, at the expense of a kopek to each one of them for every bow, was napping on a lounge close by the front door. Hear-

ing my footsteps, he awoke, rubbed his eyes, bowed
habitually, and then stared at me with a vacant and
somewhat startled expression. It was not a common
thing evidently for lodgers to go out of the hotel at that
time of night, or rather morning—it must have been
nearly two o'clock—for, after gazing a while at what he
doubtless took to be an apparition or an absconding
boarder whose bill had not been settled, he grumbled
out something like a dissent, and stood between me and
the door. A small fee of ten kopeks, which I placed in
his hand, aided him in grasping at the mysteries of the
case, and he unlocked the door and let me out, merely
shaking his head gravely, as if he divined my purpose,
but did not altogether approve of it in one of my age
and sedate appearance. In that, however, he was mistaken : I had no disposition to form any tender alliances
in Moscow.

The streets were almost deserted. An occasional drosky, carrying home some belated pleasure-seeker, was all
that disturbed the silence. I walked some distance in
the direction of the Kremlin. The air was deliciously
cool and refreshing, and the sky wore a still richer glow
than I had noticed a few hours before at the gardens of
the Peterskoi. The moon had not yet gone down, but
the first glowing blushes of the early morning were stealing over the heavens, mingled with its silvery light. I
took off my hat to enjoy the fresh air, and wandered
along quite enchanted with the richness and variety of
the scene. Every turn of the silent streets brought me
in view of some gilded pile of cupolas, standing in glowing relief against the sky. Churches of strange Asiatic
form, the domes richly and fancifully colored ; golden
stars glittering upon a groundwork of blue, green, or
yellow ; shrines with burning tapers over the massive
doors and gateways, were scattered in every direction
in the most beautiful profusion. Sometimes I saw a solitary beggar kneeling devoutly before some gilded saint,
and mourning over the weariness of life. Once I was

RUSSIAN BEGGARS.

startled by the apparition of a poor wretch lying asleep
—I thought he was dead—a crippled wreck upon the
stone steps — his eyes closed in brief oblivion of the
world and its sorrows, his furrowed and pallid features
a ghastly commentary upon the glittering temples and
idols that surround him. For above all these things
that are " decked with silver and with gold, and fastened with nails and with hammers that they move not,"
there is One who hath "made the earth by His power and established the world by His wisdom;" man is
but brutish in his knowledge; "every founder is confounded by the graven image; for his molten image is
falsehood, and there is no breath in them." Such extremes every where abound in Moscow—magnificence
and filth; wealth and poverty; a superstitious belief in
the power of images in the midst of abject proofs of
their impotence. And yet, is it not better that men

should believe in something rather than in nothing? The glittering idol can not touch the crippled beggar and put health and strength in his limbs, but if the poor sufferer can sleep better upon the cold stones in the presence of his patron saint than elsewhere, in charity's name let him,

> "O'erlabored with his being's strife,
> Shrink to that sweet forgetfulness of life."

I wandered on. Soon the cupolas of the mighty Kremlin were in sight, all aglow with the bright sheen of the morn. Passing along its embattled walls, which now seemed of snowy whiteness, I reached the grand plaza of the Krasnoi Ploschod. Standing out in the open space, I gazed at the wondrous pile of gold-covered domes till my eyes rested on the highest point — the majestic tower of Ivan Veliki. And then I could but think of the terrible Czar — the fourth of the fierce race of Ivans, who ruled the destinies of Russia; he who killed his own son in a fit of rage, yet never shook hands with a foreign embassador without washing his own immediately after; the patron of monasteries, and the conqueror of Kazan, Astrakan, and Siberia. This was the most cruel yet most enlightened of his name. I am not sure whether the tower was built to commemorate his fame or that of his grandfather, Ivan the Third, also called " the Terrible," of whom Karasmin says that, " when excited with anger, his glance would make a timid woman swoon; that petitioners dreaded to approach his throne, and that even at his table the boyars, his grandees, trembled before him." A terrible fellow, no doubt, and thoroughly Russian by the testimony of this Russian historian, for where else will you find men so terrible as to make timid women swoon by a single glance of their eye? Not in California, surely! If I were a Czar this soft summer night (such was the idea that naturally occurred to me), I would gaze upon the fair flowers of creation with an entirely different expression of countenance. They should neither wilt nor swoon unless overcome by the delicacy and tenderness of my admiration.

From the green towers of the Holy Gate, where neither Czar nor serf can enter without uncovering his head, I turned toward the Vassoli Blagennoi—the wondrous maze of churches that gathers around the Cathedral of St. Basil. Not in all Moscow is there a sight so strange and gorgeous as this. The globular domes, all striped with the varied colors of the rainbow; the glittering gold-gilt cupolas; the rare and fanciful minarets; the shrines, and crosses, and stars; the massive steps; the iron railing, with shining gold-capped points—surely, in the combination of striking and picturesque forms and colors, lights and shades, must ever remain unequaled. The comparison may seem frivolous, yet it resembled more, to my eye, some gigantic cactus of the tropics, with its needles and rich colors, its round, prickly domes and fantastic cupolas, than any thing I had ever seen before in the shape of a church or group of churches. While I gazed in wonder at the strange fabric, I could not but think again of Ivan the Terrible, by whose order it was built; and how, when the architect (an Italian) was brought before him, trembling with awe, the mighty Ivan expressed his approval of the performance, and demanded if he, the architect, could build another equally strange and beautiful; to which the poor Italian, elated with joy, answered that he could build another even stranger and more beautiful than this; and then how the ferocious and unprincipled Czar had the poor fellow's eyes put out to prevent him from building another.

But this is not the adventure. I have nothing to do at present with the Church of St. Basil or Ivan the Terrible except in so far as they affected my imagination. The business on hand is to tell you how the dire catastrophe happened.

Bewildered at length with gazing at all these wonderful sights, I turned to retrace my steps to the hotel. A

few droskies were still plying on the principal thoroughfares, and now and then I met gay parties trudging
homeward after their night's dissipation; but I soon
struck into the less frequented streets, where a dreary
silence reigned. There was something very sad and
solitary in the reverberation of my footsteps. For the
first time it occurred to me that there was not much security here for life, in case of a covert attack from some
of those footpads said to infest the city. I began to reflect upon the experience of my young American friend,
and regret that it had not occurred to me before I left
the hotel. You may think this very weak and foolish,
good friends, surrounded as you are by all the safe-
guards of law and order, and living in a country where
men are never knocked on the head of nights—with occasional exceptions; but I can assure you it is a very
natural feeling in a strange, half-barbarous city like Moscow, where one doesn't understand the language. Had
I been well versed in Russian, the probability is I should
not have felt the least alarmed; but a man experiences a
terrible sensation of loneliness when he expects every
moment to be knocked on the head without being able
to say a word in his own defense. Had my guide, Dominico, been with me, I should not have felt quite so
helpless—though I never had much confidence in his
courage—for he could at least have demanded an explanation, or, if the worst came to the worst, helped me
to run away. The fact is—and there is no use attempting to disguise it—I began to feel a nervous apprehension that something was going to happen. I was startled
at my own shadow, and was even afraid to whistle with
any view of keeping up my spirits, lest something unusually florid in my style of whistling might lead to the
supposition that I was from California, and therefore a
good subject for robbery.

Which, by the way, puts me in mind of a remarkable
fact, well worth mentioning. The State of California
owes me, at the least calculation, two hundred dollars,

paid in sums varying from six kreutzers up to a pound sterling to hotel-keepers, porters, lackeys, and professional gentlemen throughout Europe, exclusively on the ground of my citizenship in that state. In Paris—in Spain—in Africa—in Germany (with the exceptions of the beer-houses and country inns), I had to pay a heavy percentage upon the capital invested in my gold mines solely on the presumption that no man could come from so rich a country without carrying off a good deal of treasure on his person, like the carcass that carried the diamonds out of the rich valley for Sinbad the Sailor. Yet I never could forego the pleasure of announcing . myself as an embassador to foreign parts from that noble state, commissioned by the sovereigns generally to furnish them with the latest improvements in morals, fashions, and manners for the public benefit—an extremely onerous and responsible duty, which I have executed, and shall continue to execute, with the most rigid fidelity.

After walking quite far enough to have reached the hotel, I became confused at the winding of the streets. The neighborhood was strange. I could not discover any familiar sign or object. The houses were low, mean, and dark looking; the street was narrow and roughly paved. I walked a little farther, then turned into another street still more obscure, and, following that for some distance, brought up amid a pile of ruined walls. There could no longer be a doubt that I had missed the way, and was not likely to find it in this direction. It was a very suspicious quarter into which I had strayed. Every thing about it betokened poverty and crime. I began to feel rather uneasy, but it would not do to stand here among the ruins as a mark for any midnight prowler who might be lurking around. Turning off in a new direction, I took a by-street, which appeared to lead to an open space. As I picked my way over the masses of rubbish, a dark figure crossed in front, and disappeared in the shadow of a wall. I was entirely unarmed. What was to be done? Perhaps the man might be able to tell me the way to my lodgings; but I could not speak a word of Russian, as before stated, and, besides, was rather averse to making acquaintance with strangers. After a moment's reflection, I walked on, cautiously and distrustfully enough, for the notion was uppermost in my mind that this fellow was not there for any good purpose. As I passed the spot where he had disappeared, I looked suspiciously around, but he did not make his appearance. With a few hasty strides I reached the open space—a vacant lot, it seemed, caused by a recent fire. The houses were burnt down, and nothing but a blackened mass of beams, rafters, and ashes covered the ground. The only exit was through a narrow alley. Before entering this, I looked back and saw the same figure stealthily following me. On I went as rapidly as I could walk. Closer and closer came the figure. He was a man of gigantic stature, and was probably armed. Soon I heard the heavy tramp of his feet within a few paces. It was evident I must either run or stand my ground. Perhaps, if I had known what direction to take, or could have placed more reliance upon my knees, which were greatly weakened by tea, I might have chosen the former alternative, inglorious as it may seem; but, under the circumstances, I resolved to stand. Facing around suddenly, with my back to the wall, I called to the ruffian to stand off, as he valued his life. He halted within a few feet, evidently a little disconcerted at my sudden determination to make battle. His face was the most brutal I had ever seen; a filthy mass of beard nearly covered it; two piercing white eyes glistened beneath the leaf of his greasy cap; a coarse blouse, gathered around the waist by a leather belt, and boots that reached nearly to his hips, were the most striking articles of his costume. For a moment he gazed at me, as if uncertain what to do; then brushed slowly past, with the design, no doubt, of ascertaining if I was armed. I could not see whether he carried any deadly weapons himself; but a man of his gigantic stature needed none to be a very unequal opponent in a struggle with one whose most sanguinary conflicts had hitherto been on paper, and who had never wielded a heavier weapon than a pen.

Proceeding on his way, however, the ruffian, after going about a hundred yards, disappeared in some dark recess in among the houses on one side. I continued on, taking care to keep in the middle of the alley. As I approached the spot where the man had disappeared, I heard several voices, and then the terrible truth flashed upon me that there must be a gang of them. I now saw no alternative but to turn back and run for my life. It was an inglorious thing to do, no doubt, but which of you, my friends, would not have done the same thing?

Scarcely had I started under full headway when three or four men rushed out in pursuit. I will not attempt to disguise the fact that the ground passed under my feet pretty rapidly; and the probability is, the hostile party would have been distanced in less than ten minutes but for an unfortunate accident. It was necessary to cross the ruins already described. Here, in the recklessness of my flight, I stumbled over a beam, and fell prostrate in a pile of ashes. Before I could regain my feet the ruffians were upon me. While two of them held my arms, the third clapped his dirty hand over my mouth, and in this way they dragged me back into the alley. As soon as they had reached the dark archway from which they had originally started, they knocked at a door on one side. This was quickly opened, and I was thrust into a large room, dimly lighted with rude lamps of grease hung upon the walls. When they first got hold of me, I confess the sensation was not pleasant. What would the Emperor Alexander say when he heard that a citizen of California had been murdered in this cold-blooded manner? My next thought was, in what terms would this sad affair be noticed in the columns of the Sacramento *Union?* Would it not be regarded by the editor as an unprovoked disaster inflicted upon soci-

GAMBLING SALOON.

ety? My fears, however, were somewhat dispelled upon looking around the saloon into which I had been so strangely introduced. Several tables were ranged along the walls, at each of which sat a group of the most horrible-looking savages that probably ever were seen out of jail—the very dregs and offscourings of Moscow. Their faces were mostly covered with coarse, greasy beards, reaching half way down their bodies; some wore dirty blue or gray blouses, tied around the waist with ropes, or fastened with leather belts; others, long blue coats, reaching nearly to their feet; and all, or nearly all, had caps on their heads, and great heavy boots reaching up to their knees, in which their pantaloons were thrust, giving them a rakish and ruffianly appearance. A few sat in their shirt-sleeves; and, judging by the color of their shirts, as well as their skins, did not reckon soap among the luxuries of life. Several of these savage-looking Mujiks were smoking some abominable weed, intended, perhaps, for tobacco, but very much unlike that delightful narcotic in the foul and tainted odor which it diffused over the room. They were all filthy and brutish in the extreme, and talked in some wretched jargon, which, even to my inexperienced ear, had but little of the gentle flow of the Russian in it. The tables were dotted with dice, cards, fragments of black bread, plates of grease, and cabbage soup, and glasses of vodka and tea; and the business of gambling, eating, and drinking was carried on with such earnestness that my entrance attracted no farther attention than a rude stare from the nearest group. No wonder they were a little puzzled, for I was covered with ashes, and must have presented rather a singular appearance. The three ruffians who had brought me in closed the door, and motioned me to a seat at a vacant table. They then called for tea, vodka, and quass, together with a great dish of raw cucumbers, which they set to work devouring with amazing voracity. During a pause in the feast they held a low conversation with the man who served them, who went out and presently returned with a small tea-pot full of tea and a glass, which he set before me. They motioned to me, in rather a friendly way, to drink. I was parched with thirst, and was not sorry to get a draught of any thing—even the villainous compound the traktir had set before me; so I drank off a tumblerfull at once. Soon I began to experience a whirling sensation in the head. A cold tremor ran through my limbs. Dim and confused visions of the company rose before me, and a strange and spectral light seemed shed over the room. The murmur of voices sounded like rushing waters in my ears. I gradually lost all power of volition, while my consciousness remained unimpaired, or, if any thing, became more acute than ever. The guests, if such they were, broke up their carousal about this time, and began to drop off one by one, each bowing profoundly to the landlord, and crossing himself devoutly, and bowing three times again before the shrine of the patron saint as he passed out. It was really marvelous to see some of these ruffians, so besotted with strong drink that they were scarcely able to see the way to the door, stagger up before the burnished shrine, and, steadying themselves the best they could, gravely and solemnly go through their devotions.

But I see you are beginning to yawn, and, notwith-standing the most exciting part of the adventure is about to commence, it would be extremely injudicious in me to force it upon you under circumstances so disadvantageous to both parties. You will therefore oblige me by finishing your nap, and, with your permission, we will proceed with our narrative as soon as it may be mutually agreeable. In the mean time, I beg you will regard what I have already told you as strictly confidential. My reputation, both for veracity and general good character, is involved in this very extraordinary affair, and it would be unfair that either the one or the other should be prejudiced by a partial exposition of the facts.

CHAPTER XIII.

THE DENOUEMENT.

I NOTICED that the traktir, in settling accounts with his customers, made use of a peculiar instrument commonly seen in the shops and market-places throughout the city. Behind a sort of bar or counter at the head of the room he kept what is called a *schot*, upon which he made his calculations. This is a frame about a foot square, across which run numerous wires. On each wire is a string of colored pieces of wood somewhat resembling billiard-counters, only smaller. The merchant, trader, traktir, or craftsman engaged in pecuniary transactions uses this instrument with wonderful dexterity in making his calculations. He believes it to be the only thing in the world that will not lie or steal. If you have purchased to the amount of thirty kopeks, you would naturally conclude that out of a ruble (one hundred kopeks) your change would amount to seventy. Not so the sagacious and wary Russian. He takes nothing for granted in the way of trade. Your calculations may be erroneous—figures obtained through the medium of mental arithmetic may lie, but the schot never. The experience of a lifetime goes for nothing. He must have proof positive. Taking his schot between his knees, he counts off thirty balls out of a hundred. Of course there is no mistake about that. Neither you nor he can dispute it. Then he counts the remainder, and finds that it amounts to seventy—therefore your change is seventy kopeks! Do you dispute it? Then you can count for yourself. You might cover pages with written calculations, or demonstrate the problem by the four cardinal rules of arithmetic; you might express the numbers by sticks, stones, beans, or grains of coffee, but it would be all the same to this astute and cautious calculator—facts can only reach his understanding through the colored balls of his beloved schot. I don't think he would rely with certainty upon the loose verbal statement that two and two make four without resorting to the schot for a verification. But to proceed:

A few of the guests, too far gone with "little water" to get up and perform their devotions, rolled over on the floor and went to sleep. The lights grew dim. A gloomy silence began to settle over the room, interrupted only by the occasional grunting or snoring of the sleepers. The ruffians who sat at the table with me had been nodding for some time; but, roused by the cessation of noises, they called to the man of the house, and in a low voice gave him some orders. He got a light and opened a small door in a recess at one side of the room. I was then lifted up by the others and carried into an adjoining passage, and thence up a narrow stairway. In a large dingy room overhead I could see by the flickering rays of the lamp a bed in one corner. It was not very clean—none of the Russian beds are—but they laid me in it, nevertheless, for I could offer no remonstrance. What they had hitherto done was bad enough, but this capped the climax of outrages. Were the cowardly villains afraid to murder me, and was this their plan of getting it done, and at the same time getting rid of the body? Great heavens! was I to be devoured piecemeal by a rapacious horde of the wild beasts that are said to infest the Russian beds! And utterly helpless, too, without the power to grapple with as much as a single flea—the least formidable, perhaps, of the entire gang! It was absolutely fearful to contemplate such an act of premeditated barbarity; yet what could I do, unable to speak a word or move a limb.

I am reminded by this that the Russians derive the most striking features of their civilization from the French and Germans. Their fashions, their tailors, their confectioners, their perfumeries, their barbers, are nearly all French or Germans; but their baths are a national institution, derived originally, perhaps, from the Orientals. We hear a good deal of Russian baths, especially from enthusiastic travelers, and are apt to suppose that where such a thorough system of scrubbing and boiling prevails, the human cuticle must present a very extraordinary aspect of cleanliness. Perhaps this is so in certain cases, but it is not a national characteristic. A Russian bath, in the genuine style, is rather a costly luxury. There are, to be sure, in St. Petersburg and Moscow, public bath-houses for the rabble, where the filthiest beggar can be boiled out and scrubbed for a few kopeks; but people who wear a coating of dirt habitually must become attached to it in the course of time, and hate very much to dispose of it at any price. At least there seemed to be a prejudice of this kind in Moscow, where the affection with which this sort of overlining is preserved is quite equal to that with which the Germans adhere to their old household furniture. It may be, perhaps, that the few summer months which they enjoy are insufficient for the removal of all the strange things that accumulate upon the body during the long winters. The poorer classes seldom remove their furs or change their clothing till warm weather and the natural wear and tear of all perishable things cause them to drop off of their own accord. I have seen on a scorching hot day men wrapped in long woolen coats, doubled over the breast and securely fastened around the waist, and great boots, capacious enough and thick enough for fire-buckets, in which they were half buried, strolling lazily along in the sun, as if they absolutely enjoyed its warmth; and yet these very articles of clothing, with but little addition, must have borne the piercing winds of midwinter. A suspicion crossed my mind that they were trying in this way to bag a little heat for winter use, as the old burghers of Schilda bagged the light to put in their town hall because they had no windows. These strange habits must have something to do with the number of ferocious little animals—I will not degrade their breed and variety by calling them vermin—which infest the rooms and beds.   But the Russian skin is like Russian leather —the best and toughest in the world.   Something in the climate is good for the production of thick and lasting cuticles.   It is doubtless a wise provision of nature, based upon the extremes of heat and cold to which these people are exposed.   There is no good reason why animals with four feet should be more favored in this respect than bipeds.   I doubt if an ordinary Russian would suffer the slightest inconvenience if a needle were run into the small of his back.   All those physical torments which disturb thin-skinned people from other countries are no torments at all to him; and I incline to the opinion that it is the constant experience he enjoys in a small way that enables him to endure the wounds received in battle with such wonderful stoicism.   A man can carry a bull if he only commences when the animal is young.   Why not, on the same principle, accustom himself to being stabbed every night till he can quietly endure to be run through with a bayonet?   The Russian soldiers possess wonderful powers of passive endurance.   Being stabbed or cut to pieces is second nature to them—they have been accustomed to it, in a degree, from early infancy. Who does not remember how they were hewed and hacked down in the Crimean War, and yet came to life again by thousands after they were given up for dead? Perhaps no other soldiers in the world possess such stoicism under the inflictions of pain.   They stand an enormous amount of killing; more so, I think, than any other people, unless it may be the Irish, who, at the battle of Vinegar Hill, in the rebellion of '98, were nearly all cut to pieces and left for dead on the field, but got up in a day or two after and went at it again as lively as ever. This, however, was not owing to the same early experience, but to the healthy blood made of potatoes, with a slight sprinkling of Irish whisky.   In fine, I don't think a genuine Muscovite could sleep without a bountiful supply of vermin to titillate his skin any more than a miller bereft of the customary noise of his hoppers.

Which brings me back again to the adventure. On that filthy bed the ruffians laid me down to be devoured by the wild beasts by which it was infested. Then they turned about to a shrine that stood in a corner of the room, and each one bowed down before it three times and crossed himself, after which they all left the room and quietly closed the door behind them. I was penetrated with horror at the thought of the terrible death before me, but not so much as to avoid noticing that the chief furniture of the room consisted of a stove in one corner, of cylindrical form, made of terra-cotta or burnt clay, and glazed outside. It was colored in rather a fanciful way, like queensware, and made a conspicuous appearance, reaching from the floor to the ceiling. This was the genuine Russian stove, with which these people no doubt kept themselves warm during the winter. The windows are composed of double glasses, and between the sashes the space is filled with sand to keep out the air, so that to be hermetically sealed up is one of the necessities of existence in this rigorous climate. While I was pondering over the marvelous fact that people can live by breathing so many thousand gallons of air over and over so many thousand times, a whole legion of fleas, chinches, and other animals of a still more forbidding aspect commenced their horrid work, and would probably soon have made an end of me but for a new turn in this most extraordinary affair. The door gently opened. A figure glided in on tiptoe. It was that of a female, I knew by the grace and elegance of her motions, even before I could see her face or trace the undulating outline of her form in the dim light that pervaded the room. My senses were acutely alive to every movement, yet I was utterly unable to move, owing to the infernal drug with which they had dosed me. The woman, or rather girl — for she could not have been over eighteen or nineteen — cautiously approached the bed, with her finger to her lips, as if warning me not to speak. She was very beautiful—I was not insensible to that fact. Her features were wonderfully aristocratic for one in her position, and there was something in the expression of her dark, gleaming eyes peculiarly earnest and pathetic. Her hair was tossed wildly and carelessly back over her shoulders—she had evidently just risen from bed, for her costume consisted of nothing more than a loose night-wrapper, which fell in graceful folds around her limbs, revealing to great advantage the exquisite symmetry of her form. I was certain she did not belong to the house. Approaching timidly, yet with a certain air of determination, she bent down and gazed a moment in my face, and then hurriedly whispered in French, "Now is the time—let us escape! They lie sleeping by the door. A servant whom I bribed has disclosed the fact of your capture to me; I also am a prisoner in this horrid den. Will you save me? Oh, will you fly with me?" Of course, being unable to move a muscle, except those of my eyes, I could not open my mouth to utter a word in reply. The unhappy young woman looked profoundly distressed that I should thus gaze at her in silence. "Oh, what am I to do? Who will save me?" she cried, wringing her hands in the deepest anguish: "I have not a friend upon earth!" Then, clasping me by the hand, she looked in my face appealingly, and said, "Monsieur, I know you are a Frenchman. I see it in the chivalrous lines of your countenance. Ah! have pity on a friendless young girl, and do not gaze at her with such chilling indifference. I also am French. These wretches have waylaid and imprisoned me, and they hope to obtain a ransom by my detention. My friends are ignorant of my miserable fate. What can I do, monsieur, unless you assist me?"

Utterly helpless—drugged—yet perfectly conscious of all the lovely creature was saying, I was truly in a most deplorable situation. Again and again she begged me, if there was a spark of French chivalry left in my nature,

not to respond to her appeals by such a look of unutterable disdain. She was thrillingly beautiful; and beauty in
tears is enough to melt the hardest heart that ever was
put in the breast of man. I could feel her balmy breath
upon my face, and the warmth of her delicate hand in
mine, as she struggled to arouse me; and I declare it is
my honest conviction that, had I been simply a corpse,
life would have come back to my assistance; but this diabolical drug possessed some extraordinary power against
which not even the fascinations of beauty could successfully contend. Under other circumstances, indeed, there
is no telling—but why talk of other circumstances?
There I lay like a log, completely paralyzed from head
to foot. At length, unable to elicit an answer, a flush
of mingled indignation and scorn illuminated her beautiful features, and, drawing herself back with a haughty
air, she said, "If this be the boasted chivalry of my
countrymen, then the sooner it meets with a merited reward the better. Allow me to say, monsieur, that while
I admire your prudence, I scorn the spirit that prompts
it!" and, with a glance of fierce disdain, she swept with
queenly strides out of the room. A moment after I
heard some voices in the passage, and scarcely five minutes had elapsed before the door was opened again. To
my horror I saw the ruffian who had first followed me
enter stealthily with a darkened lantern, and approach
toward my bed. He carried in his right hand a heavy
bar of iron. Stopping a moment opposite a shrine on
one side of the room, he laid down his lamp and bar,
and, bowing down three times, crossed himself devoutly,
and then proceeded to accomplish his fiendish work. No
conception can be formed of the agony with which I now
regarded my fate. Crouching low as he approached, the
wretch soon reached my bedside, peered a moment into
my face with his hideous white eyes, laid down the lamp,
then grasped the bar of iron firmly in both hands, and
raised himself up to his full height. I made a desperate
effort to cry out for help. My voice was utterly gone.

I could not even move my lips. But why prolong the dreadful scene? One more glance with the fierce white eyes, a deep grating malediction, and the ruffian braced himself for his deadly job. He tightened his grip upon the bar, swung it high over his head, and with one fell blow—DASHED MY BRAINS OUT!!

*   *   *   *   *   *   *

Don't believe it, eh?

Well, sir, you would insist upon my telling you the adventure, and now I stand by it! If it be your deliberate opinion that my statement is not to be relied upon, nothing remains between us but to arrange the preliminaries. I have no disposition to deprive my publishers of a valuable contributor, or society of an ornament; but, sir, the great principles of truth must be maintained. As it will not be convenient for me to attend to this matter in person, you will be pleased to select any friend of mine in California who may desire to stand up for my honor; place him before you at the usual distance of ten paces; then name any friend of yours at present in Europe as a similar substitute for yourself—the principals only to use pistols—notify me by the Icelandic telegraph when you are ready, and then, upon return of signal, pop away at my friend. But, since it is not my wish to proceed to such an extremity unnecessarily, if you will admit that I may possibly have been deceived—that there may have been some hallucination about the adventure—that strong tea and nervous excitement may have had something to do with it, then, sir, I am willing to leave the matter open to future negotiation.

It is true I found myself in my room at the Hotel de Venise when I recovered from the stunning effects of the blow; also, that the door was locked on the inside; but I am by no means prepared to give up the point on such flimsy evidence as that. Should the physiological fact be developed in the course of these sketches that there is still any portion of the brain left, and that it performs its legitimate functions, of course I shall be forced to admit that the case is at least doubtful; yet even then it can not be regarded in the light of a pure fabrication. Has not Dickens given us, in his "Dreams of Venice," the most vivid and truthful description of the City of the Sea ever written; and what have I done, at the worst, but try in my humble way to give you a general idea of Moscow in the pleasing form of a midnight adventure, ending in an assassination? You have seen the Kremlin and the Church of St. Basil, and the by-streets and alleys, and the interior of a low traktir, and the cats, and the Russian beds, and many other interesting features of this wonderful city, in a striking and peculiar point of view, and I hold that you have no right to complain because, like Louis Philippe, I sacrificed my crown for the benefit of my subject. Besides, has not my friend Bayard Taylor given to the world his wonderful experiences of the Hasheesh of Damascus; his varied and extraordinary hallucinations of intellect during the progress of its operations? And why should not I my humble experiences of the tchai of Moscow?

Reader. Slightly sprinkled with *vodka*, or "the little water."

Oh, that was just thrown in to give additional effect to the tea!

Reader. It won't do, sir—it won't do! The deception was too transparent throughout.

Well, then, since you saw through it from the beginning, there is no harm done, and you can readily afford to make an apology for impugning my veracity.

Lady Reader. But who was the heroine? What became of her?

Ah! my dear madam, there you have me! I suspect she was a French countess, or more likely an actress engaged in the line of tragedy. Her style, at all events, was tragical.

Lady Reader (elevating her lovely eyebrows superciliously). She was rather demonstrative, it must be admitted. You brought her in apparently to fulfill your promise, but sent her off the stage very suddenly. You should, at least, have restored her to her friends, and not left her in that den of robbers.

That, dear madam, was my natural inclination; but the fact is, d'ye see, I was drugged—

Lady Reader (sarcastically). It won't do, Mr. Butterfield—your heroine was a failure! In future you had better confine yourself to facts—or fresh water.

Madam, I'd confine myself to the Rock of Gibraltar or an iceberg to oblige you; therefore, with your permission, I shall proceed to give you, in my next, a reliable description of the Kremlin.

CHAPTER XIV.

THE KREMLIN.

NOT the least of the evils resulting from this harum-scarum way of traveling and writing is the fact that one's impressions become sadly tumbled together and very soon lose their most salient features. To be whirled about the world by land and sea, as I have been for the last year, is enough to turn one's brain into a curiosity shop. When I undertake to pick out of the pile of rubbish some picture that must have been originally worth a great deal of money, I find it so disfigured by the sheer force of friction that it looks no better than an old daub. The pity of it is, too, that the very best of my gatherings are apt to get lost or ruined; and sometimes it happens that when I varnish up what appears to be valuable, it turns out not a groat. Want of method would ruin a Zingalee gipsy or a Bedouin Arab. No doubt you have already discovered to your sorrow that when we start on a visit to the Kremlin, it is no sure indication that we will not spend the day in the Riadi or the old-clothes market. If either you or I ever reach our destination, it will be by the sheerest accident. And yet one might as well undertake to see Rome without the Capitoline Hill, or Athens without the Acropolis, as Moscow without the Kremlin. We have had several glimpses of it, to be sure, in the course of our rambles, but you must admit that they were very vague and indefinite—especially the last, when, if you remember, we were laboring under some strange mental hallucination.

The Kremlin has been fully described by many learned and accomplished travelers. Coxe, Atkinson, Kohl, and various others, have given elaborate accounts of it; yet why despair of presenting, in a homely way, some general idea of it, such as one might gather in the course of an afternoon's ramble? After reading all we find about it in books of travel, our conceptions are still vague and unsatisfactory. Probably the reason is, that minute details of history and architecture afford one but a very faint and inadequate idea of the appearance of any place. Like the pictures of old Dennen, they may give you every wrinkle with the accuracy of a daguerreotype, but they fail in the general effect, or resemble the corpse of the subject rather than the living reality. I must confess that all I had read on Russia previous to my visit afforded me a much less vivid idea of the actual appearance of the country, the people, or the principal cities, than the rough crayon sketches of Timm and Mitreuter, which I had seen in the shop windows of Paris. This may not be the fault of the writers, who, of course, are not bound to furnish their own eyes or their own understanding to other people, but it seems to me that elaborate detail is inimical to strong general impressions. I would not give two hours' personal observation of any place or city in the world for a hundred volumes of the best books of travel ever written upon it; and next to that comes the conversation of a friend who possesses, even in an ordinary degree, the faculty of conveying to another his own impressions. A word, a hint, a gesture, or some grotesque comparison, may give you a more vivid picture of the reality than you can obtain by a year's study. Now, if you will just consider me that friend, and resign yourself in a genial and confiding spirit to the trouble of listening; if you will fancy that I mean a great deal more than I say, and could be very learned and eloquent if I chose; if you will take it for granted that what you don't see is there nevertheless, the Kremlin will sooner or later loom out of the fogs of romance and mystery that surround it, and stand before you, with its embattled walls and towers, as it stood before me in the blaze of the noonday sun, when Dominico, the melancholy guide, led the way to the Holy Gate. You will then discover that the reality is quite wonderful enough in its natural aspect, without the colored spectacles of fancy or the rigid asperities of photographic detail to give it effect.

Like many of the old cities of Europe, Moscow probably had its origin in the nucleus of a citadel built upon the highest point, and commanding an extensive sweep of the neighborhood. Around this houses gathered by degrees for protection against the invasions of the hostile tribes that roamed through Russia at an early period of its history. The first object of the Kremlin was doubtless to form a military strong-hold. It was originally constructed of wood, with ramparts thrown up around it for purposes of defense, but, in common with the rest of Moscow, was destroyed by the Tartars in the fourteenth century. Under the reign of Dimitri it was rebuilt of stone, and strongly fortified with walls and ditches, since which period it has sustained, without any great injury, the assaults of war, the ravages of fire, and the wear and tear of time. Kief and Vladimir, prior to that reign, had each served in turn as the capital of the empire. After the removal of the capital to Moscow, that city was besieged and ravaged by Tamerlane, and suffered from time to time during every succeeding century all the horrors of war, fire, pestilence, and famine, till 1812, when it was laid in ashes by the Russians themselves, who by this great national sacrifice secured the destruction of the French army under Napoleon.

During the almost perpetual wars by which Moscow was assailed for a period of four centuries, the Kremlin seems to have borne almost a charmed existence. With the exception of the Grand Palace, the Bolshoi Drovetz, built by the Emperor Alexander I., and the Maloi Drovetz, or Little Palace, built by the Emperor Nicholas, and the Arsenal, it has undergone but little change since the time of the early Czars. In 1812, when the French, after despoiling it of whatever they could lay their hands upon, attempted, in the rage of disappointment, to blow up the walls, the powder, as the Russians confidently assert, was possessed by the devil of water, and refused to explode; and when they planted a heavily-loaded cannon before the Holy Gate, and built a fire on top of the touch-hole to make it go off, it went off at the breech, and blew a number of Frenchmen into the infernal regions, after which the remainder of them thought it best to let it alone.

The Kremlin, as it now stands, is a large collection of palaces, public buildings, and churches, situated on the crown of a high bank or eminence on the left side of the Moskwa River, nearly in the centre of the city. It is surrounded by a high embattled wall, forming something of a triangle, about a mile in circumference, through which are several massive gateways. This wall is very strongly constructed of stone, and is about twenty-five or thirty feet in height. It forms many irregular sub-angles, and is diversified in effect by numerous towers, with green pyramidal roofs; abutments and buttresses; and a series of guard-houses at intervals along the top. The general color is white, making rather a striking contrast with the green-roofed towers, and the gilded domes and many-colored cupolas of the interior churches. Outside of this wall, on the upper side of the main angle, are some very pleasant gardens, handsomely laid out, with fine shady walks, in which many of the citizens spend their summer evenings, strolling about, enjoying the fresh air. Other parts of the exterior spaces are devoted to drosky stands, markets, and large vacant spaces for public gatherings on festa days and great occasions of military display. From every point streets diverge irregularly, winding outward till they intersect the inner and outer boulevards. These boulevards are large circular thoroughfares, crossing the Moskwa River above and below. They are well planted with trees, and have spacious side-walks on each side; but, unlike the boulevards of Paris, are only dotted at irregular intervals with houses. To the eastward lies the Kitai Gorod, or Chinese City, and to the westward the Beloi Gorod, or White City.

Isolated in a great measure from the various quarters of the city, Russian and Tartaric, by the gardens, the large open spaces, the markets, and the river, the Kremlin looms up high over all in solitary grandeur—a mass of churches, palaces, and fortifications, surmounted by the tower of Ivan Veliki, which stands out in bold octagonal relief against the one with its numerous bells swung in the openings of the different stages, thundering forth the hours of the day, or tolling a grand chorus to the chanting of innumerable priests in the churches below. Approaching the Spass Vorota, or Gate of the Redeemer, through which none can enter save with uncovered heads — such is the veneration in which this Holy Gate is held by all classes — we witness a strange and impressive spectacle. Over this wonderful gate, incased in a frame covered with glass, stands the holiest of all the pictured relics of this sacred place, a painted figure of the Savior, emblazoned with gilding, and with a lamp swung in front, which burns night and day, as it has burnt since the days of Ivan the Terrible. Before this sacred image all true believers bow down and worship. While the great bells of the tower are booming out their grand and solemn strains, it is a profoundly impressive spectacle to witness the crowds that gather before this holy shrine, and bend themselves to the earth — the rich and the poor, the decorated noble and the ragged beggar—all alike glowing with an all-pervading zeal; no pretense about it, but an intense, eager, almost frantic devotion. Many a poor cripple casts his crutches aside, and prostrates himself on the paved stoneway, in the abandonment of his pious enthusiasm. Men and women, old and young, kneel on the open highway, and implore the intercession of the Redeemer. From the highest officer of state to the lowest criminal, it is all the same. The whole crowd are bowing down in abject humiliation, all muttering in earnest tones some prayer or appeal for their future salvation. And now, as we enter the gate, the stranger, whatever may be his persuasion or condition, whether a true believer or a heretic of high or low degree, must join in the general torrent of veneration so far as to uncover his head as he walks beneath that sacred portal; for, as I said before, none can pass through the Spass Vorota without this token of respect for its sacred character. The greatest of the Czars have done it through a series of centuries. The conqueror of Kazan, Astrakan, and Siberia has here bared his imperial head; Romanoff, Peter the Great, even the voluptuous Catharine, have here done reverence to this holy portal; and all the later sovereigns of Russia, Alexander I., Nicholas, and Alexander II., ere they received their kingly crowns, have passed bareheaded through the Spass Vorota. Need we hesitate, then, profane scoffers as we may be, when such precedents lie before us? Apart from the fact that I always found it convenient to do in Rome as the Romans do, and in Moscow to conform as far as practicable to the customs of the Moscovites, I really have no prejudice on any subject connected with the religious observances of other people. In pleasant weather I would walk a mile bareheaded to oblige any man who conscientiously thought it would do him the least good; more especially in a case like this, where, if one fails to doff his shlapa, a soldier stands ready to remind his "brother" or "little friend," or possibly "little father," that he (the brother, little friend, or little father) has forgotten his "beaver."

We have now, thanks to Dominico, who has touched us up on all those points, gotten safely and becomingly through the Holy Gate without committing the sin of irreverence toward any of the saints, living or dead. We have passed through a high archway, about twenty paces in length, roughly paved with stones, and now put on our hat again as we ascend the sloping way that leads to the grand esplanade in front of the palaces and churches. This is a broad paved space, walled on the outer edge, forming a grand promenade overlooking the Moskwa River, and from which a magnificent view is had of the lower city, that sweeps over the valley of the south. Standing here, we have a grand *coup d'œil* of the river above and below, its bridges covered with moving crowds, its barges and wood-boats, and many-colored bath-houses, glittering in the sun; farther off, a dazzling wilderness of the innumerable churches of the lower city, with their green, yellow, red, and gilded cupolas and domes; still beyond, the trees and shrubberies of the outer boulevards; to the left, the great Foundling Asylum, fronting on the river, with its vast gardens in the rear; to the right, the Military Hospital, the Barracks, and, far in the distance, over the gleaming waters of the river, the Sparrow Hills, from which Napoleon caught the first glimpse of Moscow; and then the grand Convent of the Donskoi, within the outer wall, near the Kalouga Road; from which, sweeping over toward the right, once more we catch a glimpse of the wooded shade of the Race-course, the Hospital of St. Paul, and the Convent of St. Daniel; and to the left, beyond the outer wall, of various grand convents and fortifications, till the eye is no longer able to encompass all the wondrous and varied features of the scene. Turning now toward the north, after we have feasted upon this brilliant and glittering series of views, each one of which we might linger over for hours with increased delight, we stand facing the principal palaces and churches of the Kremlin — the Terema, containing the audience chambers, and the Granovitaya Palata, the coronation halls of the Czars; the new palaces; the Cathedral of the Assumption; the tower of Ivan Veliki; the Treasury and Arsenal; with innumerable glimpses of other and scarcely less prominent buildings, which unite in forming this wonderful maze of sacred and royal edifices. It would be very difficult, if at all practicable, to convey by mere verbal description a correct and comprehensive idea of the strange mingling of architectural styles here prevailing. The churches present, no doubt, the most picturesque effects, but this is not owing to any grandeur in their proportions. None of them are either very large or very high; but they are singularly varied in form, as if thrown together in bunches, without regard to order; some with Gothic gables, some round, some acutely angular, and all very rudely and roughly constructed, even the perpendicular lines being irregular. The walls are whitewashed, and in many places stained with age. The roofs are for the most part of earthen tiles, imburnt with strong prismatic colors, and shining like the inner surfaces of abalone shells. The domes are white, green, red, and yellow, and each church has a number of gilded or striped cupolas, rising irregularly from the roofs, shaped like bunches of globular cactus, such as one sees on the hill-sides of San Diego. If the comparison were not a little disparaging to their picturesque beauty, I should say that some of the cupolas—especially those of a golden cast—reminded me of mammoth pumpkins perched on the top of a Mexican Mission-house, for even the buildings themselves have something of a rude Mexican aspect about them. The new palace of the Bolshoi Dvoretz, built by the Emperor Alexander over a portion of the site of the old Tartar palace, is a large, square, uninteresting building, with nothing beyond its vast extent and grand façade to recommend it. The Terema and the Granovitaya Palata—both remains of the old Tartar palace—are highly ornamented with trellised work, and are interesting as well from their style of architecture as their contents. It was from the terraced roof of the Terema that Napoleon took his first grand view of the city of Moscow, after entering the gates of the Kremlin. The one contains a fine collection of curiosities, including various portraits of the Czars; the other the royal chamber, magnificently decorated with embroidered velvet hangings, candelabras, frescoes, gildings, and carved eagles bearing thunderbolts, and the great chair of state, in which the emperors sit enthroned to receive the homage of their vassals after the imposing ceremony of the coronation. But it would be an endless task to undertake an account of even a day's ramble through the interior of these vast palaces and public buildings. I paid five rubles for tickets and fees to porters, and, with the aid of Dominico's enlightened conversation, came out after my grand tour of exploration perfectly bewildered with jeweled crowns, imperial thrones, gilded bedsteads, slippery floors, liveried servants, stuffed horses, old guns, swords, and pistols, glassware and brassware, emeralds and other precious stones, and altogether disgusted with the childish gimcrackery of royalty. Great Alexander, I thought to myself, who would be a Czar of Russia, and have to make his living at the expense of all this sort of tom-foolery? Who would abide even for a day in a bazar of curiosity-shops, bothered out of his wits by servants and soldiers, and the flare and glitter of jewelry? It certainly all looked very shallow and troublesome to a plain man, destitute by nature of kingly aspirations. To confess the truth, I was utterly unable to appreciate any thing but the absurdity of these things. I can not discover much difference, save in degree, between barbaric show on the part of savages and on that of civilized people. For what, after all, do these coronation halls and gewgaws amount to? Who is truly king upon earth, when there is "an everlasting King at whose breath the earth shall tremble?"

Strange, indeed, and not calculated to exalt one's im-

pression of royalty, is the fact that, after purchasing a
ticket to see all these relics of the great Czars of Russia,
a horde of officers, servants, and lackeys, in imperial livery, must be feed at every turn. It is a perfect system
of plunder from beginning to end. At the door of the
new palace I was stopped by some functionary in white
stockings, polished slippers, plush breeches and plush
coat, actually blazing with golden embroidery; his head
brushed and oiled to the intensest limits of foppery, and
his hands adorned with white kid gloves, who refused
to permit me to enter until he had arranged some infernal compact of pay with my guide, Dominico. After
showing me through the grand chambers, pointing out
the beds, bed-quilts, writing-desks, chairs, and wash-ba-
sins of the Czars, he finished up his half hour's labor by
making a profound bow and holding out his hand, beggar fashion, for his fee. I gave him half a ruble (about
87½ cents), at which his countenance assumed an expression of extreme pity and contempt. Dominico had informed him that I was a stranger from California, which
had the effect of eliciting from him various passages of
exceeding politeness up to that moment. But he now
came out in his true colors, and demanded haughtily,
"Was this pitiful sum what the gentleman intended as a
recompense for his services?" Dominico shrugged his
shoulders. The liveried gentleman became excited and
insolent—assuring me, through the guide, that no stranger of any pretensions to gentility ever offered him less
than a ruble. I must confess I was a little nettled at
the fellow's manner, and directed Dominico to tell him
that, having no pretensions to gentility, I must close my
acquaintance with him, and therefore bid him good-morning. There never was an instance in which I disappointed any beggar with so much good will. I have no doubt,
if he has read any thing of California, he labors under
the impression that I am an escaped convict from San
Quentin.

O most potent Alexander, Czar of all the Russias, is

this the only way you have of paying your servants? Do you thus make a raree-show of the palace of your forefathers, and require every man who enters it for the purpose of enlightening his benighted understanding to pay your imperial lackeys the sum of three bits? Is it not enough that your soldiers and retainers should hawk old clothes through the markets of the Riadi for a decent living, without making a small speculation out of the beds and wash-stands in which your noble fathers slept and (possibly) washed their faces?

One of the most remarkable objects of interest within the walls of the Kremlin is the Tzar Kolokol, or King of Bells, cast in 1730 by order of the Empress Anne, and said to be not only the largest bell, but the largest metal casting in existence. This wonderful bell is formed chiefly of contributions of precious metals, bestowed as religious offerings by the people from all parts of the Russian empire. Spoons, plates, coins, and trinkets were thrown by the devout inhabitants into the melting mass, and thus, each having a share in it, the monarch bell is regarded with feelings of peculiar affection and veneration throughout Russia. Writers differ as to its original use and location, some contending that it was first hung in a tower, which was destroyed by fire in 1737, and that the large fragment was broken out of it in the fall, which is now exhibited by the side of the bell; others that it never was hung at all, but that this fragment resulted from a failure in the casting. Be that as it may, it was all dug out of the ground in 1837, and placed in its present position on a pedestal of granite, close by the tower of Ivan Veliki.

Standing in an open space, where the eye necessarily takes in many larger objects, including the great tower, but a very inadequate idea can be formed of the extraordinary dimensions of this bell. Cast in the usual form, its appearance at the distance of fifty or a hundred yards is not at all striking; but when you draw near and compare the height of the groups of figures usually gathered around it with that of the bell, it is easy to form some conception of its gigantic proportions. The fragment placed upright against the granite pedestal looks at a little distance scarcely three feet high, but as you approach you perceive that it is at least six. The bell itself is twenty-one feet three inches high, by twenty-two feet five inches in diameter, and varies from three feet to three inches in thickness. Underneath this immense metallic canopy is a chapel, in which is a shrine at which many thousands of the Russians every year offer up their devotions. The entrance to this is through an iron gateway, and the visitor descends several stone steps before he stands upon the paved floor of the chapel. Looking upward and around him, he then for the first time realizes the vast magnitude of this wonderful casting. It is almost impossible to conceive that such a prodigious body of metal was ever at one time a molten mass, seething over vast furnaces. Imagine a circular room more than twenty feet in diameter, and of proportionate height, and you have some faint idea of the interior of the Tzar Kolokol. It is said that it required ten strong men to draw the clapper from the centre to the inner rim, by means of ropes, so as to produce the ordinary sounds of which the bell was capable. This I can very well credit; for the great bell of the Ivan Tower, not a third of the size of this, has an iron tongue which requires the strength of three men to strike against the rim. The tremendous depth and volume of the tones sent forth for many leagues around by the monarch bell must have been sublime beyond conception, judging by this single fact, that while in Moscow, the largest bell I heard sounded was far inferior in size and weight to that of the Ivan Tower, which is rung only on state occasions, yet the sounds were so deep and powerful that they produced a reverberation in the air resembling the distant roar of thunder, mingled with the wailing of the winds in a storm. When all the bells of the tower, save the largest, were tolled together, the

G

effect was absolutely sublime, surpassing in the grandeur and majesty of their harmony any thing I had ever heard produced through human agency. Judge, then, what must have been the effect when the Tzar Kolokol rolled forth a jubilee or a death-knell from his iron tongue!

I do not wonder that the Russians regard this bell with such peculiar feelings of reverence. There is something to arouse the most profound and reverential emotions of our nature in the simple, grand, and mysterious melody of all great bells—something of the infinite that exalts our thoughts and aspirations from the earth. In my recollections of travel I have few purer or more endearing pleasures than the impressions produced by sounds like these. Often the grand old strains of the bells of Lima, Mexico, and Spain seem still to linger on my ear, and I never dream the wild and varied dream of my travels over without feeling that these mysterious voices from many lands have not spoken without a meaning, that "Life, with all its dreams, shall be but as the passing bell."

From the Tzar Kolokol I took my way, under the guidance of Dominico, to the tower of Ivan Veliki, which we ascended by the winding stairway of stone. The view from the top of this tower is incomparably the finest to be had from any point within the limits of Moscow. Here, outspread before us in one vast circle, lay the whole wondrous city of the Tzars—a perfect sea of green roofs, dotted over with innumerable spires and cupolas. The predominant features are Asiatic, though in the quarter to the west, called the Beloi Gorod, or White City, are the evidences of a more advanced civilization. Apart from the churches, which give the city its chief interest and most picturesque effect, the public buildings, such as the theatres, hospitals, military barracks, colleges, and riding-school possess no great attractions in point of architectural display, and add but little to the scenic beauties of the view. In gazing over this bewildering maze of habitations and temples of worship,

I was again strongly impressed with some two or three leading characteristics, which, being directly opposed to the idea I had formed of Moscow before seeing it, may be worthy of repetition. The general colors of the buildings, roofs, and churches are light, gay, and sparkling, so that the whole, taken in one sweep of the eye, presents an exceedingly brilliant appearance, more like some well-contrived and highly-wrought optical illusions in a theatre—such, for example, as the fairy scenery of the "Prophete"—than any thing I can now remember. The vast extent of the city, compared with its population (the circuit of its outer wall being twenty miles, while the population is but little over 300,000), is another characteristic feature; but this is in some measure accounted for by the great average of small houses, the amount of ground occupied by the Kremlin, the inner and outer boulevards, and the suburbs within the outer wall, the number of gardens and vacant lots, and the large spaces occupied by the ploschads or public squares.

Looking beyond the city and its immediate suburbs, a series of undulating plains lies outstretched toward the eastward and southward, while toward the northward and westward the horizon is bounded by low pine-covered hills and occasional forests of birch. No high mountains or abrupt outlines are any where visible—all is broad and sweeping, conveying some premonition of the vastness of the steppes that divide this region from the Ural Mountains. Waving fields of grain, pastures of almost boundless extent, and solitary farm-houses lie dim in the distance, while in the immediate vicinity of the city cultivation has been carried to considerable perfection, and the villas and estates of the nobility present something more of the appearance of civilization than perhaps any thing of a similar kind to be seen in Russia. Contrasted with the country around St. Petersburg, and the desert of scrubby pines and marshes lying for a distance of nearly five hundred miles along the line of the railway between the two great cities, the neighborhood of Moscow is wonderfully rich in rural and pastoral beauties. Viewing it in connection with the city from the tower of Ivan Veliki, I certainly derived the most exquisite sensations of pleasure from the novelty, extent, and variety of the whole scene. Yet, calmly and peacefully as it now slumbers in the genial sunshine of a summer's afternoon, what visions it conjures up of bloodshed and rapine, plague, pestilence, and famine, and of all the calamities wrought by human hands, and all the appalling visitations of a divine power by which this ill-fated spot has been afflicted. Looking back through the wide waste of years, the mighty hosts of Tamerlane uprise before us, pouring through the passes of the Ural, and sweeping over the plains with their glittering and bloodstained crests like demons of destruction carrying death and desolation before them. Then the giant Czars, half saints, half devils, loom through the flames of the ill-fated city, with their myriads of fierce and defiant warriors stemming the torrent of invasion with the bodies of the dying and the dead. Then are the streets choked with blackened ruins and putrid masses, and the days of sorrow and wailing come, when the living are unable to bury the dead. Again, a great famine has come upon the city after the days of its early tribulations have passed away, and strong men, driven to desperation by the pangs of hunger, slay their wives and children, and feed upon the dead bodies, and mothers devour the sucking babes in their arms; and horror grows upon horror, till, amid the slaughter, ruin, and madness wrought by this unparalleled calamity, a hundred thousand corpses lie rotting in the streets in a single day, and the city is decimated of its inhabitants! The scene changes again. Centuries roll on; a dreary day has come, when the foreign invader once more holds possession of the citadel. With the prize in his hands, fires burst from every roof in every quarter. Three hundred thousand of the inhabitants have fled; a wind arises and fans the devouring flame; churches and

houses, temples and palaces, are wrapped in its relentless embraces; the convicts and the rabble run like demons through the streets, drunk with wine and reveling
in excesses; soldiers, slaves, and prostitutes pillage the
burning ruins, all wild and mad with the unholy lust of
gain. Soon nothing is left but blackened and smoking
masses, the ruins of palaces, temples, and hospitals, and
the scared and mutilated corpses of the dead who have
been crushed by the falling walls or burnt in the flames.
Then the invading hosts, stricken with dismay, fly from
this fated and ill-starred city to darken the snows of
Lithuania with their bodies; and of five hundred thousand men—the flower of French chivalry—but forty
thousand cross the Beresina to tell the tale! Surely
Moscow, like Jerusalem, hath "wept sore in the night."

While lounging about through the gilded and glittering mazes of the Uspenski Sabor, almost wearied by the
perpetual glare of burnished shrines, my attention was
attracted by a curious yet characteristic ceremony within these sacred precincts. In a gold-cased frame, placed
in a horizontal position in one of the alcoves or small
chapels, was a picture of a saint whose cheeks and robes
were resplendent with gaudy colors. This must have
been St. Nicholas or some other popular personage belonging to the holy phalanx. His mouth was very nearly obliterated by the labial caresses of the worshipers
who came there to bestow upon him their devotions. A
stone step, raised about a foot from the flagged pavement, was nearly worn through by the knees of the penitents, who were forever dropping down to snatch a kiss
from his sacred lips—or at least what was left of them,
for his mouth was now little more than a dirty blotch,
without the semblance of its original outline. While
pondering over the marvelous ways in which men strive
to cast off the burden of their sins, I observed a very
graceful and elegantly-dressed female approach, and with
an air of profound humility kneel in the accustomed place.
As she drew back her veil she displayed a remarkably

pretty face, and there was something quite enchanting in the coquetry with which she ignored the presence of a stranger. Of course she could have had no idea that any person of the opposite sex would dare to think of female loveliness in such a place, and the charming unconsciousness of her manner, as she adjusted the folds of her dress, and revealed the exquisitely rounded contour of her form, was the very best proof of that fact. A perfect withdrawal of self from the world and all its vanities was her ruling expression. Thrice did this lovely creature gracefully incline her head and kiss the blotched countenance of that inanimate saint. Ah me! what a luxury it must be to be a saint! What a lucky fellow is St. Nicholas, to be kissed by such honeyed and pouting lips as these! Chaste and pious kisses they may be, but, notwithstanding that, it must be very hard to keep cool, under the circumstances. Who would not suffer a life of martyrdom, and be turned into a picture or an image on such terms? Surely this bewitching damsel must have committed some dreadful sin to be thus soliciting the saintly intercession of a little picture with a dirty mouth! Perhaps she had recently suffered her own delectable lips to be pressed by the bearded mouth-piece of some tender and persuasive lover, and now sought to make atonement by kissing St. Nicholas! By all the powers of beauty, I'll forswear sack, Dominico, and try —ha! here comes a devotee of another sort. Let us wait a while. For, as I live, it is a great puncheon of a woman, weighing over three hundred pounds—puffing and steaming as she waddles toward the shrine—a perfect Falstaff in petticoats. Shade of Venus! what a face and figure! Carbuncled with wine, and bloated with quass and cabbage soup, I'll bet my head, Dominico, she's a countess! How the juices of high living roll from her brow as she stoops down, and gives the unfortunate St. Nicholas a greasy dish-cloth of her fat lips! Faugh! I'll consider about my course of life, Dominico. There are some inconveniences in being a saint. Next comes an old and toothless crone, all draggled with dirt, limping on crutches — a most pitiful object to look upon. She hobbles slowly and painfully up to the place just vacated — puts her crutches aside, kneels down, and, bowing low her palsied head, presses a dry, shriveled, and leathery kiss upon the grease-spot left by the fat woman. Thrice she performed this ceremony, mumbling over in her guttural way the prescribed formula; and then rising, regained her crutches, and begged for alms. Well, of course I gave the alms; but the other part of the performance suggested some painful thoughts. It was surely enough to moderate the ardor of one's aspirations toward a saintly life. Yet, after all, Dominico, every sweet must have its bitter. Let us not despair yet. Next comes a great bearded Mujic, all tattered and torn—a regular grizzly bear on his hind legs, and drunk at that. This horrid monster has evidently not known the use of either soap or water for many a long day. His accustomed beverage must be vodka, and grease the only application ever used to purify his skin. He, too, kneels down and gives the image three cordial smacks —a pretty heavy penalty to endure on the part of any saint. Upon my word, Dominico, I don't think it would be possible for me to stand that! But hold — here comes a fellow who caps the climax. A bilious, yellow-skinned, black-eyed fop, dressed in the height of fashion, with frizzled black hair, divided behind, and smelling strong of pomatum, a well-oiled mustache, and a simpering, supercilious expression—one of those nasty creatures that old Kit North says never can be washed clean. He looks conceited and silly enough to be an attache to the court of his imperial highness the emperor. When this fellow knelt before the picture and slavered it with his ugly mouth, a dizzy sensation of disgust came over me. Upon a general review of all the circumstances, Dominico, I have concluded that it might not be so pleasant, after all, to be a saint—in Russia.

It must not be supposed from this little sketch of a

characteristic scene that I wish to ridicule any form of religion. I saw precisely what I state, and am in no way responsible for it. If people imagine this sort of thing does them any good, they are quite welcome to enjoy it; but they must not expect every body else to be impressed with the profound sensations of solemnity which they feel themselves. The Russians may kiss the heads off every saint in Moscow without the slightest concern or opposition on my part. The Romans have kissed a pound of brass off the big toe of St. Peter, in the grand Cathedral at Rome, and I see no reason why other races should not enjoy similar privileges, only it does not produce the same effect upon every body.

Yet, in some sense, such scenes are not without an aspect of sadness. It is melancholy to look upon such a mingling of glitter and barbarism, wealth and poverty, sincerity, debasement, and crime. No human being is truly ridiculous, however grotesque may be the expression of his feelings, when they are the genuine outpouring of a contrite heart. These nobles, common citizens, and beggars, thus meeting upon common ground, in a country where the distinctions of rank are so rigidly observed, and for the time being disregarding all differences of condition; forgetting their ambitions, their jealousies, and animosities, and giving themselves up with such unselfish zeal to all the demands made upon them by their forms of religion, is, in itself, a touching and impressive sight. I confess that when the first shock of grotesqueness, so strikingly connected with all I saw, passed away, the feeling left was one of unutterable sadness. These people were all fellow-beings, and, right or wrong, they were profoundly in earnest; yet, while thinking thus, I could not but fancy the same divine strain of warning that was wafted to the house of Israel still lingered in the air: "Every man is brutish in his knowledge; every founder is confounded by the graven image; for his molten image is falsehood, and there is no breath in them; they are vanity and the work of errors; in the time of their visitation they shall perish."

In reference to the interiors of the churches of the Kremlin, I can only find space to say, after having visited them all, that they present a confusion of gilded and glittering aisles, pillars, alcoves, chapels, and painted domes, which baffles any thing like accurate description. The Cathedral of the Assumption is literally lined with gilding, daubs of paintings representing scriptural scenes, figures and pictures of saints, dragons and devils of every conceivable color and oddity of design and costume, and burnished shrines and candelabras. Through the dazzling mazes of this sacred edifice crowds of devotees, priests, and penitents are continually wandering; here, casting themselves upon their knees, and bowing down before some gold-covered shrine; there standing in mute and rapt adoration before some pictured symbol of eternity—grandees, beggars, andall; the priests bearing tapers and chanting; the air filled with incense; the whole scene an indescribable combination of moving appeals to the senses. All the churches of the Kremlin partake, more or less, of this character. In some of them, the old bones and other relics held peculiarly sacred are inclosed within iron gratings or railings, and are only accessible to the visitor through the services of a priestly guide. Every visitor must, of course, pay for the gratification of his curiosity; so that the bones of the most venerated characters in the history of the Russian Church are turned into a considerable source of profit. It may well be said that every saint pays his own way, so long as there is a fragment of him left in this world. If one could be assured of the truth of all he learns during a tour of inspection through these receptacles of sacred relics, it would indeed confound all his previous impressions that the days of miracles had passed. There is a picture in the Uspenski Saber, the bare contemplation of which, combined with a fervent appeal, it is confidently asserted, recently effected a sudden and wonderful cure in the case of a crippled man, who was carried there from his bed, but after his devotions before this picture walked out of the door as well as ever; and every where about these sacred precincts pictures and carved images are abundant which at stated intervals shed tears and manifest other tokens of vitality.

Outside, on the steps of these churches, the stranger encounters innumerable gangs of beggars, who watch his incoming and his outgoing with the most intense eagerness—rushing toward him with outstretched hands, calling upon all the saints to bless him and his issue forever and ever, and sometimes bowing down to the earth before him, in their accustomed way, as if he himself partook of some sacred attributes. Apart from the wretched aspect of these poor creatures, among which were the lame, the halt, and the blind from all the purlieus of Moscow, there was something very revolting in the debasement of their attitudes. To assist them all was impossible; and I often had to struggle through the crowds with feelings akin to remorse in being compelled to leave them thus vainly appealing to my charity. When alone, hours after, the weary and pathetic strain of their supplications would haunt me, bearing in its sorrowful intonations a weird warning that we are all bound together in the great fellowship of sin.

And now, while we are taking our last lingering look at the Kremlin, the mighty bells of the tower toll forth a funeral knell. A priest lies dead in one of the churches, his coffin draped in the habiliments of woe. The chanting rises ever and anon above the death-knell that sweeps through the air. Standing aloof, we listen to the solemn sounds of mourning. The funeral cortége comes forth from the church. The hearse, with its plumed horses all draped in black, receives the coffin; priests and mourners, bearing lighted tapers, lead the way, chanting a requiem for the departed; and thus they pass before us—the living and the dead—till they reach the Holy Gate. Then the priests and the crowd bow down and pray; and when they have passed out from under the sacred arch, they turn before the image of the Savior and pray again; then rising, they cross themselves devoutly and pass on to the last earthly rest-ing-place of their friend and brother.

Surely death draws us nearer together in life. I thought no more of forms. What matters it if we are all true to our Creator and to our convictions of duty! Life is too short to spend in earthly contentions.

"In the morning it flourisheth and groweth up; in the evening it is cut down and withereth."

CHAPTER XV.

RUSSIAN MANNERS AND CUSTOMS.

RUDE and savage as the lower orders are in their ex-ternal appearance, they certainly can not be considered deficient in politeness, if the habit of bowing be taken as an indication. In that branch of civilization they are well entitled to take rank with the Germans and French, from whom, doubtless, they have acquired many of their forms of etiquette. Something, however, of Asiatic grav-ity and courtliness mingles with whatever they may have adopted from the more sprightly and demonstrative races of the South; and a certain degree of dignity, ac-companied though it may be with rags and filth, is al-ways observable in their manners. The alacrity, good nature, and enthusiasm so characteristic of the Germans, and the dexterous play of muscles and vivacious suavity of the French, are wholly deficient in the Russians—such of them, at least, as have retained their nationality. The higher classes, of course, who frequently spend their summers at the watering-places of Germany and their winters in Paris, come home, like all traveled gentlemen, with a variety of elegant accomplishments, the chief of which is a disgust for their own language and customs. This, indeed, seems to be a characteristic of several other

nations—an inordinate desire to become denationalized
by imitating whatever is meretricious and absurd in
other people; and you need not be surprised should you
fail to recognize even your unpretending friend and cor-
respondent on his return to California; for although I
still pretend to write a little English, I no longer speak
it except in broken accents. Having also worn out
three good hats practicing the art of bowing on the
boulevards of Paris and the glacis of Frankfort, I never
pretend now to recognize any body without striking the
top of my tile against the cap of my knee.

This, you see, is all in the way of excuse for the Russians, and arises rather from an excess of good nature
than an excess of egotism. Constant practice in the so-
lemnities of street-worship—uncovering their heads and
bowing low before their numerous saints and shrines—
may have some influence upon the stateliness of Russian politeness. It is, however, a very prominent and
characteristic trait, and in some of its phases rather astounding to a stranger. A common thing in the streets
of Moscow is to see a couple of sturdy beggars, uncouth
as grizzly bears, meet and stop before each other with
the utmost and most punctilious gravity. Beggar number one takes his greasy cap from his head slowly and
deliberately, gives it a graceful sweep through the air,
and, with a most courtly obeisance, exhibits the matted
tuft, or the bald spot on the top of his head, to his
ragged friend. Beggar number two responds in a similar courteous style, neither uttering a word. Each then
gravely replaces his cap, touches the brim of it once or
twice by way of representing a few extra bows, and
passes on his way with an expression of profound dignity, utterly unconscious of the grotesque effect of all this
ceremony to a stranger. I have seen the most vaga-
bond-looking istrovoschik, or drosky-drivers, jump out
of their drosky and perform similar courtesies toward
each other; and where men of this craft are given to
politeness, one may rest assured that it must be a na-

A PASSAGE OF POLITENESS.

tional characteristic. All seem to be the slaves of ceremony, from the Czar down to the Mujik. Porters, wagoners, water-carriers, butchers, bakers, and chimney-sweeps are equally skilled in the noble art of bowing. At first, judging by the uncouth faces and the grimy costumes of these interesting people, such passages of politeness have very much the effect of burlesque. It seems impossible that men of such rude aspect can be in earnest. One soon gets used to it, however, and regards it as a matter of course. I could not but think how strange it would look to see a couple of Sacramento or San Francisco hack-drivers meet in some populous part of the town, and each one take off his hat to the other, and, with a graceful flourish, make a courtly salaam; or a pair of draymen stop their drays, get down leisurely, approach each other in an attitude of impressive dignity, take off their hats, and double themselves up before an admiring audience. They would certainly be suspected in our rude country of poking fun at each other. I can very well understand why butchers and chimney-sweeps should be polite, since they are accustomed to scraping; and the custom looks appropriate enough with many other classes, including barbers, who are generally men of oily manners, and tailors and printers, who are naturally given to forms; but with men whose business is intimately associated with horse-flesh, I must say it has something of a satirical aspect. Never in this world can I force myself to believe that a hack-driver is in earnest in any thing short of his fare. Do not understand me as casting any injurious reflection upon this valuable class of men; but it is a melancholy feature in humanity—of which sad experience enables me to speak feelingly—that integrity and horse-flesh are antagonistical, and can never go together. For the hack-driver personally I have great respect. He is a man of the world—knows a thing or two about every body and every thing; is constitutionally addicted to cheating, and elevates that noble propensity into one of the fine arts; maintains his independent character, and pockets his extraordinary profits in the face of all municipal restrictions; scoffs at the reign of the law, and drinks his regular bitters. I consider him a persecuted and an injured man; but of such elastic stuff is he made that he rises above all persecutions and all injuries, and still is, and ever will be, master of that portion of the human race which travels and abounds in cities. He is given to humor, too, is the hackman. Nobody better understands how to give a joke, or to resent one. An adept in ridicule, he always enjoys it when not applied to himself. If he is deficient in any one quality, perhaps it is piety. Hack-drivers, as a class, are not pious men; they may be very good men in their way, but, strictly speaking, they are not pious. Neither are they much given to mutual courtesies, especially at steam-boat landings. Therefore I say that to see hack-drivers bow down before shrines and stop on public thoroughfares, and with the utmost gravity uncover their heads and interchange courtly salaams—nay, even kiss hands in certain cases—is a novel and peculiar spectacle, suggestive of improvements which might be beneficially imported into our country.

There was an impassive, abstracted air about Dominico very difficult to describe, but very impressive to a stranger. All these peculiarities were developed the first or second day of our acquaintance. About the third he seemed to grow impatient, hummed over a few gems from unknown operas, and was less disposed than usual to unbend himself. There was evidently a coolness growing up between us. I suspected it originated in my hat, which was really very shabby; and fancied I detected a supercilious expression in his eye as it ranged over my coat and down to my boots. At length he said, "Monsieur, you appear to travel with very little baggage!"

Myself. Yes, only a knapsack.

Dominico (after a pause). Pray what business may Monsieur be engaged in?

M. None at all—just ranging about miscellaneously.

Dom. May I be so bold as to ask what part of England does Monsieur come from?

M. Oh, I didn't come from England at all!

Dom. (puzzled). Pray where does Monsieur come from?

M. Oh, just come from over the way there — California!

Dom. (elevating his eyebrows and stopping suddenly). California? The great gold country? Where they dig gold out of the ground?

M. Yes—that's my country.

Dom. (admiringly). Oh, then, Monsieur is a gentleman of fortune, just traveling for pleasure?

M. Precisely; for pleasure and information combined. My estates are situated in the city of Oakland.

Dom. Is that a large city?

M. Well, it covers a good deal of ground—as much, I think, as Moscow.

Dom. If Monsieur pleases, we will take a drosky and visit some of the gardens?

M. Agreed.

And so ended the conversation. It was marvelous, the change it produced in Dominico; how his dignity evaporated; how vivacious he became; how frank and unreserved he was in his descriptions of the wonders of Moscow; how he scorned to take trifles of change, and how magnificently he disregarded expenses. Wherever we went, however grand the domestics, soldiers, or police, Dominico was always high above them, and I could hear him descanting constantly on the wonderful richness of California. Doubtless the strain of his conversation ran about thus: "Behold, gentlemen, I have brought before you a living Californian! Notwithstanding the shabbiness of his hat, and the strange and uncivilized aspect of his clothes, he is the richest man in that land of gold! Yes, gentlemen, his income can scarcely fall short of ten millions of rubles per annum. Make way, if you please!"

All things considered, Dominico let me off pretty well at the close of our acquaintance, upon my explaining to him that a draft for five hundred thousand rubles which ought to be on the way had failed to reach me, owing doubtless to some irregularity in the mail service, or some sudden depression in my Washoe stocks.

In the way of food the hotels are well supplied, and the fare is not bad in the principal cities. Fish and game are abundant, but veal is the standard dish. I called for a beef-steak at the hotel in St. Petersburg, and was furnished with veal. The soup was made of veal. After salad we had veal cutlets. Then came a veal stew; next in order was a veal pie; and before the courses were finished I think we had calf's head baked and stuffed. At a station-house on the way to Moscow I hurriedly purchased a sandwich. It was made of veal. I asked for mutton-chops at the hotel in Moscow, and got veal. In fact, I was surfeited with veal in every possible shape wherever I went.

Now I am not particular in matters of diet. In a case of emergency I can relish buzzard, but if there is any one kind of food upon earth that I think never was designed to be eaten, it is veal. No very young meat is good, to my notion—not even young pig, so temptingly described by the gentle Elia; nor young dog, so much esteemed by Chinese and Russian epicures. It has neither the consistency nor the flavor of the mature animal, and somehow suggests unpleasant images of flabby innocence. There is something horribly repugnant to one's sense of humanity in killing and devouring a helpless little calf. Who but a cannibal can look the innocent creature in the face, with its soft confiding eyes, its gentle and baby-like manners, and calculate upon devouring its brains, or satisfying the cravings of hunger upon its tender ribs? Who can see the butcher, with his murderous knife in such a connection, without a sting of remorse at the idea of the mother's grief—her great eyes swimming in tears, her lowing cries haunting him for days? I never see a gang of these helpless little creatures driven to the shambles without thinking of that touching picture, the Murder of the Innocents.

In vain I tried to escape this veal passion in Russia. Nay, even in Finland and Sweden it pursued me. I actually began to feel flabby, and felt ashamed to look the poor cows in the face. It was a marvel how the cattle, of which there seemed to be no lack, ever arrived at maturity. If the people kill all the calves, as appeared to be the case, in the name of wonder, where do the cows come from? This question puzzled me exceedingly for some time, and was only solved when I asked a Russian to explain it. "Oh," said he, smiling at my simplicity, "they only kill the male calves. They allow the cow calves to grow up!"

Still, when I came to reflect upon the reason given, it occurred to me that they must be a very singular race of cows. Perhaps they were Amazonian cows.

This leads me by an easy and not ungraceful transition to the Foundling Asylum of Moscow, one of the largest and most remarkable institutions of the kind in the world. In other public places throughout Europe, especially in picture-galleries and museums, the visitor is required to deliver up his walking-stick at the door, in return for which he receives a ticket corresponding with one fastened upon the article itself—as in baggage-cars upon the railway, so that he may redeem it when he thinks proper. But I had little thought, in my experience of foreign travel, that a similar system should prevail in regard to the deposit of living beings, as in the foundling establishment of Moscow. Here, any body with a surplus baby can carry it and have it labeled around the neck, receive a ticket in return corresponding in number with the deposit, and call for it at any future time, certain that it will be delivered up—if alive. The building is of immense extent, and is situated on the banks of the Moskwa River, near the lower part of the town. The grounds around it are tastefully laid out, and must occupy twenty or thirty acres, the whole being surrounded by a high wall, and comprising numerous and substantial outhouses, workshops, etc., for the use of the establishment. Many thousand children are annually taken in and nursed at this institution, no restriction being imposed upon the parents, who may be either married or single, to suit their own taste or condition. The regular force of wet-nurses employed is about six hundred, besides which there are numerous dry-nurses and teachers for the older children. It is estimated that the entire expense of conducting the establishment is not less than five or six hundred thousand rubles per annum, most of which is defrayed by voluntary contributions and interest received on loans.

I spent a forenoon rambling through the various wards, and can safely say I never before saw such an extraordinary collection of human squabs within one inclosure. It was certainly one of the strangest and saddest spectacles I had ever witnessed—so many infant specimens of humanity, bundled up like little packages of merchandise, labeled, numbered, and nursed with a mathematical regularity fearfully inconsistent with one's notions of the softness and tenderness of babyhood. To be sure, they are well treated—kindly and gently treated, perhaps; but it is pitiful to see these helpless little creatures bereft of the gentle motherly touch; washed, physicked, nursed, and too often buried by hired and unsympathizing hands; and no more thought of them, save in the way of duty, than so many little animals destitute of souls. The very idea of attachments formed by nurses is of itself a painful subject of contemplation; for of what avail is it that a child should be loved by its nurse, or find in her a new mother, when by the rules of the establishment there must be constant separations. It is said that over twenty-five thousand children derive, either directly or indirectly, support from this establishment. About six thousand are taken in annually, of which perhaps one fourth die. Many of them are not far from dead when admitted; and it is only surprising, considering the deprivations they must endure in being so suddenly withdrawn from the mother's care, that so large a proportion should survive.

If it be a wise child that knows its own father, it would be a very remarkable father who could recognize his own child among such a variegated collection as I saw here. Never upon earth was there a more astonishing mixture of baby flesh—big babies and little babies, pug-nosed, black-eyed, blue-eyed, fat and lean, red, yellow, and white babies—all sorts ever invented or brought to light in this curious world of ours. Yet the utmost order was observed, and the beds, nurses, cribs, and feeding apparatus looked wonderfully clean for a Russian institution, where cleanliness is not generally the prevailing characteristic. But, great guns! what music they must make when they all get started in one grand simultaneous chorus! five or six hundred babies, of both sexes, from one to two or three years old, in one department; as many girls from three to five in another; boys of the same age in another; older boys and older girls innumerable in another! What a luxury it must be to hear them all together! In general, however, they do not make as much noise as might be supposed. I only heard about forty or fifty small choruses while there; but, trifling as that was, it enabled me to form an idea of the style of music that might be made when five or six thousand gave their whole mind to it. I am personally acquainted with one small baby not over a couple of years old, who, when excited of nights, can very nearly raise the roof off the house, and am certain that five hundred of the same kind would burst the whole city of Moscow sky-high if ever they got at it together. These Russian foundlings, however, are generally heavy-faced, lymphatic babies, and fall naturally into the machine existence which becomes their fate; otherwise it would seem a hard life for the poor nurses, who are not always gifted with the patient endurance of mothers. I was told that the children only cried periodically, say at intervals of every four hours, but hardly credit that statement. Being for the most part soggy little animals, they spend a goodly portion of their time in sleep, and doubtless, when not sleeping, are much given to eating and drinking.

During the summer months several thousand of these children are sent out in the country to nurse, after which they are returned in due order. As soon as they become old enough, they are taught reading and writing, and the most intelligent are selected to become teachers. The boys usually receive a military education, and a certain proportion of them furnish recruits for the imperial army.

CHAPTER XVI.

DESPOTISM *versus* SERFDOM.

THE reader has probably discovered by this time that I have no great affection for the political institutions of Europe, and am pretty strong in my prejudices against despotic governments of all sorts. The fact is, I believe our own, with all its faults, is the best system of government ever devised by man.

The Emperor Alexander II. is admitted on all hands to be a most estimable and enlightened sovereign. He possesses, in a greater degree, perhaps, than any of his predecessors, the confidence and affection of his people. All his labors since he ascended the throne in February, 1855, have been directed to the emancipation of the serfs and the general welfare of his country. No fault can be found with him by the most ardent advocate of human liberty. His sympathies are—as far as it is practicable for those of an autocrat, clothed with absolute powers, to be—in favor of freedom. Toward the people and the government of the United States he entertains the most kindly feeling, and would doubtless sincerely regret the overthrow of our republican system. He has, moreover, devoted himself with unceasing zeal to the abolition of many onerous and unnecessary restrictions upon the liberty of the press and the civil rights of his subjects; encouraged institutions of learning; prohibited to a considerable extent cruelty and oppression in the subordinate branches of the public service; and in all respects has proved himself equal to the great duty imposed upon him, and worthy the esteem and commendation of the civilized world. Yet I can not see what there is in a despotic form of government, under the very best circumstances, to enlist our admiration or win our sympathies. We may respect and appreciate a good ruler, but every autocrat is not good of his kind; nor is every country in a happy condition because it may be exempt from the horrors of commotion. But no sovereign power can ever attain a rank among the civilized nations of the earth—beyond the respect to which its brute force may entitle it—so long as the very germ of its existence is founded in the suppression of civil and political liberty among its subjects.

What, after all, does the emancipation of the serfs amount to? They are only to be nominally free. The same power that accords them the poor privilege of tilling the earth for their own subsistence may at any time withdraw it. They are not to be owned by individual proprietors, and bought and sold like cattle; but they possess none of the privileges of freemen; have no voice in the laws that govern them; must pay any taxes imposed upon them; may be ordered, at any time, to abandon their homes and sacrifice their lives in foolish and unnecessary wars in which they have no interest; in short, are just as much slaves as they were before, with the exception that during the pleasure of the emperor they can not be sold. But will every emperor be equally humane? There is nothing to prevent the successor of Alexander the Second from restoring the system of serfage, with all its concomitant horrors. It will not be difficult to find a predominating influence among the nobles to accomplish that object; for this has been a long and severe struggle against their influence, and owes its success entirely to the unremitting labors of the sovereign. The next autocrat may labor with equal earnestness to undo this good work; but it matters little, save in name. Despotism and freedom are antipodes, and can not be brought together. It may be said that it would be difficult to enslave a people who had once even partially tasted the sweets of liberty, but the history of Russia does not furnish testimony to that effect.

Since the publication of the ukase abolishing serfdom, there has been a great deal of trouble in the more remote districts between the serfs and their masters, arising chiefly from ignorance on the one side, and discontent and disaffection on the other. Every possible obstacle has been thrown in the way of a fair understanding of its terms. Some idea may be formed of the extreme ignorance and debased condition of the serfs when I mention that in many parts of the country, where the influence of the court is not so immediately felt by the proprietors, they have assumed such despotic powers over their dependents, and exercise to this day such an inexorable command over their lives, liberties, and persons, that the poor creatures have almost learned to regard them as demigods. When a nobleman of high position, owning large tracts of land and many serfs, visits his estates, it is not an uncommon thing to see the enslaved peasantry, who are taught to believe that they exist by his sufferance, cast themselves prostrate before him and kiss the ground, in the Oriental fashion, as he passes. It is a species of idolatry highly soothing to men in official position, who are themselves subjected to almost similar debasement before their imperial master. In some instances, especially at a distance from the capital, the acts of cruelty perpetrated by these cringing and venal nobles, as an offset to the arbitrary rule under

SERFS.

which they themselves exist, are enough to make the
blood curdle. The knout, a terrible instrument made of
thick, heavy leather, and sometimes loaded with leaden
balls, is freely used to punish the most trifling offense.
Men and women, indiscriminately, are whipped at the
pleasure of their masters, the only real restrictions being
that if they die within twenty-four hours the owners are
subjected to trial for murder; but even that is nearly
always evaded. The present emperor has done much
to meliorate these abuses; but his orders have to go a
great way and through a great many unreliable hands,
and it is very difficult to carry them into effect unless
they accord with the views of a venal and corrupt bureaucracy and an unprincipled corps of subordinates.

In some of the districts where the serfs were purposely kept in ignorance of the true meaning and intention

of the emperor's ukase, a vague idea took possession of their minds that they were free, and that the proprietors had no right to compel them to labor, or in any way curtail their liberty. Many of them left the estates to which they were attached, and sought occupation elsewhere on their own account; others refused to obey the orders given them by their seigneurs, and a great deal of trouble and bloodshed ensued. In some instances it became necessary to call in the military forces of the district to subdue the mutinous serfs and preserve order. Protests and remonstrances innumerable were addressed to the emperor, pointing out the absolute impracticability of carrying his beneficent scheme into effect, based chiefly on the ground that the serfs themselves were opposed to emancipation. This, of course, occasioned a great deal of anxiety and trouble at head-quarters. It was rather a hard state of things that the very peasants whom he was striving with all his power to serve should, by their insubordination—arising sometimes, it was true, from ignorance, but too often from willful misconduct—do even more than their masters to frustrate his beneficent designs. These troubles went on from time to time, till eventually a deputation of three hundred serfs made their way to St. Petersburg and solicited an audience of the emperor. His majesty, probably in no very amiable mood, called the deputation before him, and demanded what they desired. They answered that they wished an explanation in regard to his order of emancipation, which many of their people did not understand. Some thought they were to be free in two years, but many thought they were free from the date of the order, with the simple condition that they were to pay sixty rubles to their masters the first year, and thirty the second; others, again, that they were free without any condition whatever. All they wanted to know was, were they free or not? If free, why were they forced to labor for other people; and if not free, was there any prospect that they ever would be? The emperor asked, "Can you read?" Some answered that they could read, others that they could not. "Have you read my order?" demanded the emperor of those who could read. "Yes, your majesty," they replied, "we have read your order, but we don't understand it." All who could read and had read the order were removed on one side. "Now," said the emperor, turning to the others, "has this order been read to you?" "Yes, your majesty," they replied, "but we don't understand it." "Very well," observed the emperor; "you seem to be an intelligent set of men, capable of learning, and we shall see that the order is made intelligible. We had supposed it was perfectly clear in its terms; but, since you do not or will not comprehend it, all you who can read must be whipped." The literary portion of the deputation were then taken off by a file of soldiers, treated to a score or two of lashes each, and sent back to their people to explain the manifesto. "And all you," said the emperor, turning to the unlearned members of the deputation, "must serve three years as soldiers, during which time we shall see that you are taught to read." They were accordingly taken off, and furnished with a general outfit of uniforms, and are now serving their imperial master in a military capacity.

Summary justice, that, one might say. It seems, at all events, a pretty prompt method of explaining official documents, and could probably be adopted beneficially in other countries.

CHAPTER XVII.

REFORM IN RUSSIA.

In my last chapter I took occasion to acknowledge, in terms of sincere respect and admiration, the noble efforts of the present emperor, Alexander II., in the great cause of human freedom. He has already gone very far beyond any of his predecessors in the extension of civil liberty among his subjects, but a great crisis has now arrived which will practically test his sincerity. What he has heretofore done will be worse than nothing unless he remains true to himself and the noble cause which he has espoused. History shows us that the sovereigns of Russia have not always been indifferent to public opinion; but, with one or two honorable exceptions, it also shows us that they have been more liberal in their professions than in their acts. I ventured the assertion that there are insuperable obstacles to a very high order of civilization in Russia. Perhaps this is too gloomy a view of the case, and, considering the wonderful natural capacities of the people, it may be thought rather illiberal for an American; but I must confess the difficulties strike me as very serious. The severity of the climate in the middle and northern parts of the empire, the vast proportion of desert and unavailable lands, and the diversity of fierce and ignorant races to be governed, are certainly obstacles not easily overcome, if we are to understand by civilization a predominance of moral and intellectual cultivation, combined with material prosperity and a reasonable share of liberty and happiness among the mass of the people. It is not that a few shall be learned, and intelligent, and privileged above all others, but that the broad fields of knowledge shall be open to all; that education shall be general, and the right of every class to the fruits of their labor and the enjoyment of civil, political, and religious liberty shall be recognized and protected by the laws of the land. In this view, it seems to me that the most serious obstacle to civilization in Russia is presented by the despotic nature of the government, and the difficulty, under the existing state of things, of substituting another for which the ignorant masses are prepared. The aristocracy are constantly clamoring for increased powers and privileges, but it is very certain they have no affinity, beyond pecuniary interest, with the middle and lower classes, and that their sole aim is to interpose every possible obstacle to the progress of freedom. The emperor is now practically the great conservative power who stands between them and their dependents. Any increase of authority to the aristocracy would deprive the masses of the limited protection which they now enjoy. Already the head and front of Russian despotism are the camarilla and the bureaucracy, who practically administer the affairs of the government. So long as they hold their power, they stand as a barrier to all progress on the part of the people. Thoroughly aristocratic and tyrannical in all their instincts, they have every thing to lose and nothing to hope from a constitutional form of government. Why, it may be asked, if the emperor is sincere in his professions of regard for freedom and civilization, does he not make use of the aristocratic powers vested in him, and cast away from him all these obstacles to the perfection of his plans? The question is easier asked than answered. We are but little enlightened upon the secret councils that prevail at the court of St. Petersburg. Whatever is done there is only known by its results; whatever finds its way into the public press is subject to a rigid censorship, and is worth little so far as it conveys the remotest idea of facts. What you see demonstrated you may possibly be safe in believing, but nothing else. It may be easier to speak of removing obstacles than to do it; or it may be that the emperor has no fixed policy for the future, and therefore hesitates to encounter difficulties through which he can not see his way without any adequate or well-defined object.

No country in the world presents such an anomalous condition of affairs as that presented by Russia at this time. The preliminary steps have been taken to set free over twenty-three millions of white people, so accustomed to a condition of servitude, so generally ignorant, and so incapable of thinking or acting for themselves, that many, if not most of them, look with dread upon the movement made for their emancipation. The rights reserved to them are so little understood, and, indeed, so visionary under any circumstances—for two rights to the same land would be as impracticable in Russia between the proprietors and the peasant as in our country between the whites and the Indians—that they can see nothing beyond abandonment to increased oppressions and sufferings in the proposed movement. Degraded as they are, accustomed from infancy to obey their rulers, kept in a condition of brutish ignorance in order that they may be kept in subjection, it is natural they should be unable to realize the mysterious benefits about to be conferred upon them. In their present abject position they enjoy a certain kind of protection from their owners, who, if not always governed by motives of humanity, are at least generally susceptible of the influences of self-interest, and take care to feed and clothe them, and provide for them in cases of sickness; and although this is done at the expense of their labor, it relieves them from responsibilities which they are scarcely prepared to assume. To set them free against their own will, or even admitting that, in common with all mankind, they must have some general appreciation of liberty—to undertake so radical a change in their condition and future prospects without a practical definition of their rights and the substitution of some substantial benefits for the withdrawal of responsibilities now borne by their owners, is an anomalous movement attended by no ordinary difficulties. When we add to this the adverse influences of the landed proprietors; their determined hostility to the abrogation of rights and privileges which they have so long enjoyed; their entire conviction that, without direct powers of coercion, they can not depend upon the labor of the peasantry; that the natural tendency of free labor is to elevate the masses, and render them less subservient to the will of the aristocracy, then, indeed, it may well be conceived that the natural difficulties arising from the ignorance and improvident habits of the class now held in bondage will be greatly augmented. Believing, however, that all men have a

right to their freedom; that such a right is the gift
of the Creator, which can only be wrongfully withheld
from them by any earthly power; that it is superior
to any casual influences or considerations of policy, we
can not but admire the moral courage of the movement,
and the apparent zeal and constancy with which the
emperor has labored, in the face of every obstacle, to
carry it into effect. But the question now arises, is it
to end before it assumes a substantial form? Is it to
be a mere chimera gotten up to entertain and delude
the world? If Alexander aspires to the approval of all
enlightened people beyond the limits of his own empire,
he must make good his claim to it by a determined policy, carrying in it the germ of civil and political liberty.
It will not do to "tickle the ears of the groundlings"
with high-sounding phrases of human progress, while he
fetters their limbs with manacles of iron. There can be
no such thing as a graduated despotism — a stringent
form of controlling the ignorant and a mild form of controlling the intelligent — under one system of government. The ways to knowledge, to honorable distinction, to wealth and happiness, must be open to all; justice must be administered with impartiality, and wherever there is taxation there must be representation.
There can not be one kind of justice for the rich and
another for the weak; constitutions for some and des-
potisms for others. The machine must be complete in
all its parts, and work with a common accord, or it will
soon become deranged and break to pieces.

Peter the Great did much toward the physical improvement of the country. He built up cities, created
a navy, organized an army, extended his dominions, encouraged education, and fostered the mechanical arts;
but he held a tight rein upon his subordinate officers,
and suppressed what little freedom the masses enjoyed.
He was ambitious, and liked to enjoy a reputation for
enlightenment, but no regard for civilization beyond the
power it gave him to extend his dominions. His sub-

jects were merely his instruments. All he learned in
other countries was to sharpen them and keep them in
order, that he might use them to the best advantage.
His ambition was not of the highest or noblest kind.
The page he has left in history is interesting and instructive, but there is nothing in it to warrant the belief that it will be selected by a remote posterity to be
bound up among the lives of truly great and good men.
Catharine II. extended the privileges of the nobility,
made wars upon inoffensive nations, corrupted the morals of her people, and manifested her regard for the serfs
by giving large numbers of them away to her paramours.
The Emperor Alexander I. was ambitious of distinction,
as the most cultivated and enlightened sovereign of his
time. He issued liberal edicts, but seldom observed
them. He wished to be thought friendly to liberty,
without sacrificing any of his despotic privileges. He
gave a Constitution to the Poles, but surrounded it by
such forms and influences that they could derive no advantage from it. He was weak, cunning, and conceited;
given rather to the delicate evasions of diplomacy than
to the bold straightforwardness of truth and honor. The
Emperor Nicholas was utterly selfish and despotic in all
his instincts. He professed to take a profound interest
in the cause of emancipation, but it was purely a question
of policy with him. He cared nothing about human
rights. His dark and cruel nature was unsusceptible of
a noble or generous impulse. While he preached liberal
generalities, he ruled his subjects with an iron rod. He
was bigoted, narrow-minded, and brutal. The sense of
right was not in his nature. His ambition was to be an
object of heathenish idolatry to his subjects—whether as
a god or devil it mattered nothing; fear was the only
incense he was capable of craving; and if such a nature
can be susceptible of enjoyment, his consisted in the
abasement of his fellow-creatures. The severity of his
decrees, the rigor of his administration, and the attributes of infallibility which he cast around his person,

caused him to be regarded with awe, but not with love.
He could brook no opposition nor survive a failure.
Few tears were shed when he was stricken down in his
pride. He left but a small legacy of good deeds to en-
dear him in the memory of his subjects. The haughty
Czar lies dead in his sepulchre—cold, stern, and solitary
as he lived.

Nicholas left his country in a distracted and unhappy
condition — deeply in debt; commerce deranged; the
military service in the worst possible condition, and
nearly every branch of the public service in the hands
of corrupt and incapable men. Well might he say to
his own son upon his dying bed, "Poor Alexander, my
beloved son, where lie the ills of unhappy Russia?"
Well might he endeavor to make atonement for his errors by recommending at his last hour the emancipation
of the serfs.

The milder spirit of Alexander reigns in his place.
What future, then, does this humane young sovereign
propose to himself and his country? He gives personal
liberty to the serfs, but he can not allow them to become
intelligent and responsible beings. If they do, they will
no longer acknowledge his right to deprive them of political liberty. He removes various restrictions from the
press, and the moment the light of intelligence strikes
upon the minds of his subjects, they call for a constitution
and the overthrow of a despotic camarilla. He undertakes to restrain a powerful, intelligent, and unscrupulous
aristocracy, who by instinct, education, and self-interest
hate the very name of freedom, and they turn against
him, and provoke those whom he would serve to acts of
rebellion against his authority. We can scarcely wonder that this is the case when we consider the interests
they have at stake. It is not likely that they will quietly
relinquish their accustomed source of revenue. On the
other hand, the argument is advanced, and with a good
share of reason, that the emancipation of the serfs is really a benefit to the owners. It relieves them of enor-

mous responsibilities, and, by encouraging industry, increasing the intelligence, self-reliance, and capacity of the serfs themselves, makes their labor more profitable to the landed proprietors. This is a view of the case, however, in which they have no faith. Believing in nothing free except the free use of authority in their own persons, they can not be brought to understand the advantages of free labor.

But these considerations do not, by any means, comprise all the difficulties in which Russia is now placed. The dependencies are constantly in revolt. Constant troubles are going on in the remote districts. Nine millions of the population—the old believers who do not profess the prevailing religion—have their secret conferences, their plans and purposes, all antagonistical to the existing form of government. A reign of terror exists in Poland. The Finns detest their rulers, and are only kept in a partial state of quietude by a total subversion of the liberties guaranteed to them under the Constitution. The municipal franchises existing in the various provinces of Russia are a mere mockery; mayors and corporate officers are imprisoned or banished without cause or process of law. The councils of the government are secret, and nobody can conjecture how long he may be permitted to enjoy his personal liberty. The exchequer is annually deficient from thirty to forty millions of rubles. Public credit is growing worse and worse every day, and the whole country is falling into a condition of bankruptcy. It is evident, even to the most superficial observer, that a great crisis is at hand. The Poles are united in their resistance to the despotic sway of the government. Witness the late bloody massacres in Warsaw (1862), against which the whole civilized world cries aloud in horror! They will not now be satisfied with empty professions and still emptier concessions. They demand a Constitution—not a mere paper Constitution, like that of 1815, made to be violated by every lackey of the government sent to coerce them.

They demand civil, political, and religious liberty. Can the emperor grant it to a dependency, and withhold it from the body of his people?

This has been tried for nearly half a century — ever since 1815 — and what has it resulted in? Are the Poles any better satisfied now than they were then? Are they benefited and enlightened by being cut down and hacked to pieces by a set of drunken and blood-thirsty Cossacks in the name of the great Russian government?

The Emperor Alexander must adopt some other system. He will never reduce the Poles to submission in that way. Overpowered and cut to pieces they may be, but not conquered. They belong to the unconquerable races of mankind. The blood that heroes, and heroines, and martyrs are made of runs in the veins of every man, woman, and child of the Polish nation. If they can not govern themselves, it is equally certain they can not be governed by any despotic power. It is not by slaughtering defenseless women and children; not by forcing churches to be opened; not by sending savage and heartless minions to crush the people down in the dust, that Alexander II. is to win a reputation for humanity and liberality. It is not by issuing edicts of emancipation to his serfs, and then, at the instigation of a cruel and ruthless camarilla, deluging the country with their blood to keep them quiet, that he is going to do it. It is not by extending privileges to the press and the universities, and then, by a sudden and violent suppression of all liberty, undertake to arrest some abuses, that he is likely to achieve it. It is not by countenancing venal and unscrupulous writers to sustain every outrage that his nobles may choose to perpetrate, and banishing all who respectfully remonstrate against their misconduct, that he is to attain the highest eminence as a civilized sovereign. It is not by keeping up a system of foreign surveillance, by which Russians in other countries are watched and their lives threatened, that these glorious results are to be achieved. His secret police may (on their own responsibility or his, it matters little to the victims which) assassinate M. Herzain, the editor of the *Kolokol*, in London; but if they do, a thousand Herzains will rise in his place. No; it is by no such means as these that the name of Alexander II. is to be transmitted to posterity as the most liberal and enlightened sovereign of the age.

If he would regenerate Russia—if he would avert the dismemberment of a great empire — if he would accomplish the noble mission upon which the world gives him the credit of having started, he must banish from his presence all evil councils; he must be true to himself and the great cause of humanity; he must give all his people, and all his dependencies, a liberal and equitable constitution, which will protect them from the despotic sway of military governors and the aristocracy. He must establish a constitutional government, complete in all its parts; abolish secret tribunals, and open the avenues of knowledge and justice to all. He must see that the laws are fairly and equitably administered. He must enlarge the liberty of the press, and proscribe no man for his opinions, unless in cases of treason, and under peculiar circumstances of civil commotion endangering the public safety. He must abolish the censorship of the colleges, universities, and places of public amusement, and leave them to be regulated by the municipal authorities. In short, he must cease to be a despot and become a constitutional monarch. Will he do it? Can he do it? Does he possess the moral courage to do it? Time alone can answer these questions. I sincerely believe the emperor is a good man, actuated by the best motives, but not always governed by the wisest counsels. I believe he now has an opportunity of earning a name that enlightened men will bless through all time to come. So far, it is to be regretted that he has not pursued the most consistent course, but it is not yet too late to retrieve his errors. One thing is certain—there can be no half-way measures of reform in Russia. The spirit of the age—the general increase of intelligence—requires a radical change. He can not be autocrat and king at the same time. He must be one or the other. If he tries both, the empire will be dismembered before many years.

Whatever may be the extent and variety of those hidden restraints, which doubtless exist, and must, from the very nature of the government, be exempt from the scrutiny of a stranger as well as from popular discussion, it is beyond question that in the principal cities, at least, very little is visible in that respect which would be considered objectionable in the municipal regulations of any city in the United States. From this, of course, must be excepted the presence in every public place and thoroughfare of vast numbers of soldiers and officers; but that is a feature which St. Petersburg shares in common with all the cities of Europe, and the traveler can scarcely regard it as an indication of the depressed condition of Russian civilization. I think I have seen in the streets of Pesth, Vienna, Berlin, and Frankfort quite as many soldiers, according to the population, as in St. Petersburg. I would say something about Paris, but I expect to go there after a while, and would dislike very much to be placed in the position of Mr. Dick Swiveller, who was blockaded at his lodgings, and never could go out without calculating which of the public ways was still left open. But if there be officers enough of all kinds in Paris to keep the public peace and suppress objectionable correspondence and pamphlets against members of the reigning family, there are also enough in Lyons and Marseilles, as well as other cities of France, to prove that civilization and soldiers, however inimical to each other, may, by the force of circumstances, be reduced to a partnership. The question that troubles me most is to determine precisely what is the highest condition of civilization. It can not be to enjoy fine palaces and have a great many soldiers, for Marco Polo tells us that the great Kubla Khan had palaces of gold and precious stones of incredible extent and most sumptuous magnificence, such as the world has never seen from that day to this, and could number his troops by millions; yet nobody will undertake to say that the Tartars of the tenth century were in advance of the French of the nineteenth century. It can not consist in the enjoyment of freedom, and the general dissemination of education and intelligence among the people; for where will you find a freer or more intelligent people than those of the United States, who are rated by the Parisians as little better than savages? I think civilization must consist in the perfection of cookery, and a high order of tailoring and millinery. If the French excel in the manufacture of cannons and iron-cased ships, and devote a good deal of attention to surgery, it is a necessity imposed upon them by the presence of Great Britain and their natural propensity for strong governments; but I am disposed to believe that their genius lies in gastronomy and tailoring, and in the construction of hats and bonnets. Since the latter articles cover the heads of the best classes of mankind, they must be the climax or crowning feature of all human intelligence. I am greatly puzzled by the various opinions on this subject entertained by the most cultivated people of Europe. The English seem to think the perfection of civilization consists in preaching against slavery and then trying to perpetuate it, in order to get hold of some cotton; the French in suppressing family pamphlets, annulling the sacred contract of marriage, building iron-cased ships, cooking frogs, snails, and cats, making fancy coats, and topping off the human head with elegant hats and bonnets; the Austrians in the manufacture of shin-plasters for their soldiers, and the making and breaking of constitutions for ungovernable dependencies; the Prussians in the blasphemous necromancy of receiving crowns for their kings direct from God; and all in some shape or other professing devotion to human liberty, and doing every thing in their power to subvert it. Truly it is enough to puzzle one who seeks for truth amid the prevailing fogs of error that seem to have descended upon mankind. If there be any degree in honesty, I really think the Emperor of Russia is entitled to the palm of being the most sincere in his profession of regard for the advancement of human freedom. He imposes no restrictions upon his own subjects which he does not consider necessary for the maintenance of his despotic power, and, while struggling against the influence of a wealthy, intelligent, and refractory aristocracy to extend the boon of personal liberty to twenty-three millions of serfs, is the only sovereign who boldly and openly manifests a generous sympathy for the cause of freedom in the United States. While I can see nothing to admire in any form of despotism, or any thing in common between us and the government of Russia beyond the common bond of humanity that should connect the whole human race, I am forced to admit, with all my hatred of despotic institutions, that they are not always a sure indication of an illiberal and insincere spirit on the part of the rulers, or of a base, sordid, and groveling spirit on that of the subjects. It is a matter of regret, calculated to shake our faith in the beneficial effects of a high order of intelligence among men, that the course of England and France, since the commencement of our difficulties, presents a very unfavorable contrast with that of Russia; for, although self-interest has restrained them from actual participation in the overthrow of our government, they have given its enemies the full benefit of their sympathy.

You will smile, perhaps, at the oddity of the idea, considering the roughness of our country, the scarcity of palaces, fine equipages, liveried servants with white kid gloves and cocked hats, and the absence of a perfect railroad system in our remote quarter of the world; but I am perfectly in earnest in saying that, if asked to lay my hand upon my heart and declare, in all sincerity, what country upon earth I do consider the most highly favored

and enlightened at the present stage of the nineteenth
century, I should not hesitate one moment to name the
State of California. The idea has been growing in my
head ever since I came to Europe. It is based upon considerations which are susceptible of the clearest demonstration. For example, assuming our population to be
five hundred thousand, where will you find the same
number of educated, enterprising, and intelligent men in
any one district or state of Europe, not excepting any
given part of France or England? If we have fewer
learned and scientific men than older countries can boast,
we have a greater number above mediocrity, according
to our population, and a vastly higher average of general
intelligence. If our laws are too often loosely administered, it is at least in the power of the people to remedy
the difficulty by substituting good and faithful for corrupt and inefficient officers ; and if any law should prove
burdensome, it can be repealed at the will of the majority. So far as injustice is concerned, I have seen more
of it in Europe, where individual rights were concerned,
than I ever saw in California. We have a public sentiment in favor of the right which can not be shaken by
corrupt, factious, and transitory influences. If our governors and public men are not furnished with gilded palaces and fine equipages, the labor of the toiling poor is
not taxed to supply them. If we are backward in the
higher branches of literature and the fine arts, there is
scarcely a mechanic or a miner in the state who does not
know more of the history of his own country, possess a
more accurate knowledge of its institutions, read more
of the current intelligence of the day from all other countries—who, in short, is not better versed in every branch
of practical knowledge applicable to the ordinary purposes of life, than the average of the most intelligent
classes in Great Britain or France. If we are deficient
in the dandyism of dress and the puppyism of manners,
which so generally pass for refinement and politeness on
the Continent of Europe, there is scarcely a boor among

us who would not be hooted out of the lowest society
for the indifference, rudeness, and disrespect toward
women, which form the rule rather than the exception
among the polished nations of Europe. I have seen
more absolute selfishness, coarseness, and innate vulgar-
ity under the guise of elegant manners, since my arrival
on this side of the water, than I ever saw in California
under any guise whatever. If that be civilization, I do
not want to see it prevail in our country. It would be
difficult, indeed, to say in what respect a comparison
would not show a heavy balance in our favor. Wealth
is more equally diffused, fortune is more accessible to all,
the honors and emoluments of political position are within the reach of every man, the press is unrestrained in its
freedom save in so far as individual rights and the well-
being of society may be concerned; no class is oppressed
by inequitable burdens, and none endowed with exclusive privileges; a rich soil, a prolific mineral region, a
climate unequaled for its salubrity, and a promising future, afford profitable occupation, health, and happiness
to the whole community; none need suffer unless from
their own misconduct, or the visitation of the Supreme
Power by which all are ruled; and none need despond
who possess energy of character and the capacity to appreciate the many blessings bestowed upon them. What
nation in Europe possesses a future at all, much less such
a future as that which lies before us? Russia may improve and prosper to a certain extent; beyond that, no
human eye can discern the glimmerings of a higher and
more enlarged civilization. England has reached her
culminating point. The States of Germany—what future have they? Alas! the past and the present must
answer. France—where is her future? Another revolution—another emperor—another and another bloody
history of revolutions, barricades, kings, emperors, and
demagogues, reaching, so far as human eye can penetrate, through the dim vistas of all time to come. If, on
the one side, we see the type of human perfection and

the maturity of all worldly knowledge, and if we see on the other only the presumption that springs from ignorance, want of cultivation, or want of reverence for the example of others, then I earnestly pray that we may forever remain in our present benighted condition, or, if we advance at all, that it may not be in the direction taken by any of the governments of Europe. As our present is unlike theirs, so I trust may be our future.

CHAPTER XVIII.

A BOND OF SYMPATHY.

THE Russians, doubtless, have a natural appetite for tobacco, in common with all races of mankind, whether Digger Indians, Caffirs, Hindoos, Persians, Turks, Americans, or Dutchmen; for I never yet have met with a people who did not take to the glorious weed, in some shape or other, as naturally as a babe to its mother's breast. *Vodka*, or native brandy, is their favorite beverage, when they can get it. In that respect, too, they share a very common attribute of humanity—a passion for strong drinks. Nevertheless, although the love of intoxicating liquors is pretty general in Russia, the habit of smoking which usually accompanies it is not so common as in the more southern parts of Europe. A reason for this may be found in the prohibitions established by the government against the general use of tobacco. It is true, any person who pleases may enjoy this luxury, but by a rigid ukase of the emperor the restrictions amount very nearly to an absolute prohibition, so far as the common people are concerned. Smoking is prohibited in the streets of every town and city throughout the empire, and any infraction of the law in this respect, whether by a native or foreigner, is visited by a heavy penalty. I hear of several instances in St. Petersburg and Moscow of arrests by the police for violations of the imperial decree. The reason given by the Russians themselves for this despotic regulation is, that the cities being built mostly of wood, extensive and disastrous conflagrations have arisen from carelessness in street-smoking. It is difficult to see how the risk is lessened in this way, for the prohibition does not extend to smoking within doors. A carpenter may indulge his propensity for cigars over a pile of shavings, provided it be in his workshop, but he must not carry a lighted cigar in his mouth on any of the public thoroughfares. The true reason perhaps is, that the emperor considers it a useless and expensive habit, and thus makes use of his imperial power to discountenance it, as far as practicable, among his subjects. They may drink *vodka* if they please, because that only burns their insides out; but they must not smoke cigars, as a general rule, because that impairs their moral perceptions. Hence cigars are not permitted to be sold at any of the tobacco-shops in packages of less than ten. Few of the lower classes ever save up money enough to buy ten cigars at a time, so that if they desire to smoke they must go to a cheap groggery and indulge in cheap cigaritos. Owing to the want of opportunity, therefore, smoking is not a national characteristic, as in Germany and the United States.

This, I must confess, gave me a rather gloomy impression of Russia, and accounted in some measure for the grave and uncongenial aspect of the people. One always likes to find some bond of sympathy between himself and the inhabitants of the country through which he travels. I remember reading somewhere of a Scotchman who had occasion to visit the United States on business connected with an establishment in Glasgow. He was disgusted with the manners and customs of the people; had no faith in their capacity for business; found nothing to approve; considered them vulgar, impertinent, irresponsible, and irreligious; and finally was about to take his departure with these unfavorable views, when he discovered, from some practical experience, that they possessed, in addition to all these traits, wonderful shrewdness in the art of swindling. New dodges that he had never dreamt of turned up in the line of debits and credits; he was interested—delighted! A familiar chord was touched. He retracted all he had said; formed the most exalted opinion of the people; reluctantly returned to Glasgow, and there made a fortune in the course of a few years! It is said that he now swears by the eternal Yankee nation—the only oath he was ever known to make use of—and expresses a desire to settle in the United States, if he can find a suitable part of the country abounding in fogs, rain, sleet, snow, and wind.

Somewhat akin to this is the affection with which a traveler in a foreign land regards every mountain, tree, or flower that reminds him of his own country. The most pleasant parts of my experiences of mountain scenery are those that most resemble similar experiences at home. Some suggestion or hint of a familiar scene has often caused me to enjoy what would otherwise perhaps have attracted no particular attention. I remember once, while traveling in Brazil, near the Falls of Tejuca, some very pleasant scenes of early life came suddenly to mind, without any thing that I could perceive at the moment to give rise to such a train of thought. The aspect of the country was different from any I had ever seen before; and it was not till I discovered a bunch of violets close by my feet that I became aware that it was a familiar perfume which had so mysteriously carried me back to by-gone days. On another occasion, when at sea in the Indian Ocean, after many dreary months of absence from home, I one day accidentally found in the pocket of an old coat a paper of fine-cut chewing tobacco. With what delight I grasped the glittering treasure and applied it to my nose can only be conceived by a true lover of the weed—I speak not of your voracious chewers, who masticate this delectable narcotic as if it were food for the stomach instead of nutriment for the soul, but of the genuine devotee, who can appreciate the divinest essence, the rarest delicacies of tone and touch, the most exquisite shades of sentiment in this wondrous weed. What a luxury, after months of dreary longing —what an oasis in the desert of life! No attar of roses could be sweeter than that paper of fine-cut. I played with it—just titillating the nostrils—for hours before I dared to descend to the coarse process of chewing. And then—ah heavens! can mortal mixture ever equal that first chew again! How bright and beautiful the world looked! What happy remembrances I reveled in all that day, of serenades, and oyster-suppers, and pretty girls, and a thousand other fascinations of early youth, all of which grew out of a paper of fine-cut.

My experiences in Sweden were even more delightful in this respect than in Russia. At Stockholm I saw drunken men every day, and at Gottenburg it was the prevailing trait. The trouble was to see a man who was not laboring under a pressure of bricks in his hat. On one occasion I must have seen in the course of a single afternoon several hundred reeling home in the highest possible condition of ecstasy—either that, or the streets were so badly paved, and the roads so devious and undulating, that they made people stagger to keep straight. It was on the occasion of a fair, and may perhaps have been an exception to the general rule. One thing is certain—it looked very natural, and made me cotton wonderfully to these good people. There was something really homelike in a reeling, staggering crowd —their shouts and uproarious songs, their boozy faces and tobacco-stained mouths. Every body seemed to be on a regular "bender." The only point of difference between the Swedish and the California "bender" was in the way the boys hugged and kissed the peasant-girls; but even in this respect a similitude may sometimes be found in the vicinity of the Indian Reservations, where I have seen Digger damsels treated quite as affectionately. However, it was all right, so long as both parties were willing. I rather liked the Gottenburg custom myself—as a spectator, of course.

My last and perhaps most agreeable experience connected with the pleasures of sympathy occurred in Norway, on the road from Christiania to Trondjhem. With profound humiliation I make the confession that I have never yet been able to eradicate a natural passion for tobacco. Once, after reading the Rev. Dr. Cox's terrific book on the Horrors of Tobacco, in which it was conclusively shown that a single drop of the oil of this noxious weed put upon a cat's tongue killed the cat, I resolved to master this vicious propensity for poison. For six months I neither smoked, snuffed, nor chewed. But it came back somehow. Care, I think, revived it, and every body knows that care, as well as tobacco, killed a cat. A man might as well be killed one way as another. We must all eat our peck of dirt, and in some shape or other swallow our peck of poison. One learned gentleman proves that tobacco is poison; another, that coffee and tea are equally fatal; another, that meat is no better, and so on; our food and drink are pretty much composed of poison, so that we are constantly killing ourselves, and the result is, we die at last. Still, it is marvelous how long some people survive all these deadly stimulants; how fat and hearty the Germans are in spite of their meerschaums; how wonderfully the French survive their strong coffee; how the Russians deluge their stomachs with hot tea and yet still live; how the English get over their porter and brown stout; and how long it takes the various poisons to which the various nations of the earth are addicted to produce any sensible diminution in the population. Sometimes I am inclined to think people would die if they never ate a particle of any thing—either food or poison. It seems to be one of those debts that we incur on coming into the world, and can only discharge by going out of it.

All of which leads you gradually to the main point— my experience in Norway. First, however, I must tell you that on my arrival in Europe, not being able to find a plug of genuine Cavendish, I was forced to satisfy the

cravings of this morbid appetite by nibbling bad cigars.
But a new difficulty soon became manifest—there was
not a spot in all Germany where it was possible to get
rid of a quid without attracting undue attention. No
man likes to be stared at as an outlaw against the recognized decencies of life. One may smoke cigars under
a lady's nose, dress like a popinjay, or kiss his bearded
friend in most Continental cities, but he must not chew
tobacco, because it is considered a barbarous and filthy
habit. He may guzzle beer, take snuff, and wear dirty
shirts, but if he would avoid reproach as an unclean animal he must abandon his quids. Now, as a general rule,
I dislike to violate public sentiment, or inconvenience
people with whom I associate. If they are nonsensical
and inconsistent in their notions, I agree with them for
the sake of harmony, if not for politeness. Nothing
pleases me better than to annoy an Englishman by doing
every thing that he most dislikes, because he makes it a
point to be disagreeable and unmannerly; carries his
nationality wherever he goes, and it does me good to
furnish him with material for criticism. Out of pure
good nature, I meet him half way; chew and spit that
he may grumble, and put my legs over the back of the
nearest chair to see him enjoy a good hearty fit of disgust, and talk loud that he may find material for ill-
natured reflections on American manners—all of which,
I know, is exactly what obliges him. It affords him
such undeniable grounds for the depreciation of others,
and the indulgence of his own weak vanity !

In like manner I obliged my German friends, who,
however, are altogether different in their exactions, and
only require Americans to drop all their uncivilized habits, and become like themselves—quiet, decent, and respectable old fogies. Therefore I obeyed the laws,
doffed my savage California costume, quit whisky, took
to beer, avoided all passages of tenderness toward the
female sex, and herded mostly with men. For a time,
however, I held on to my beloved quid of cigar. It was

such a solace in the midst of all these privations! But,
alas! I had to give that up too; there was not a spot in
all Germany suitable for the purpose of expectoration!
The floors of the houses are so dreadfully clean—not a
piece of carpet bigger than a rug to sit upon; the porce-
lain stoves so inaccessible; the windows always shut;
every nook and corner blazing with little ornaments;
the lady of the house so severely conscious of every
movement; even the little earthen pans near the stove,
filled with white sand nicely smoothed over to represent
salt-cellars—the ostensible spittoons of the establishment
—staring one in the face with a cold, steady gaze amounting to a positive prohibition—no, the thing was impossible! I saw plainly that a good, old-fashioned squirt of
tobacco-juice would ruin such a country as this, where
every room in every house was inimical to the habit,
and every speck of ground throughout the length and
breadth of the land adapted to some useful or ornamental purpose. Why, sir, I assure you that in the little
duchy of Nassau—where it is said the grand-duke is unable to exercise his soldiers at target-shooting without
obtaining permission to place the target in some neighboring state—I found the garden-walks and public roads
so fearfully clean, every leaf and twig being swept up
daily, and preserved to manure the duchy, that during
a pedestrian tour of three days I was absolutely ashamed
to spit any where. There was no possible chance of
doing it without expunging a soldier or a policeman, or
disfiguring the entire province. The result was, between
tobacco-juice, salt water, iron water, sulphur water, soda-
water, and all other sorts of water that came out of the
earth from Brunnens of Nassau, I got home as thin as a
snake, and was forced to deny myself even the poor consolation of a Frankfort cigar. So matters went on for
nearly a year. I became a morose and melancholy man.
This will account for all the bitter and ill-natured things
I said of the Germans in some of my sketches, every
word of which I now retract.

But to come to the point of the narrative. In the due course of a vagabond life, after visiting Russia and Sweden, I found myself one day on the road from Lillchammer to the Dorre Fjeld in Norway. I sat in a little cariole—an old peasant behind. The scenery was sublime. Poetry crept over my inmost soul. The old man leaned over and said something. Great heavens! What a combination of luxuries! His breath smelled of whisky and tobacco. I was enchanted. I turned and gazed fondly and affectionately in his withered old face. Two streams of rich juice coursed down his furrowed chin. His leathery and wrinkled mouth was besmeared with the precious fluid; his eyes rolled foolishly in his head; he hung on to the cariole with a trembling and unsteady hand; a delicious odor pervaded the entire man. I saw that he was a congenial soul—cottoned to him at once —grasped him by the hand—swore he was the first civilized human I had met in all my travels through Europe —and called upon him, in the name of the great American brotherhood of chewers, to pass me a bite of his tobacco. From that moment we were the best of friends. The old man dived into the depths of a greasy pocket, pulled out a roll of black pigtail, and with joy beaming from every feature, saw me tear from it many a goodly mouthful. We talked—he in Norwegian, I in a mixture of German and English; we chewed; we spat; we laughed and joked; we forgot all the discrepancies of age, nativity, condition, and future prospects; in short, we were brothers, by the sublime and potent free-masonry of tobacco. All that day my senses were entranced. I saw nothing but familiar faces, gulches, canons, barrooms, and boozy stage-drivers; smelt nothing but whisky and tobacco in every flower by the wayside; aspired to nothing but Congress and the suffrages of my fellow-citizens. I was once again in my own, my beloved California.

"Such is the patriot's boast, where'er we roam,
His first, best country ever is at home."

CHAPTER XIX.

CIVILIZATION IN RUSSIA.

IT may be a little startling to set out with the general proposition that Russia is not only very far from being a civilized country, but that it never can be one in the highest sense of the term. The remark of Peter the Great, that distance was the only serious obstacle to be overcome in the civilization of Russia, was such as might well be made by a monarch of iron will and unparalleled energy, at whose bidding a great city arose out of the swamps of Courland, where Nature never intended a city to stand. But the remark is not true in point of fact. Distance can be annihilated, or nearly so; and although Peter the Great was probably aware of that fact, he might well have reasoned that facility of intercommunication is not so much the cause as the result of civilization. The wilderness may be made to blossom as the rose through human agency, but it can only be done by divine permission. I think that permission has been withheld in the case of a very considerable portion of Russia. No human power can successfully contend against the depressing influences of a climate scarcely paralleled for its rigor. Where there are four months of a summer, to which the scorching heats of Africa can scarcely bear a comparison, and from six to eight months of a polar winter, it is utterly impossible that the moral and intellectual faculties of man can be brought to the highest degree of perfection. There must, of course, always be exceptions to every general rule; but even in the dark and bloody history of Russia we find that the exceptions of superior intelligence and enlightenment have been chiefly confined to those who availed themselves of the advantages afforded by more temperate

I

climes.   Peter himself, the greatest of the Czars, and
certainly the most gifted of his race in point of intellect,
perfected his education in other countries, and in all his
grand enterprises of improvement availed himself of the
intellect and experience of other races.   Every important improvement introduced into Russia during his
reign was the product of some other country, executed
under foreign supervision.   This, perhaps, more than
any thing else, may be said to afford the most striking
evidence of the enlarged and progressive character of
his mind.   Yet the very same practice has been followed
to a greater or less extent by all his successors, and still,
with the exception of a railroad built by Americans, a
telegraph system, a few French fashions, and a movement professing to have for its object the emancipation
of the serfs, the country, beyond the limits of the sea-
port districts and those parts bordering on the States
of Germany, has advanced but little toward civilization
since the reign of Peter.

With such a vast extent of territory, and such a variety of climates as it must necessarily embrace, it may
seem rather a broad assertion to say that climate can be
any obstacle to Russian civilization ; but let us glance
for a moment at the general character of the country.
Between the sixtieth and seventy-eighth degrees of north
latitude, embracing a considerable portion of European
and Asiatic Russia, the winters are exceedingly long and
severe, the summers so short that but little dependence
can be placed upon crops.   The greater part of this region consists of lakes, swamps, forests of pine, and extensive and barren plains.   The mines of Siberia may be
regarded as the most valuable feature in this desolate
region.   The production of flax and hemp in the province of Petersburg, and the lumber products of the forests which are accessible to the capital, give some importance to such portions as border on the southern and
European limit of this great belt; but its general features are opposed to agricultural progress.   Whatever

of civilization can exist within it must be of forced growth, and be maintained under the most adverse circumstances. South of this, between the fifty-fifth and sixtieth degrees of latitude, comes a still wider and more extensive region, comprising St. Petersburg, Riga, Moscow, Smolensk, and a portion of Irkutsk and Nijni Novgorod. Here the summers are longer and the winters not quite so severe; but a large portion of the country consists of forests, sterile plains, and extensive marshes, and much of it is entirely unfit for cultivation. The European portions are well settled, and corn, flax, and hemp are produced wherever the land is available, and large bands of cattle roam over many parts of the country. In its general aspect, however, considering the duration and severity of the winters, and the large proportion of unavailable lands, I do not think it can ever become very productive in an agricultural point of view. Between fifty and fifty-five degrees latitude, embracing the valley of the Volga, is a more favored region, abounding in fertile lands, and the summers are longer, but the winters are still severe, especially in the eastern portions. From latitude forty-three to fifty, embracing portions of Kief, the Caucasus, and other southern possessions of the empire, the winters are comparatively temperate, and the summers warm and long; but here, again, a great portion of this country consists of mountains, arid plains, and deserts, and it is subject to extreme and terrible droughts. Here is a vast extent of territory, comprising about one hundred and sixty-five degrees of longitude and thirty-five of latitude, which contains within its limits a greater variety of bad climates, and a greater amount of land unavailable for any purposes of human life, than any equal compass of territory upon the globe, if we except Africa, which is at least doubtful. Within the limits of this vast, and, for the most part, inhospitable region, we find nearly all the races who, as far back as the history of mankind dates, have been the most addicted to predatory wars, and the indulgence of every savage propensity growing out of an untamable nature — Tartars, Cossacks, gipsies, Turks, Circassians, Georgians, etc., and the Russians proper, whose wild Sclavonic blood contains very nearly all the vices and virtues that circulate through the veins of all these races, besides many enterprising and unscrupulous traits of character to which the inferior tribes could never aspire. Here we have a mixed population, estimated in 1856 at seventy-one millions, including North American possessions and tributary tribes, a great part of it composed of totally incongruous elements, and with a variety of religions, embracing about nine millions of Roman, Armenian, and irregular Greek Catholics, Lutherans, Mohammedans, Israelites, and Buddhists — the national creed being the Greco-Russe, which, it is estimated, is professed by about fifty millions of the inhabitants, including, of course, infants and young children, and many others who know nothing about it. To keep all these incongruous elements in order, and provide against foreign invasion, requires a standing army of 577,859 troops "for grand operations," as the last almanac expresses it, besides various *corps de reserve*, and a navy of 186 fron steamers, 41 large sailing vessels, and numerous gun-boats and smaller vessels, in the Baltic, the Black Sea, the Caspian Sea, the White Sea, and the Sea of Azof. More than seven eighths of these are frozen up and totally unavailable for six months every year. It is estimated that, after allowing for the forces necessary to protect the home possessions of the empire, of which Russian Poland is the most troublesome, the number of troops that can be brought into active offensive operation does not, under ordinary circumstances, exceed two hundred thousand men, and it must be obvious, considering that Russia has but little external seaboard, and must submit to the rigors of a climate which locks up the best part of her navy at least half of every year, that she can never attain any great strength as a naval power. I am inclined to believe, therefore, that while this great nation, or combination of nations, is, from the very nature of its climate and topography, almost impregnable to foreign invasion, it can never become a very formidable power at any great distance from home; and there are considerations connected with its form of government, and the difficulty or impracticability of changing it, which, in my opinion, forms an insuperable obstacle to the education of the people, and such general dissemination of intelligence among the masses as will entitle them to take the highest rank among civilized nations. Nor does the history of Russia during past ages afford much encouragement for a different view of the future. Democracy existed for several centuries before the country became subject to despotic rule, and from the ninth to the fifteenth century the aristocracy possessed no hereditary privileges; the offices of state were accessible to all, and the peasantry enjoyed personal liberty. It was not until the reign of Peter the Great—the high-priest of civilization—that the serfs became absolute slaves subject to sale, with or without the lands upon which they lived. In respect to political liberty, there has been little, if any advance since the reign of the Empress Catharine, who accorded some elective privileges to certain classes of her subjects in the provinces, and reduced the administration of the laws to something like a system. The absurd pretense of Alexander I. in according to the Senate the right of remonstrating against imperial decrees is perfectly in keeping with all grants of power made by the sovereigns of Russia to their subjects. There is not, and can not be in the nature of things, a limited despotism. As soon as the subjects possess constitutional rights at all binding upon the supreme authority, it becomes another form of government. The great difficulty in Russia is, that the sovereign can not divest himself of any substantial part of his power without adding to that of the nobles and the aristocracy, who are already, by birth, position, and instinct, the class most to be feared, and most inimical to the progress of freedom. It is not altogether the ignorance of the masses, therefore, that forms an insuperable barrier to the introduction of more liberal institutions, but the wealth, intelligence, and influence of the higher classes, who neither toil nor spin, but derive their support from the labor of the masses whom they hold in subjection. It is natural enough they should oppose every reform tending to elevate these subordinate classes upon whom they are dependent for all the powers and luxuries of their position. Admitting that the present emperor may have a leaning toward free institutions, and possibly contemplate educating forty or fifty millions of his subjects to run him into the Presidency of Russia, it is obvious that the path is very thorny, and that the position will be well earned if ever he gets there. But these acts of sovereign condescension, although they read very well in newspapers, and serve to entertain mankind with vague ideas of the progress of freedom, are generally the essence of an intense egotism, and amount to nothing more than cunning devices to subvert what little of liberty their subjects may be likely to extort from them by the maintenance of their rights. I do not say that Alexander II. is governed by these motives, but, having no faith in kings or despots of any kind, however good they may be, I can see no reason why he should prove any better than his predecessors. Upon this point let me tell you an anecdote. You are aware, perhaps, that the Finns have a Constitution which allows them to do what they please, provided it be pleasing to the emperor. Like the ukase of Alexander I. to the Senate, and all similar grants of authority, it is not worth the parchment upon which it is written, and in its practical operation is no better than a practical joke. The Finns, however, are a brave, simple minded, and rather superstitious people, and take some pride in this Constitution. It is the ghost of liberty at all events, and they indulge in the hope that some day or other it will fish up the dead body. Not more than a few weeks ago, a small party of these worthy people, on their way to Stockholm for purposes of business or pleasure, were arrested and put in prison by the Russian authorities on the supposition that they differed from the emperor in his interpretation of this liberal Constitution, and were going to Sweden to lay their grievances before their old compatriots. It is quite possible that this was true. I heard complaints made when I was in Helsingfors that there was quite a difference of opinion on the subject. But it is a marvel how they could misunderstand their right under the Constitution, when there is a strong military force stationed at the principal cities of Finland to make it intelligible. So thought the emperor or his subordinates, and put them in jail to give them light. The point in the transaction which strikes me most forcibly is, that a power like that of Russia, after having wrested the province of Finland from Sweden, with an army and navy far inferior to what she now possesses, should be afraid that a handful of Finns should tell a pitiful tale to the King of Sweden, and prevail upon him to take their country back again. If this be the freedom granted under the free Constitution of Finland, the restraints upon personal liberty must be pretty stringent in dependencies where no Constitutions at all exist.

By a natural law, the waves of despotism gather strength and volume as they spread from the central power. It is scarcely an exaggeration to say that the Autocrat of Russia is the least despotic of all the despots in authority. The landed proprietors in the remote provinces too often rule their dependents with an iron rod, and the strong arm of the supreme authority is more frequently exercised in the protection than in the oppression of the lower classes. The tribunals of justice in these districts are corrupt, and the laws, as they are administered by the subordinate officers of the government, afford but little chance of justice to the ignorant masses. The landed proprietors are subjected to various exactments and oppressions from the governors, and these again are at the mercy of the various colleges or departments above them, and so on up to the imperial council and imperial presence. Each class or grade becomes independent, despotic, and corrupt in proportion as they recede from the central authority, having a greater latitude of power, and being less apprehensive of punishment for its abuse. In truth, the nobles and aristocracy are the immediate oppressors of the ignorant masses, who are taught to regard them as demigods, and bow down before them in slavish abasement. Now and then, in extreme cases, where the autocrat discovers abuses which threaten to impair his authority, he sends some of these aspiring gentlemen on a tour of pleasure to Siberia, and thus practically demonstrates that there is a ruling power in the land. As all authority emanates from him, and all responsibility rests with him, so all justice, liberality, fair dealing, and humanity are apt to find in a good sovereign, under such a system, their best friend and most conscientious supporter. The success of his government, the prosperity and happiness of his people, even the perpetuity of the entire political system, depend upon the judicious and equitable use which he makes of his power. There are limits to human forbearance, as sovereigns have discovered by this time. The Czar is but a man, a mere mortal, after all, and can only hold his authority through the consent, indifference, or ignorance of his subjects; but should he oppress them by extraordinary punishments or exactions, or withdraw from them his protection against the petty tyranny of his subordinates, he would find, sooner or later, that the most degraded can be aroused to resentment. It is the belief on the part of the peasantry, of which the population of Russia is in so large a part formed, that the emperor is their friend—that he does not willingly or unnecessarily deprive them of their liberties. This tends to keep them in subjection. Indeed, they have but faint notions of liberty, if any at all, born as they are to a condition of servitude, and reared in abject submission to the governing authorities. They are generally well satisfied if they can get enough to eat; and, when they are not subjected to cruel and unusual abuses, are comparatively happy.

The unreasonable assumptions of power on the part of their immediate governing authorities present a trait common to mankind. We know from experience in our own country that the negro-driver on a Southern plantation—a slave selected from slaves—is often more tyrannical in the use of authority than the overseer or owner. We know that there are hard and unfeeling overseers on many plantations, where the owner is comparatively mild and humane. So far as he knows any thing of the details of his own affairs, his natural disposition accords with his interest, and he is favorable to the kind treatment of his slaves. But he can not permit them to become intelligent beings. They may study all the mechanical arts which may be useful to him—become blacksmiths, carpenters, or machinists, but they must not learn that they are held in servitude, and that the Almighty has given him no natural right to live upon their earnings, or enjoy his pleasure or power at the expense of their labor and their freedom. The same condition of things, with some variation, of course, arising from differences of climate and races, exists in Russia, and the results are not altogether dissimilar. We find idleness, lack of principle, overbearing manners, ignorance, and sensualism a very common characteristic of the superior classes, mingled though it may be with a show of fine manners, and such trivial and superficial accomplishments as may be obtained without much labor. It is a great negro plantation on a large scale, in which the gradation of powers has a depressing tendency, causing them to increase in rigor as they descend, like a stone dropped from a height, which at first might be caught in the open hand, but soon acquires force enough to brain an ox.

One of the effects of the strong coercive powers of the

government is perceptible in this, that the greatest latitude prevails in every thing that does not interfere with the maintenance of political authority; and although it is difficult, in such a country, to find much that comes within that category, occasional exceptions may be found. Thus drunkenness, debauchery, indecency, and reckless, prodigal, and filthy habits, are but little regarded, while the slightest approach to the acquisition of a liberal education, or the expression of liberal opinions on any subject connected with public polity, is rigidly prohibited. Most of the English newspapers are excluded from the empire, although if admitted they would have but few general readers among the Russians—certainly not many among the middle or lower classes. No publication on political economy, no work of any kind relating to the science of government or the natural rights of man; nothing, in short, calculated to impair the faith of the people in the necessity of their political servitude, is permitted to enter the country without a most careful examination. A rigid censorship is exercised over the press, the libraries, the public colleges, the schools, and all institutions having in view the education of the people and the dissemination of intelligence. The Censorial Bureau is in itself an important branch of the government, having its representatives diffused throughout every province, in every public institution, and even extending its ramifications into the sacred realms of private life; for it is a well-known fact that a family can not employ a private tutor whose antecedents and political proclivities have not undergone the scrutiny and received the official sanction of the censorial authorities.

How can a country, under such circumstances, be expected to take a high rank among the enlightened nations of the earth? The very germ of its existence is founded in the suppression of intelligence. It may enjoy a limited advancement, but there can be no great progress in any direction which does not tend at the same time to the subversion of a despotic rule. Even the

theatres, operas, *cafés*, and all places of public amusement, are under the same rigid surveillance. No play
can be performed, no opera given, no *café* opened, no
garden amusements offered to the public, unless under
the supervision and with the sanction of the censorial
authorities. In all well-regulated communities there
must be, of course, some local or municipal restrictions
respecting popular amusements, based upon a regard for
public morals, but in this case the question of morality
is not taken into much account. Provided there is nothing politically objectionable in the performance, and it
has no tendency to make the people better acquainted
with the rottenness of courts, the selfishness, wickedness,
and insincerity of men in authority, and their own rights
as human beings—provided the theme be *Jishn za Zara*
—"Your life for your Czar," or the exhibition a voluptuous display—provided it be merely a matter of abject
adulation or fashionable sensation, the most fastidious
censor can find no fault with it. What, then, does the
education of the masses amount to? We read of lectures for the diffusion of knowledge among the people;
of colleges for young men; of various institutions of
learning; of a liberal system of common schools for the
poor. All this is very well in its way. A little light
is better than none when the road is crooked, and the
country abounds in ruts and deep pitfalls. But the
lights shed by these institutions are much obscured by
the official glasses through which they shine. The building of fortifications; the manufacture of gunpowder;
the use of guns and swords; the beauties of rhetoric
abounding in the drill manual; the eloquence of batteries and broadsides; the poetry of ditching and drain-
ing; the ethics of primary obedience to the authorities,
and afterward to God and reason; all that pertains to
rapine, bloodshed, and wholesale murder—the noble art
of mutilating men in the most effective manner, and the
best method of cutting them up or putting them together again when that is done; the horrid sin of using one's

own lights on any internal problem of right or wrong, religion or public policy, when the emperor, in the plenitude of his generosity, furnishes light enough out of his individual head for sixty-five millions of people—these are the principal themes upon which the intellects of the rising generation of Russia are nourished. In the primary schools a select and authorized few are taught reading, writing, and arithmetic, but they seldom get much farther, and not always that far, before subordinate positions in the army or navy are found for them. Their education is indeed very limited, and may be set down as an exception to the general ignorance.

It will thus be seen that the whole system of education has but one object in view, the maintenance of a military despotism. In this it would scarcely be reasonable to search for cause of complaint. Doubtless the acquisition of knowledge is encouraged as far as may be consistent with public security and public peace. But it is obvious that under such a system these people can never emerge from their condition of semi-barbarism. They must continue behind the spirit of the age in all that pertains to the highest order of civilization. Science, in a limited sense, may find a few votaries; the arts may be cultivated to a certain degree; a feeble school of literature may attain the eminence of a national feature; but there can be no general expansion of the intellectual faculties, no enlarged and comprehensive views of life and of human affairs. Whatever these people do must be subservient to military rule; beyond that there can be little advance save in what is palpable to the grosser senses, or what panders to the savagery of their nature. A statesman or a philosopher, with independence enough to think and speak the truth if his views differed from those of the constituted authorities, would be a very dangerous character, and be very apt to pursue his career, in company with all who have hitherto aspired to distinction in that way, beyond the confines of Siberia. Russia may produce many Karasmins to write glowing histories of her wars and conquests, but her Burkes, her Pitts, and her Foxes will be few, and her Shakspeares and her Bacons fewer still. Her Pascal's Reflections will be tinged with Siberian horrors; her Young's Night Thoughts will be of the dancing damsels of St. Petersburg; her Vicars of Wakefield will abound in the genial humor of devils and dragons, saints and tortures; and the wit of her Sidney Smiths will have a crack of the knout about it, skinning men's back's rather than their backslidings; effective only when it draws human blood, and best approved by the censors when it strikes at human freedom.

We find the results of such a system strongly marked upon the general character. While equals are jealous of each other, inferiors are slavish and superiors tyrannical. It is often the case that overbearing manners and abject humility are centred in the same class or person. Thus the Camarilla are overbearing to the bureaucracy, the bureaucracy to the provincial nobility, and the provincial nobility to the inferior classes. As I said before, it is a sliding-scale of despotism. The worst feature of it is seen in the treatment of women. Among the better classes conventionality has, doubtless, somewhat meliorated their condition. Absolute physical cruelty would be, perhaps, a violation of etiquette and good breeding; but neglect, selfishness, innate coarseness of thought, and a general want of chivalrous appreciation, are too common in the treatment of Russian women not to strike the most casual observer. Certainly the impressions of one who has been taught from infancy to regard the gentler sex as entitled to the most profound respect and chivalrous devotion—to look upon them as beings of a more delicate essence than man, yet infinitely superior in those moral attributes which rise so high above intellect or physical power—are not favorable to the assumptions of Russian civilization. Yet, since the condition of woman is but little better in any part of Europe, it may be that this is one of the fashions imported from France or

Germany, and since these two claim to be the most polite and cultivated nations in existence, it is even possible that the Americans—a rude people, who have not yet had time to polish their manners or perfect their customs—may be mistaken in their estimate of the ladies, and will, some day or other, become more Europeanized.

But, in all fairness, if the Russians be a little uncouth in their way, they possess, like bears, a wonderful aptness in learning to dance; if the brutal element is strong in their nature, so also is the capacity to acquire frivolous and meretricious accomplishments. Like all races in which the savage naturally predominates, they delight in the glitter of personal decoration, the allurements of music, dancing, and the gambling-table, and all the luxuries of idleness and sensuous folly—traits which they share pretty generally with the rest of mankind. Tropical gardens, where the thermometer is twenty degrees below zero; feasts and frolics that in a single night may leave them beggars for life; military shows; the smoke and carnage of battle; the worship of their saints and Czars—these are their chief pleasures and most genial occupations.

But, with all this folly and prodigality, there is really a great deal of native generosity in the Russian character. Liberal to a fault in every thing but the affairs of government, they freely bestow their wealth upon charitable institutions, and, whether rich or poor, are ever ready to extend the hand of relief to the distresses of their fellow-creatures. It is rarely they hoard their gains. There are few who do not live up to the full measure of their incomes, and most of them very far beyond. Whether they spend their means for good or for evil, they are at least free from the groveling sin of stinginess. I never met more than one stingy Russian to my knowledge; but let him go. He reaped his reward in the dislike of all who knew him. Toward each other, even the beggars are liberal. There is nothing little or contemptible in the Russian character. Overbearing and despotic they may be; deficient in the gentler traits which grace a more cultivated people; but meanness is not one of their failings. In this they present a striking contrast to a large and influential portion of their North German neighbors, for whose sordid souls Beelzebub might search in vain through the desert wastes that lie upon the little end of a cambric needle.

In some respects the Russians evince a more enlarged appreciation of the world's progress than many of their European neighbors. They have no fixed prejudices against mechanical improvements of any kind. Quick to appreciate every advance in the useful arts, they are ever ready to accept and put in practical operation whatever they see in other countries better than the product of their own. Thus they adopt English and American machinery, railways, telegraphs, improvements in artillery, and whatever else they deem beneficial, or calculated to augment their prosperity and power as a nation. While in Germany it would be almost an impossibility to introduce the commonest and most obvious improvement in the mechanical arts—if we except railways and telegraphs, which have become a military and political necessity, growing out of the progress of neighboring powers—while many of their fabrics are still made by hand, and their mints, presses, and fire-engines are of almost primeval clumsiness, the Russians eagerly grasp at all novelties, and are wonderfully quick in the comprehension of their uses and advantages. A similar comparison might be made in reference to the freedom of internal trade, and the encouragement given to every industrial pursuit among the people, being the exact reverse of the policy pursued by the German governments. Thus, while we find them backward in the refinements of literature and intellectual culture, it is beyond doubt that they possess wonderful natural capacity to learn. They lack steadiness and perseverance, and are not always governed by the best motives; but in boldness of spirit, disregard of narrow prejudice, ability to conceive and execute what they desire to accomplish, they have few equals and no superiors. Combined with these admirable traits, their wild Sclavonic blood abounds in elements which, upon great occasions, arise to the eminence of a sublime heroism. Brave and patriotic, devoted to their country and their religion, we search the pages of history in vain for a parallel to their sacrifices in the defense of both. Not even the wars of the Greeks and Romans can produce such an example of heroic devotion to the maintenance of national integrity as the burning of Moscow. When an entire people, devoted to their religion, gave up their churches and their shrines to the devouring element; when princes and nobles placed the burning brands to their palaces; when bankers, merchants, and tradesmen freely yielded up their hard-earned gains; when women and children joined the great work of destruction to deliver their country from the hands of a ruthless invader, it may well be said of that sublime flame—

> "Thou stand'st alone unrivall'd, till the fire,
>   To come, in which all empires shall expire."

Truly, when we glance back at the national career of the Russians, they can not but strike us as a wonderful people. While we must condemn their cruelty and rapacity; while we can see nothing to excuse in their ferocious persecution of the Turks; while the greater part of their history is a bloody record of injustice to weaker nations, we can not but admire their indomitable courage, their intense and unalterable attachment to their brave old Czars, and their sublime devotion to their religion and their nationality.

CHAPTER XX.

PASSAGE TO REVEL.

It was not without a feeling of regret that I took my departure from St. Petersburg. Short as my visit to Russia had been, it was full of interest. Not a single day had been idly or unprofitably spent. Indeed, I know of no country that presents so many attractions to the traveler who takes pleasure in novelties of character and peculiarities of manners and customs. The lovers of picturesque scenery will find little to gratify his taste in a mere railroad excursion to Moscow; but with ample time and means at his disposal, a journey to the Ural Mountains, or a voyage down the Volga to the Caspian Sea, would doubtless be replete with interest. For my part, much as I enjoy the natural beauties of a country through which I travel, they never afford me as much pleasure as the study of a peculiar race of people. Mere scenery, however beautiful, becomes monotonous, unless it be associated with something that gives it a varied and striking human interest. The mountains and lakes of Scotland derive their chief attractions from the wild legends of romance and chivalry so inseparably connected with them; and Switzerland would be but a dreary desert of glaciers without its history. In Russia, Nature has been less prodigal in her gifts; and the real interest of the country centres in its public institutions, the religious observances of the people, and the progress of civilization under a despotic system of government. Of these I have endeavored to give you such impressions as may be derived from a sojourn of a few weeks in Moscow and St. Petersburg — necessarily imperfect and superficial, but I trust not altogether destitute of amusing features.

On a pleasant morning in August, I called for my "rechnung" at the German gasthaus on the Wasseli-Ostrow. The bill was complicated in proportion to its length. There was an extra charge of fifteen kopeks a day for the room over and above the amount originally specified. That was conscientious cheating, so I made no complaint. Then there was a charge for two candles when I saw but one, and always went to bed by daylight. That was customary cheating, and could not be disputed. Next came an item for beefsteaks, when, to the best of my knowledge and belief, nothing but veal cutlets, which were also duly specified, ever passed my lips in any part of Russia. Upon that I ventured a remonstrance, but gave in on the assurance that it was Russian beefsteak. I was too glad to have any ground for believing that it was not Russian dog. Next came an item for police commissions. All that work I had done myself, and therefore was entitled to demur. It appeared that a man was kept for that purpose, and when he was not employed he expected remuneration for the disappointment. Then there was an item for domestic service, when the only service rendered was to black my boots, for which I had already paid. No matter; it was customary, so I gave in. Then came sundry bottles of wine. I never drink wine. "But," said the proprietor, "it was on the table." Not being able to dispute that, I abandoned the question of wine. Various ices were in the bill. I had asked for a lump of ice in a glass of water on several occasions, supposing it to be a common article in a country on the edge of the Arctic circle, but for every lump of ice the charge was ten kopeks. Upon this principle, I suppose they attach an exorbitant value to thawed water during six months of the year, when the Neva is a solid block of ice. I find that ice is an uncommonly costly luxury in Northern Europe, where there is a great deal of it. In Germany it is ranked with fresh water and other deadly poisons; in Russia it costs too much for general use; and in Norway and Sweden, where the snow-capped mountains are always in sight, the people seem to be unacquainted with the use of iced water, or, indeed, any other kind of water as a beverage in summer. They drink brandy and schnapps to keep themselves cool. However, I got through the bill at last, without loss of temper, being satisfied it was very reasonable for St. Petersburg. Having paid for every article real and imaginary; paid each servant individually for looking at me; then paid for domestic services generally; paid the proprietor for speaking his native language, which was German, and the commissioner for wearing a brass band on his cap, and bowing several times as I passed out, the whole matter was amicably concluded, and, with my knapsack on my back, I wended my way down to the steam-boat landing of the Wasseli-Ostrow. As I was about to step on board the Russian steamer bound for Revel — an eager crowd of passengers pressing in on the plankway from all sides—I was forcibly seized by the arm. Supposing it to be an arrest for some unconscious violation of the police regulations, a ghastly vision of Siberia flashed upon my mind as I turned to demand an explanation. But it was not a policeman who arrested me — it was only my friend, Herr Batz, the rope-maker, who, with a flushed face and starting eyes, gazed at me. "Where are you going?" said he. "To Revel," said I. Almost breathless from his struggle to get at me, he forcibly pulled me aside from the crowd, drew me close up to him, and in a hoarse whisper uttered these remarkable words: "*Hempf is up!* It took a rise yesterday—*Zweimal zwey macht vier, und sechsmal vier macht vier und zwanzig! verstehen sie?*" "Gott im Himmel!" said I, "you don't say so?" "*Ya, freilich!*" groaned Herr Batz, hoarsely: "*Zwey tausent rubles! verstehen sie? Sechs und dreissig, und acht und vierzig.*" "Ya! ya!" said I, grasping him cordially by the hand, for I was afraid the steamer would leave—"*Adjeu, mein Herr! adjeu!*" and I darted away into the crowd. The last I saw of the unfortunate rope-maker, he was standing on the quay, waving his red cotton handkerchief at me. As the lines were cast loose, and the steamer swung out into the river, he put both hands to his mouth, and shouted out something ·which the confusion of sounds prevented me from hearing distinctly. I was certain, however, that the last word that fell upon my ear was "*hempf!*"

The Neva at this season of the year presents a most animated and picturesque appearance. A little above the landing-place of the Baltic steamers, a magnificent bridge connects the Wasseli-Ostrow with the main part of the city, embracing the Winter Palace, the Admiralty, and the Nevskoi, generally known as the Bolshaia, or Great Side. Below this bridge, as far as the eye can reach in the direction of the Gulf of Finland, the glittering waters of the Neva are alive with various kinds of shipping—merchant vessels from all parts of the world; fishing smacks from Finland and Riga; lumber vessels from Tornea; wood-boats from the interior; Russian and Prussian steamers; row-boats, skiffs, and fancy colored canoes, with crews and passengers representing many nations of the earth, are in perpetual motion; and while the sight is bewildered by the variety of moving objects, the ears are confounded by the strange medley of languages.

Through this confused web of obstacles, the little steamer in which I had taken passage worked her way cautiously and systematically, catching a rope here and there for a sudden swing to the right or to the left, stopping and backing from time to time, and feeling with her nose for the narrow channels of the river, till she was fairly out of danger, when, with a blast of the whistle and a heavy pressure of steam, she dashed forth into the open waters of the gulf.

As we gradually receded, I turned to take a last look at the mighty Venice of the North. The gold-covered domes of the churches, rising high above the massive ranges of palaces, were glittering brilliantly in the sunlight; the variegated shipping of the Neva was growing dim in the distance; the masses of foliage that crowned the islands were of tropical luxuriance, and the whole city, with its palaces, fortifications, and churches, seemed to rest upon the surface of the waters. It was a sight not soon to be forgotten. I turned toward the dark and stern fortresses of Cronstadt, now breaking in strong outline through the golden haze of the morning, and thought of the grim old Czar who had thus battled with Nature, and planted a mighty city in the wilderness; and thus musing, sighed to think that such a man should have lacked the warmth divine which sheds the only true and enduring lustre upon human greatness.

After the usual detention at Cronstadt for the examination of passports, the steamer once more started on her way, and in a few hours nothing was in sight save the shores of the gulf dim on the horizon, and the sails of distant vessels looming up in the haze.

I now, for the first time, had leisure to look at my fellow-passengers.

A Russian steamer during the pleasure season is a floating Babel. Here, within the limits of a few dozen feet, were the representatives of almost every nation from the Arctic circle to the tropics—Finns and Swedes, Norwegians and Danes, Tartars and Russians, Poles and Germans, Frenchmen and Englishmen, South Americans, and —I was going to say North Americans, of which, however, I was the sole representative.

It was a motley assemblage—a hodge-podge of humanity, a kind of living pot-pourri of dirty faces and dirty shirts, military uniforms, slouched hats, blowses, and big boots. There was a Russian general, who always stood at the cabin door to show himself to the rest of the passengers. I don't know for the life of me what he was angry about, but his face wore a perpetual frown of indignation, scorn, and contempt; his black brows were constitutionally knit; his eyes seemed to be always trying to overpower and knock somebody under; his lips were firmly compressed, and his mustaches stood out like a dagger on each side, with the handles wrapped in a bundle of dirty hair under his nose. So tight was his uniform around the body and neck that it forced all the blood up into his face, and wouldn't let it get back again; and it seemed a miracle that the veins in his forehead did not burst and carry away the top of his head, brains and all. Opposite to this great man, in an attitude of profound humility, stood his liveried servant—a very gentlemanly-looking person, with an intellectual baldness covering the entire top of his cranium. This deferential individual wore a coat beautifully variegated before and behind with gold lace; a pair of plush knee-breeches, white stockings, and white kid gloves; and was continually engaged in bowing to the great man, and otherwise anticipating his wants. When the great man looked at a trunk, or a carpet sack, or any thing else in the line of baggage or traveling equipments, the liveried servant bowed very low, looked nervously about him, and then darted off and seized hold of the article in question, gave it a pull or a push, put it down again, looked nervously around him, hurried back and bowed again to his august master, who by that time was generally looking in some other direction with an air of great indifference—as much as to say that he was accustomed to that species of homage, and did not attach any particular value to it. The passengers regarded him with profound awe and admiration, and seemed to be very much afraid he would, upon some trifling provocation, draw his sword and attack them. I was determined, if ever he undertook such a demonstration of authority as that, to resent it with the true spirit of a Californian, and cast about me for some weapon of personal defense, but saw nothing likely to be available in an emergency of that kind except a small bucket of slush, with which, however, it would be practicable to "douse his glim." This great man, with his attendant, was bound for the sea-baths of

Revel, where he would doubtless soon be buffeting the waves like a porpoise—or possibly, in virtue of the commanding powers vested in him by nature and the Czar of Russia, would sit down by the sea-shore like Hardicanute the Dane, and order the waves to retire.

Then there was an old lady and her three daughters who sat on the camp-stools by the step-ladder; the same fat old lady, bedizened with finery, and the same three young ladies, with strong features and dismal dresses, which the traveler encounters all over the Continent of Europe. The old lady was in a state of chronic agony lest the young ladies should be forcibly seized and carried away by some daring youth of the male sex; and the young ladies were conscious that such was the general purpose of mankind, and that they were in imminent danger of being preyed upon in that way, and, consequently, must always hold down their heads and look at the seams in the deck upon the approach of any gallant-looking cavalier with a handsome face and a fine figure, to say nothing of the expressive tenderness of his eyes and the gracefulness of his manner, and many other fascinating features in the young gentleman's appearance, of which they could not be otherwise than entirely unconscious, since they had not taken the slightest notice of him, and never contemplated encouraging his advances. The old lady was a very discreet and proper old lady, and the young ladies were very discreet and proper young ladies, and they were going to the baths of Revel after their last winter's campaign in the fashionable circles of St. Petersburg; and any body could see at a glance that they were of a distinguished and fashionable family, because they had a courier and two lapdogs, and carried a coat of arms on their trunks and bandboxes, and were taken with violent headaches soon after leaving Cronstadt, and used smelling-salts.

Next was the man who belongs to no particular nation, speaks every language, and knows every body — a shabby-genteel, middle-aged man, of no ostensible occupation, but always occupied. "Sare," said he, "I perceive you are an Englishman. I always very glad am to meet with Englishmen. I two years spent in London." "Indeed!" said I; "you speak English very well, considering you learned it in England!" "Yes, sare — in London—I was in business there. "Mercantile?" said I. "No, sare; I attended to mi-lor Granby's 'orses." "Oh! that indeed!" "Yes, sare;" and so the conversation went on in a manner both entertaining and instructive. In the course of it, I gathered that my shabby-genteel friend was going to Revel to attend a 'orse-race.

Another conspicuous group on the deck soon after attracted my attention — the hungry people. This group consisted of some six or eight persons, male and female, of a very Jewish cast of features, well-dressed and lively, evidently Germans, since they spoke in the German language. Scarcely had the steamer cast loose from the quay when they opened the pile of baskets, boxes, and packages by which they were surrounded, and, taking out sundry loaves of bread, lumps of cheese, sausages, and wine-bottles, began to eat and drink with a voracity perfectly amazing. I was certain I had seen them a thousand times before. Every feature was familiar; and even their constitutional appetite was nothing new to me. I had never seen this group, or their prototype, in any public conveyance, or in any part of the world, without a feeling of envy at the extraordinary vigor of their digestive functions. Here were pale, cadaverous-looking men, and sallow women, who never stopped eating from morning till night, in rough or calm weather, in sunshine or storm; ever hungry, ever thirsty, ever cramming and guzzling with a degree of zest that the sturdiest laborer in the field could never experience; and yet they neither burst nor dropped down dead, nor suffered from sea-sickness. Doubtless they had just breakfasted before they came aboard; but, to make sure of it, they immediately breakfasted again. As soon as they

were through that, they lunched; then they dined; after
dinner they drank coffee and ate cakes; after coffee and
cakes they lunched again; then they ate a hearty supper, and after supper whetted their appetites on tea and
cakes; and before bedtime appeased the cravings of
hunger with a heavy meal of sausages, brown bread, and
cheese, which they washed down with several bottles
of wine. I don't know how many times they got up to
eat in the night, but suppose it could not have been
more than twice or three times, since they were at it
again by daylight in the morning as vigorously as ever.
I am inclined to think that some people are physically
so organized as to be insensible to the difference be-
.tween a pound of food and ten pounds, as others are unconscious of the difference between wit and stupidity,
sense and nonsense; such, for instance, as the humorous group, who sit by the companion-way, and keep
themselves and every body around them in a continued
roar of laughter. It is good to be merry; but I must
confess it is not within the bounds of my capacity to
discover a source of merriment in such pranks of wit as
these people enjoy. A young fellow makes a face like
an owl — every body roars laughing, the idea is so exquisitely comical. Another pulls his comrades by the
hair, and every body shouts with uproarious merriment.
One sly chap shoves another off his seat and takes possession of it—a feat so humorous that the whole crowd
is convulsed. A bad orange, pitched across the deck,
strikes an elderly gentleman on the bald pate — well, I
had to laugh at that myself. By-and-by, a stout, florid
young gentleman turns pale and groans; three or four
officious friends, with twinkling eyes, seize him by the
arms, and drag him over to the lee-scuppers, where he
manifests still more decided symptoms of sea-sickness.
IIis friends hold him, rub him, chafe him, and pat him
on the back; one offers him a meerschaum pipe to
smoke; another, a bunch of cigars; a third, a piece of fat
meat; while a fourth tempts him with a bottle of some

wine, all of which is uncommon fun to every body but the unfortunate victim. Thus the time passes away pleasantly enough, after all, taking into view the variety of incidents and scenes which constantly occupy the attention of a looker-on. I had taken a deck-passage for cheapness, and made out to get through the night by bundling myself up on a pile of baggage, and catching a few cat-naps whenever the noise created by these lively young gentlemen would permit of such a feat.

By seven o'clock in the morning we were steering into the harbor of Revel.

CHAPTER XXI.

REVEL AND HELSINGFORS.

FEW cities within the limits of the Russian dominions possess greater historic interest than Revel. Although its commerce is limited to a few annual shipments of hemp, flax, and tallow, produced in the province of Esthonia, and the importation of such articles of domestic consumption as the peasants require, it occupies a prominent position as a naval dépôt for Russian vessels of war, and is much frequented in summer by the citizens of St. Petersburg as a bathing-place and general resort of pleasure. A steamer leaves daily for Revel and Helsingfors, which, during the bathing season, is crowded with passengers, as in the case of my own trip, of which I have already given you a sketch. The approach to the harbor, in the bright morning sun, is exceedingly picturesque. Beyond the forest of masts and spars, with gayly-colored flags and streamers spread to the breeze, rises a group of ancient buildings on the rocky eminence called the Domberg, comprising the castle, the residences of the governor and commandant, and various palaces and quarters of the nobility, surrounded by Gothic walls and strong fortifications. This ancient and picturesque pile has been termed the Acropolis of Revel, though beyond the fact that it overlooks the lower town and forms a prominent feature in the scenic beauties of the place, it is difficult to determine in what respect it can bear a comparison with the famous Acropolis of Athens. However, I have observed that travelers find it convenient to discover resemblances of this kind where none exist, as a means of rounding off their descriptions; and since the Kremlin is styled the Acropolis of Moscow, I see no reason why Revel should not enjoy the same sort of classic association. It is to be hoped that when Russian travelers visit San Francisco, they will, upon the principle adopted by tourists in their country, do us the justice to designate Russian Hill as the Acropolis of San Francisco; and should they visit Sacramento during the existence of a flood, I have no doubt they can find a pile of bricks or a whisky barrel sufficiently elevated above the general level to merit the distinctive appellation of an Acropolis. Revel has suffered more frequent changes of government, and passed through the hands of a greater variety of rulers, than any city, perhaps, in the whole of Northern Europe. In the twelfth and thirteenth centuries it was a province of Denmark; subsequently it fell into the hands of the Swedes, and in 1347 became a possession of the Livonian Knights, a chivalrous and warlike order, who built castles, lived in a style of great luxuriance, killed, robbed, and plundered the people of the surrounding countries, and otherwise distinguished themselves as gentlemen of the first families, not one of them having ever been known to perform a day's useful labor in his life. Such, indeed, was the heroic character of these doughty knights, that, having plunged the whole country into ruin and distress, the peasants, driven to desperation, rose upon them in 1560, and completely routed and destroyed them, killing many, and compelling the remainder to seek some other occupation. This was rough treatment for gentlemen, but it happens from time to time in the course of history, and shows to what trials chivalrous blood is exposed when it can't have its own way. Finally Esthonia and Livonia fell into the hands of Charles II. of Sweden, from whom they were wrested by Peter the Great. Since that period these provinces have continued under the Russian dominion. From the time of Peter to the reign of the present emperor, Revel has been a favorite summer resort of the Czars. It has been rebuilt, patched, fortified, and improved to such an extent that it now represents almost every style of architecture known in Northern Europe since the Middle Ages. The people partake of the same characteristics, being a mixture of every Northern race by which the place has been inhabited since the reign of Eric XIV. of Denmark. I spent some hours visiting the churches and other objects of interest, a detailed description of which would scarcely be practicable within the brief limits of a letter. The Ritterschaftshaus, containing the armorial bearings of the nobility, is a place of great historical interest; but I saw nothing that afforded me so much amusement as the scenes in the Jahrmarket, where the annual summer fair is held. Here were booths and tents, and all sorts of wares, much in the style of the markets of the Riadi in Moscow, of which I have already given a description. The crowds gathered around those places of barter and trade appeared to enjoy a very free-and-easy sort of life. I could see nothing about them indicative of an oppressed condition. Most of them were reeling drunk, and such as were not drunk seemed in a fair way of speedily arriving at that condition of beatitude.

From the Jahrmarket I strolled out to the Cathermthal, a favorite resort of the citizens during the heat of the day. The shady promenades of this magnificent garden, its natural beauties, and the display of equipages and costumes, render it an exceedingly agreeable lounging-place for a stranger. Every thing is in the Russian style—the pavilions, the music, the theatrical exhibitions, and the predominance of naval and military uniforms throughout the grounds. The scarcity of flowers is remedied to some extent by the profusion of epaulettes and brass buttons, which the emperor seems to regard as superior to any thing in nature. No garden that I have yet seen in Russia is destitute of ornaments of this kind.

Gambling was going on every where—at every tea-table and in every pavilion. This department of civilization is well represented in Revel by the Russians. Horse-racing, cards, dominoes, and other amusements and games of hazard, are their ruling passion. A Russian who will not bet his head after he has lost all his valuable possessions must be a very poor representative of his country indeed. I have rarely seen such a passionate devotion to the gaming-table, even in California, which is not usually behind the nations of Europe in all that pertains to the cultivation of the human mind. Revel must be a heaven to a genuine Russian. All is free and unreserved, and morals are said to be unknown, save to a few of the old-fashioned citizens and gentry. Visitors usually leave their own behind them, and depend upon chance for a fresh supply in case of necessity.

The afternoon was warm, and it occurred to me that a stroll on the beach would be pleasant. Accompanied by my friend the horse-jockey, who seemed determined to hold on to me as long as I remained in Revel, under the conviction, no doubt, that I was secretly engaged in the horse business, and would come out in my true character before long, I sauntered down in the direction of some bathing tents, scattered along the beach a little below the port. My jockey friend was continually trying to pump out of me upon which of the horses in the approaching race it was my intention to bet, urging me as a friend not to throw away my money on the roan or chestnut, although appearances were in their favor, but to go in heavy on the black mare; and notwithstanding I assured him it was not my intention to risk any portion of my capital on this race, he was pertinacious in giving me his advice, and could not be convinced that I knew nothing about the horses, and never bet on races of any kind. "Sare," said he, "you are a stranger. These Russians are great rascals. They will cheat you out of your eyes. I speakee English. I am your friend." I thanked him very cordially, but assured him there was no danger of my being cheated. He then went into a dissertation on the relative merits of the horses, to prove that it was impossible for me, a perfect stranger, to escape bankruptcy among so many sharpers. "But," said I, "the horse-race takes place to-morrow, does it not?" "Yes, sare, to-morrow at three o'clock! You will be there? I shall also be there!" "But, my good friend, I leave to-night in the steamer; therefore all your kindness is thrown away!" "Oh! you must not leave to-night. You must see the horse-race!" In vain I assured him it was impossible for me to remain. He was not to be put off on any pretext, and, having made up his mind that I must remain, I was forced to drop the subject and let him have his way. While he was enlarging upon the merits of the black mare, my attention was attracted by a group of bathers—ladies, as I judged by their voices, though, as they were dressed in rather a fantastic style, I could not perceive any other indication of the sex. One of the party—a lively young girl of sixteen or seventeen—seemed to be a perfect mermaid. She plunged and swam, ducked and dived, kicked up her delicate little feet, and disappeared under the surf in a way that struck me with awe and admiration. Never was there such an enchanting picture of perfect abandonment to the enjoyment of the occasion. A poetic feeling took possession of me. Visions of grottoes under the deep sea waves, and beautiful princesses and maidens, filled my soul. I thought of Gulnare in the Arabian Nights, and felt disposed, like Mirza, the King of Persia, to "embrace her with great tenderness." It was really a very pretty sight. "Sare," said my companion, confidentially, "take my advice. She is blind of one eye, and has a strain in the fore leg, but you may bet on her! I jockeyed her for six months before the last race." He was still talking about the black mare. I turned away to hide my impatience. After a few words of desultory conversation, I excused myself on the plea of sickness, and bade him good-evening.

At 8 P.M. I took my departure from Revel. A new batch of passengers had come on board. We were soon steaming our way across the Gulf of Finland. I had rarely spent a more pleasant day, and, if time had permitted, would gladly have prolonged my sojourn in the quaint old city of Revel. The summer nights were still incomparably beautiful. A glow of sunshine was visible in the sky as late as eleven o'clock. At two, the rays of the rising sun began to illuminate the horizon. A dead calm gave to the sleeping waters of the Gulf the appearance of a lake; and as we approached the shores of Helsingfors, the illusion was heightened by innumerable little islands, clothed with verdant slopes of grass and groves of pine. The harbor of Helsingfors derives a peculiar interest from its system of fortifications. Nature seems to have done much to render it impregnable; and what Nature has not done has been accomplished by the military genius of the Russians. Immense masses of rock rise from the water in every direction, leaving deep narrow passages between for vessels. Every rock is a fortress. The steamer passed through a perfect maze of fortifications. Guns bore upon us from all sides—out of the forts, out of holes in the rocks—in short, out of every conceivable nook and crevice in the bay. The very rocks seemed to be alive with sentinels and to bustle with armories. Probably there is no part of the Russian dominions, except Cronstadt, more thoroughly fortified than Sweaborg. The system of engineering displayed upon this point evinces the highest order of military genius. The fortifications embrace a series of forts, castles, barracks, and military establishments of various kinds, situated on seven islands of solid rock, forming the different channels of approach to the harbor. Count Ehrensuerd, Field-marshal of Sweden, is entitled to the credit of having devised the original system of fortifications, afterward so successfully carried out by the Czars of Russia. This was the last rallying-point of the Swedes during the war with Russia. In 1808, Admiral Cronstadt, the commander of the Swedish forces, who had hitherto proved himself a brave and patriotic officer, submitted to terms of capitulation and delivered over the forts to the Russians. History scarcely furnishes a parallel to such a wanton and unaccountable act of treachery. Cronstadt had fifteen hundred men, two frigates, and all the munitions of war to hold his position against any force that could be brought against him; while the Russians were reduced to great extremities, and, it is said, had scarcely force enough left to man the forts after they were evacuated by the Swedes. Sufficient testimony has been gathered by historians to show that Cronstadt bartered his honor for money; yet, strange to say, such is the high estimation in which he was originally held by the Swedes, that many of them to this day profess to disbelieve that he was capable of such an infamous crime. It is thought by some that he must have been laboring under some mental hallucination at the time of the capitulation. Be that as it may, the success of the Russian arms was doubtless greatly facilitated by this act of treason. Cronstadt, like Benedict Arnold, died an isolated and broken-hearted man. His ill-gotten gains were but a poor recompense for the infamy entailed upon his name. Such, indeed, as all history shows, has been and must ever be the fate of all traitors to their country.

Helsingfors was founded by Gustavus Vasa in the sixteenth century. A portion of the old town is still visible, though there is little about it beyond a few ruined walls possessing much historical interest. After the Russians obtained possession they enlarged and improved the city upon its present site, and in 1819 it became the capital of Finland. In 1827 Abo suffered from a general conflagration, after which the grand University of that city was removed to Helsingfors, which now comprises the most important public buildings and institutions in Finland. Among these are the senate-house, the palace of the governor, the Museum, the Botanical Garden, the Observatory, etc. The streets in the lower parts of the city are broad and regular, and many of the houses are quite as good as the generality of private residences in Moscow or St. Petersburg. The principal church, which is built in the form of a Greek cross, is a conspicuous and imposing edifice, standing near the centre of the town on a rocky eminence, presenting on the approach up the harbor a peculiarly Russian effect with its gilded domes and crosses. The green roofs of the houses also remind one that he is still within the dominions of Russia; and if any doubt on that point should remain after landing from the steamer, it is speedily dispelled by the vast numbers of Russian soldiers and officers constantly marching about the streets.

I had two days to devote to the objects of interest in and around Helsingfors. For convenience and economy, I took a room in a Finnish hotel, on one of the back streets. Having deposited my knapsack, my first visit was to the Observatory, from which a beautiful view is to be had of the harbor and fortifications. From this point of observation a very good idea may be formed of the extent and general character of the town. It covers a large area of solid rocks, the entire foundation consisting of immense round boulders, forming a succession of ups and downs singularly varied in outline and picturesque at every point of view. Beyond the main part of the town, toward the interior, the country is mountainous, and covered for the most part with dense forests of pine. Cultivation has made but little progress beyond the immediate suburbs. A few miles from the waters of the bay the eye rests upon an apparently untrodden wilderness of rocky heights and pine forests, and toward the Gulf nothing can exceed the desolate grandeur of the scene. Rock-bound islands, upon which the surf breaks with an unceasing moan; points and promontories covered with dark forests; a rugged coast, dimly looming through the mist; innumerable sea-gulls whirling and screaming over the dizzy pinnacles, are its principal features. While I was seated on a bank of moss near the Observatory, enjoying the beauties of the scene, strains of music were wafted up on the breeze from the shady recesses of the Botanical Gardens, toward which I saw that the citizens were wending their way. It was Sunday, which here as well as in Germany is a day of recreation. I took a by-path and speedily joined the crowd. The people of every degree are well dressed and respectable, and I was somewhat surprised to find so much politeness, cultivation, and intelligence in such an out-of-the-way part of the world. The music was excellent, and the display of style and fashion in the gardens was quite equal to any thing I had seen in my European travels. From what little I saw of the Finns, I was greatly prepossessed in their favor. They seem to me to be a primitive, substantial, and reliable race, strong in their affections, kind and hospitable toward strangers, amiable and inoffensive, yet brave and patriotic—hating the Russians with a cordiality truly refreshing. I formed a casual acquaintance with several of them during my rambles about the Garden. No sooner did they discern my nationality than they gave me to understand that their Constitution had been violated, their liberties trampled under foot, their rights disregarded, and their patience under all these injuries misconstrued. "We only await an opportunity," they said, "to prove to the world that we are still a free-born people. The time is not distant. In the heart of every Finn burns the spirit of a freeman and a patriot! We are not a race doomed to slavery. You who are an American can understand us! We only want a chance to cast off the chains of despotism which now oppress us. It is coming: we are overpowered now, but not conquered! We hate the

Russians! No true Finn can ever amalgamate with such a race!"

This was the strain in which I was constantly addressed. Notwithstanding the electoral privileges guaranteed to the Finns under their Constitution, and the fact that many of the municipal offices are filled by themselves, there is no more community of interest between them and their rulers than between the Italians and the Austrians. Their hatred of the government and of all its concomitants is implacable. It seemed a luxury to some of these poor people to find a sympathizing listener. I met many intelligent Finns, both in Helsingfors and Abo, who spoke good English, and never conversed with one for five minutes without hearing the same strong expressions of dislike to the present condition of affairs, and sanguine hopes for the future. There is only hope for them, that I can see—that the emancipation of the serfs may lead to the establishment of a more liberal system of government throughout the Russian dominions. All hopes based upon isolated revolutions are futile.

CHAPTER XXII.

A BATHING SCENE.

I DEVOTED the afternoon to a stroll on the sea-shore, which presents many interesting features in the neighborhood of Helsingfors. A considerable portion of the town, as already stated, is built upon immense boulders of solid rock, and some of the streets are entirely impracticable for wheeled vehicles, owing to the rugged masses of stone with which Nature has thought proper to pave them. Indeed, it is no easy task for a pedestrian to make his way through the suburbs, over the tremendous slippery boulders that lie scattered over the earth in every direction, the trail being in some instances higher than the houses. I can not conceive how people can travel over such streets in wet weather; it seems a task only fit for goats under favorable circumstances; but the Finns are an ingenious people, and probably ride on the backs of the goats when walking is impracticable. Passing the straggling lines of fishermen's huts forming the outskirts of the town, I rambled over two or three miles of rocky fields till I found myself on the shores of the gulf, at a point sufficiently lonesome and desolate to be a thousand miles from any inhabited portion of the globe. Taking possession of a natural chair, worn in the rocks by the rains of many centuries, I seated myself upon its mossy cushion, and, baring my head to the pleasant sea-breeze, quietly enjoyed the scene. Perhaps this very seat was the throne of an old viking! Here were sea-shells, and glittering pebbles, and tufts of moss for his crown ; and here were sea-gulls to make music for him, and the spray from the wild waves to keep him cool; and a thousand rock-bound islands, lying outspread to the north, with grottoes in them for his ships ; and piles upon piles of rocky palaces all around, covered with golden roofs of moss ; and every thing, in short, that could make glad the heart of a grim old viking residing on the edge of the arctic circle. And if this summer scene, with its blue sea, and wood-capped islands, and warm sun, and balmy breeze, could not make glad his heart, it would not be difficult to imagine what changes winter could bring over it, and how the old viking, sitting on his throne by the sea-shore, could enjoy the dead and icy waste before him ; and how the winter drifts would whistle through his hair ; and how cheery the jagged rocks would look peeping up out of the snow-drifts ; and how balmy would be the night-air at sixty degrees below freezing-point; and how the old viking would shake his beard with laughter as he warmed his hands in a mid-day sun, only ten feet above the horizon, and make the icicles rattle on his chin ; and sit thus laughing and blowing his fingers, and rattling his icy beard, and saying to himself, "What a blessing to be a Finlander! How horribly the natives of Spain and Italy must suffer from bad climate! What a pity it is Finland is not large enough to accommodate the whole human race." With such thoughts as these I amused myself for some time, soothed and charmed by the pleasant sea-breeze and the music of the waves upon the rocks. The air was deliciously pure, and the odor of the sea-weeds had something in it so healthful and inspiring that I was insensibly carried back to by-gone days. How short a time it seemed since I was a wanderer upon the rock-bound shores of Juan Fernandez, yet how many strange scenes I had passed through since then—how much of the world I had seen, with its toils, and troubles, and vicissitudes! Here I was now, after years of travel in every clime, among the various nations of the earth, sitting solitary and alone upon an isolated rock on the shores of Finland! Whither was I going? What was the object? Where was the result? When was it to end? Years were creeping over me; I was no longer in the heyday of youth, yet the vague aspirations of boyhood still clung to me— the insatiable craving to see more and more of the world —the undefined hope that I would yet live to be cast away upon a desolate island, and become a worthy disciple of the immortal Robinson Crusoe! Ah me! What a lonesome feeling it is to be a visionary, enthusiastic boy all one's life, in this practical world of dollars and cents, where other boys are men, and men forget that they ever were young! But this, you say, is all sentimental nonsense. Of course it is. I admit the full folly of such thoughts. It would be a pitiable spectacle indeed to see every body inspired by the vagabond spirit of Robinson Crusoe. No doubt, if you were sitting upon a rock on the Gulf of Finland, my respected Californian friend, you would be hammering off the croppings and trying to discover the indications. You consider that the true philosophy of life—to dig, and delve, and burrow in the ground, and get gold and silver out of it, and suffer rheumatism in your bones and cramps in your stomach, and wear out your life in a practical way, while we visionaries are dreaming sentimental nonsense! But, after all, does the one pay any better than the other in the long run? Will gold or silver make you see farther into a millstone, or give you a better appetite, or put youth and health into your veins, or cause you to sleep more soundly of nights, or prolong your life to an indefinite period beyond the span allotted to the average of mankind? Will you never be convinced of the truth of these inspired words, which can not be repeated too often: As you brought nothing into the world, so you can take nothing out of it?

Come, then, let us be young again, and dash into the blue waters of Finland, and buffet the sparkling brine as it seethes and boils over the rocks! Away with your gold and your silver, and your toils and cares, and let us play Robinson Crusoe and Friday here in this solitary little glen, where "our right there is none to dispute"— unless it may be the Czar of Russia. Off with your shirt, your boots, your drawers, your all, and be for once a genuine savage—be my man Friday, and I'll teach you how to enjoy life. Ye gods! doesn't it feel fine—that plunge in the foaming brine! Why, you look like a boiled lobster already; the glow of health is all over you; your eyes sparkle, your skin glistens; you shoot out the salt sea-spray from your nostrils in a manner that would surprise any porpoise; you whoop and you yell like a young devil let loose! Never in the world would I take you to be a hard, money-making, lucre-loving man! Why, my dear Friday, you are a perfect jewel of a savage! I didn't know it was you, and doubt if you knew it yourself! Isn't it glorious? I feel a thousand years younger! Don't you hear me singing,

> "Oh, poor Robinson Crusoe!
> Tinky ting tang, tinky ting tang,
> Oh, poor Robinson Crusoe!"

But the water is rather fresh—considering how much salt there is in it. We had better take a race over the rocks. Run, Friday, for your life. If I catch you, overboard you go into the sea again. Run, you savage, run! Voices? you say, human voices?

Great heavens! Where are you, Friday? Gone! disappeared behind that projecting ledge of rocks. And here am I, all alone, up to my arm-pits in the water, with a group of Finnish ladies standing there, not a hundred yards off, looking at me!—ay, gazing steadfastly at me, and, what is worse, splitting their sides laughing at my confusion! What in the world is to be done? The water seems to be growing colder and colder. I am chilled through. My jaws begin to chatter. Suppose a shark should seize me by the leg—or a sudden and violent cramp should take possession of me? My gracious! what are those women doing now? Actually seating themselves on the rocks, within ten steps of my clothes, and spreading several packages of bread, cheese, and cakes around them! They are going to enjoy a picnic while I enjoy my bath! I hear their merry voices; I can imagine the general drift of their jokes. How innocently they eat, and drink, and laugh. Possibly they take me for a seal or a walrus! Certainly nothing is visible but my head, on the crown of which, I regret to say, is a bald spot about the size of your hand. It may be very funny to see it dodging up and down among the breakers—but I can't stand it much longer. Already the spray has wellnigh strangled me; I shiver all over; a horrible presentiment is uppermost in my mind that polypi, and sea-leeches, and shiny jelly-fish are fastening their suckers upon my legs; I jump, and kick, and plunge in an agony of apprehension, while those fair creatures on the rock imagine, no doubt, that I am disporting myself in sheer exuberance of joy. If they only knew that I had been full half an hour in the water before they appeared, there might be some hope of a release; but that does not seem to have entered their heads.

Never in all my experience, reader, was I in such a predicament. This is no fancy sketch. It is true, every word of it. Had the picnickers been old ladies, I might have shut my eyes, and made a break out of the water for my clothes; but three of them, at least, were young, and, worse than that, very pretty! The courage for so daring and monstrous an act was not in me. I felt that it would be easier to die; and yet to die in this way is pretty hard when it comes to a practical test. What the deuce was to be done? I could not speak a word of Finnish, otherwise I might have implored them to retire a few hundred yards and let me get my clothes. With a shirt, or even a pocket-handkerchief, I might have charged upon the enemy; but I had nothing—not even a hat—as a shield against the battery of sparkling eyes that bore down upon me! A thousand expedients flashed through my mind in the extremity of my sufferings. I would slip out of the water on all-fours, and creep over the rocks like a seal, but that would be an extremely ungraceful way of approaching a bevy of strange ladies. Then it occurred to me if I could get hold of a bunch of sea-weeds, it might serve as a temporary substitute for a costume; but the weeds had all drifted away by this time, and not a patch was in sight. Even a large oyster-shell might have afforded some assistance; but who ever heard of oyster-shells in the Gulf of Finland? Nothing remained save to dive down and seize a big rock, detach it from the bottom, and, holding it up before me, make a break for the pile of clothes; yet when I came to consider the preposterous spectacle that a middle-aged man would present in a state of nudity charging full tilt upon a party of ladies, with a big rock in his hands and a gleam of desperation in his eye, the idea seemed too monstrous to be entertained, and I was forced to give it up. The difficulty was becoming really serious. Doubtless it appears very funny to my California friends, but I can assure them it was pretty near death to me. I would have given ten dollars for the poorest cotton shirt that was ever dealt out by an Indian agent to a Reservation Digger; nay, transparent as the blankets are, I might have made one serve my purpose by doubling it three or four times and holding it up in front.

All this, however, though very well in its way, did not relieve me from my embarrassing predicament. Something must be done, and that very speedily. I was rapidly wilting under the chilling influence of the water. Ten minutes more would render me a fit subject for a coroner's inquest. I saw but one alternative: to work my course a few hundred yards up the shore, and then creep out the best way I could, and run for my life till I found some friendly nook among the rocks in which I could conceal myself till these fair Finns took a notion to depart.

Acting upon this idea, I ducked down as low as possible, and crept over the jagged and slippery rocks, in mortal dread all the time that some receding wave would leave me a dripping spectacle for these fair damsels to laugh at; till, bruised and scarified beyond farther endurance, I worked my way to a landing-place, where I paused in a recumbent position — that is to say, on all-fours—to take an observation. They must have perceived something ludicrous in my attitude. A wild scream of laughter saluted my ears. I could stand no more. What little warmth was left in my blood forced itself into my head and face as I sprang to my feet. With a groan of shame and mortification, I took to my heels; and never before, so help me Jupiter! did I run so fast in my life. Scream after scream of laughter followed me! It is impossible for me to conjecture how I looked, but I felt dreadfully destitute of sail as I scudded over the rough pathway that wound around the shore. Blushing, panting, and utterly overwhelmed with conflicting emotions of modesty and despair, I darted behind the friendly shelter of a rock, and inwardly resolved that if ever I went bathing in Finland again, I would at least perform my ablutions in a more appropriate costume than Nature had bestowed upon me.

The next question was, how long were these people

going to enjoy themselves at my expense? Was I to be blockaded from my clothes all the rest of the afternoon? I could not, upon any principle of international law, undertake to break the blockade on the ground that it was not effectual, and yet it was pretty hard to do without my cotton. What I had suffered from the cold while in the water was nothing to what I now began to experience from the unobstructed rays of the sun. My skin was rapidly assuming every variety of color supposed to exist in the rainbow, and a painful consciousness possessed me that in half an hour more I would be blistered from head to foot. There was no shade on my side of the rock, and nothing any where in sight that could afford the least protection. Racked with renewed anguish, I peeped out to see if there was any earthly prospect of reaching my clothes. Horror upon horror! what were they doing now? Did my eyes deceive me? As sure as fate, they were all quietly undressing themselves! Hats, scarfs, parasols, and dresses were scattered all around them; there they sat, on the moss-covered rocks, their alabaster necks and limbs glistening in the sun, looking for all the world like a bevy of mermaids, laughing and chattering in the highest glee, perfectly indifferent to my presence! I saw no more. A dizziness came over me. Consternation seized my inmost soul. Drawing back behind the rock, I held my face close up to it and shut both my eyes. Don't talk to me about courage! Every man is a coward by nature. Of what avail was it that I had killed whales and chased grizzly bears? Here I was now, hiding my face, shutting my eyes, trembling in the hot sun like a man with an ague, both knees knocking together, and my heart ready to pop out of my mouth from abject fear! Strange— wasn't it?—especially after having made the grand tour of Europe, in many parts of which live men and women are ranked with statuary. What harm is there, after all, in discarding those artificial trappings which disfigure the human form divine? Many a man who looks like an Apollo Belvidere in his natural condition, becomes a very commonplace fellow the moment he steps into his conventional disguise. He is no longer heroic; he may be a very vulgar-looking mortal, not at all calculated to produce classical impressions on any body. His form divine has fallen into the hands of a tailor, who may be neither an artist or a poet. And since we can admire an Apollo Belvidere, why not a Venus de Medici, or, still more, the living, breathing impersonation of beauty buffeting the waves with

"Shapely limb and lubricated joint."

But, hang it all! though not an ill-shaped man, I don't flatter myself there was any thing in my personal appearance, as I crouched behind the rock, shutting both eyes as hard as I could, to remind the most enthusiastic artist of the Apollo Belvidere! Nay, the gifted Hawthorne himself could scarcely have made a Marble Faun out of so unpromising a subject. And as for the fair bathers, who by this time were plunging about in the water like naiads, it would of course be impossible for me to say how far they were improved by lack of costume, since I looked in another direction, and kept my eyes faithfully closed from the very beginning. The question now occurred to me, Would I not be justified by the law of nations in breaking the blockade? It was now or never. If they once commenced dressing, farewell to hope! Well, I did it. Heaven only knows how I got through the terrible ordeal. I only remember that desperation gave strength and speed to my limbs, and I ran with incredible velocity. A moment of terrible confusion ensued as I grasped at my scattered habiliments. There came a scream of laughter from the wicked naiads who were sporting in the waves. I fled over the hills—my bundle in my arms—and never once stopped till I reached a small valley about half a mile distant. Breathless, mortified, and bewildered at the oddity of the adventure, I hurriedly dressed, and walked back to town. Arrived at my hotel, I called for a bottle of schnapps, retired to

my room, locked the door, and fervently ejaculated,
"'All's well that ends well!' Here's to the ladies of
Helsingfors! But if ever you catch me in such a scrape
again, my name's not Browne!"

CHAPTER XXIII.

ABO—FINLAND.

I was strongly inclined to spend several weeks in Helsingfors. The bathing is delightful, and the manners and
customs of the people are primitive and interesting. My
adventure on the sea-shore, as I soon discovered, was
nothing uncommon. I mentioned the matter to my landlady—a Finnish woman of very sociable manners, who
spoke a little English. I asked her if it was customary
for the ladies to dispense with bathing-dresses. She said
they generally wore something when they bathed in public, but beyond the limits of the regular bath-houses, at
the end of the Botanical Gardens, they seldom troubled
themselves about matters of that kind ; in fact, they preferred going in without any obstruction, because "they
could swim so much better."

Having procured my passport at the Bureau of the
Police, I took passage in a Swedish steamer bound for
Abo and Stockholm. Next morning by daylight the
steamer arrived from St. Petersburg. I went on board,
and in a few hours more the fortifications of Sweaborg
were dim in the distance.

The accommodations on board the Swedish steamers
are excellent. I took passage in the second cabin, for the
sake of economy, and found every thing as clean and
comfortable as I could desire. The waiters are polite
and attentive, the fare is good, and the company quiet
and respectable. The difference in this respect is very
striking between first and second class passengers on
board of American and Swedish steamers. In the latter
there is no rowdyism—no incivility from officers or serv-

ants; and, so far as the passengers are concerned, I could not perceive that they were debarred from any of the privileges enjoyed by passengers of the first class. They had the entire range of the vessel, and were treated with the same respect and consideration shown to others who possessed the means of indulgence in a little more style. I have been particularly pleased with this trait in the management of public conveyances throughout Europe. In Sweden and Norway it is especially characteristic. The commonest deck-passenger on board a Swedish or Norwegian steamer is treated with courtesy. Indeed, I have seen instances of care and tenderness toward the poorer classes, whose circumstances compelled them to travel in this way, that I regret to say would excite astonishment in our own democratic country. I can scarcely understand why it is that the captain and officers of a steam-ship on our side of the water consider it their duty to harass passengers who do not pay the highest price with all sorts of vexatious restrictions, and to render their condition as uncomfortable as possible. To be overbearing, insolent, and ungentlemanly seems to be the only aim of these important functionaries, and, so far as my experience goes, they succeed so well in this respect that if they do not actually prove themselves brutes and blackguards during the passage, they are usually rewarded for their forbearance, on reaching the port of destination, by a card of thanks. I have seen no such insolence on the part of officers and slavishness on that of passengers on board of any Swedish or Norwegian steamer, as I have often seen on the Panama and California coast steamers. Yet cards of thanks are not common in Europe. In fact, they would be regarded as a reflection upon the officers rather than an evidence of complimentary appreciation.

The coast of Finland from Helsingfors to Abo abounds in small rocky islands, covered, for the most part, with a stunted growth of pine. The outline of the main land is extremely rugged and irregular, presenting a succession of promontories, bays, and inlets, weather-beaten cliffs of granite, and gloomy pine forests. No sign of habitation is to be seen during the entire voyage, with the exception of an occasional group of fishermen's huts or a custom-house station. The whole country has the appearance of an unbroken wilderness. The steamer plows her way, hour after hour, through the narrow and winding passages that lie between the islands—sometimes so close to the overhanging cliffs and rugged boulders of granite as almost to touch—and often apparently land-locked amid the maze of islands and promontories. While there is nothing grand or imposing in the scenery, the coast of Finland is certainly one of the most interesting portions of the world, in a geological point of view. The singular formation of the rocks, their rich and varied colors, and the strange manner in which Nature has grouped them together, afford an endless variety of interesting studies. The utter isolation of the inhabitants from the busy world, their rude and primitive mode of life, their simplicity, hardihood, and daring ; the rigors of climate to which they are subject, and their strong attachment to their sea-girt homes and perilous pursuits, render the trip interesting to the general tourist, who, though not skilled in geology, may be supposed to possess, like myself, a fancy for gathering up odds and ends touching the condition of his fellow-beings.

The people of this coast region are a hardy race, whose wild habits of life and isolation from the great outer world develop in them many striking and peculiar traits of character. During the long winters, when the bays, inlets, and harbors are blocked with ice, they become wood-choppers or lumbermen, and spend their time chiefly in the forests. Upon the breaking up of winter they prepare their nets and fishing-gear, and, as soon as the season permits, set forth in their little smacks, and devote the principal part of the summer to catching and curing fish, for which they find a ready sale at the stations along the shore, frequented by traders from St.

Petersburg. They live in small cabins, built of pine logs, rarely consisting of more than two rooms. Each family owns a small patch of ground, with an unlimited range of forest. A few cows or goats, a vegetable garden, and some chickens or ducks, constitute all they require for domestic use, and these are usually attended by the women and children during the absence of the men on their fishing expeditions. Education is at a low ebb among them, though the rudimental branches are not altogether neglected. They are a simple, hospitable, and kind-hearted people, ignorant and superstitious, yet by no means deficient in natural capacity. No better sailors than the Finns are to be found in any part of the world, and there is scarcely a sea throughout the arctic regions which has not been visited by their vessels. Although the climate is rigorous during a considerable portion of the year, the Finns prefer it to any other in the world, and conscientiously believe the garden of Paradise must have been originally located in Finland. The lower classes are contented and happy, caring little for affairs of government, unless they happen to be subjected to some peculiar or oppressive restraints. As the traveler approaches the Gulf of Bothnia, they assimilate very closely to the same classes in Sweden, and but little difference is perceptible either in their language or costume. The educated classes, such as the professional men, merchants, bankers, traders, etc., are as polished as most people throughout the North of Europe, and many of them are distinguished for their cultivated manners and general intelligence. Such of these as I conversed with on board the steamer impressed me very favorably. I found them liberal in their sentiments, and devoted admirers of our American institutions. Yet, strange to say, the only secessionist I met in the course of my wanderings in this region was a Finn. Hearing me speak English, he immediately opened a conversation on the subject of the revolutionary movement in the United States. He did not know what we were fighting for ; thought the North was acting very badly; regarded the people of the South as an oppressed and persecuted race; believed in slavery; considered the Lincoln government a perfect despotism, etc. In short, his views were a general epitome of the speeches, proclamations, and messages of the leading rebels throughout the South. I listened to him with great patience. He had an interesting family on board, all of whom spoke English; and what struck me as peculiar, a species of negro English common in the Southern States. "Sir," said I, at length, "you surprise me! I had not expected to meet so strong an advocate of slavery and slave institutions in this latitude. Can it be possible that you are a Finn?" "Yes, sir," he answered, "a genuine Finn—now on a visit to my native country after an absence of twenty-five years." "Then you must have lived in the South?" "Yes, sir; in Montgomery, Alabama. I have property there. It was getting pretty bad there for a family, and I thought I had better pay a visit to Finland while the war was going on." This accounted for the peculiar sentiments of my fellow-traveler! He seemed to be a very nice old gentleman, and I was sorry to find him tinctured with the heresies of rebellion. Farther conversation with him satisfied me that if he could get his property out of Montgomery, and put it in Massachusetts, he would be a very respectable Union man. I don't think his heart was in the movement, though his pocket, doubtless, felt a considerable interest in it.

The town of Abo, formerly the capital of Finland—now a place of no great importance except as a customhouse and military station — is beautifully situated on the banks of a river called the Aurajoki, about three miles above its mouth. Vessels of medium draught, including the coasting steamers, have no difficulty in ascending as far as the bridge, where they lie alongside the wharves and receive or discharge freight. Those of larger draught usually anchor off the village of Boxholm, a picturesque gathering of red cottages, with

high peaked roofs, situated at the entrance of the river.
Above the village, on the summit of a rocky cliff, stands
the fort of Abohus, ready at a moment's notice to pour
a broadside into any enemy of Imperial Russia that may
undertake to pass up the river.

Abo, since the removal of the capital and University
to Helsingfors and the great conflagration of 1827, which
destroyed two thirds of the town, has fallen into decay,
and now does not contain a population of more than ten
or twelve thousand souls. Spread over an area of several miles square, with a sufficient number of houses to
accommodate twice or three times the population, its
broad, stone-paved thoroughfares and numerous unten-
anted buildings have a peculiarly desolate appearance.
Back a little from the river the pedestrian may walk
half a mile at midday without meeting a single soul in
the streets. A dead silence reigns over these deserted
quarters, as if the prevailing lethargy had fallen upon
the few inhabitants that remain. Grass grows on the
sidewalks, and the basement walls of the houses are covered with moss. A dank, chilly mildew seems to hang
in the air. One might become green all over, like a neglected tomb-stone, should he forget himself and stand
too long in one spot. I spent a considerable portion of
the day rambling through these melancholy by-ways, and
must admit that the effect upon my spirits was not cheering. Now and then the apparition of some cadaverous
old woman, wrinkled with age—a greenish hue upon her
features—would appear unexpectedly at some unexpected opening in one of the ruinous old houses, and startle
me by a gaze of wonder or some unintelligible speech
addressed to herself. Probably a human being had not
been seen in that vicinity for the last month. Sometimes a slatternly servant-girl would appear in the distance, her dress bedraggled with slops, a tub of water
on the pavement close by, and a long-handled mop in her
hand, with which she seemed to be vigorously engaged
in scrubbing the green slime and tufts of moss off the

window-sills; but catching a sight of the strangers, down would go the mop, and then the usual hasty attempt would be made at fixing her hair and otherwise increasing her personal charms. As I drew near, this useful member of society would naturally take a sidelong glance at the strange gentleman, and, perceiving that he was uncommonly attractive in personal appearance, it was quite natural she should make a neat little courtesy and say "*Got Aften!*" to which, of course, I always responded in the most affable manner, not forgetting to say to myself, in an audible tone, "Sken Jumfru!"—a pretty girl. No harm in that, is there?

In the afternoon I walked out to a public garden about two miles from town, where there are some very pleasant promenades, a large building containing a ballroom, and numerous pavilions for refreshments. It was a festive occasion, and the élite and fashion of Abo were assembled there in their best attire. The music was inspiring. Dancing seemed contagious. The ballroom was crowded, and old and young were whirling about on the light fantastic toe with a zest and spirit truly inspiring. Old gentlemen with bald heads seemed to have forgotten their age and infirmities, and whirled the blooming damsels around in the dizzy mazes of the waltz as dexterously as the youngest; and young gentlemen hopped about quite frantic with joy, and altogether bewildered with the beauty of their partners. It was really a pretty sight. Rarely had I seen so many pleasant faces of both sexes, especially those of the ladies. Good-humor, simplicity, and frankness were their predominant traits. All ceremony seemed to be cast aside, and every body participated in the dance as if it were one great family frolic. The formality of introduction was dispensed with, or probably most of the guests were already acquainted. The fiddlers scraped louder and louder; wilder and faster blew the horns, and on went the dance with increasing vigor. I was getting excited—the spirit of the thing was contagious. Though not much of a

dancer, yet I had occasionally in my life filled a place in
a reel or a cotillon. Waltzing, to be sure, was a little
beyond my experience, but I had a general idea of the
figure, and could not perceive that there was any thing
very difficult about it. Most of the waltzers here whirled around with great ease, and I could see no reason
why it would not be entirely practicable for an active
man like myself, who thought nothing of climbing high
mountains or jumping across small rivers, to do the
same. Besides, these people were strangers; it would
be a good opportunity to try my skill. Doubtless, any
of the young ladies would oblige me if I asked them to
dance. They seemed to oblige every body that asked
them, and showed no signs of fatigue. Indeed, they
looked fresher and more vigorous after every bout. I
was particularly charmed with the appearance of one
young lady. Her complexion was florid, and her figure
absolutely magnificent. At a rough guess she must
have weighed a hundred and eighty pounds. Every
time she whirled past me I could feel the floor give way.
Her partner was rather small, and revolved around her
like a planet round the sun. When she laughed, which
was nearly all the time, her beautiful mouth opened at
least two thirds of the way across her face, revealing a
set of teeth to which flakes of snow, pearls, or any thing
of that kind could bear no comparison. The extraordinary vigor of this girl, her tremendous powers of endurance, her weight, beauty, and good-humor, rendered
her a general favorite. She was, in fact, the belle of the
room. To dance with her would be an honorable distinction. Now I am naturally a modest man, but of late
years that defect has been gradually disappearing from
my character. I resolved to dance with this girl—if she
would consent. As soon as there was a pause, therefore, I made bold to go up to her, and, with a very polite bow, solicited her hand—in English. She didn't understand English, but she understood dancing, and answered me very politely in Swedish, "Ja!" I think my

dress and manner, together with my ignorance of the Swedish language, had rather a favorable effect. She certainly looked complimented and gratified. I saw her turn round her head as we stood up, and laugh at the other girls, which I interpreted to mean that she, of all in the room, had succeeded in catching the distinguished stranger. Well, the music started — it was a German waltz. I stood holding on to my partner as the ivy clings to the solid oak. Never did I feel so firm a girl. Had she been formed of lead she could not have felt more substantial. Now, thought I, away we'll spin over the floor, a living duet, altogether accidental, but beautiful to behold—

> "Like the sweet tunes that wandering meet,
> And so harmoniously they run,
> The hearer dreams they are but one."

There was only one consideration that gave me any particular anxiety. Being of a light and slender figure, I had some apprehensions that in the giddy whirl of the waltz this powerful young lady might accidentally throw me out of balance and create an unpleasant scene. However, there was no time for reflection. At a given signal, away she started with tremendous energy. I did my best to whirl her round, and don't think it would be possible for any body to do any better under the circumstances; but she didn't keep time—or I didn't. Round and round the room we flew, to the inspiring strains of the music, with an undulating motion very difficult to conceive, and still more difficult to execute without danger to the other dancers. The warm blood rushed to my face; my head grew dizzy: the only thing I saw was that this style of waltzing must end in destruction to myself or somebody else. I was fairly lifted off my feet at every turn, and found myself absolutely hanging on to my partner to keep from falling. She never relaxed in her vigorous movements one moment; but as the music increased in spirit, so did she. The room was filled with waltzers. It was impossible to be flying about in this way without hitting somebody. I knew it from the very beginning, but what could I do? The first man down was an old gentleman. I begged his pardon, and helped him up again. Next I was dashed against a young lady. She and her partner both went down. I helped them up, and begged pardon again, which was granted with great good-humor. After that, most of the waltzers began to get out of the way, so that we presently had a more enlarged scope of operations. I fancy there was something uncommon in my style of waltzing that attracted attention. It was not long before we had the entire circle to ourselves, the crowd standing around and manifesting the most intense appreciation of our efforts. All went on very well for a while, Up and down the room, and round and round we whirled, and at every whirl there was a murmur of admiration and applause. My beautiful partner shook her sides as if convulsed with an earthquake—I could feel the motion, but was unable to conjecture the cause. Possibly she was getting agitated—or it might be that sentiments of tenderness were stealing over her heart. That idea, or something else, confused me. I struck out one foot a little awkwardly. She tripped against it, whirled me half round in attempting to gain her balance, and then we fell. It was very awkward. What rendered it still more unpleasant, every body began to laugh. People always do laugh at the misfortunes of others. I would have picked the young lady up at once, or at least tried it (for she was rather heavy), but the fact is, I fell underneath, and was utterly unable to move. Had I been pinned and riveted to the floor, I could not have been in a more helpless position. A man whose natural instincts are polite is surely a subject of sympathy and commiseration under such a pressure of difficulties as this. I breathed hard, but was unable to get out a single word of apology, till, with a laugh and a bound, my fair partner regained her feet, and then she very good-naturedly assisted me in regaining mine. Mortified beyond measure, I conducted her to a seat. As I was passing out of the room soon after, a new waltz struck up. The dancers went at it again as lively as ever. I turned to see what had become of my partner. She was whirling over the floor with undiminished energy in the arms of a young gentleman in military uniform. He may have been more accustomed to waltzing than I was, but I think any person present—not excepting the young lady herself—would have been willing to admit that his style did not compare with mine in force and individuality. It certainly produced no such effect upon the audience.

I walked back to town a sober and thoughtful man. This dancing business is a very foolish pastime. It may do very well for giddy and thoughtless young persons, but for men of mature years it is the height of folly. I am surprised that they should be led aside from their customary propriety by the fascinations of beauty.

The sun was just setting. Its last rays rested upon the ruined walls of the Observatory. I followed a crowd of citizens who were slowly toiling up the stone steps, and, after a pretty hard climb, was rewarded with a magnificent view of the city and surrounding country. The rocky pinnacle upon which the Observatory stands rises some three hundred feet above the banks of the river, and overlooks a large portion of the valley of the Aurajiki. The winding waters of the river; the green fields; patches of woodland, villas, and gardens; the blue mountains in the distance, and the silent city lying like a mouldering corpse beneath, presented a scene singularly picturesque and impressive. I sat down upon the ruined walls and thought of Abo in its glory—the ancient head-quarters of Christianity in Finland; the last abiding-place of the beautiful Caroline Morsson, the peasant queen of Sweden, wife of Eric XII., who died here, and whose remains lie in the Cathedral—the city of the mighty hosts of warlike Finns who fought under the banner of Charles XII., and made a funeral pyre of their

bodies upon the bloody field of Puttara. The present
Finns are of this heroic race. Not less brave, yet less
fortunate than the Spartans of Thermopylæ, they have
lost their country and their freedom, and now groan under the oppression of a despotic government.

While thus musing on the past, a strain of delicious
music broke the stillness. I rambled over the granite
cliffs in the direction of the sound, and soon came to a
grove of trees, with an open space in the middle, occupied by a band of musicians, who were surrounded by a
group of citizens, thus pleasantly passing the summer
evening. Booths and tents were scattered about in every
direction, in which cakes and refreshments were to be
had; and gay parties of young people were seated on
long planks so arranged as to make a kind of spring seats,
upon which they bounced up and down to the time of
the music. Children were playing upon the grass, their
merry shouts of laughter mingling pleasantly with the
national air performed by the band. On the moss-covered rocks sat groups of young ladies, guarded by their
amiable mothers or discreet duennas, as the case might
be, trying hard not to see any of the young gentlemen
who lounged about in the same vicinity; and young gentlemen prowled about puffing cigars as if they didn't
care a straw whether the young ladies looked at them or
not—both being, of course, according to the established
usages of society, natural enemies of each other. For the
life of me, I can't tell why it is that young ladies and gentlemen should be thus everlastingly at war. Would it
not be better to kiss and make it up, and try, if possible,
to get along peaceably through the world?

But the steamer blows her whistle—the bell rings—I
must hurry on board. Good-by, dear Finns, big and little, I like you all. God bless you! Good-by old Abo,
with your ancient church, and your moss-grown streets,
and deserts of houses—I feel sorry for you, but I can't
help it! Good-by, Russia! If I don't call again, attribute it to no want of interest in the great cause of civili-

zation. Just drop me a line and let me know when the serfs are free and a constitutional government is established, and I will strain a point to pay my respects to Alexander II. I rather like the young man, and have an idea that he is capable of noble deeds and heroic sacrifices. But he must abolish his secret police, punish them for whipping women, open universities upon a liberal basis, throw the camarilla and the aristocracy overboard, quit murdering the poor Poles at Warsaw, and do several other things before he can have my support. Should he accomplish these beneficial reforms, and at any future time think proper to settle in my neighborhood, where the climate is more genial, I shall cheerfully vote for him as mayor of the city of Oakland.

CHAPTER XXIV.

STOCKHOLM.

The passage from Abo to Stockholm occupies about eighteen hours, and in fine weather affords a constant succession of agreeable scenes. With the exception of about four hours of open sea in crossing the Gulf of Bothnia, the steamer is constantly surrounded by islands, many of them highly picturesque, and all interesting from their peculiar geological formation. Occasionally the island winds like a snake through a wilderness of naked granite boulders, round and slippery, and barely high enough out of the water to afford a foundation for a few fishermen's huts, which from time to time break the monotony of their solitude. Sometimes the channel opens out into broad lakes, apparently hemmed in on all sides by pine-covered cliffs; then passing between a series of frightful crags, upthrown, as it were, out of the water by some convulsion of nature, the surging waves lash their way through the narrow passages, and threaten each moment to ingulf the frail vessel, or dash it to atoms against the rocks. The greatest danger in making this trip arises from the number of sunken rocks, which often approach to within a few feet of the surface without being visible. The depth is usually marked by poles or buoys, and it often happens that the steamer plies her way for hours between these water-marks, where there is no other indication of danger. The Swedish and Finnish pilots are proverbially among the best in the world. We had an old Finn on board — a shaggy old sea-dog, rough and weatherbeaten as any of the rocks on his own rock-bound coast, who, I venture to say, never slept a wink during the entire passage, or if he did, it was all the same. He knew every rock, big and little, visible and invisible, that lay on the entire route between Abo and Stockholm, and could see them all with his eyes shut. An uncouth, hardy, honest old monster was this Finn — a Caliban of a fellow, half human, half fish — with a great sou'wester on his head, a rough monkey-jacket buttoned around his body, and a pair of boots on his legs that must have been designed for wading over coral reefs, through seas of swordfish, shovel-nosed sharks, and unicorns. His broad, honest face looked for all the world like a granite boulder covered with barnacles and sea-weed, and ornamented by a bunch of mussels for a nose, and a pair of shining blue pebbles by way of eyes; and when he spoke, which was not often, his voice sounded like the keel of a fishing-smack grating over a bank of gravel. I strongly suspect his father was a sea-lion and his mother a grampus or scragg whale, and that he was fished up out of the sea when young by some hardy son of Neptune, and subsequently trained up in the ways of humanity on board a fishing-smack, where the food consisted of polypi, lobsters, and black bread. Yet there was something wonderfully genial about this old pilot. He chewed enormous quantities of tobacco, the stains of which around his mouth greatly improved the beauty of his countenance; and when he was not chewing pigtail he was smoking it, which equally contributed to soften the asperities of his features. Having sailed in many seas, he spoke many languages, but none very intelligibly, owing to some radical defect in the muscles of his mouth. As to the channel between Abo and Stockholm, which lies partly through the Aland Islands and numerous adjacent rocks, above and below water, I believe he had traveled over it so often that he could steer a vessel through it standing backward as readily as box the compass, or shut both his eyes and tell where the deepest water lay by the smell of the air and the taste of his tobacco.

The passage across the Gulf of Bothnia was somewhat rough, and most of the passengers were sea-sick, owing, no doubt, to the short chopping motion which prevails on board of all kinds of sea-going vessels in these inland seas. Having performed various voyages in various parts of the world, I was, of course, exempt from this annoyance; but my digestion had been impaired in Russia by the vast quantity of tea, cucumbers, veal, cabbage-soup, and other horrible mixtures which I had been forced to consume while there, and which now began to tell on my constitution. Notwithstanding repeated doses of cognac, taken from time to time as I walked the decks, the sea began to whirl all round, the clouds overhead to swing about at random through the rigging, and the odor of the machinery to produce the strongest and most disagreeable sensations. I went below to see how things looked there; but, finding the atmosphere dense and the prospect gloomy, returned in great haste and looked over the bulwarks to see how fast we were going through the water. While thus engaged, an amusing thought occurred to me. Suppose the mermaids who lie down in the briny depths form their ideas of the beauty of the human countenance from the casual glimpses thus afforded of our features, would it be possible for the most susceptible of them to fall in love with us? The idea was so droll that I was almost convulsed with laughter; but, not wishing to attract attention by laughing aloud at my own thoughts, I merely clung to the bulwarks and doubled myself up, trying to avoid the appearance of eccentricity. At or about the same moment, the old Finnish pilot, with whom I had formed an acquaintance, came along, and said good-naturedly, "Hello, sir! I dink you pe sea-sick." "Sea-sick?" said I, a little nettled. "Oh no, Herr Pilot, I'm an old sailor, and never get sea-sick." "Vel, I dought you was sick—you look bad, sir," answered the good old pilot; "de sea is very rough, sir." Here the steamer took a notion to pitch down into the water and jump up again suddenly, and then rolled on one side and then on the other, and at the same time a number of the passengers began to make grotesque and disagreeable noises, which amused me so much that I had to turn away my face and look at the water again to avoid laughing. "Sir," said the old pilot, who observed the contortions of mirth by which I was moved, "vil you have some schnapps? I dink schnapps is goot for de sea-sick." "Thank you," said I, the tears streaming from my eyes, "I won't have any just now." "Vel, 'twon't last long, any how," suggested the good-natured monster. "By'm-by we be up to Vaxholm—in pout two hours. Dere's land! Don't you see it?" I saw it, and right glad I was too, for it is always refreshing to see land from the deck of a steamer. In half an hour more we entered a smooth stretch of water, and soon the wood-covered islands and shores of Sweden were close ahead.

Passing the fortress of Waxholm, we entered the magnificent fjord or arm of the sea which extends for a distance of ten or twelve miles up to the city. The scenery on this part of the route is very fine. All along the shores of the main land and adjacent islands rugged cliffs of granite reared their hoary crests over the waters of the fjord. Forests of oak and pine cover the rolling background, and beautiful villas, with parterres and blooming gardens, peep from every glen. Sometimes for miles the solitude of the forests and rock-bound shores is unbroken, save by an occasional fisherman's hut or an open patch of green pasture; then suddenly, upon turning a point, a group of red-roofed villas glimmer through the foliage; sail-boats are seen gliding over the water with gay companies of ladies and gentlemen from the city enjoying the fresh breeze that sweeps up from the Gulf; now a hay-boat or a clumsy lugger laden with wood drifts along lazily toward the grand centre of trade; and as we approach nearer to the dim smoke-cloud that hangs over the city, big and little craft gather thicker and thicker before us, till the whole fjord seems alive with masts and sails. Soon the outlines of the churches and castles break through the dim distance, and, like some grand optical illusion, the whole city gradually opens up before us.

To say that I was charmed with the first view of Stockholm would but faintly express the feelings with which I gazed upon this beautiful metropolis of the North. Though different in almost every essential particular, it has been not unaptly compared to Venice; and certainly, if the sparkling waters from which it seems to rise, the wood-covered islands, the rich and varied outlines of its churches and castles, the forests of shipping at its wharves, the many-colored sail-boats and gondolas sweeping hither and thither, the glowing atmosphere, and surrounding gardens, villas, temples, and pavilions, can entitle it to that distinction, Stockholm well deserves to rank with the Queen City of the Adriatic.

The landing for the Baltic steamers is at the head quay called the Skepsbron, which in summer is well lined with shipping, and presents rather an animated appearance. Very little formality is observed in regard to the baggage of passengers, and passports are not required, or at least no demand was made upon me for mine. All I had to do was to show my knapsack to the custom-house officer, who put a chalk-mark upon it, signifying, no doubt, that it contained nothing contraband; after which I stepped ashore, and, aided by a friendly fellow-passenger, found lodgings at a dirty little hotel close by, called the "Stadt Frankfort." If there is any worse place to be found in Stockholm, it must be the very worst on the face of the earth, for the "Stadt Frankfort" is next thing to it. Being dirty and foul of smell, and abounding in vermin, of course the charges are, as usual in such cases, proportionally high, for which reason I recommend it to any gentleman traveling in this direction whose main object is to get rid of his money for an equivalent of filth, fleas, bugs, bad bread, and worse coffee. The main part of the city, embracing the King's Palace, the Bourse, the Church of St. Nicholas, the Barracks and public buildings, is built upon an island fronting the Baltic on the one side and the Malar Lake on the other. This is the most populous and interesting part, though the streets are narrow and irregular, and the houses generally old and dilapidated, with dark, gloomy fronts, and a very fishy and primitive expression of countenance. The new parts of the city, called the Normalm to the north and the Sodmalm to the south, which are connected with the island by bridges, have some fine streets and handsome rows of buildings in the modern style, especially the Normalm, which contains the King's Garden, the Arsenal, the Opera-house, and the principal hotels and residences of the foreign ministers. This part of Stockholm will compare favorably with second or third-rate cities in Germany; for it must be borne in mind that, striking as the external aspect of Stockholm is, the interior is very far from sustaining the illusion of grandeur cast around it by the scenic beauties of its position. In nothing is the traveler more disappointed than the almost total absence of business excitement. With the exception of a few stevedores at work on the wharves and a trifling jostle at the market-places, the whole city seems to be sitting down in its Northern solitude, waiting, like Mr. Micawber, for something to turn up. In some parts one may walk half a mile without hearing a sound save the echo of his own footsteps. It is, emphatically, a "slow" place—so slow, indeed, compared with the marts of commerce to which I had been accustomed in California (especially the city of Oakland), that I was constantly impressed with the idea that every body was fast asleep, and that if three or four of them should happen to wake at the same time, it would be fearfully startling to hear their eyelids crack open and the hollow streets echo to their yawns.

But don't understand this as a reflection upon the Swedish race. They are industrious and energetic when occasion requires, but, like all people who live at the extreme North, acquire tropical habits of indolence from the climate. During the tedious winters, when the days are but six hours long, all who can afford it become torpid, like frogs, and lie up in their houses till the summer sun thaws them out. Balls, parties, and sleigh-riding occasionally rouse them up, but lethargy is the general rule. The warm weather comes very suddenly, and then the days are eighteen hours long. This being the season of outdoor pleasure, it is spent in visits to the country or lounging about the gardens, sitting on spring benches and enjoying the sunshine.

The Swedish soldiers are a fine-looking race of men, far superior in stature and general appearance to the soldiers of Russia. They are well drilled, bold, and manly, and have fine faces, full of spirit and intelligence. Wherever these men are led, they will now, as in past times, give the enemies of their country some trouble. I consider them the finest soldiers in Northern Europe.

The general aspect of the citizens of Stockholm is that of extreme plainness and simplicity. I take them to be an honest, substantial, and reliable people, well educated and intelligent ; satisfied with themselves and the world, and proud of their country and its history. Politeness is a national characteristic. Every person, of high and low degree, upon entering a shop, takes off his hat, and remains with uncovered head while making his purchase. Gentlemen who meet on the street knock the tops of their "tiles" against their knees, and continue to bow at each other long after they have passed. In feature and general appearance the Swedes are handsomer than the southern races of Europe, and for that reason wear a nearer resemblance to the Americans. I saw several men in Stockholm who would not have done discredit to California, in point of fine faces and commanding figures. The Swedish ladies are proverbially beautiful. It was really refreshing, after my visit to Russia, to see so many pretty women as I met here. Light hair, oval features, sparkling blue eyes, and forms of intoxicating grace and beauty—ah me! why should such dangers be permitted to threaten the defenseless traveler with instant destruction, when the law provides for his protection against other disasters by land and sea, assault and battery, false imprisonment and highway robbery? Yet here were lovely creatures, gliding about at large, shooting mutilation and death out of their bright blue eyes, and apparently as indifferent to the slaughter they committed as if it were the finest fun in the world! Talk of your French beauties, your Italian beauties, your Spanish beauties! Give me, for the impersonation of soul expressed in the human form divine—for features "woven from the music of the spheres and painted with the hues of the aurora borealis"—a Swedish beauty, the nearest approach upon earth to an American beauty, which, being altogether angelic, must ever remain the highest type of perfection known to mankind.

I don't wonder Swedenborg made so many heavens for his female characters. His "conjugal felicity" required at least seven. One small heaven, constructed upon the Swedish plan, would certainly afford but limited accommodations for all the beauties of Stockholm.

A day or two after my arrival in Stockholm I called to see Mr. Fristadins, the American consul, from whom I obtained the latest news in reference to the progress of the rebellion. Accustomed as we are in the United States to read the newspapers every morning, wherever we may happen to be, the deprivations in this respect to which an American traveler in Europe is subjected must be experienced to be fully appreciated. Even in the principal cities of Germany it is difficult to find a newspaper that contains any thing more than a notice of the price of stocks, a few telegraphic items about the petty court movements of neighboring cities, a rehash of slander upon our country from the London *Times*, or an item of news about the war, in which the states are misplaced, the names misspelled, and the most important points omitted. I do not think there is a village press in California that would not be ashamed to turn out such trashy little sheets as are issued in Frankfort; and as for the matter of fairness and honesty, it is rare to find an independent newspaper in any part of Europe. To suppress truth and subserve some military or financial interest is the business for which they are paid. Making due allowance for party prejudices, you may guess at the truth in most of our American journals, but it would be a waste of time to search for it in the newspapers published on this side of the water. While they studiously refrain from indecorous language, they are corrupt and unrelia-. ble beyond any thing known in California, and have not even the merit of being energetic and entertaining liars. This is the case in Russia and Finland as well as in Germany. Where the press is subjected to a rigid censorship, it is of course useless to look for reliable information, and as for late intelligence, it does not travel through official bureaus. Before leaving Frankfort I had news to the 28th of June. A week after my arrival at St. Petersburg the same news was promulgated in that city. On my return from Moscow I had the pleasure of reading the details in an American newspaper. One or two mutilated telegraphic dispatches seemed to sharpen my appetite during the trip to Revel, Helsingfors, Abo, and Stockholm; and now, arrived at the head-quarters of Swedish civilization, after searching in vain for a late English or American newspaper at the principal cafés, I

was compelled to make application to our consul, in the
faint hope that he might be an occasional reader of that
ephemeral species of literature. Fortunately, Mr. Fristadius had spent some time in the United States, and
learned to appreciate the magnitude and importance of
the struggle in which we were engaged.

I had the pleasure, during my sojourn in Stockholm,
of getting a glimpse of Swedish social life in one of its
most agreeable phases. Mr. Fristadius, who is a Swede
by birth and education, and occupies a prominent position as one of the leading iron-merchants of Stockholm,
was kind enough to invite me to an entertainment at his
villa, situated about four miles from the city, on one of
the prettiest little islands in the Malar Lake.

At an early hour in the afternoon, the company, which
consisted of thirty or forty ladies and gentlemen, assembled by appointment at a wharf near one of the principal bridges, where a small steam-boat belonging to Mr.
Fristadius was in waiting. I was a little astonished, not
to say taken aback, at the display of elegant dresses, liveried servants, and white kid gloves that graced the occasion, and looked at my dusty and travel-worn coat,
slouched hat, and sunburnt hands—for which there was
no remedy—with serious thoughts of a hasty retreat.
One doesn't like to be a savage among civilized people;
yet, if one undertakes to travel with little baggage and
less money, what can he do, unless he holds himself aloof
from the world altogether, which is not the best way of
seeing it? There was no time for reflection, however;
the whistle was blowing, and we were hurried on board
by our kind host, who seemed determined to make every
body as happy as possible. The trip down the lake was
delightful. On either side the hills and islands were
dotted with villas and gardens; sail-boats were skimming over the water with gay parties intent on pleasure;
the views of the city from every turn were picturesque
beyond description, and the weather was quite enchanting. As we swept along on our course, the gentlemen

of the party, who were nearly all Swedes, united in a wild and beautiful Scandinavian glee, the mellow strains of which swept over the water, and were echoed from the wooded islands and shores of the lake with a magnificent effect. Whether it was the scenery, the weather, or the singing, or all combined, I could scarcely tell, but this little trip was certainly an episode in life to be remembered with pleasure in after years. In about half an hour we drew near a perfect little Paradise of an island, upon which, half hidden in shrubbery and flowers, stood the villa of our friend, Mr. Fristadius. Here were winding graveled walks overhung by rich foliage; beds of flowers in full bloom; grottoes of rock laved by the waters of the lake; immense boulders of granite surmounted by rustic pavilions; hedges of privet and hawthorn to mark the by-paths; a miniature bridge from the main island across to a smaller island, upon which stood an aquatic temple for the fishing-boats and gondolas; with a wharf jutting out into the deep water at which the little steam-boat landed. Nothing could be more unique than the whole place. Nature and art seemed to have united to give it the most captivating effects of wildness, seclusion, comfort, and elegance. It was Crusoe-life idealized. As we approached the landing-place, the interesting family of our host, surrounded by numerous friends, stood upon a little eminence awaiting our arrival. While we gazed with pleasurable emotions at the pretty scene before us, a most delicate and appropriate compliment was paid to our excellent minister, Mr. Haldeman, and his accomplished wife, who were of the party. The American flag was hoisted upon a pole near the landing by Mrs. Fristadius, and the company with one accord arose and greeted with three cheers this glorious emblem of liberty. I shall never forget the mingled feelings of pride and pleasure with which I looked upon the stars and stripes once more, after months of dreary depression in countries where freedom is but a glimmering hope in the human heart. But here in Sweden the spirit of our institutions is appreciated; here I found myself surrounded by noble and trusty friends of the American Union, loyal to their own liberal government, yet devoted to the great cause of human freedom wherever it can exist consistently with the progress of the times and the capacity of the people for self-government. As the flag waved in the breeze, an inspiring song of liberty burst from the joyous company—one of those soul-stirring songs of Belman, which find a response in the breast of every Swede—wild, impassioned, and patriotic, breathing in every word and intonation the chivalrous spirit of men whose ancestry had fought under the glorious banners of Gustavus Adolphus.

As soon as the song was concluded the little steamboat drew up to the wharf, where we were most kindly and cordially greeted by the family of our host. After a pleasant ramble about the grounds we proceeded to the house, which is situated on a picturesque eminence overlooking the lake, and the adjacent shores and islands. Here, in a large and elegant saloon, opening on all sides upon a spacious veranda, a sumptuous collation was spread. The company lounged about without ceremony, eating, drinking, and enjoying themselves as they pleased; wit and wine flowed together, unrestrained by the slightest formality. In the midst of our "feast of reason and flow of soul," Mr. Fristadius made a neat and appropriate little speech of "welcome to all his friends," which was followed by a song from the musical gentlemen; after which he proposed a toast to a young married couple present. This was followed by another song. Then there was a toast to the American flag, another speech and a song, to which Mr. Haldeman, our minister, responded in such terms of enthusiasm and complimentary allusion to the Swedish nation that there was a general outburst of applause. I had hoped, in view of my rustic garb, to escape notice, and was snugly barricaded in a corner behind a table, looking on quietly and enjoying the scene, when, to my great astonishment, a toast was proposed "to the DISTINGUISHED TRAVELER FROM CALIFORNIA!" In vain I looked about me to see if any prominent gentleman of my acquaintance from California would step forward and answer to the summons, when I was gently but firmly captured by our host, and duly brought forth to respond to the charge! Never having made a speech in my life, I could only seize hold of a wine-glass (which I think belonged to somebody else), and in the confusion of the moment drink spontaneously to the great traveler from California! Then there was an inspiring glee from the lively young gentlemen who did the music.

Thus passed the time till dinner was over, when we adjourned to the garden for coffee and cigars. Seated under the wide-spreading trees, in the balmy air of this summer evening, we had songs and recitations of Scandinavian poetry, anecdotes, and humorous dissertations till nearly midnight. I do not remember that I ever participated in a more rational or delightful entertainment. After a farewell glee to our host we marched down to the wharf, where the boat was in waiting, and embarked for Stockholm. I can only add that I was charmed with the refinement and intelligence of Swedish society, as far as I could judge of it by this casual glimpse. From many of the guests I received cordial invitations to prolong my sojourn, and the next morning found two or three of the gentlemen in readiness to show me every thing of interest about the city.

We visited the Museum, where there is an interesting assortment of Scandinavian antiquities, and the palace, and some half a dozen other places, all of which came in the regular routine of sight-seeing; but the fact is, I am getting dreadfully tired of this systematic way of lionizing the cities of Europe. I turn pale at the sight of a museum, shudder at a church, feel weak in the knees at the bare thought of a picture-gallery, and as for antiquities, they make my flesh creep. Between you and myself, dear reader, I wouldn't give a sou-markee for all the old bones gathered up during the last eighteen centuries, unless to start a bone-mill and sell the dust at a remunerative profit.

After all, the more I saw of Stockholm the more the blues began to creep over me. It is depressingly slow in these far Northern cities; so slow, indeed, I don't wonder every thing has a mildewed and sepulchral aspect. The houses look like slimy tombs in a graveyard; the atmosphere, when the sun does not happen to shine—which is more than half the time—is dank and flat, and hangs upon one's spirits like a nightmare, crushing out by degrees the very germ of vitality. I am not surprised that paralysis and hip-disease are frightfully prevalent in Stockholm.

Give me California forever—the land of sunshine and progress. I have seen no country like it yet. When I think of old times there, a terrible home-sickness takes possession of me. So help me, friends and fellow-citizens, I'd sooner be a pack-mule in California with a raw back, and be owned by a Mexican greaser, employed week in and week out in carrying barrels of whisky over the Downieville trail, fed on three grains of barley per day, and turned out to browse on quartz rock and sage-bushes every night—I'd rather be a miserable little burro, kicked and cuffed by a Mariposa Chinaman—I'd rather be a dog and bay the moon in the city of Oakland, or a toad and feed upon the vapors of a dungeon at San Quentin — I'd rather be a lamp-post on the corner of Montgomery Street, San Francisco, and be leaned against, and hugged, and kissed alternately by every loafer out of the Montgomery saloon — I'd rather be any of these than a human being compelled to live permanently in Europe, with a palace in every city, town, and village, and an income of fifty thousand dollars a day to defray expenses; so don't be surprised if I should turn up again one of these fine mornings on the Pacific coast. The only difficulty at present is — a collapse in the financial department.

CHAPTER XXV.

WALKS ABOUT STOCKHOLM.

IF you expect any very lively or striking pictures of Stockholm from a tourist like myself, whose besetting trouble in life is a constitutional melancholy, I am afraid you will be disappointed. It is beyond doubt one of the most agreeable cities in the North, and, so far as public institutions are concerned, affords a fine field of research for the antiquarian and the naturalist. Any enterprising gentleman who desires to improve his mind by the study of Puffendorf can here find the original. Linnæus, Berzelius, and others will materially assist him in grasping at the mysteries of animated creation; and if he be of a poetical turn, he can enjoy Belman in the unadulterated Scandinavian metre. For me, however, the public museums and libraries possessed only an external interest. I would gladly have devoted the remainder of my life to Scandinavian researches, but, having several other important matters to attend to, I was reluctantly forced to give up the idea. The main object at present was to escape from " an eternal lethargy of woe," which seemed to grow worse and worse every day. I really had nothing particular to afflict me, yet I both felt and looked like "a man sore acquaint with grief." Day after day I wandered about the streets in search of excitement. All in vain; such a luxury is unknown to strangers in Stockholm. I visited the fruit-markets, jostled about among the simple and kind-hearted peasants, bought bunches of cherries and baskets of raspberries from the pretty peasant-girls, and then stood eating my way into their acquaintance, while they laughed, and talked, and wondered where in the world such a strange man came from, and when I told them I came from California they looked incredulous, having probably never heard of such a country. Then I strolled down through the fish-market, where there were a great many queer fish exposed for sale by ancient and slimy old men and women, whose hands and aprons were covered with fish-scales, and whose faces had a very fishy expression. They offered me fish in every shape—skinned, gutted, chopped up, or whole, just as I pleased to buy them. One wrinkled old woman, with a voice much broken by shouting against the Gulf storms from high rocks, or some such cause, called my attention to a monster fish that must have weighed at least sixty pounds, and insisted upon letting me have it at a reduced price. I shook my head and smiled. In that smile I suppose the sagacious old fishwoman discovered the pliancy of my disposition, for she immediately commenced a wild harangue on the merits of the fish, scarcely a word of which I understood. Two or three times I started to leave, but each time she made a motion to detain me. The fact is, I was afraid she would get hold of me with her fishy hands, and was considerably embarrassed what to do. The price of the fish was reasonable enough— only two marks (about forty cents); but I had no use for it, and did not like to carry it to my hotel. The worst of it was, the old woman thought the price was the only obstacle, and finally came down to a mark and a half. What was to be done? From Billingsgate to Stockholm, it is notorious that a disappointed fishwoman is a very dangerous and uncertain foe to be encountered by any man, however brave. She began to get excited at the bare prospect of having taken so much trouble for nothing. Several of her friends began to gather round. A cold tremor ran through my frame. There seemed to be no possible way of evading the purchase without creating an unpleasant scene. To make an end of it, I bought the fish. With a bunch of grass wrapped around its tail, I made my way through the crowd. To be sure, I felt a little ashamed to be perambulating the streets of a strange city with a big fish in my hand, yet I could not well throw it down on the sidewalk, and was afraid, if I offered it to some little boy, he might stick his tongue in his cheek, and ask me if I saw any thing green in the corner of his eye. The case was getting worse and worse every moment. People stopped and looked at me as I passed. My arm was getting tired. Fortunately, I was close to the quay. A happy thought struck me; I walked over to the water's edge and cast the fish into his native element. "Go," said I, in the language of my uncle Toby; "there's room enough in the world for you and me." What the by-standers thought of the act I did not wait to see. It was enough that I was clear of a very unpleasant companion, though an ancient and fish-like odor remained with me for some time after. As for the fish, I doubt if he ever came to life; he must have been dead for several days when I bought him, judging by a taint upon my hands, which the best soap could not eradicate.

After this I rambled gloomily along the quays, and wondered what every body was waiting for. There were small vessels enough lying at the wharves, but every body on board seemed to be taking it easy. Cooks were lying asleep on the galleys; skippers were sitting on the poop, smoking socially with their crews; small boys, with red night-caps on their heads, were stretched out upon the hatchways, playing push-pin, and eating crusts of black bread; stevedores, with dusty sacks on their shoulders, were lounging about on the wharf, waiting for something in the way of trade to turn up; shabby citizens, who seemed to be out of profitable employment, were sitting on the loose timbers overlooking the water, bobbing for fish, and never catching any so far as I could perceive; and scattering crowds of idlers were strolling idly along like myself, in search of something particular to look at, but, failing to discover it, they looked about at things generally, and then strolled on to look at something else. I sighed at the stagnation of business, and hoped it would never be my fate to be engaged in mercantile affairs in Stockholm. Before the Gotha Canal was completed this was a very brisk city; but since that period, Gottenburg, being more accessible, has monopolized much of the European trade. The principal trade of Stockholm now consists of exports of iron, and imports of sugar, coffee, and liquors. Throughout the interior the peasantry manufacture most of the articles required for their own use, such as clothing, implements of husbandry, etc., so that they are not large consumers of foreign commodities. Finding it very dull in town, I walked out in the suburbs, which are pretty and picturesque, though primitive enough to be a thousand miles from a commercial city. The houses are chiefly constructed of wood, painted yellow, with red roofs, and neatly ornamented with verandas; and the people have a quaint and simple look, as if they knew but little of the world, and did not care much to trouble their heads about the progress of events. Here as well as elsewhere, children continue to be born in great numbers, and groups of them were to be seen before every house playing in the mud just as little cotton-headed children play all over the world. I say cotton-headed, because these were of the blue-eyed, white-haired race who have a natural affinity for muddy places, and whose cheeks have a natural propensity to gather bloom and dirt at the same time.

I struck out on the high points of the Normalm, and on one of them discovered an old church, surrounded by trees, with benches conveniently placed beneath their shade for weary pedestrians. Here were family groups quietly enjoying the fresh air, the men smoking and drinking, while the women and girls economized time by knitting and sewing. I took a vacant seat and looked down over the city. Surely a prettier prospect could not exist upon earth. There lay the city of the sea outspread beneath, its irregular streets, quaint old houses and churches covering every available space; the numerous wooded islands in the vicinity dotted with villas;

sloops and boats floating dreamily on the Malar Lake, and larger vessels gliding over the waters of the Baltic; dense forests of pine dim in the distance; and over all a strangely colored Northern light, that gave the scene something of a spectral aspect. Yet the spirit of repose that seemed cast over this fair scene was absolutely oppressive to one like myself, accustomed to an active life. From the high points I wandered down into the low places, through narrow and tortuous streets; gazed into the stables and cow-houses; watched the tinners, and coppersmiths, and shoemakers as they wound up the labors of the day in their dingy little shops; peered into the greasy little meatshops and antiquated grocery-stores; studied the faces of the good people who slowly wended their way homeward, and bowed to several old ladies out of pure kindliness and good feeling; then wandered back into the public places, still pursued by a green and yellow melancholy. I gazed steadfastly at the statues of Gustavus Vasa, Charles XII., and Berzelius, and tried in vain to remember something of their history. I went into the picture-shops, took off my hat to small boys behind the counter, looked at the pictures, and bought several, for which I had no earthly use; then I went to the café on the bridge, drank coffee and cognac, and attempted to read the Swedish newspapers, of which I understood every letter, but not a word; after which I heard the whistle of a small steam-boat at the end of the café garden, and ran down in a hurry to get on board. The steam-boat was about equal to a good-sized yawl, and was bound for some port unknown to me; but that made no difference. I never see a boat of any kind going any where, or a locomotive, or a carriage, or any thing that moves by steam, sails, horse-power, or electricity, without feeling an unconquerable desire to be off too, so that I very much fear, if I should come across a convict vessel bound for Van Diemen's Land, it would be impossible for me to avoid jumping on board and going with the crowd. In the present case it was essentially necessary that I should keep moving. I was almost sinking under the oppressive loneliness of the place. Rather than remain another hour within the limits of such a dreary old city, I would have taken passage in a tread-mill, and relied upon the force of imagination to carry me to some other place. Nay, a hangman's cart on the way to the gallows would have presented a strong temptation. In saying this I mean nothing disrespectful to Birger Jarl, who founded Stockholm, and made it his place of residence in 1260; nor to Christina Gyllenstierna, who so heroically defended it against Christian II. of Denmark in the sixteenth century; nor to Gustavus Vasa, the brave liberator of Sweden ; nor his noble and heroic grandson, Gustavus Adolphus; nor any body else famous in Swedish history; but the truth of it is, Sweden at the present day is essentially a home country, and the people are too domestic in their habits and modes of thought to afford any peculiar interest to a casual tourist. I like their simple and genial manners, and respect them for their sterling integrity, yet these are traits of no great value to one who travels so far out of the world in search of objects of more stirring interest. The ordinary traveler, who has no time to dive very deep beneath the surface of human life, is not satisfied to find things nearly as he finds them at home; streets, shops, and houses undistinguished by any peculiarity save the inconveniences and oddities of age; people every where around him who dress like all other civilized people, and possess the standard virtues and weaknesses of humanity; the proprieties of life decently observed, and loyalty to forms and time-honored usages a national characteristic. A Swede would no more violate a rule of etiquette, smile or bow out of place, eat a beefsteak or drink his schnapps at an unusual hour, or strike out any thing novel or original in the way of pleasure, profit, or enterprise, than a German. The court circle is the most formal in Europe, and the upper classes of society are absolute slaves to conventionality. A presentation at court is an event of such signal importance that weeks of preparation are required for the impressive ordeal; and when the tailor, and shoemaker, and the jeweler have done their part, and the unhappy victim, all bedeviled with finery and befrogged with lace, is brought into the presence of royalty, it is a miracle if he gets through without committing some dire offense against the laws of etiquette. Fine carriages, coats of arms, uniforms, and badges of office, are held in high veneration; and while the government is liberal and the people profess to be independent, their slavish devotion to rank, dress, and etiquette surpasses any thing I saw in Russia. With this, to be sure, is mingled a certain simplicity of manner and kindliness of expression toward inferiors which sometimes lead the stranger to believe that he is among a democratic people, but they are as far from democracy as the Prussians or the Austrians. The very affability of the superior to the inferior is the best evidence of the inseparable gulf that lies between them. In Russia there is the charm of barbarism, savagery, filth, and show; the people are loose, ferocious, daring, and wild; here in Sweden, the quiet, decent, home-aspect of the people, their rigid observance of the rules of etiquette, their devotion to royalty, law, and order, are absolutely depressing. In the abstract, many traits in their character are worthy of admiration, but as a traveler I detest this kind of civilization. Give me a devil or a savage at all times, who outrages the rules of society and carries an advertisement of character on his back. As an artist I can make something of him, either in the way of copy or pencil-sketches.

Which brings me back to my situation, in the natural course of events. The whistle blows. The little steamboat is about to stop at the landing-place of the Djurgaard. The engineer, smutty and oily with hard service, gives a turn to the crank, pulls an iron bar with a polished handle, and then pushes it; the tea-kettle boiler fizzes and whizzes, and lets off steam; the paddles stop paddling; the gentlemen passengers stand up and adjust their shirt collars; the ladies gather their shawls around them, and pick up their scattered bundles; with a whirl and a jerk we are alongside the wharf, and the captain jumps from the bow with a rope in his hand, and makes all fast to a logger-head. And now step ashore, if you please, ladies and gentlemen, and let us take a stroll through the deer garden, where

"The ash and warrior oak
Cast anchor in the rifted rock."

The walks through this beautiful park (said to be the finest attached to any capital in Europe) are broad, and handsomely graded. Grand old forest-trees on either side make "a boundless contiguity of shade" over the greensward. Pavilions and rustic summer-houses stand on the high points of rock, commanding magnificent views of the adjacent islands and waters of the lake. Flower-gardens are numerous, and every nook and dell contains some place of refreshment, where the gay company who frequent these delightful grounds in the long summer evenings can drink their tea and enjoy the varied beauties of the scene. Wandering through these sylvan glades, the eye is continually charmed with the rare combinations of natural and artificial beauties scattered around in every direction with such wonderful prodigality. At one moment you imagine yourself in a wilderness, hundreds of miles from any human habitation, so dense are the shades of the grand old forest-trees, and so wild and rugged the moss-covered rocks; a few steps bring you suddenly upon some fairy scene, where palaces and temples, gilded carriages, gayly-dressed companies of ladies and gentlemen, and groups of children sporting upon the grass, dispel the illusion. Ascending to the highest points by the narrow and tortuous by-paths, I could almost fancy myself in the midst of the Coast Range, so perfect was the isolation; then coming out suddenly upon some projecting cliff, the change of scene from rugged grandeur to the perfection of civilization was absolutely magical. Vegetation in this northern region, where the summers are so short and warm, flourishes with an almost tropical luxuriance. The melting of the snows in spring, followed by heavy rains and sudden heat, causes the earth to give forth its products with a prodigality that compensates in some degree for the long and dreary winters. Trees burst into leaf as if by magic; flowers shoot up and bloom in a few weeks; the grass, enriched by the snows, springs forth and covers the earth like a gorgeous carpet of velvet. All nature rejoices in the coming of the long summer days. The birds sing in the groves; the bees hum merrily around the flowers; the gay butterflies flit through the sunbeams; and day and night are an almost continued period of revelry for all those beautiful and ephemeral creatures that droop and die with the flowers. I have nowhere seen such a profusion of intensely rich green and such wonderfully deep shades as in the neighborhood of Stockholm. It is almost oppressive to one accustomed to California scenery, where the whole face of the country wears a dry red-and-yellowish hue in summer. Strange how one's tastes change by association! I well remember when I first entered the Golden Gate, in August, 1849, after a long and dreary voyage round Cape Horn. Glad as I was to see land once more, it struck me that I had never looked upon so barren and desolate a country. The hill-sides had the appearance of parched and sodless deserts. Yet I soon learned to like that warm glow. I slept upon those parched hills, breathed the invigorating air, and felt the inspiration of California life. I would not now exchange the summer drapery of our hills and valleys for the deepest green upon earth. To my present frame of mind there is something flat and chilling in this redundancy of verdure that reminds one of death and the grave-yard. The moss-covered rocks jutting from the cold, grassy earth; the dripping fern; the pale, flitting gleams of sunshine struggling through the depths of foliage; the mould that seems to hang in the air—all these strike me as death-like. I long for the vital glow of a more genial sun, whose all-pervading light is reflected from the rich golden earth, shooting health and vigor through every fibre of the frame, permeating body and soul with its effulgence. Such intensity of light, such warmth of colors, fill the dullest mind with inspiration; the blood is quickened in its circulation; the respiration is full and free; the intellect becomes clearer and sharper; the whole man is quickened into the highest condition of mental and physical vitality. Is it a matter of wonder, then, that the people of California should be brave, generous, and loyal—that they should have a high sense of right, and an undying scorn of wrong? I hold that the species is improved by the climate and the country—that stronger men and better men are now undergoing the process of development in California than in any other country on the face of the earth. If we live fast and die suddenly, it is the natural consequence of increased bodily and mental vigor, which too often leads to excesses, but which, under proper training, must eventually lead to the highest moral and intellectual achievements. The fault does not lie in our climate. I have yet seen none to equal it North or South—not even in Italy. I do not think the climate of Sweden is conducive to longevity, or extraordinary mental or bodily vigor. Indeed, the same may be said of any climate abounding in such rigorous extremes. The Swedes, it is true, lead a placid and easy life, content with ordinary comforts, and worried by no exciting or disquieting ambitions; hence they enjoy good health, and generally get through the usual span allotted to man. If the same sanitary rules were observed in our country, there would be less sickness and fewer untimely deaths. Dissipation is not rare in Sweden, especially in the capital cities, but it is more methodical with us. The people have certain times and occasions for getting drunk; they make a regular business of it. Virulent and disgusting diseases are also prevalent among them, so that between the rigors of climate and other causes less excusable, they frequently appear old and decrepit before their time. That among the middle classes there are fine-looking men and beautiful women, is true; that in literature, science, and music, they can boast names that will go down to posterity, is a fact that can not be denied; but I think such a climate and the habits engendered by it are inimical to the highest order of physical and mental development among the masses. Hence we find throughout the country many diseased and deformed persons of both sexes; many weakly and not a few imbecile. The peasants are not so hardy and robust as I expected to find them; and I was told by competent judges, better informed than I could hope to become during so brief a sojourn, that they are progressively degenerating year after year, and can not now compare with the peasants of former times.

To say that I was charmed with my ramble through the Djurgaard would but faintly express the pleasure I derived from my visit to this beautiful park. Of all the resorts for recreation that I have yet seen in Northern Europe, I give it the palm for natural beauty and tasteful cultivation. In this the Swedes excel. Their villas, gardens, and parks are unsurpassed, and no people in the world better understand how to enjoy them.

Late in the evening I returned to my hotel, delighted with all I had seen. I was anxious to extend my rambles to Upsala, and to visit more in detail the various beautiful islands and places of interest in the vicinity of Stockholm; but the season was advancing, and I was reluctantly compelled to push on toward Norway.

CHAPTER XXVI.

THE GOTHA CANAL.

On a pleasant morning in August I called for my bill at the "Stadt Frankfurt." The landlady, a blooming young woman of rather vivacious and persuasive manners, wished me such a delightful journey, and looked so sorry I was going, that I could not muster resolution enough to complain of the various caudles that were never burnt, and the numerous services that were never rendered, except in the bill; and had she charged me for washing my own face and putting on my own boots, I fear the result would have been the same. Wishing her a happy future, I shouldered my knapsack, which by this time contained only two shirts, an old pair of stockings, and some few flowers and stones from celebrated places, and, thus accoutred for the journey, made my way down to Riddarholm Quay. In a dingy old office, abounding in cobwebs, a dingy old gentleman, who spoke English, sold me a second-class ticket for Gottenburg. The little steamer upon which I had the good fortune to secure a passage was called the Admiral Von Platten, a name famous in the history of Swedish enterprise. It was Von Platten who, in 1808, took charge of the great work of internal improvement known as the West Gotha Canal, and by the aid of Telford, the celebrated English engineer, carried it into successful operation in 1822. The project of connecting the lakes of Wenern and Wettern, and forming a water communication all the way between Stockholm and Gottenburg, was entertained at a very early day by the different sovereigns and scientific men of Sweden. Bishop Brask in 1516, Gustavus I., Charles IX., Swedenborg, Gustavus Adolphus, and others, took particular interest in it, and some progress was made in the building of locks and opening of short passages up to the beginning of the present century. Daniel Thunberg contributed materially to the opening of the route between Wenern and the Baltic; and Colonel N. Eriksson, the celebrated engineer whose reputation stands so high in the United States, had the direction of the work for many years. It was not, however, till 1844 that the entire work was fully completed, although some years prior to that time the two seas were connected and open to navigation. The immense expense of this

M 2

enterprise; the extraordinary natural obstacles that have been overcome; the patience and perseverance with which it has been carried into practical operation; the magnitude and durability of the work, can only be appreciated by one who has made the trip through Sweden by this route. It is certainly the grandest triumph recorded in Swedish history. It will exist and benefit generations to come, when the names of her kings, warriors, and statesmen shall be known only to antiquarians.

The steamers now plying on this route are small, but well arranged for the accommodation of passengers. There is a first and second cabin, and a restaurant at which the traveler can call for what he desires, and, provided his tastes are not eccentric, generally get what he calls for. The waiters are simple-minded, kind-hearted, and sociable; sit down and gossip with the passengers (at least those of the second class), and, what seems rather novel and amusing to a stranger, leave the bill to be made out and summed up by the passengers themselves. A general account-book is left open in the cabin, in which it is expected every traveler will set down his name and keep his own account. At the end of the trip, the head waiter goes the rounds of the cabin and deck, book in hand, and asks the passengers to designate their names and sum up their accounts. Nobody seems to think of cheating or being cheated. There is something so primitive in this way of dealing on a public highway between two commercial cities, that I was quite charmed with it, and have some thoughts of recommending it to the California Steam Navigation Company. Just think what a pleasure it would be to travel from San Francisco to Sacramento, and keep the record of your own bitters and cigars, to say nothing of your supper and berth! I am certain the plan would be approved by a majority of the traveling public throughout the state.

The company on board these little Swedish steamers is generally plain, sociable, and intelligent. Among the passengers I met many who spoke English and German, and few who did not speak at least one language in addition to their own. In midsummer the trip from Stockholm to Gottenburg usually takes three days, though it is sometimes accomplished in two. The distance is about three hundred and seventy miles by the shortest route, through the Wettern and Wenern lakes. Time, however, is no great object in Sweden, and a day or two more or less makes no great difference. The beauty of the scenery, and the diversity of land and water, render the trip one of the most agreeable in Northern Europe, and for one I can safely say it would have pleased me all the better had it lasted longer.

Leaving the Riddarholm Quay, our route lay for the first four hours through the Malar Lake. The weather was delightful, and there was scarcely a ripple on the water. Sloops and wood-boats lay floating upon its glassy surface without perceptible motion. All along on either side beautiful villas peeped from the umbrageous shores and islands. Behind us, the city loomed up in all its queenly beauty, the numerous churches and public buildings presented in majestic outline against the sky, while the forest of shipping at the quays added a more stirring and vital interest to the scene. As we turned the last promontory to the right, and took a lingering look at this charming "city of the sea," I thought I had never enjoyed a more enchanting *coup d'œil.* The suburbs of Stockholm; the numerous little islands, with their rich green shrubbery; the villas and gardens; the sparkling vistas of water, form a combination of beauties rarely to be met with in any other part of the world. No wonder the Swedes regard their capital as a paradise. I fully agree with them that in summer it deserves all their praise; but I should prefer a warmer and more genial paradise for winter quarters. Earthen stoves and hot-air furnaces are not in any of the seven heavens that occur in my imagination.

Before many hours we passed a point somewhat celebrated in Swedish history. On a high peak of rock, hanging upon a pole, is a prodigious iron hat, said to be the identical "stove-pipe" worn by one of the old Swedish kings — a terrible fellow, who was in the habit of slaying hundreds of his enemies with his own hand. This famous old king must have been a giant in stature. Judging by his hat, as Professor Agassiz judges of fish by their scales, he must have been forty feet high, by about ten or fifteen broad; and if his strength corresponded with his gigantic proportions, I fancy he could have knocked the gable-end off a house with a single blow of his fist, or kicked the head out of a puncheon of rum, and swallowed the contents at a single draught, without the least difficulty. His hat probably weighs a hundred pounds—enough to give any ordinary man a severe headache. Here it has stood for centuries, in commemoration of his last struggle. Besieged by an overwhelming force of his enemies, as the chronicle goes, he slew some thousands of them, but, being finally hard pressed, he lost his iron hat in the fight, and then plunged headlong into the lake. Some historians assert that he took to water to avoid capture; but I incline to the opinion myself that he did it to cool his head. At all events, the record ends at this point. We are unable to learn any thing more of his fate. These Northern races are strong believers in their own aboriginal history, and although there may be much in this that would require the very best kind of testimony before a California jury, the slightest hint of a doubt as to its truth would probably be taken as a personal offense by any public spirited Swede. In that respect, thank fortune, I am gifted with a most accommodating disposition. I can believe almost any thing under the sun. Giants and genii are nothing to what my credulity is capable of; and as for fairies and hobgoblins, I can swallow them by wholesale. There is only one thing in this world that I entertain the least doubt about—the title to my house and lot in Oakland. Upon that point I question if it ever will be possible for human evidence to satisfy me. Three times I paid for it, and each time every body considered it perfect except myself. I expect daily to hear of another title, of which I trust some enterprising gentleman in want of funds will advise me. It will be a source of consolation to know that I was not mistaken.

Situated near the entrance of the canal, on the left bank, is the beautiful little town of Soderkoping, celebrated for its mineral springs, to which the people of Stockholm resort in great numbers during the summer for health and recreation. The scene as we approached was very pretty. Pine and oak forests cover the granite hills' for many miles around, relieved by occasional openings dotted with villas, gardens, and farms; and the dark red wooden houses of the town have a singularly pleasant effect glimmering in the sunbeams through the rich masses of foliage by which they are surrounded. Groups of visitors stood at the locks awaiting the news from the city, or anxiously looking out for the familiar faces of relatives and friends, while the lock-men slowly and methodically performed their accustomed routine of labors. Soderkoping is a very ancient town, and in former times enjoyed considerable importance as a mart of commerce. Passing through a narrow stretch of canal, some miles in length, overhung by trees and rocks on the right, and affording some pleasant views of the rich valley to the left, the banks gradually widened 'till we entered a beautiful little lake, leading, after a short passage, to the waters of the Roxen. The narrow parts of the canal are difficult of navigation, owing to the various turns and the solid masses of rock through which it is cut; and the steamer sometimes proceeds very slowly, carefully feeling her way along, till an open space affords an opportunity of going ahead at a more rapid rate. In the mean time the passengers are all on ton the decks, shaded by an awning, enjoying themselves in the most unceremonious manner, laughing and talking in groups, sipping their coffee, or promenading up and down to enjoy the sweet-scented breeze from the neighboring hills.

The Roxen Lake, through which we next passed, is some seventeen miles long by seven broad, and is justly regarded as one of the loveliest sheets of water in all Sweden. The shores are neither very high nor very grand, but it would be difficult to find any thing more charming than the rich coloring of the rocks, their varied outlines, the luxuriance of the forests, and the crystal clearness of the water. Villages and farms are seen at occasional intervals in the distance, and sloops, with their sails hanging idly against their masts, float upon the placid surface of the lake as upon a mirror. Indeed, so perfect is the inversion, that the eye can scarcely determine how much is real and how much the result of optical illusion. Passing in sight of the town of Linkoping, which lies to the left, we soon reached the entrance of the West Gotha Canal, which here makes a direct ascent from the waters of the Roxen of seventy-five feet. At this point there are eleven locks, seven of which are closely connected, and the remainder separated by short stretches of canal. Near at hand is a pretty little village to the left, famous for its church, the Vretakloster, built in the Gothic style in 1128, by Inge II., one of the early kings of Sweden. While the steamer was slowly toiling through the locks, a party of the passengers, including myself, paid a visit to the church, and, aided by a venerable sacristan, saw all that was to be seen in it, chief among which are the tombs of the kings and the arms of the Douglas family, those warlike Scots who took such an active part in the military exploits of Sweden during the Thirty Years' War. The walk was a pleasant relief after our trip across the lake, and on our return by a short cut to the upper locks we had a splendid view of the wood-covered shore and glistening waters of the Roxen, now fading away in the rich twilight. The steamer occupies about an hour and a half in getting through the locks, and most of the passengers take advantage of the delay to stroll about among the neighboring cottages and gardens, and enjoy the various refreshments offered

for sale at the pavilions and tents erected near the upper
extremity for the accommodation of travelers. Fresh
milk, raspberries, coffee, sweet cakes, and ale are the principal articles furnished at these places. Notwithstanding there was an abundant supply of luxuries on board,
every body seemed to be hungry and thirsty on getting
ashore. The rapidity with which the plates, cups, and
glasses were emptied was really surprising, and would
have done credit to a crowd of Californians, who, I think,
can eat more and drink more in a given time than any
race of men upon the earth.

The canal for some distance beyond the locks is quite
narrow—often barely wide enough for two steamers to
pass. On the left the banks rise to a considerable height,
and then gradually decline till the canal passes along a
ridge, high above the surrounding country. The effect
in these places is very peculiar. The overhanging trees
almost unite their branches over the chimney of the
steamer as she wends her way slowly and steadily along;
deep ravines extend downward into an impenetrable
abyss on either side; the sky glimmers through the foliage in a horizontal line with the eye, and one can almost
fancy the world has been left below somewhere, and that
a new highway has been entered, upon which passengers
steam their way to the stars. I am quite certain, if we
had kept a direct course long enough, we would have
reached the moon or some of the heavenly bodies.

It was late at night when we reached the Boren Lake,
another of those natural highways that lie between the
Baltic and the North Sea. This lake is comparatively
small, but it abounds in rocky islands and shoals which
render the navigation through it rather intricate. A pilot is taken on board at the entrance of each lake, and
discharged upon reaching the next canal station.

I remained on deck until midnight, enjoying the
strange and beautiful lights spread over the heavens in
this latitude, and was reluctant even then to lose the
views during any part of the journey. Nature, however,

can not be defrauded of her legitimate demands even by the beauties of scenery, and I went below to sleep out the remainder of the night. My berth was in the forward cabin, where twenty or thirty passengers were already stretched out—some on the tables, some on the floor, and as many as could find room were snoring away in the temporary berths erected on the seats for their accommodation. Toward morning I was suddenly aroused by a strange and jarring motion of the boat, accompanied by a grating sound. It seemed as if an earthquake were throwing us up out of the water; yet the shocks were more sudden and violent than any I had ever before experienced. Many of the passengers were cast out of their berths, and the glass and crockery in the pantry went crashing over the floor. Scarcely conscious whether I was dreaming or awake, I grasped a post, and sprang out on a pile of baggage, but was immediately precipitated across the cabin. Fortunately I fell against the chambermaid, and suffered no injury. Amid the confusion worse confounded, the screams of the women down below, the crash of broken glasses, and the general struggle to get to the cabin door, a German Jew sprang from his berth, and in frantic accents begged that his life might be spared. "Take my money!" cried he; "take it all, but for God's sake don't murder me!" The poor fellow had evidently been aroused out of some horrible dream, and between actual and imaginary dangers was now quite bewildered with terror. I could not help but be amused at the grotesque expression of his face, even at such a moment. It would have provoked a smile had we been going to the bottom. There was no fear of that, however, as I quickly ascertained. We were already hard and fast on the bottom. We had run upon a sunken rock, and were so firmly wedged between its crevices that it seemed likely we should remain there some time. As soon as all was still, I quietly dressed myself and went on deck to take an observation. It was just daylight. We were in the middle of a lake, surrounded by small rocky islands. One of these was only a stone's throw distant on our starboard. The stakes between which our course lay were close by on the larboard. We had missed the channel by some twenty or thirty yards, and run upon a bed of solid boulders. The pilot, it seemed, had been drinking a little too freely of schnapps, and had fallen asleep at the helm. It was a miracle that we were not all dashed to pieces. A few yards to the right stood a sharp rock, which, had we run against it, would have crushed in the entire bow of the boat, and probably many of us would have perished.

Although there was no fear of our sinking any deeper unless the bed of rocks gave way, it was not a pleasant prospect to be detained here, perhaps for several days. The main shore was some five or six miles distant, and presented an almost unbroken line of granite boulders and dense pine forests. Most of the passengers were on deck, in a state of high excitement; the gentlemen running about in their shirt sleeves and drawers, and the ladies in those indescribable costumes which ladies usually wear when they go to sleep. The captain was mounted on the poop-deck, with his pipe in his mouth, giving orders to the men, who were pulling and tugging at big ropes, and trying to be very busy knocking things about; the pilot stood a little apart from the captain, pale and moody, having in a single moment destroyed his prospects for life. I felt very sorry for the poor fellow, though there was really no excuse for him. Every now and then the captain turned to him and gave him a broadside of curses, which he bore very meekly.

In vain the engineer put on additional steam; in vain the captain shouted "Back!" "Ahead!" "Stop!" We did nothing but stop. It was stop all the time. As there is no tide in these inland waters, the prospect was that we would continue to stop as long as the rocks remained stationary.

All hope of progress being at an end, the engineer slackened down the fires; the deck-hands went to breakfast, and the passengers went down below to dress and talk over their misfortune. The sun rose as usual, and the sky was as clear and the lake as placid as if nothing had happened. I had been trying all my life to get shipwrecked on a desolate island; now there seemed a fair prospect of success. The only difficulty was, that there was no heavy sea to break the vessel to pieces, and she was too substantial to go to pieces of her own account. The nearest island was little more than a barren rock. A few birds wheeled about over it, or sat perched upon its rugged points, but with that exception I doubt if it furnished a foothold for a living creature.

After a good breakfast of sausages and veal cutlets, brown bread and coffee, we again turned out on deck. This time the joyful tidings reached us from aloft that a Gottenberg steamer was approaching. Soon the smoke of her chimneys was perceptible from the deck, and in an hour or so she was alongside. A stout hawser was bent on to her, and after another hour of pulling and tugging, backing and filling, we slipped off the rocks, and floated out into the channel. I was destined, after all, never to be decently shipwrecked. We had suffered but little injury, and proceeded on our way as quietly as if nothing had interrupted our course. On our arrival at the next pilot station the captain put the pilot ashore, with a parting malediction in the Swedish vernacular.

The next place of importance on our route was the pretty little town of Motala, at which we stopped for some hours to take in freight and passengers. The neighborhood is undulating and picturesque, and abounds in rich farms. Motala is an old-fashioned place, with paved streets and wooden houses, much like the suburbs of Stockholm. It is celebrated chiefly for its manufactures of iron. The founderies are numerous, and cutlery of a very good quality is manufactured here. Besides these, it possesses many other objects of interest. The churches are well worth visiting, and the ruins of the fortifications erected in 1567, to resist the Danes, are among the finest in Sweden. From Motala, after another narrow stretch of canal, we soon reached the Wettern Lake, the next largest to the Wenern, and the waters of which are three hundred and four feet above the level of the sea.

In my recollections of travel I can scarcely call to mind any experience more pleasant than I enjoyed during this part of the trip. The lake scenery of Sweden, although not very grand compared with that of the Norwegian fjords, is certainly unsurpassed in the softness and beauty of its coloring, the crystal clearness of the water, the luxuriance of the surrounding forests, the varied labyrinths of charming little islands through which the channel winds, and the delicate atmospheric tints cast on the distant shores. By this time, too, the passengers have become better acquainted. The wonderful sights that we have seen together; the perils and dangers through which we have passed; the breakfasts, dinners, and suppers that we have eaten at the same board; the amount of solid sleeping that we have done in the same little cabin; the promenades we have had up and down the decks, and the rambles we have enjoyed together, have bound us together as one family, and now we come out with our individual histories and experiences, our accomplishments and humors. We (the gentlemen) drink schnapps together, smoke cigars, talk all the languages under the sun, tell our best anecdotes, and sing glees under the awning. The ladies look more beautiful than ever, and although they are still a little shy of us, as ladies in Europe generally are of the male sex, they sometimes favor us with a smile or a pleasant word, and thus contribute to our happiness. I don't know, for the life of me, what dire offense the man who founded European society was guilty of; but it is certain his successors, from Algeria to the North Pole, are sadly mistrusted by the unmarried ladies. This, I regret to say, is the case in Sweden, as well as in Germany and France. A gentleman is generally regarded as a ferocious cannibal, ready without the slightest provocation to devour and swallow up defenseless maidens. The married ladies are free and easy enough, having discovered probably that men are not half so dangerous as they are reported to be. But, all things considered, the Swedish ladies are exceedingly polite and affable, and on occasions of this kind seem well disposed toward our rapacious sex.

The next important point in our route was the fortress of Wanas, which commands the channel entering the lake on the eastern side. This is considered a work of great importance in view of invasion by any foreign power. We did not stop long enough to examine it in detail, merely touching to put the mail ashore and take in a few passengers. Leaving the Wettern Lake, our route lay through a series of smaller lakes, beautifully diversified with wood-covered islands, till we entered the Viken, another magnificent stretch of water of less extent than the Wettern, but still more beautiful than any we had yet seen. Here the rocks and islands are innumerable, rising from the water in every direction; the smaller ones covered with moss, lichens, shrubbery, and flowers; and the larger darkened with a dense growth of fir, pine, and other evergreens, while the oak, elm, and ash occasionally enliven the masses of shade with their more lively foliage.

At the end of the Viken, which is some fifteen miles in length, the West Gotha Canal commences, and continues through a rich and beautiful farming country to the waters of the great Wenern Lake, some twenty miles distant. The passage through this portion of the route is less interesting than others through which we had passed —so far, at least, as the scenery is concerned. The country is undulating, but not sufficiently diversified for fine scenic effects. Farms and meadows extend nearly all the way to the shores of the Wenern; and the canal passes at frequent intervals through farming districts, which, in point of cultivation, are quite equal to any thing I had seen in more southern parts of Europe. The peasants' houses along the route are neat and comfortable, and reminded me occasionally of our New England farm-houses. Villages enliven the route at intervals of a few miles, but generally they are of inconsiderable size, and may properly be regarded as mere gatherings of farm-houses around the nucleus of a church or post station. In this respect, I was struck with the difference between Sweden and Germany. The German peasantry, as a general thing, live in villages, and carry on their farming outside, sometimes at a distance of several miles. In the Thuringenwald, the Schuartzwald, the Spessart, and some other mountainous districts, it is true, exceptions may be found to this rule; but throughout the best cultivated districts of Germany there are but comparatively few farm-houses in which isolated families live. Hence villages, and, in many cases, large towns, form the head-quarters of each agricultural parish. The pedestrian, in traveling through Germany, is scarcely ever more than a "halp-stund" from one town or village to another. I think the longest stretch I ever made between two villages was two hours, or six and a half miles. In Sweden (and the same may be said of Norway) the farming districts have more of an American aspect. The houses are scattered about on the different farms, and the peasants do not seem to be so gregarious in their habits as those of Germany. This arises in part from the fact that the population is not so dense in Sweden as in the more central parts of Europe, and in part from the greater abundance of wood and pasture, and the predominance of the lumbering, mining, and stock-raising interests. Many of the farmers are also lumbermen and miners, and nearly all have a good supply of blood cattle. The extent of arable land in Sweden is comparatively small. It presents few attractions as an agricultural country. Its chief wealth consists in its vast forests and mines. The climate is too severe and the production of cereal crops too uncertain to render farming on a large scale a profitable pursuit. This is especially the case in the northern

parts. South of Stockholm, between the lakes of Wettern and Wenern, and along the banks of the Gota River, farming is carried to considerable perfection; but
with this exception, and some small and sheltered valleys
to the north, in which the peasants manage with great
care and labor to raise a sufficient supply of grain and
potatoes for domestic consumption, but little is produced
for exportation. The land generally throughout Sweden
is barren and rocky, and it is only by great labor and
constant manuring that fair crops can be produced. In
the populous districts, where the soil possesses some natural advantages, the farms are mostly small, averaging
from ten to seventy-five acres. A tract of forest is usually attached to these farming-lands, from which the peasants derive their supplies of lumber and fuel. Saw-mills
are numerous on all the rivers, and a large trade in lumber is carried on in the lake regions. The main lumber
region lies north of Stockholm, on the various small rivers emptying into the Gulf of Bothnia. Sundswall,
Umea, Lulea, and Haparanda are the principal places of
exportation on the eastern shore, and Gottenburg on the
west. The fisheries are also an important branch of industry, and large quantities of stromung and herrings are
exported. Salmon abound in the rivers, and the lakes
and mountain streams furnish a very fine quality of trout.
Game is more abundant in the densely wooded regions
of Sweden than in Norway, being less accessible to English sportsmen. Of late years Norway has become the
favorite hunting and fishing ground of the English, and
every summer they swarm all over the country with
their guns and fishing-rods. In Sweden, however, comparatively few have yet made their appearance. Bear,
elk, red deer, ptarmigan, and wild-fowl abound in the
forests and along the shores of the lakes. The Swedes
themselves are not so much given to this kind of recreation as the English. Their chief amusements consist in
Sunday afternoon recreations, such as theatrical repre-
sentations, dancing, singing, drinking, and carousing. In

their religious observances they are very strict, but after church they consider themselves privileged to enjoy a little dissipation in the Continental style. It too often happens that their frolics are carried to an excess. More brandy and other strong liquors are consumed in Sweden, according to the population, than in New Orleans or San Francisco, which is saying a good deal for the civilization of the people. Another good sign is that they chew tobacco. The better classes usually smoke this delightful weed, but the peasants both smoke it and chew it, showing conclusively that they are advancing rapidly toward emancipation from the narrow prejudices of European society. I saw drunken men and tobacco-chewers in Sweden who would have done credit to any little mining district in California. The habit of drinking is almost universal. The peasants drink to get drunk, the better classes drink for excitement, and all drink because they like it. At the principal restaurants in Stockholm and Gottenburg there is usually an anteroom opening into the main saloon. Here every gentleman who enters deposits his hat and cane. In the centre of the room stands a small table, upon which are several decanters containing "schnapps," a pile of brown bread sliced, various plates of biscuit and thin flour-cake, butter, and pickled fish. Around this the customers gather to acquire an appetite, which they accomplish by drinking one or two glasses of schnapps, eating a few small fish (stromung) spread upon their bread and butter, and then drinking some schnapps. They then go in to dinner, and call for what they want, including the various wines necessary for the process of digestion. Having eaten heartily and emptied a few bottles of wine, they wind up with coffee and cognac or maraschino. One would think such a process every day would burn the lining off the best stomach in the world; but the Swedes, like the Russians, have gutta-percha stomachs. The same system, it is true, prevails in San Francisco, only in a different form, and the same consequences generally ensue.

People are very apt to get up from the table with a rush of blood to the head, a general obliquity of vision, and a peculiar weakness in the knees. I tried it myself by way of experiment, and was sick of a headache for three days after. Somehow I can travel a long distance on foot without getting tired, but my stomach is not lined with sheet iron. I have seen women and children drink at a single sitting enough of intoxicating beverages, since my arrival in Europe, to have capsized me for a month. This, I think, will account for the prevalence of bloated bodies and red noses in these highly civilized countries.

I had read somewhere, before visiting Sweden, that the Swedes are not very sociable toward strangers. Perhaps in this respect they do not produce so favorable an impression as the Germans, but my experience has been such as to give me a very pleasant idea of their social qualities. It is true they are not so demonstrative in their manners as the French, or so enthusiastic as the Germans; but I found no difficulty in becoming acquainted with them, and was invariably treated with kindness and hospitality. When a Swede manifests an interest in your behalf, it is pretty certain that he feels it. If you become acquainted with one respectable family, you have a general entree into the entire social circle. No pains are spared to render your visit agreeable; and although the demonstrations of kindness are never intrusive, you feel that they are cordial and sincere. There may be among the more polished classes a certain degree of formality which to a stranger bears the appearance of reserve; but this quickly passes away, and the pleasure is all the greater in finding that there is really very little reserve about them. With all their adhesion to forms and ceremonies, they are simple and unaffected in their manners, and have a natural repugnance to whatever is meretricious. In a word, the Swedes are an honest, straightforward, sterling people, resembling more, in certain points of character, the English than any of their Continental neighbors, though I must do them the justice to say that they rarely have so unpleasant a way of manifesting their best traits. I can readily believe that the longer they are known the better they may be liked. It is true I saw nothing of Swedish society beyond what a casual tourist can see in passing rapidly through the country, yet that little impressed me very favorably, and disposes me to rely with confidence upon what I gathered from others who have enjoyed a more extended experience.

The home sketches of Fredrika Bremer give a more thorough insight of Swedish life and manners than perhaps those of any other writer. Of late years, however, Miss Bremer does not appear to have maintained her early popularity. She is said to have written some things which have given offense and provoked severe criticism, and I was surprised to hear her productions mentioned by several of her countrymen in somewhat disparaging terms. This was a source of disappointment to me, for I had supposed she was the most popular writer in Sweden; and I could not easily forget the pleasure I had derived from the perusal of "The H—— Family," "Nina," "The Professor," and other of her charming delineations of domestic life. As no man is a prophet in his own valley, I suppose the same may be said of women. To this, however, Jenny Lind is an exception.

But, as usual, I find myself steering out of the channel. We were now in the great Wenern Lake, a vast sheet of water fifty miles broad by one hundred in length. The elevation of this lake is 147 feet above the sea level. Its shores are densely wooded, and it abounds in islands, many of which are inhabited and cultivated. Several rivers of considerable size empty their waters into the Wenern, among which is the Klar, a large and rapid stream having its source in the mountains of Norway, at a distance of two hundred and fifty miles to the north. Fishing and lumbering are the principal occupations of the inhabitants living on the islands and shores. All these interior waters are frozen over in winter, and communication is carried on by means of sledges. The winters are very severe; and it is said that great numbers of wolves, driven from their usual haunts by starvation, prowl along the public highways during the winter months in search of prey. Traveling parties are sometimes attacked, and it is considered dangerous for children to go from one farm-house to another. The government, however, by a system of rewards for the destruction of these vicious animals, has succeeded of late years in greatly reducing their numbers.

In speaking of the severity of Swedish winters, it may be well to state that the cold is uniform, and consequently more easily endured than if the temperature were subject to sudden variations. There is, of course, considerable difference between the northern and southern parts of the country; but, taking the average or central parts, the winters may be considered as lasting about five months. During that period the snow covers the earth, and the lakes and rivers are frozen. At Stockholm the thermometer averages in summer about 70 degrees above, and in winter 20 degrees below zero, of Fahrenheit. At Gottenburg the summers are not quite so warm and the winters not so cold. The temperature of the Norwegian coast facing the Atlantic is less rigorous than that of the Swedish coast on the Baltic, arising from the influence of the Gulf Stream, and partly from the proximity of the open sea. Even at Wammerfest, which lies within the arctic circle, the winters are comparatively mild. At Bergen it rains over two hundred days in the year, and the fjords are seldom frozen over.

Passing along the eastern shore of the Wenern, we passed a series of rocky islands, well wooded till we reached the town of Wenersberg—an important dépôt for the commerce and products of the lake. At this place a brisk trade in iron and lumber is carried on during the summer months, and the wharves present quite a lively appearance, with their shipping, and piles of lumber and merchandise. The population of Wenersberg is about 2500; the houses are neat, and the general appearance of the town is thrifty. We stopped long enough to enjoy a ramble through the streets, and take a look at the inhabitants, after which our little steamer proceeded on her way through the Wassbottom Lake. At the end of this we entered the Carls Graf, or that portion of the canal built by Charles IX., to avoid the upper falls of the Gota River. The canal is here cut through solid masses of rock, and must have been a work of great difficulty and expense.

Late in the evening we arrived at the Falls of Trolhætta.

CHAPTER XXVII.

VOYAGE TO CHRISTIANIA.

I SHALL not stop to describe the Falls of Trolhætta. Better word-painters have so often pictured the beauties of this region that there is nothing left for an unimaginative tourist like myself.

A few hours' travel by the river steamer brought me to Gottenburg, where, for the first time since my arrival in Europe, I really began to enjoy life. Not that Gottenburg is a very lively or fascinating place, for it abounds in abominations and smells of fish, and is inhabited by a race of men whose chief aim in life appears to be directed toward pickled herring, mackerel, and codfish. There was much in it, however, to remind me of that homeland on the Pacific for which my troubled heart was pining. A grand fair was going on. All the peasants from the surrounding country were gathered in, and I met very few of them, at the close of evening, who were not reeling drunk. Besides, they chewed tobacco—an additional sign of civilization to which I had long been unaccustomed.

At Gottenburg, in the absence of something better to do, I made up my mind to visit Norway. The steamer

IN NORSELAND.

from Copenhagen touches on her way to Christiania. She has an unpleasant habit of waking people up in the middle of the night; and I was told that if I wanted to make sure of getting on board, I must sit up and watch for her. This is abominable in a mercantile community; but what can be expected of a people whose noblest aspirations are wrapped up in layers of dried codfish? By contract with the kellner at my hotel the difficulty was finally arranged. For the sum of two marks, Swedish currency, he agreed to notify me of the approach of the Copenhagen steamer. I thought he was doing all this solely on my account, but afterward discovered that he had made contracts at a quarter the price with about a dozen others.

It was very late in the night, or very early in the morning, when I was roused up, and duly put on board the steamer. Of the remainder of that night the least said the better. A cabinful of sea-sick passengers is not a pleasant subject of contemplation. When the light of day found its way into our dreary abode of misery, I went on deck. The weather was thick, and nothing was to be seen in any direction but a rough, chopping sea and flakes of drifting fog. A few doleful-looking tourists were searching for the land through their opera-glasses. They appeared to be sorry they ever undertook such a stormy and perilous voyage, and evidently had misgivings that they might never again see their native country. Some of them peeped over the bulwarks from time to time, with a faint hope, perhaps, of seeing something new in that direction; but from the singular noises they made, and the convulsive motions of their bodies, I had reason to suspect they were heaving some very heavy sighs at their forlorn fate. The waiters were continually running about with cups of coffee, which served to fortify the stomachs of these hardy adventurers against sea-sickness. I may here mention as a curious fact that in all my travels I have rarely met a sea-going gentleman who could be induced to acknowledge that he suffered the least inconvenience from the motion of the vessel. A headache, a fit of indigestion, the remains of a recent attack of gout, a long-standing rheumatism, a bilious colic to which he had been subject for years, a sudden and unaccountable shock of vertigo, a disorganized condition of the liver—something, in short, entirely foreign to the known and recognized laws of motion, disturbed his equilibrium, but rarely an out-and-out case of sea-sickness. That is a weakness of human nature fortunately confined to the ladies. Indeed, I don't know what the gentler sex would do if it were not for the kindness of Providence in exempting the ruder portion of humanity from this unpleasant accompaniment of sea-life, only it unfortunately happens that the gentlemen are usually afflicted with some other dire and disabling visitation about the same time.

Toward noon the fog broke away, and we sighted the rocky headlands of the Christiania Fjord. In a few hours more we were steaming our way into this magnificent sheet of water at a dashing rate, and the decks were crowded with a gay and happy company. No more the pangs of despised love, indigestion, gout, and bilious colic disturbed the gentlemen of this lively party; no more the fair ladies of Hamburg and Copenhagen hid themselves away in their state-rooms, and called in vain to their natural protectors for assistance. The sea was smooth; the sun shot forth through the whirling rain-clouds his brightest August beams. All along the shores of the Fjord, the rocky points, jutting abruptly from the water, rose like embattled towers, crowned with a variegated covering of moss, grim and hoary with the wild winds and scathing winters of the North. Beautiful little valleys, ravines, and slopes of woodland of such rich and glittering green opened out to us on either side, as we swept past the headlands, that the vision was dazzled with the profusion and variety of the charms bestowed upon this wilderness of romantic scenery. A group of fishermen's huts, behind a bold and

THE STEAMER ENTERING THE FJORD.

jagged point of rocks—a rude lugger or fishing-smack, manned by a hardy crew of Norskmen, rough and weather-beaten as the ocean monsters of their stormy coast, gliding out of some nook among the rocky inlets —here the cozy little cottage of some well-to-do sea-captain, half fisher, half farmer, with a gang of white-headed little urchins running out over the cliffs to take a peep at the passing steamer, the frugal matron standing in the door resplendent in her red woolen petticoat and fanciful head-dress, knitting a pair of stockings, or some such token of love, for her absent lord—there, a pretty little village, with a church, a wharf, and a few store-houses, shrinking back behind the protecting wing of some huge and rugged citadel of rocks, the white cottages glittering pleasantly in the rays of the evening sun, and the smoke curling up peacefully over the surrounding foliage, and floating off till it vanished in the rich glow of the sky—all so calm, so dreamy in colors and outline that the imagination is absolutely bewildered with the varied feast of beauties: such are the characteristic features of this noble sheet of water.

The Christiania Fjord is one of the largest in Norway. Commencing at Frederickstadt on the one side and Sandesund on the other, it extends into the interior a distance of seventy or eighty miles, making one of the finest natural harbors in the world. The water is deep, and the shores are almost rock-bound. In many places the navigation is somewhat intricate, owing to the numerous rocky islands and rugged headlands; but the Norwegian pilots are thoroughly experienced in their business, and know every foot of the way as familiarly as they know their own snug little cabins perched up among the rocks.

Touching at the picturesque little town of Horten on the left, we discharged some passengers and took in others, after which we proceeded without farther incident to the town of Drobak on the right. Here the Fjord is narrow, presenting something the appearance of a river. A group of fortifications on the cliffs pro-

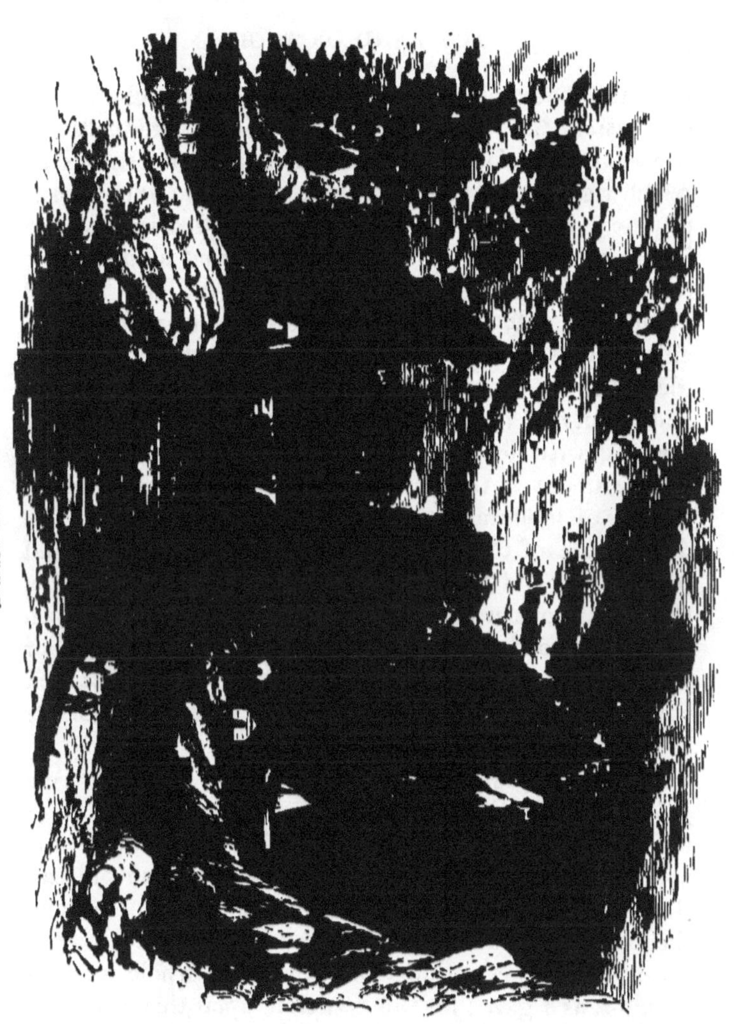

N 2

tects this passage. The view on leaving Drobak is inexpressibly beautiful. The Fjord widens gradually till it assumes the form of an immense lake, the shores of which rise abruptly from the water, covered with forests of pine. Moss-covered rocks, green wooded islands, and innumerable fishing-craft, give variety and animation to the scene. Range upon range of wild and rugged mountains extend back through the dim distance on either side till their vague and fanciful outlines are mingled with the clouds. Nothing can exceed the richness and beauty of the atmospheric tints. A golden glow, mingled with deep shades of purple, illuminates the sky. In the distance the snowy peaks of the vast interior ranges of mountains glisten in the evening sun. The deep green of the foliage which decks the islands and promontories of the Fjord casts its reflected hues upon the surface of the sleeping waters. In the valleys, which from time to time open out as we sweep along on our way, rich yellow fields of grain make a brilliant and striking contrast to the sombre tints of the pine forests in the rear.

It was long after sunset, but still light enough to enjoy all the beauties of the Fjord, when we saw before us the numerous and picturesque villas that adorn the neighborhood of Christiania. Passing the fine old castle of Aggershuus on the left, we rounded a point, and then came in full view of the town and harbor.

Surely there is nothing like this in the whole world, I thought, as I gazed for the first time upon this charming scene. The strange oldfashioned buildings, the castle, the palace on the hill-top, the shipping at the wharves, the gardens on every slope, the varied outlines of the neighboring cliffs and hills, covered with groves and green slopes of rich sward; every nook glimmering with beautiful villas; the whole reflected in the glowing waters that sweep through the maze of islands and headlands in every direction; can there be any thing more beautiful in all the world?

THE ISLANDS.

The steamer was soon hauled alongside the wharf, where a crowd of citizens was gathered to see us land. Here again was a scene characteristic of Norway. No hurry, no confusion, no shouting and clamoring for passengers, but all quiet, primitive, and good-humored. How different from a landing at New York or San Francisco! Three or four sturdy hack-drivers stood smoking their pipes, watching the proceedings with an air of philosophical indifference truly refreshing. Fathers, mothers, sisters, brothers, and cousins of various parties on board, waved their handkerchiefs and nodded affectionately to their friends and relatives, but kept their enthusiasm within limits till the plank was put out, when they came on board, and kissed and hugged every body of their acquaintance in the most affectionate manner. The officers of the customs, good easy souls! also came on board, books in hand, and made a kind of examination of the baggage. It was neither severe nor formal, and I felt an absolute friendship for the chief officer on account of the jolly manner in which he looked at me, and asked me if I had any thing contraband in my little knapsack. I offered to open it, but with a wave of his hand he chalked a pass upon it and I walked ashore. For the first time in my life I here felt the inconvenience of not being persecuted by porters and hack-drivers. The few who were on hand seemed to be particular friends or relatives of parties on board, and were already engaged. I walked up the queer, grass-grown old streets, looking around in the dim twilight for a hotel; and after stumbling into half a dozen odd-looking shops and store-houses, contrived to make my way to the Hotel Victoria, said to be the best in Christiania.

As it is no part of my purpose to write a book on Christiania, I shall only say that for the next three days I rambled about enjoying all the objects of interest in this quaint northern city—the churches, the museum, the castle, the palace, the ups and downs of the streets, the market-places, wharves, and gardens, and the magic beauties of the neighborhood. There is a plainness and simplicity about the people of Christiania, a good-humor of expression, a kindliness of manner and natural politeness that impressed me very favorably. The society is said to be genial and cultivated. I have no doubt of the fact, though my stay was too short to afford an opportunity of making many acquaintances.

At the Hotel Victoria I met Ole Bull, who was on a tour through his native land. He sat near me at the *table d'hôte*, and I had an opportunity of noticing the changes which time has made in his appearance. The last time I had seen him was in Columbus, Ohio, in 1844. He was then in the very prime of life, slender and graceful, yet broad of shoulder and powerful of limb; with light straight hair, clear blue eyes, and a healthy Northern complexion. He is now quite altered, and I am not sure that I would have recognized him had he not been pointed out to me. In form he is much stouter, though not so erect as he was in former years. His hair is sprinkled with gray. He retains the same noble cast of features, and deep, dreamy, and genial expression of eye as of old, but his complexion is sallow, and his face is marked by lines of care. There is something sad and touching in his manner. I do not know what his misfortunes in America may have to do with his present dejected expression, but he seems to me to be a man who has met with great disappointments in life. Although I sat beside him at the table, and might have claimed acquaintance as one of his most ardent American admirers, I was deterred from speaking to him by something peculiar in his manner—not coldness, for that is not in his nature—but an apparent withdrawal from the outer world into himself. A feeling that it might be intrusive to address him kept me silent. I afterward sent him a few lines, expressing a desire to renew my early acquaintance with him; but he left town while I was absent on an excursion to the Frogner-assen, and, much to my regret, I missed seeing him.

CHAPTER XXVIII.
FROM CHRISTIANIA TO LILLEHAMMER.

The population of Christiania is something over 40,000, and of late years it has become quite a place of resort for tourists on the way to the interior of Norway. The houses built since the fire of 1858, which destroyed a considerable portion of the town, are large and substantial, built of stone and covered with cement. The streets for the most part are broad and roughly paved. Very little of characteristic style is observable in the costume of the citizens. Plainness of dress, simple and primitive manners, and good nature, are the leading traits of the Norwegians. Christiania is the modern capital of Norway, and was founded by Christian IV. of Denmark, near the site of the ancient capital of Osloe, which was founded in 1058 by King Harold Hardraade. Some of the old buildings still remain in a state of good preservation; but the chief interest of the city consists in its castle, university, library, and museum of Northern antiquities. A traveler from the busy cities of America is struck with the quiet aspect of the streets, and the almost death-like silence that reigns in them after dark. In many places the sidewalks are overgrown with grass, and the houses are green with moss. Stagnation broods in the very atmosphere. Christiania is in all respects the antipodes of San Francisco. A Californian could scarcely endure an existence in such a place for six weeks. He would go stark mad from sheer inanity. Beautiful as the scenery is, and pleasantly as the time passed during my brief sojourn, it was not without a feeling of relief that I took my departure in the cars for Eidsvold.

The railway from Christiania to Eidsvold is the only

APPROACH TO CHRISTIANIA.

one yet in operation in Norway. It was a pretty heavy
undertaking, considering the rough country and the limited resources of the people; but it was finally completed, and is now considered a great feature in Norwegian civilization. Some idea may be formed of the back-
wardness of facilities for internal communication throughout this country when I mention the fact that beyond
the distance of forty miles to Eidsvold and the Lake of
Miösen, the traveler is dependent upon such vehicles as
he takes with him, unless he chooses to incur the risk of
procuring a conveyance at Hamar or Lillehammer. The
whole country is a series of rugged mountains, narrow
valleys, desolate fjelds, rivers, and fjords. There are no
regular communications between one point and another
on any of the public highways, and the interior districts
are supplied with such commodities as they require from
the sea-board solely by means of heavy wagons, sledges,
boats, and such other primitive modes of transportation
as the nature of the country and the season may render
most available.

Like every thing else in Norway, the cars on the Eidsvold railway have rather more of a rustic than a metro-
politan appearance. They are extremely simple in construction and rural in decoration; and as for the road,
it may be very good compared with a trail over the Sierra Nevada Mountains, but it is absolutely frightful
to travel over it by steam. Three hours is the allowance of time for forty miles. If I remember correctly,
we stretched it out to four, on account of a necessary
stoppage on the way, caused by the tumbling down of
some rocks from an overhanging cliff. The jolting is
enough to dislocate one's vertebræ; and I had a vague
feeling all the time during the trip that the locomotive
would jump off the track, and dash her brains out against
some of the terrible boulders of granite that stood frowning at us on either side as we worried our way along
from station to station.

It was nearly dark when we came to a saw-mill by the

roadside. The scenery is pretty all the way from Christiania, but not very striking till the train passes the narrow gorge in which the saw-mill is situated, where there is a tunnel of a few hundred feet that penetrates a bluff on the left. Emerging from this, we are close upon the charming little village of Eidsvold, one of the loveliest spots in this land of beauty. A few minutes more brought us to the station-house, where the railway ends. Here we found ourselves at a good hotel, picturesquely situated on the bank of the Wormen, a river flowing from the Miösen Lake.

At eleven o'clock on a fine Sunday forenoon I took my departure from Eidsvold on board one of the little lake steamers. These vessels are well managed, and not inconveniently arranged, but they are so very small that on particular occasions, when there is an unusual pressure of travelers, it is difficult to find room for a seat. Owing to the facilities afforded by the railway from Christiania, an excursion to Lillehammer is the most popular way of passing a Sunday during the summer months, and this being the height of the season, the crowd was unusually great. It also happened that two hundred soldiers, who had served out their time, were returning to their homes in the interior, so that there was no lack of company on board. If the soldiers were somewhat lively and frolicsome, it was nothing more than natural under the circumstances. A good many were intoxicated—at the idea, perhaps, of getting home once more, and their songs and merry shouts of laughter kept every body in a good humor. I am unable to account for a curious fact, which I may as well mention in this connection. Whenever the authorities of any country through which I chance to travel have occasion to send their troops from one point to another, they invariably send them upon the same boat or in the same railway train upon which I have the fortune to take passage. There must be something military in my appearance, or some natural propensity for bloodshed in my nature, that causes this affinity to exist between us, for it has happened altogether too often to be accidental. The King of Sicily, some years ago, sent a party of troops to keep me company to Palermo. Subsequently the King of Greece favored me with a large military convoy to one of the Greek islands. After that I had an independent supervision of various bodies of Turkish soldiers on board of different vessels within the Turkish dominions. Recently Napoleon III. sent down by the same train of cars, from Paris to Marseilles, about four hundred of his troops for Algiers. Being detained at Marseilles by some unforeseen circumstance, I had the pleasure of seeing these men shipped off on the first steamer. I took passage in the next. By some extraordinary fatality, for which there is no accounting, there were upward of five hundred additional troops shipped on this vessel. It was a consolation to know that a storm was brewing, and that they would soon be all seasick. Before we got out of the Gulf of Lyons I could have slain every man of them with a pocket-knife. It was therefore with a spirit of resignation that I saw the Norwegian soldiers come on board at Eidsvold. Fate had ordained that we should travel together, and it was no use to complain. Besides, I liked their looks. As stalwart, blue-eyed, jovial, and hearty-looking a set of fellows they were as ever I saw in any country—men of far higher intelligence and physical capacity than the average of soldiers in Continental Europe. That these were the right sort of men to fight for their country there could be no doubt. I have rarely seen finer troops any where than those of Norway.

The Miösen Lake is sixty-three miles in length, extending from Minde to Lillehammer, and varies in width from five to ten miles. The broadest part is opposite to Hamar, nearly at the centre, and not far from the island of Helgeö. The shores embrace some of the finest farming lands in Norway; and after passing Minde, the sloping hill-sides are dotted with pretty little farm-houses, and beautifully variegated with fields and orchards. In many places, so numerous are the cottages of the thrifty farmers hung in this favored region, that they resemble a continuous village, extending for many miles along the hill-sides. There is not much in the natural aspect of the country to attract the lover of bold mountain scenery. The beauties of the shores of Miösen are of a gentle and pastoral character, and become monotonous after a few hours. Near Hamar, on the right, there are the ruins of an old cathedral, burned and plundered by the Swedes in 1567.

Apart from the ordinary interest of the Miösen Lake, arising from the quiet, pastoral character of its shores, it possessed a peculiar charm to me, owing to the fact that, in 1755, when the great earthquake occurred at Lisbon, its waters rose twenty feet, and suddenly retreated. Only a few months previously I had visited the city of Lisbon, and stood upon the very spot where, in six minutes, over sixty thousand souls had been buried beneath the ruins. I was now, so to speak, following up an earthquake.

It was late at night when we arrived at the pretty little town of Lillehammer, at the head of the lake. Leaving the steamer here, I found myself, for the first time, beyond the limits of the English language. A Norwegian with whom I had become acquainted on board the boat was kind enough to walk up town with me and show me the way to the post station, where I had some difficulty in procuring accommodations, owing to the number of recent arrivals.

The town of Lillehammer contains twelve or fifteen hundred inhabitants, whose principal industry consists in the lumber business. Immense rafts are towed down the lake every day by the returning steamers, and carried by rail from Eidsvold to Christiania. The logs are drifted down the Logen River from the interior, and cut up at Lillehammer and Eidsvold. Such as are designed for spars are dressed and shipped at the latter place. There are many other points on the lake from which supplies of timber are also transferred to Christiania, so that, between farming, fishing, and lumbering, the inhabitants of this region make out a very comfortable subsistence, and generally own the lands upon which they reside. Many of them are wealthy—for this part of the world.

Lillehammer is prettily situated on an eminence, and consists of log and frame houses, presenting much the appearance of a Western lake village in the United States. The view of the Miösen and its verdant shores is very fine from the top of the hill. It was ten o'clock at night when I arrived, although the sky was still lighted up with a purple glow from the departed sun. Something of the wonderful scenic beauties of the country were still visible. A party of French tourists, who had come to Norway to make a three days' visit, set off at this late hour to see the torrent which breaks from the side of the mountain, about half a mile beyond the town. I was solicited to join them; but my passion for sight-seeing was rather obscured by the passion of hunger and thirst. At such times I am practical enough to prefer a good supper to the best waterfall in the world. Waterfalls can be postponed. Hunger must be promptly satisfied. Thirst makes one dry. A distant view of falling water is a poor substitute for a glass of good ale. There is no fear that any ordinary cataract will run itself out before morning.

This was my first experience of a post station, and very pleasant I found it. The inns of Norway are plain, cheap, and comfortable; not very elegant in appearance, but as good in all respects as a plain traveler could desire. I had a capital supper at Lillehammer, consisting of beef-steak, eggs, bread, butter, and coffee—enough to satisfy any reasonable man. The rooms are clean, the beds and bedding neat and comfortable, and the charge for supper, lodging, and breakfast not exceeding an average of about fifty cents. At some of the interior stations I was charged only about twenty-five cents, and in no instance was I imposed upon. The innkeepers are so generally

obliging and good-natured that there is very little difficulty in getting along with them. A few words always
sufficed to make my wants understood, and the greatest
kindness and alacrity were invariably shown in supply-
ing them. But I anticipate my journey.

After a pleasant night's rest I arose bright and early;
and here, being for the first time thrown completely upon
my own resources in the way of language, was obliged
to have recourse to my vocabulary to get at the means
of asking for breakfast and a horse and cariole. Fancy
a lean and hungry man standing before a substantial
landlord, trying to spell out a breakfast from his book in
some such way as this:

"Jeg vil Spise [I will eat]!"

"Ya, min Herr!" the landlord politely answers.

"Jeg vil Frokost [I will breakfast]!"

"Ya, min Herr;" and the landlord runs off into a perfect labyrinth of birds, fish, eggs, beefsteak, hot cakes,
and other luxuries, which the inexperienced traveler is
vainly attempting to follow up in his book. In despair,
he at length calls out,

"Ja! Ja!—that's all right! any thing you say, my fine
old gentleman!"

At which the landlord scratches his head, for he doesn't
understand precisely what you have selected. Now you
take your book, and explain slowly and systematically:

"Kaffee!"

"Ja."

"Œgg!"

"Ja."

"Fisk!"

"Ja."

"Smör og Brod!"

Here the landlord is staggered, and scratches his head
again. *Smör* he gets a glimmering of, but the bread
stuns him. You try it in a dozen different ways—broad,
breyd, breed, brode, braid. At length a light flashes upon
his mind. You want bread! Simple as the word is, and

though he pronounces it precisely according to one of your own methods, as you suppose, it is difficult to get the peculiar intonation that renders it intelligible.

"Ja!" And thus you lay the foundation of your breakfast; after which, having progressed so far in the language, there is no great difficulty in asking for a "Heste og Cariole" [a horse and cariole].

A little practice in this way soon enables the traveler to acquire a sufficient knowledge of the language for the ordinary purposes of communication along the road. With a smattering of the German it comes very readily to one who speaks English, being something of a mixture between these two languages. I was really astonished to find how well I could understand it, and make myself understood, in the course of a few days, though candor obliges me to say that if there is any one thing in the world for which nature never intended me it is a linguist.

I was in hopes of finding at Lillehammer a party of tourists bound over the Dovre Fjeld to Trondhjem, of whom I had heard in Christiania. In this I was disappointed. They had started a few days previously. An omnibus was advertised to run as far as Elstad, some thirty-five miles up the valley of Gudbransdalen, which would be so much gained on my route. It seemed, however, that it only ran whenever a sufficient number of passengers offered—so I was obliged to give up that prospect.

CHAPTER XXIX.

HOW THEY TRAVEL IN NORWAY.

NOTHING can be more characteristic of Norwegian seclusion from the world than the rude means of inland communication between the principal cities. Here was a public highway between two of the most important sea-ports in the country—Christiania and Trondhjem—without as much as a stage to carry passengers. Every traveler has to depend upon his own vehicle, or upon such rude and casual modes of conveyance as he can find at the stations by the wayside. I asked the reason of this backward state of things, and was informed that the amount of travel is insufficient to support any regular stage line. The season for tourists lasts only about three months, and during the remainder of the year very few strangers have occasion to pass over the roads. In winter—which, of course, lasts very long in this latitude—the whole country is covered with snow, and sledges are altogether used, both for purposes of traveling and the transportation of merchandise from the sea-board. The products of the country—such as logs, spars, and boards—are prepared during these months for rafting down the rivers during the spring floods. Once, as I was told, an enterprising Englishman had started a regular stage-line from Christiania to Trondhjem, in consequence of the repeated complaints of the traveling public, who objected to the delays to which they were subject; but he was soon obliged to discontinue it for want of patronage. When travelers had a convenient way of getting over, they grumbled at being hurried through, and preferred taking the usual conveyances of the country, which afforded them an opportunity of enjoying the scenery and stopping wherever they pleased. People did not come all the way to Norway, they said, to fly through it without seeing any of its wonders and beauties. There was some philosophy in this, as well as a touch of human nature. It reminded me of the Frenchman in Paris who lived to be eighty years of age without ever leaving the city; when the king, for the sake of experiment, positively forbid him from doing so during the remainder of his life. The poor fellow was immediately seized with an inordinate desire to see something of the outside world, and petitioned so hard for the privilege of leaving the city that the king, unable to resist his importunities, granted him the privilege, after which the man was perfectly satisfied, and remained in Paris to the day of his death.

By reference to a copy of the laws on the subject of post-travel, which I had procured in Christiania from a Mr. Bennett, I discovered that the system is singularly complicated and hazardous, as well as a little curious in some of its details. The stations are situated along the road about every eight or ten miles (counted in Norwegian by so many hours). Nothing that we could call a village is to be seen in any part of the interior, unless the few straggling farm-houses occasionally huddled together, with a church in the centre, may be considered in that light. The stations usually stand alone, in some isolated spot on the wayside, and consist of a little log or frame tavern, a long shambling stable, innumerable odds and· ends of cribs, store-houses, and outbuildings, forming a kind of court or stable-yard; a rickety medley of old carts and carioles lying about basking in the sun; a number of old white-headed men smoking their pipes, and leathery-faced women on household duties intent, with a score or so of little cotton-headed children running about over the manure pile in the neighborhood of the barn, to keep the pigs company; here and there a strapping lout of a boy swinging on a gate and whistling for his own amusement; while cows, sheep, goats, chickens, and other domestic animals and birds browse, nibble, and peck all over the yard in such a lazy and rural manner as would delight an artist. This is the ordinary Norwegian station.

There is always a good room for the traveler, and plenty of excellent homely fare to eat. At some few places along the route the station-houses aspire to the style and dignity of hotels, but they are not always the best or most comfortable. Then there are "fast" and "slow" stations—so called in the book of laws. At the fast stations the traveler can procure a horse and cariole without delay—fifteen minutes being the legal limit. At the slow stations he must wait till the neighborhood, for a distance of three or four miles perhaps, is searched for a horse—sometimes for both horse and cariole. If

O

he chooses to incur the expense he can send forward a *Forbad*, or notice in advance, requiring horses to be ready at each station at a specified time; but if he is not there according to notice, he must pay so much per hour for the delay. A day-book is kept at each of these post-houses, in which the traveler must enter his name, stating the time of his arrival and departure, where he came from, his destination, how many horses he requires, etc. In this formidable book he may also specify any complaint he has to make against the station-holder, boy, horse, cariole, or any body, animal, or thing that maltreats him, cheats him, or in any way misuses him on the journey; but he must take care to have the inn-keeper or some such disinterested person as a witness in his behalf, so that when the matter comes before the Amtmand, or grand tribunal of justice, it may be fairly considered and disposed of according to law. When the inn-keeper, station-holder, posting-master, alderman, or other proper functionary on the premises, fails to present this book and require the traveler to sign his name in it, he (the arrant violator of laws) is fined; but the traveler need not flatter himself that the rule does not work both ways, for he also is fined if he refuses or intentionally neglects to write his name in the said book. The number of horses to be kept at fast stations is fixed by law, and no traveler is to be detained more than a quarter of an hour, unless in certain cases, when he may be detained half an hour. At a slow station he must not be detained over three hours—such is the utmost stretch of the law. Think of that, ye Gothamites, who complain if you are detained any where on the face of the earth three min-utes—only detained three hours every eight or ten miles! But for delay occasioned by any insuperable impediment, says the Norwegian law-book—such as a storm at sea, or too great a distance between the inns—no liability is incurred on either side. A Philadelphia lawyer could drive six-and-thirty coaches-and-four, all abreast, through such a law as that, and then leave room enough for a

Stockton wagon and mule-team on each side. Who is to judge of the weather or the distance between the inns? When the traveler holds the reins he is responsible for the horse, but when the post-boy does the holding, he, the said boy, is the responsible party. Should any post-horse be ill treated or overdriven when the traveler holds the reins, so that, in the language of the law, "the station-holder, inn-keeper, or two men at the next station can perceive this to be the case, the traveler shall pay for the injury according to the estimation of these men, and he shall not be allowed to be sent on until the payment is made." The traveler pays all tolls and ferry charges. "When the road is very hilly, or is in out-of-the-way districts where there are but few horses in proportion to the travel, and the distance between the stations is unusually long, or under other circumstances where the burden on the people obligated to find horses is evidently very oppressive, etc.," "it may be ordered by the king, after a declaration to that effect has been procured by the authorities, that payment for posting may be reckoned according to a greater distance, in proportion to the circumstances, as far as double the actual distance."

In addition to all these formidable regulations—against which it seems to me it would be impossible for any ordinary man to contend—the tariff fixes the price of posting for fast and slow stations in the country, the only difficulty being to find where the towns are after you get into them, or to know at what stage of the journey you leave them. The Amtmand, by letter to all the authorities, likewise requires the tariff to be hung conspicuously in all the inns; which tariff, says the law, "is altered according to the rise and fall of provisions."

When I came to study out all this, and consider the duties and obligations imposed on me as a traveler going a journey of three or four hundred miles; that I was to be subject to contingencies and liabilities depending upon the elements both by land and sea; that serious responsibilities fell upon me if I held the reins of the post-horse, and probably heavy risks of life and limb if the post-boy held them; that the inn-keeper, station-holder, alderman, or two men chosen miscellaneously from the ranks of society, were to judge of damages that might be inflicted upon the horse; that I must register my name in a day-book, and enter formal complaints against the authorities on the way about every ten miles; that the tariff might rise and fall five hundred times during the journey, for aught I knew, according to the rise and fall of provisions or the pleasure of the Amtmand; that conspiracies might be entered into against me to make me pay for all the lame, halt, blind, and spavined horses in the country, and my liberty restrained in some desolate region of the mountains; that I could not speak a dozen words of the language, and had no other means of personal defense against imposition than a small pen-knife and the natural ferocity of my countenance—when all these considerations occurred to me, I confess they made me hesitate a little before launching out from Lillehammer.

However, the landlord of the post, a jolly and good-natured old gentleman, relieved my apprehensions by providing such a breakfast of coffee, eggs, beefsteak, fish, and bread, that my sunken spirits were soon thoroughly aroused, and I felt equal to any emergency. When I looked out on the bright hill-sides, and saw the sun glistening on the dewy sod, and heard the post-boys in the yard whistling merrily to the horses, I was prepared to face the great Amtmand itself. In a little while the horse and cariole designed for my use were brought up before the door, and the landlord informed me that all was "*fertig.*"

Now, was there ever such a vehicle for a full-grown man to travel in? A little thing, with a body like the end of a canoe, perched up on two long shafts, with a pair of wheels in the rear; no springs, and only a few straps of leather for a harness; a board behind for the skydskaarl, or post-boy, to sit upon; and a horse not bigger than a large mountain goat to drag me over the road! It was positively absurd. After enjoying the spectacle for a moment, and making a hurried sketch of it, wondering what manner of man had first contrived such a vehicle, I bounced in, and stretched my legs out on each side, bracing my feet against a pair of iron catches, made expressly for that purpose. Fortunately, I am a capital driver. If nature ever intended me for any one profession above all others, it must have been for a stage-driver. I have driven buggies, wagons, and carts in California hundreds of miles, and never yet killed any body. Like the Irishman, I can drive within two inches of a precipice without going over. Usually, however, I let the horse take his own way, which, after all, is the grand secret of skillful driving.

My baggage consisted of a knapsack containing two shirts and an extra pair of stockings, a sketch-book and some pencils, and such other trifling knick-knacks as a tourist usually requires in this country. I carried no more outside clothing than what common decency required: a rough hunting-coat, a pair of stout cloth pantaloons, and an old pair of boots—which is as much as any traveler needs on a Norwegian tour, though it is highly recommended by an English writer that every traveler should provide himself with two suits of clothes, a Mackintosh, a portable desk, an India-rubber pillow, a few blankets, an opera-glass, a musquito-net, a thermometer, some dried beef, and a dozen boxes of sardines, besides a stock of white bread, and two bottles of English pickles.

CHAPTER XXX.

A NORWEGIAN GIRL.

With a crack of the whip that must have astonished the landlord, and caused him some misgivings for the fate of his horse and cariole, I took my departure from

Lillehammer.   About half a mile beyond the town we (the skydskaarl, myself, horse, and cariole) passed the falls—a roaring torrent of water tumbling down from the mountain side on the right.   Several extensive saw-mills are located at this point.   The piles of lumber outside, and the familiar sounds of the saws and wheels, reminded me of home.   The scene was pretty and picturesque, but rather disfigured by the progress of Norwegian civilization.   Passing numerous thriving farms in the full season of harvest, the road winding pleasantly along the hill-side to the right, the foaming waters of the Logen deep down in the valley to the left, we at length reached the entrance of the Gudbransdalen—that beautiful and fertile valley, which stretches all the way up the course of the Logen to the Dovre Fjeld, a distance of a hundred and sixty-eight miles from Lillehammer.   It would be an endless task to undertake a' description of the beauties of this valley.   From station to station it is a continued panorama of dashing waterfalls, towering mountains, green slopes, pine forests overtopping the cliffs, rich and thriving farms, with innumerable log cottages perched up among the cliffs, and wild and rugged defiles through which the road passes, sometimes overhung by shrubbery for miles at a stretch.   Flying along the smoothly-graded highway at a rapid rate; independent of all the world except your horse and boy; the bright sunshine glimmering through the trees; the music of the wild waters falling pleasantly on your ear; each turn of the road opening out something rich, new, and strange; the fresh mountain air invigorating every fibre of your frame; renewed youth and health beginning to glow upon your cheeks; digestion performing its functions without a pang or a hint of remonstrance; kind, genial, open-hearted people wherever you stop—is it not an episode in life worth enjoying?   The valley of the Logen must surely be a paradise (in summer) for invalids.

. At each station the traveler is furnished with a stunted little boy called the skydskaarl, usually clothed in the cast-off rags of his great-grandfather; his head ornamented by a flaming red night-cap, and his feet either bare or the next thing to it; his hair standing out in every direction like a mop dyed in whitewash and yellow ochre, and his face and hands freckled and sunburned, and not very clean, while his manners are any thing but cultivated. This remarkable boy sits on a board behind the cariole, and drives it back to the station from which it starts. He is regarded somewhat in the light of a high public functionary by his contemporary ragamuffins, having been promoted from the fields or the barn-yard to the honorable position of skydskaarl. His countenance is marked by the lines of premature care and responsibility, but varies in expression according to circumstances. The sum of four cents at the end of an hour's journey gives it an extremely amiable and intelligent cast. Some boys are constitutionally knowing, and have a quick, sharp look; others again are dull and stolid, as naturally happens wherever there is a variety of boys born of different parents. For the most part, they are exceedingly bright and lively little fellows. Mounted on their seat of honor at the back of the cariole, they greatly enliven the way by whistling and singing, and asking questions in their native tongue, which it is sometimes very difficult to answer when one is not familiar with the language.

I had at Moshuus a communicative little boy, who talked to me incessantly all the way to Holmen without ever discovering, so far as I could perceive, that I did not understand a single word he said. Another, after repeated efforts to draw me out, fell into a fit of moody silence, and from that into a profound slumber, which was only broken off toward the end of our journey by an accident. The cariole struck against a stone and tilted him out on the road. He was a good deal surprised, but said nothing.

Another little fellow, not more than six or seven years of age—a pretty fair-haired child—was sent with me over a very wild and broken stage of the journey. He was newly dressed in a suit of gray frieze with brass buttons, and was evidently a shining light at home. On the road a dog ran out from the bushes and barked at us. The poor little skydskaarl was frantic with terror, and cried so lustily that I had to take him into the cariole, and put him under my legs to keep him from going into fits. He bellowed all the way to the next station, where I endeavored to make the inn-keeper understand that it was cruel to send so small a boy on such a hazardous journey. The man laughed and said "Ja! he is too little!" which was all I could get out of him. I felt unhappy about this poor child all day.

On another occasion I had a bright, lively little fellow about twelve years of age, who was so pleased to find that I was an American that he stopped every body on the road to tell them this important piece of news, so that it took me about three hours to go a distance of seven or eight miles. There was a light of intelligence in the boy's face that enabled me to comprehend him almost by instinct, and the quickness with which he caught at my half-formed words, and gathered my meaning when I told him of the wonders of California, were really surprising. This boy was a natural genius. He will leave his mountain home some day or other and make a leading citizen of the United States. Already he was eager to dash out upon the world and see some of its novelties and wonders.

At Laurgaard I was favored with a small urchin who must have been modeled upon one of Hogarth's pictures. He was a fixed laugh all over. His mouth, nose, ears, eyes, hair, and chin were all turned up in a broad grin. Even the elbows of his coat and the knees of his trowsers were wide open with ill-concealed laughter. He laughed when he saw me, and laughed more than ever when he heard me "*tale Norsk*." There was something uncommonly amusing to this little shaver in the cut of a man's jib who could not speak good Norwegian. All the way up the hill he whistled, sang lively snatches of song, joked with the horse, and when the horse nickered laughed a young horse-laugh to keep him company. It did me good to see the rascal so cheery. I gave him an extra

STATION-BOY.

shilling at Braendhangen for his lively spirit, at which he grinned all over wider than ever, put the small change in his pocket, and with his red night-cap in one hand made a dodge of his head at me, as if snapping at a fly, and then held out his spare hand to give me a shake. Of course I shook hands with him.

Shaking hands with small boys, however, is nothing uncommon in Norway. Every boy on the entire route shook hands with me. Whenever I settled the fare the skydskaarl invariably pulled off his cap, or, if he had none, gave a pull at the most prominent bunch of hair,

GOOD-BY—MANY THANKS!

and holding forth a flipper, more or less like a lump of raw beef, required me, by all the laws of politeness, to give it a shake. The simplicity with which they did this, and the awkward kindliness of their manner, as they wished me a pleasant trip, always formed an agreeable episode in the day's travel. I have shaken a greater variety of boys' hands in Norway—of every size, kind, and quality, fat, lean, clean, and dirty, dry and wet—than ever I shook all over the world before. Notwithstanding the amount of water in the country, I must have carried away from Trondhjem about a quarter of a pound of the native soil. Between the contortions of body and limb acquired by a brief residence in Paris, the battering out of several hats against my knee in the process of bowing throughout the cities of Germany, and the shaking of various boys' hands on my trip through Norway, I consider that my politeness now qualifies me for any society.

It must not be understood, however, that I was always favored with the society of little boys. At one of the stations, which, for obvious reasons, it would be indiscreet to name, there was no boy visible except the ragamuffin who had accompanied me. He, of course, was obliged to return with the horse and cariole. Three white-headed old men were sitting on a log near the stable basking in the sun, and gossiping pleasantly about by-gone times or the affairs of state, I could not understand which. Each of these venerable worthies wore a red night-cap, which in this country answers likewise for a day-cap, and smoked a massive wooden pipe. It was a very pleasant picture of rural content. As I approached they nodded a smiling "*God Aften!*" and rose to unharness the horse. An elderly lady, of very neat appearance and pleasing expression, came to the door and bade me a kindly welcome. Then the three old men all began to talk to me together, and when they said what they had to say about the fine weather, and the road, and the quality of the horse, and whatever else came into

NORWEGIAN PEASANT FAMILY.

their antiquated heads, they led the horse off to the stable and proceeded to get me a fresh one. While they were doing that the elderly lady went back into the house and called aloud for some person within. Presently a fine buxom young girl, about seventeen years of age, made her appearance at the door. I flattered myself she wore rather a pleased expression when she saw me; but that might have been the customary cast of her features, or vanity on my part. At all events, there was a glowing bloom in her cheeks, and a penetrating brilliancy in her large blue eyes, wonderfully fascinating to one who had not recently looked upon any thing very attractive in the line of female loveliness. She was certainly a model of rustic beauty—I had rarely seen her equal in any country. Nothing could be more lithe and graceful than her form, which was advantageously set off by a tight bodice and a very scanty petticoat. A pair of red woolen stockings conspicuously displayed the fine contour of her—ankles I suppose is the conventional expression, though I mean a great deal more than that. As she sprang down the steps with a light and elastic bound, and took hold of the horse, which by this time the three old men were fumbling at to harness in the cariole, I unconsciously thought of Diana Vernon. She had all the daring grace and delicacy of the Scotch heroine—only in a rustic way. Seizing the horse by the bridle, she backed him up in a jiffy between the shafts of the cariole, and pushing the old gray-heads aside with a merry laugh, proceeded to arrange the harness. Having paid the boy who had come over from the last station, and put my name and destination in the day-book, according to law, I refreshed myself by a glass of ale, and then came out to see if all was ready. The girl nodded to me smilingly to get in and be off.

I looked around for the boy who was to accompany me. Nobody in the shape of a boy was to be seen. The three old men had returned to their log by the stable, and now sat smoking their pipes and gossiping as usual,

and the good-natured old landlady stood smiling and
nodding in the doorway. Who was to take charge of
the cariole? that was the question. Was I to go alone?
Suppose I should miss the road and get lost in some awful wilderness? However, these questions were too much
for my limited vocabulary of Norsk on the spur of the
moment. So I mounted the cariole, resolved to abide
whatever fate Providence might have in store for me.
The girl put the reins in my hand and off I started, wondering why these good people left me to travel alone. I
thought that they would naturally feel some solicitude
about their property. Scarcely was I under way, when,
with a bound like a deer, the girl was up on the cariole
behind, hanging on to the back of the seat with both
hands. Perfectly aghast with astonishment, I pulled the
reins and stopped. "What!" I exclaimed, in the best
Norsk I could muster, "is the *Jomfru* going with me?"
"*Ja!*" answered the laughing damsel, in a merry, ringing voice—"*Ja! Ja! Jeg vil vise de Veien!*—I will
show you the way!"

Here was a predicament! A handsome young girl
going to take charge of me through a perfectly wild and
unknown country! I turned to the old lady at the door
with something of a remonstrating expression, no doubt,
for I felt confused and alarmed. How the deuce was I,
a solitary and inexperienced traveler from California, to
defend myself against such eyes, such blooming cheeks,
such honeyed lips and pearly teeth as these, to say nothing of a form all grace and agility, a voice that was the
very essence of melody, and the fascinating smiles and
blandishments of this wild young creature! It was
enough to puzzle and confound any man of ordinary
susceptibility, much less one who had a natural terror
of the female sex. But I suppose it was all right. The
old lady nodded approvingly; and the three old men
smoked their pipes, and, touching their red night-caps,
bid me—*Farrel! meget god reise!*—a pleasant trip! So,
without more ado, I cracked the whip, and off we start-

ed. It was not my fault, that was certain. My conscience was clear of any bad intentions.

We were soon out of sight of the station, and then came a steep hill. While the pony was pulling and tugging with all his might, the girl bounced off, landing like a wood-nymph about six feet in the rear of the cariole; when, with strides that perfectly astonished me, she began to march up the hill, singing a lively Norwegian ditty as she sprang over the ruts and ridges of the road. I halted in amazement. This would never do. Respect for the gentler sex would not permit me to ride up the hill while so lovely a creature was taking it on foot. Governed by those high principles of gallantry, augmented and cultivated by long residence in California, I jumped out of the cariole, and with persuasive eloquence begged the fair damsel to get in and drive up the hill on my account; that I greatly preferred walking; the exercise was congenial—I liked it. At this she looked astonished, if not suspicious. I fancied she was not used to that species of homage. At all events, she stoutly declined getting in; and since it was impossible for me to ride under the circumstances, I walked by her side to the top of the hill. A coolness was evidently growing up between us, for she never spoke a word all the way; and I was too busy trying to keep the horse in the middle of the road and save my breath to make any farther attempts at conversation.

Having at length reached the summit, the girl directed me to take my place, which I did at once with great alacrity. With another active bound she was up behind, holding on as before with both hands to the back of the seat. Then she whistled to the horse in a style he seemed to understand perfectly well, for away he dashed down the hill at a rate of speed that I was certain would very soon result in utter destruction to the whole party. It was awful to think of being pitched out and rolling down the precipice, in the arms perhaps of this dashing young damsel, who, being accustomed to the road, would doubtless exert herself to save me.

"*Nu! Reise! Reise!*—travel!" cried this extraordinary girl; and away we went, over rocks, into ruts, against roots and bushes; bouncing, springing, splashing, and dashing through mud-holes; down hill and still down; whirling past terrific pits, jagged pinnacles of rock, and yawning gulfs of darkness; through gloomy patches of pine, out again into open spaces, and along the brinks of fearful precipices; over rickety wooden bridges, and through foaming torrents that dashed out over the road, the wild girl clinging fast behind, the little pony flying along madly in front, the cariole creaking and rattling as if going to pieces, myself hanging on to the reins in a perfect agony of doubt whether each moment would not be our last. I declare, on the faith of a traveler, it beat all the dangers I had hitherto encountered summed up together. Trees whirled by, waterfalls flashed upon my astonished eyes, streaks of sunshine fretted the gloom with a net-work of light that dazzled and confounded me. I could see nothing clearly. There was a horrible jumble in my mind of black rocks and blue eyes, pine forests and flaming red stockings, flying clouds and flying petticoats, the roar of torrents and the ringing voice of the maiden as she cried "*Flue! Gaae! Reise!*—Fly! Go it! Travel!" Only one thought was uppermost— the fear of being dashed to pieces. Great heavens, what a fate! If I could only stop this infernal little pony, we might yet be saved! But I dared not attempt it. The slightest pull at the reins would throw him upon his haunches, and cariole and all would go spinning over him into some horrible abyss. All this time the wild damsel behind was getting more and more excited. Now she whistled, now she shouted "*Skynde pa!*—Faster! faster!" till, fairly carried away by enthusiasm, she begged me to give her the whip, which I did, with a faint attempt at prayer. Again she whistled, and shouted "*Skynde pa!*—Faster! faster!" and then she cracked the most startling and incomprehensible Norwegian melodies with the whip, absolutely stunning my ears, while she shouted " *Gaae! Flue! Reise!*—Go it! Fly! Travel!" Faster and still faster we flew down the frightful hill. The pony caught the infection of enthusiasm, and now broke into a frantic run. "Faster! faster!" shrieked the wild girl in a paroxysm of delight.

By this time I was positively beside myself with terror. No longer able to distinguish the flying trees, waterfalls, and precipices, I closed my eyes and gasped for breath. Soon the fearful bouncing of the cariole aroused me to something like consciousness. We had struck a rock, and were now spinning along the edge of a mighty abyss on one wheel, the other performing a sort of balance in the air. I looked ahead, but there was neither shape nor meaning in the country. It was all a wild chaos of destructive elements—trees, precipices, red stockings, and whirling petticoats—toward which we were madly flying.

But there is an end to all troubles upon earth. With thanks to a kind Providence, I at length caught sight of a long stretch of level road. Although there were several short turns to be made before reaching it, there was still hope that it might be gained without any more serious disaster than the breaking of a leg or an arm. Upon such a casualty as that I should have compromised at once. If this extraordinary creature behind would only stop whistling and cracking the whip, and driving the little pony crazy by her inspiring cries, I might yet succeed in steering safely into the level road; but the nearer we approached the bottom of the hill the wilder she became—now actually dancing on the little board with delight, now leaning over to get a cut at the pony's tail with the whip, while she whistled more fiercely than ever, and cried out, from time to time, "*Flue! Gaae! Reise!*" Already the poor animal was reeking with sweat, and it was a miracle he did not drop dead on the road.

However, by great good fortune, aided by my skill in driving, we made the turns, and in a few minutes more

THE POST-GIRL.

were safely jogging along the level road. Almost breath-less, and quite bewildered, I instinctively turned.round to see what manner of wild being this girl behind was. If you believe me, she was leaning over my shoulder, shaking her sides laughing at me, her sparkling blue eyes now all ablaze with excitement, her cheeks glowing like peonies, her lips wide apart, displaying the most exqui-site set of teeth I ever beheld, while her long golden tress-es, bursting from the red handkerchief which served as a sort of crowning glory to her head, floated in wavy ringlets over her shoulders. Hermosa! it was enough to thaw an anchorite! She was certainly very pretty—there was no doubt of that; full of life, overflowing with health and vitality, and delighted at the confusion and astonishment of the strange gentleman she had taken in charge.

Can any body tell me what it is that produces such a singular sensation when one looks over his shoulder and discovers the face of a pretty and innocent young girl within a few inches of his own, her beautiful eyes spark-ling like a pair of stars, and shooting magic scintillations through and through him, body and soul, while her breath falls like a zephyr upon his cheek? Tell me, ye who deal in metaphysics, what is it? There is certainly a kind of charm in it, against which no mortal man is proof. Though naturally prejudiced against the female sex, and firmly convinced that we could get along in the world much better without them, I was not altogether insensible to beauty in an artistical point of view, other-wise I should never have been able to grace the pages of HARPER with the above likeness of this Norwegian sylph. After all, it must be admitted that they have a way about them which makes us feel overpowered and irresponsible in their presence. Doubtless this fair dam-sel was unconscious of the damage she was inflicting upon a wayworn and defenseless traveler. Her very innocence was itself her chiefest charm. Either she was the most innocent or the most designing of her sex. She

thought nothing of holding on to my shoulder, and talked
as glibly and pleasantly, with her beaming face close to
my ear, as if I had been her brother or her cousin, or
possibly her uncle, though I did not exactly like to regard
it in that point of view. What she was saying I could
not conjecture, save by her roguish expression and her
merry peals of laughter.

"*Jeg kan ikke tale Norsk!*—I can't speak Norwegian"—was all I could say, at which she laughed more
joyously than ever, and rattled off a number of excellent
jokes, no doubt at my helpless condition. Indeed, I
strongly suspected, from a familiar word here and there,
that she was making love to me out of mere sport, though
she was guarded enough not to make any intelligible
demonstration to that effect. At last I got out my vocabulary, and as we jogged quietly along the road, by
catching a word now and then, and making her repeat
what she said very slowly, got so far as to construct
something of a conversation.

"What is your name, *skën Jumfru?*" I asked.

"Maria," was the answer.

"A pretty name; and Maria is a very pretty girl."

She tossed her head a little scornfully, as much as to
say Maria was not to be fooled by flattery.

"What is *your* name?" said Maria, after a pause.

"Mine? Oh, I have forgotten mine."

"Are you an Englishman?"

"No."

"A Frenchman?"

"No."

"A Dutchman?"

"No—I am an American."

"I like Americans—I don't like Englishmen," said the
girl.

"Have you a lover?"

"Yes."

"Are you going to be married to him?"

"Yes, in about six months."

"I wish you joy."

"Thank you!"

At this moment a carriage drawn by two horses hove
in sight. It was an English traveling party—an old
gentleman and two ladies, evidently his wife and daughter. As they drew near they seemed to be a little per-
plexed at the singular equipage before them—a small
horse, nearly dead and lathered all over with foam; a
cariole bespattered with mud; a dashing fine girl behind,
with flaunting hair, a short petticoat, and a flaming pair
of red stockings; myself in the body of the cariole, covered from head to foot with mire, my beard flying out
in every direction, and my hair still standing on end
from the effects of recent fright—a very singular spectacle to meet in the middle of a public highway, even in
Norway. The road was very narrow at the point of
meeting. It became necessary for one of the vehicles to
pull up the side of the hill a little in order to allow room
for the other to pass. Being the lighter party as well
as under obligations of gallantry, I at once gave way.
While endeavoring to make a passage, the old gentleman
gruffly observed to the public generally,

"What an excessively bad road!"

"Very!" said I.

"Beastly!" growled the Englishman.

"Abominable!" said I.

"Oh, you are an Englishman?" said the elderly lady.

"No, madam—an American," I answered, with great
suavity.

"Oh, an American!" said the young lady, taking out
her note-book; "dear me, how very interesting!"

"From California," I added, with a smile of pride.

"How very interesting!" exclaimed the young lady.

"A great country," said I.

"Gray," observed the elderly lady, in an under tone,
looking very hard at the girl, who was still standing on
the little board at the back of the cariole, and who coolly and saucily surveyed the traveling party, "Gray, is
that a Norwegian girl?"

"Yes, madam; she is my postillion, only she rides behind, according to the Norwegian custom."

"Dear me!" cried the young lady, "how very interesting!"

"And dangerous too," I observed.

The elderly lady looked puzzled. She was thinking of dangers to which I had no reference.

"Dangerous?" exclaimed the young lady.

"Yes; she came near breaking my neck down that hill;" and here I gave the party a brief synopsis of the adventure.

"Devilish odd!" growled the old Englishman, impatiently. "Good-day, sir. Come, get up!"

The elderly lady said nothing, but looked suspicious.

"Dear me!" exclaimed the young lady, as they drove off; "how very—" This was the last I heard, but I suppose she considered it interesting. The whole affair, no doubt, stands fully recorded in her note-book.

The way being now clear, we proceeded on our journey. In a little while the station-house was in sight, and after a few minutes' drive I was obliged to part from my interesting companion. At first I hesitated about proffering the usual fee of four shillings; but, upon reflection, it occurred to me that I had no right to consider her any thing more than a post-boy. It was worth something extra to travel with one so lively and entertaining, so I handed her double the usual allowance, at which she made a very polite courtesy, and greatly relieved my embarrassment by giving me a hearty shake of the hand and wishing me a pleasant journey. This was the last I saw of my Norwegian Diana. She is a young damsel of great beauty and vivacity, not to say a little wild. I trust she is now happily married to the object of her affections.

CHAPTER XXXI.

HOW THEY LIVE.

EVERY where on the route through the interior I found the peasants kind, hospitable, and simple-hearted. Sometimes I made a detour of several miles from the main road for the purpose of catching a glimpse of the home-life of the farmers; and, imperfect as my means of communication were, I never had any difficulty in making acquaintance with them after announcing myself as a traveler from California. They had all heard, more or less, of that wonderful land of gold, and entertained the most vague and exaggerated notions of its mineral resources. It was not uncommon to find men who believed that the whole country was yellow with gold; that such quantities of that ore abounded in it as to be of little or no value. When I told them that the country was very rich in the precious metals, but that every hill was not a mass of gold, nor the bed of every river lined with rocks and pebbles of the same material, they looked a little incredulous, not to say disappointed. Many of them seemed surprised that a Californian should be traveling through a distant land like Norway merely for amusement, and few seemed to be entirely satisfied when I assured them, in answer to their questions, that I was not very rich; that I was neither a merchant, nor a speculator, nor the owner of gold mines, but simply an indifferent artist making sketches of their country for pastime. French, German, and English artists they could believe in, for they saw plenty of them in the wilds of Norway every summer; but what use would such a poor business be in California, they said, where every man could make a thousand dollars a day digging for gold? I even fancied they looked at my rough and dust tume as if they thought it concealed a glittering uniform, such as the rich men of my country must naturally wear when they go abroad to visit foreign lands. It was impossible to convince them that I was not extravagantly wealthy. On any other point there might be room for doubt, but the pertinacity with which they insisted upon that afforded me much amusement; and since I could not dispel the illusion, it generally cost me a few extra shillings when I had any thing to pay to avoid the stigma of meanness. Not that my extraordinary wealth ever gave them a plea for imposition or extortion. Such an idea never entered their heads. On the contrary, their main purpose seemed to be to show every possible kindness to the distinguished stranger; and more than once, at some of the post-stations, I had to remind them of things which they had omitted in the charge. For this very reason I was in a measure compelled to be rather more profuse than travelers usually are, so that the state from which I have the honor to hail owes me a considerable amount of money by this time for the handsome manner in which I have sustained its reputation. At some of the stopping-places on the road, where I obtained lodgings for the night, it was not uncommon to find intelligent and educated families of cultivated manners. Education of late years has made considerable progress in Norway; and the rising generation, owing to the facilities afforded by the excellent school system established throughout the country, but especially in the principal towns, will not be in any respect behind the times, so far as regards intellectual progress. It is the simplicity and honesty of these good people, however, that form their principal and most charming characteristic. To one long accustomed to sharp dealing and unscrupulous trickery, it is really refreshing their confidence in the integrity of a stranger. Usually they left the settlement of accounts to myself, merely stating that I must determine what I owed by adding up the items according to the tariff; and, although my knowledge of the language

was so limited, I nowhere had the slightest approach to
a dispute about the payment of expenses. On one occasion, not wishing to forfeit this confidence, I was obliged
to ride back half a mile to pay for two cigars which I
had forgotten in making up the reckoning, and of which
the inn-keeper had not thought proper to remind me, or
had forgotten to keep any account himself. No surprise
was manifested at this conscientious act—the inn-keeper
merely nodding good-naturedly when I handed him the
money, with the remark that it was "all right."

In the districts remote from the sea-ports, the peasants, as may well be supposed, are extremely ignorant
of the great outside world. Sweden and Denmark are
the only countries known to them besides their own
"Gamle Norge," save such vague notions of other lands
as they pick up from occasional travelers. To them
"Amerika" is a terra incognita. A letter once or twice
a year from some emigrant to the members of his family
goes the rounds of the district, and gives them all the
knowledge they have of that distant land of promise;
and when they listen, with gaping eyes and open mouths,
to the wonderful stories of adventure, life, enterprise, and
wealth detailed by the enthusiastic rover, it is no wonder they shake their heads and say that Christian, or
Hans, or Olé (as the case may be), "always was a capital fellow at drawing a long bow." They firmly believe
in ghosts and supernatural visitations of all sorts, but
are very incredulous about any country in the world
being equal to "Gamle Norge." Naturally enough, they
consider their climate the most genial, their barren rocks
the most fertile, their government the best and most liberal on the face of the earth, and themselves the most
highly favored of the human race. Goldsmith must have
had special reference to the Norwegians when he sang
of "that happiest spot below:"

> "The shuddering tenant of the frigid zone
> Boldly proclaims the happiest spot his own."

And why should they be otherwise than contented—

if such a thing as contentment can exist upon earth?
They have few wants and many children; a country free
from internal commotion, and too far removed from the
great scenes of European strife to excite the jealousy
of external powers; sufficient food and raiment to satisfy the ordinary necessities of life, and no great extremes
of wealth or poverty to militate against their independence, either in a political or social point of view. With
good laws, an excellent Constitution, and a fair representation in the Storthing, they are justly proud of their
freedom, and deeply imbued with the spirit of patriot-
ism.

Very little of poverty or beggary is to be seen by the
wayside during a tour through Norway. Only at one
point between Kringelen and Laurgaard—a wild and
barren district exceedingly savage in its aspect, situated
in a narrow gorge of the mountains near the head of the
Logen—was I solicited for alms. A portion of this route,
after passing Sinclair's Monument, is rudely fenced in,
so as to render available every foot of the narrow valley.
The road passes directly through the little farms, which
at this stage of the journey are poor and unproductive.
The climate is said to be very severe in this district, in
consequence of its altitude, and the sharp winds which
sweep down from the mountain gorges. At every gateway a gang of ragged little children always stood ready
to open the gate, for which, of course, they expected a
few shillings; and as these gates occur at intervals of
every few hundred yards for some distance, it produces
a sensible effect upon one's purse to get through. Passing through some wretched hamlets in this vicinity,
crowds of old women hobbled out to beg alms, and I did
not get clear of the regiments of children who ran along
behind the cariole to receive the remainder of my small
change for several miles. Strange to say, this was the
only place during my rambles through the interior in
which I saw any thing like beggary. Generally speaking, the farming lands are sufficiently productive to sup-

ply all the wants of the peasants, and many of the farmers are even comfortably situated.

The houses in which these country people reside are not altogether unlike the small log cabins of the early settlers on our Western frontier. I have seen many such on the borders of Missouri and Kansas. Built in the most primitive style of pine logs, they stand upon stumps or columns of stone, elevated some two or three feet from the ground, in order to allow a draft of air underneath, which in this humid climate is considered necessary for health. They seldom consist of more than two or three rooms, but make up in number what they lack in size. Thus a single farming establishment often comprises some ten or a dozen little cabins, besides the large barn, which is the nucleus around which they all centre ; with smaller cribs for pigs, chickens, etc., and here and there a shed for the cows and sheep, all huddled together among the rocks or on some open hill-side, without the least apparent regard to direction or architectural effect. The roofs are covered with sod, upon which it is not uncommon to see patches of oats, weeds, moss, flowers, or whatever comes most convenient to form roots and give consistency and strength to this singular overtopping. The object, I suppose, is to prevent the transmission of heat during the severe season of winter. Approaching some of these hamlets or farming establishments during the summer months, the traveler is frequently at a loss to distinguish their green-sodded roofs from the natural sod of the hill-sides, so that one is liable at any time to plunge into the midst of a settlement before he is aware of its existence. Something of a damp, earthy look about them, the weedy or grass-covered tops, the logs green and moss-grown, the dripping eaves, the veins of water oozing out of the rocks, give them a peculiarly Northern and chilling effect, and fill the mind with visions of long and dreary winters, rheumatisms, colds, coughs, and consumptions, to which it is said these people are subject. Nothing so wild and primitive is to be seen in any other part of Europe. A silence almost death-like hangs over these little hamlets during a great part of the day, when the inhabitants are out in the hills attending their flocks or cultivating their small patches of ground. I passed many groups of cabins without seeing the first sign of life, save now and then a few chickens or pigs rooting about the barn-yard. The constant impression was that it was Sunday, or at least a holiday, and that the people were either at church or asleep. For one who seeks retirement from the busy haunts of life, where he can indulge in uninterrupted reflection, I know of no country that can equal Norway. There are places in the interior where I am sure he would be astonished at the sound of his own voice. The deserts of Africa can scarcely present a scene of such utter isolation. With a rod in his hand, he can, if given to the gentle art, sit and dream upon some mossy bank,

> "In close covert by some brook,
> Where no profaner eye may look,
> And hide him from day's garish noon."

Thus you often come upon an English sportsman waiting for a nibble.

The food of the peasants consists principally of black bread, milk, butter, and cheese. Meat is too expensive for very general use, though at certain seasons of the year they indulge in it once or twice a week. Coffee is a luxury to which they are much addicted. Even the poorest classes strain a point to indulge in this favorite narcotic, and in no part of Norway did I fail to get a good cup of coffee. It is a very curious fact that the best coffee to be had at the most fashionable hotels on the Continent of Europe—always excepting Paris—is inferior to that furnished to the traveler at the commonest station-house in Norway. This is indeed one of the luxuries of a tour through this part of Scandinavia. The cream is rich and pure, and it is a rare treat to get a large bowlful of it for breakfast, with as much milk as you please, and no limit to bread and butter. Your appetite is not

WAITING FOR A NIBBLE.

measured by infinitesimal bits and scraps as in Germany. A good wholesome meal is spread before you in the genuine backwoods style, and you may eat as much as you please, which is a rare luxury to one who has been stinted and starved at the hotels on the Continent. I remember, at one station beyond the Dovre Fjeld, Bennett's Hand-book says, "Few rooms, but food supplied in first-rate style when Miss Marit is at home. She will be much offended if you do not prove that you have a good appetite." On my arrival at this place, not wishing to offend Miss Marit—for whom I entertained the highest respect in consequence of her hospitable reputation—I called for every thing I could think of, and when it was placed upon the table by that accomplished young lady (a very pleasant, pretty young woman, by-the-way), fell to work and made it vanish at a most astonishing rate. Miss Marit stood by approvingly. During a pause in my heavy labors I called the attention of this estimable person to her own name in the printed pamphlet, at which she blushed and looked somewhat confused. Possibly there might be a mistake about it.

"Your name is Miss Marit?" I asked, very politely.

"Ja."

"And this is Miss Marit in print?"

"Ja."

She took the book and tried to read it.

"Nikka Forstoe!"—she didn't understand.

"What does it say?" she asked, rather gravely.

Here was a job—to translate the paragraph into Norwegian! Besides, it would not do to translate it literally, so I made a sort of impromptu paraphrase upon it.

"Oh! it says Miss Marit is a very pretty young lady."

"Ja!"—blushing and looking somewhat astonished.

"And Miss Marit is a very nice housekeeper."

"Ja."

"And Miss Marit makes splendid coffee, and thoroughly understands how to cook a beefsteak."

"Ja!"

"And Miss Marit would make a most excellent wife for any young gentleman who could succeed in winning her affections!"

"Nei!" said the young lady, blushing again, and looking more astonished than ever.

"Ja," said I, "it is all in print"—adding, with an internal reservation, "or ought to be."

Who can blame me for paying tribute to Miss Marit's kindness and hospitality? She is certainly deserving of much higher praise than that bestowed upon her, and I hope Mr. Bennett will pardon me for the liberal style of my translation. If he didn't mean all I said, let the responsibility rest upon me, for I certainly meant every word of it.

The farming districts are limited chiefly to the valleys along the river-courses, and such portions of arable lands as lie along the shores of the Fjords. A large proportion of the country is extremely wild and rugged, and covered, for the most part, with dense pine forests. The peasants generally own their own farms, which are small, and cut up into patches of pasture, grain-lands, and tracts of forest. Even the most unpromising nooks among the rocks, in many parts of the Gudbransdalen Valley, where plows are wholly unavailable, are rooted up by means of hoes, and planted with oats and other grain. I sometimes saw as many as forty or fifty of these little arable patches perched up among the rocks, hundreds of feet above the roofs of the houses, where it would seem dangerous for goats to browse. The log cabins peep out from among the rocks and pine-clad cliffs all along the course of the Logen, giving the country a singular speckled appearance. This, it must be remembered, is one of the best districts in the interior. The richest agricultural region is said to be that bordering on the shores of the Miösen. One of the comforts enjoyed by the peasants, and without which it would scarcely be possible for them to exist in such a rigorous climate, consists in the unlimited quantity of fuel to which they have such easy access. This is an inconceivable luxury during the long winter months; and their large open fireplaces and blazing fires, even in the cool summer evenings, constantly remind one of the homes of the settlers in the Far West. When the roads are covered with snow the true season of internal communication commences. Then the means of transportation and travel are greatly facilitated, and the clumsy wagons used in summer are put aside for the lighter and more convenient sledges with which every farmer is abundantly provided. All along the route the snow-plows may be seen turned up against the rocks, ready to be used during the winter to clear and level the roads. In summer the means of transportation are little better than those existing between Placerville and Carson Valley.

SNOW-PLOW.

It was during the height of the harvesting season that
I passed through the Gudbransdalen. One of the most
characteristic sights at this time of the year is the extraordinary amount of labor imposed upon the women,
who seem really to do most of the heavy work. I thought
I had seen the last of that in the Thuringerwald, Odenwald, and Schwartzwald, while on a foot-tour through
Germany ; but even the Germans are not so far advanced
in civilization in this respect as the Norwegians, who do
not hesitate to make their women cut wood, haul logs,
pull carts, row boats, fish, and perform various other kinds
of labor usually allotted to the stronger sex, which even
a German would consider rather heavy for his " frow."

The men, in addition to this ungallant trait, are much
addicted to the use of tobacco and native corn-brandy—
which, however, I can not but regard as a sign of civili-

A DRINKING BOUT.

zation, since the same habits exist, to some extent, in our
own country. Chewing and drinking are just as common as in California, the most enlightened country in the

world.   Wherever I saw a set of drunken fellows roaring and rollicking at some wayside inn, their faces smeared with tobacco, and their eyes rolling in their heads, I naturally felt drawn toward them by the great free-masonry of familiar customs.

The system of farming followed by the peasants is exceedingly primitive, though doubtless well adapted to the climate and soil.   Nothing can be more striking to a stranger than the odd shapes of the wagons and carts, and the rudeness of the agricultural implements, which must be patterned upon those in vogue during the time of Odin, the founder of the Norwegian race.   Owing to the humidity of the climate, it is necessary in harvest time to dry the hay and grain by staking it out in the fields on long poles, so that the sun and air may penetrate every part of it.   The appearance of a farm is thus rendered unique as well as picturesque.   In the long twilight nights of summer these ghostly stakes present the appearance of a gang of heathenish spirits standing about in the fields, with their long beards waving in the air, and their dusky robes trailing over the stubbles.   The figures thus seen at every turn of the road often assume the most striking spectral forms, well calculated to augment those wild superstitions which prevail throughout the country.   It was impossible for me ever to get quite rid of the idea that they were descendants of the old Scandinavian gods, holding counsel over the affairs of the nation, especially when some passing breeze caused their arms and robes to flutter in the twilight, and their heads to swing to and fro, as if in the enthusiasm of their ghostly deliberations.

Mingled with the wild superstitions of the people their piety is a prominent trait.   Their prevailing religion is Episcopal Lutheran, though Catholicism and other religions are tolerated by an act of the Storthing, with the exception of Mormonism, which is prohibited by law.   A considerable number of proselytes to that sect have emigrated to Salt Lake.   This prevailing spirit of piety

A NORWEGIAN FARM

is observable even in the wildest parts of the country, where every little hamlet has its church, and neither old nor young neglect their religious services. Most of these

NORWEGIAN CHURCH.

churches are built of wood, with a steeple of the same material, shingled over and painted black, so as to present the most striking contrast to the snows which cover the face of the country during the greater part of the year.

The parish schoolmaster is a most important personage in these rural districts. He it is who trains up the rising generation, teaches the young idea how to shoot, and

"Out of great things and small draweth the secrets of the universe."

PARISH SCHOOLMASTER.

He is greatly revered by the simple-minded old farmers, is cherished and respected by the mothers of families, enthusiastically admired and generally aspired to by the village belles, and held in profound awe by all the little urchins of the neighborhood. He speaketh unknown

tongues; he diveth into the depths of abstruse sciences;
he talketh with the air of one burdened with much learning; he "argueth the cycles of the stars from a pebble
flung by a child;" he likewise teacheth reading, writing,
and arithmetic, and applieth the rod to the juvenile seat
of understanding, as shown on the preceding page.

Soon after leaving Storkterstad, a station about two
days' journey from Lillehammer, on the main road to
Trondhjem, I passed through a very steep and rugged
defile in the mountains, with jagged rocks on the right
and the foaming waters of the Logen on the left, where
my attention was called by the skydskaarl to a small
monument by the roadside bearing an inscription com-
memorative of the death of Colonel Sinclair. If I remember correctly, a fine description is given of this celebrated passage by Mögge, whose graphic sketches of
Norwegian scenery I had frequent occasion to admire,
during my tour, for their beauty and accuracy. I fully
agree with my friend Bayard Taylor, that the traveler
can find no better guide to the Fjelds and Fjords of this·
wild country than "Afraja" and "Life and Love in Norway." Laing has also given an interesting account of
the massacre of Colonel Sinclair's party. From his ver-
sion of this famous incident in Norwegian history it appears that, during the war between Christian the Fourth
of Denmark and Gustavus Adolphus of Sweden, while
the Danes held the western coast of Norway, Colonel
Sinclair, a Scotchman, desiring to render assistance to
the Swedes, landed at Romsdalen, on the coast, with a
party of nine hundred followers. Another detachment
of his forces landed at Trondhjem. It was their intention to fight their way across the mountains and join the
Swedish forces on the frontier. Sinclair's party met with
no resistance till they arrived at the pass of Kringelen,
where three hundred peasants, hearing of their approach,
had prepared an ambush. Every thing was arranged
with the utmost secrecy. An abrupt mountain on the
right, abounding in immense masses of loose rock, fur-

nished the means of a terrible revenge for the ravages committed by the Scotch on their march from Romsdalen. The road winds around the foot of this mountain, making a narrow pass, hemmed in by the roaring torrents of the Logen on the one side and abrupt cliffs on the other. Across the river, which here dashes with frightful rapidity through the narrow gorge of the mountains, the country wears an exceedingly weird and desolate aspect; the ravines and summits of the mountains are darkened by gloomy forests of pine, relieved only by hoary and moss-covered cliffs overhanging the rushing waters of the Logen. On the precipitous slopes of the pass, hundreds of feet above the road, the peasants gathered enormous masses of rock, logs of wood, and even trunks of trees, which they fixed in such a way that, at a moment's notice, they could precipitate the whole terrible avalanche upon the heads of the enemy.

Such was the secrecy with which the peasants managed the whole affair, that the Scotch, ignorant even of the existence of a foe, marched along in imaginary security till they reached the middle of the narrrow pass, when they were suddenly overwhelmed and crushed beneath the masses of rocks and loose timbers launched upon them by the Norwegians. Rushing from their ambush, the infuriated peasants soon slaughtered the maimed and wounded, leaving, according to some authorities, only two of the enemy to tell the tale. Others, however, say that as many as sixty escaped, but were afterward caught and massacred. Attached to this fearful story of retribution, Laing mentions a romantic incident, which is still currently told in the neighborhood. A young peasant was prevented from joining in the attack by his sweetheart, to whom he was to be married the next day. She, learning that the wife of Colonel Sinclair was among the party, sent her lover to offer his assistance; but the Scotch lady, mistaking his purpose, shot him dead. Such is the tragic history that casts over this wild region a mingled interest of horror and romance.

The road from Laurgaard beyond the pass of the Kringelen ascends a high mountain. On the right is a series of foaming cataracts, and nothing can surpass the rugged grandeur of the view as you reach the highest eminence before descending toward Braendhagen. Here the country is one vast wilderness of pine-clad mountains, green winding valleys, and raging torrents of water dashing down over the jagged rocks thousands of feet below. It was nearly night when I reached Dombaas, the last station before ascending the Dovre Fjeld.

A telegraphic station at Dombaas gives something of a civilized aspect to this stopping-place, otherwise rather a primitive-looking establishment. The people, however, are very kind and hospitable, and somewhat noted for their skill in carving bone and wooden knife-handles. I should have mentioned that, wild as this part of the country is, the traveler is constantly reminded by the telegraphic poles all along the route that he is never quite beyond the limits of civilization. Such is the force of habit that I was strongly tempted to send a message to somebody from Dombaas; but, upon turning the matter over in my mind, could think of nobody within the limits of Norway who felt sufficient interest in my explorations to be likely to derive much satisfaction from the announcement that I had reached the edge of the Dovre Fjeld in safety. The name of a waiter who was good enough to black my boots at the Victoria Hotel occurred to me, but it was hardly possible he would appreciate a telegraphic dispatch from one who had no more pressing claims to his attention. I thought of sending a few lines of remembrance to the Wild Girl who had come so near breaking my neck. This notion, however, I gave over upon reflecting that she might attach undue weight to my expressions of friendship, and possibly take it into her head that I was making love to her —than which nothing could be farther from my intention. I had a social chat with the telegraph-man, however—a very respectable and intelligent person—who

DOYLE FIELD.

gave me the latest news; and with this, and a good supper and bed, I was obliged to rest content.

CHAPTER XXXII.

JOHN BULL ABROAD.

LEAVING Dombaas at an early hour, I soon began to ascend a long slope, reaching, by a gradual elevation, to the Dovre Fjeld. The vegetation began to grow more and more scanty on the wayside, consisting mostly of lichens and reindeer moss. I passed through some stunted groves of pine, which, however, were bleached and almost destitute of foliage. The ground on either side of the road was soft, black, and boggy, abounding in springs and scarcely susceptible of cultivation. At this elevation grain is rarely planted, though I was told potatoes and other esculents are not difficult to raise. On the left of the road, approaching the summit, lies a range of snow-capped mountains between the Dovre Fjeld and Molde; on the right a series of rocky and barren hills of sweeping outline, presenting an exceedingly desolate aspect. In the course of an hour after leaving Dombaas, having walked most of the way, I fairly reached the grand plateau of the Dovre Fjeld. The scene at this point of the journey is inexpressibly desolate.

Bare, whitish-colored hills bound the horizon on the right; in front is a dreary waste, through which the road winds like a thread till lost in the dim haze of the distance; and to the left the everlasting snows of Snaehatten. A few wretched cabins are scattered at remote intervals over the desert plains, in which the shepherds seek shelter from the inclemency of the weather, which even in midsummer is often piercingly raw. Herds of cattle, sheep, and goats were grazing over the rocky wastes of the Fjeld. Reindeer are sometimes seen in this vicinity, but not often within sight of the road. The only vegetation produced here is reindeer moss, and a

coarse sort of grass growing in bunches over the plain.
I met several shepherds on the way dressed in something
like a characteristic costume—frieze jackets with brass
buttons, black knee-breeches, a red night-cap, and armed
with the usual staff or shepherd's crook, represented in
pictures, and much discoursed of by poets:

> "Methinks it were a happy life
> To be no better than a homely swain;"

but not on the Dovre Fjelds of Norway. It must be
rather a dull business in that region, taking into consideration the barren plains, the bleak winds, and desolate
aspect of the country. No sweet hawthorn bushes are
there, beneath which these rustic philosophers can sit,

> "Looking on their silly sheep."

Shepherd life must be a very dismal reality indeed. And
yet there is no accounting for tastes. At one point of
the road, beyond Folkstuen, where a sluggish lagoon
mingles its waters with the barren slopes of the Fjeld, I
saw an Englishman standing up to his knees in a dismal
marsh fishing for trout.

The weather was cold enough to strike a chill into
one's very marrow; yet this indefatigable sportsman
had come more than a thousand miles from his native
country to enjoy himself in this way. He was a genuine specimen of an English snob—self-sufficient, conceited, and unsociable; looking neither to the right nor the
left, and terribly determined not to commit himself by
making acquaintance with casual travelers speaking the
English tongue. I stopped my cariole within a few paces
and asked him "what luck?" One would think the
sound of his native tongue would have been refreshing
to him in this dreary wilderness; but, without deigning
to raise his head, he merely answered in a gruff tone,
"Don't know, sir—don't know!" I certainly did not suspect him of knowing much, but thought that question at
least would not be beyond the limits of his intelligence.
Finding him insensible to the approaches of humanity,
I revenged myself for his rudeness by making a sketch

of his person, which I hope will be recognized by his friends in England should he meet with any misfortune in the wilds of Norway. They will at least know where to search for his body, and be enabled to recognize it when they find it. This man's sense of enjoyment re-

PLAYING HIM OUT.

minded me of the anecdote told by Longfellow in Hyperion, of an Englishman who sat in a tub of cold water every morning while he ate his breakfast and read the newspapers.

I met with many such in the course of my tour. Is it not a little marvelous what hardships people will encounter for pleasure? Here was a man of mature age, in the enjoyment perhaps of a comfortable income, who had left his country, with all its attractions, for a dreary desert in which he was utterly isolated from the world. He was not traveling—not reading, not surrounded by a few congenial friends who could make a brief exile pleasant, but utterly alone; ignorant, no doubt, of the language spoken by the few shepherds in the neighborhood; up to his knees in a pool of cold water; stubbornly striving against the most adverse circumstances of wind and weather to torture out of the water a few miserable little fish! Of what material can such a man's brain be composed, if he be gifted with brain at all? Is it mud, clay, or water; or is it all a bog? Possibly he was a lover of nature; but if you examine his portrait you will perceive that there is nothing in his personal appearance to warrant that suspicion. Even if such were the case, this was not the charming region described by the quaint old Walton, where the scholar can turn aside "toward the high honeysuckle hedge," or "sit and sing while the shower falls upon the teeming earth, viewing the silver streams glide silently toward their centre, the tempestuous sea," beguiled by the harmless lambs till, with a soul possessed with content, he feels "lifted above the earth." Nor was the solitary angler of the Dovre Fjeld a man likely to be lifted from the earth by any thing so fragile as the beauties of nature. His weight —sixteen stone at least—would be much more likely to sink him into it.

As I approached the neighborhood of Djerkin on the Dovre Fjeld, famous as a central station for hunting expeditions, I met several English sportsmen armed with rifles, double-barreled guns, pistols, and other deadly weapons, on their way to the defiles of the adjacent mountains in search of the black bears which are said to infest that region. One of these enthusiastic gentlemen was seated in a cariole, and traveled for some distance in front of me. Taking into view the rotundity of his person, which overhung the little vehicle on every

side, I could not but picture to myself the extraordinary
spectacle that would be presented to any observant eye
in case this ponderous individual should suddenly come
in contact with one of those ferocious animals.

ENGLISH SPORTSMAN.

Here you have him, just as he sat before me—a back
view, to be sure, but the only one I could get in the emergency of the moment. It will be easy to imagine, from
the dexterous grace of his figure, how he will bound over
the rocks, climb up the rugged points of the precipices,
hang by the roots and branches of trees, dodge the at-
tacks of the enemy, crawl through the brush, and, in the
event of an unfavorable turn in the battle, retreat to some
position of security.

No man can be blamed for running when he is sure to be worsted in an encounter of this kind. Many a brave Californian has taken to his heels when pursued by a grizzly, and I have scarcely a doubt that I would pursue the same course myself under similar circumstances. Only it must look a little ludicrous to see a fat Englishman, a representative of the British Lion, forced to adopt this mortifying alternative rather than suffer himself to be torn into beef-steaks. It may be, however, that in this instance our Nimrod has suddenly discovered that it is about dinner-time, and is hurrying back to camp lest the beef should be overdone.

BEAR CHASE.

These bear-hunting Englishmen take care to have as many chances on their own side as possible. Hence they usually go into the mountains well provided with guides, ammunition, provisions, etc., and prepare the way by first securing the bear in some favored locality. This is done by killing a calf or hog, and placing the carcass in the required position. A hired attendant lies in wait until he discovers the bear, when he comes down to the station or camp, and notifies the hunter that it is time to start out. Thus the risk of life is greatly reduced, and the prospect of securing some game proportionally augmented. The black bears of Norway are not very dangerous, however, and, hunted in this manner, it requires no great skill to kill them. They are generally to be found in the higher mountains and defiles, a few miles

from some farming settlement. In winter, when their customary food is scarce, they often commit serious depredations upon the stock of the farmers. Every facility is freely afforded by the peasants for their destruction, and every bear killed is considered so many cattle saved.

It was late in the afternoon when I descended a rocky and pine-covered hill, and came in sight of the station called Djerkin, celebrated as one of the best in the interior of Norway. This place is kept by an old Norwegian peasant family of considerable wealth, and is a favorite resort of English sportsmen bound on fishing and hunting excursions throughout the wilds of the Dovre Fjeld. The main buildings and outhouses are numerous and substantial, and stand on the slope of the hill which forms the highest point of the Fjeld on the road from Christiania to Trondhjem. The appearance of this isolated group of buildings on the broad and barren face of the hill had much in it to remind me of some of the old missionary establishments in California; and the resemblance was increased by the scattered herds of cattle browsing upon the parched and barren slopes of the Fjeld, which in this vicinity are as much like the old ranch lands of San Diego County as one region of country wholly different in climate can be like another. A few cultivated patches of ground near the station, upon which the peasants were at work gathering in the scanty harvest, showed that even in this rigorous region the attempts at agriculture were not altogether unsuccessful. As usual, the principal burden of labor seemed to fall upon the women, who were digging, hoeing, and raking with a lusty will that would have done credit to the men.

CHAPTER XXXIII.

WOMEN IN NORWAY AND GERMANY.

I must say that of all the customs prevailing in the different parts of Europe, not excepting the most civilized states of Germany, this one of making the women do all the heavy work strikes me as the nearest approximation to the perfection of domestic discipline. The Diggers of California and the Kaffres of Africa understand this thing exactly, and no man of any spirit belonging to those tribes would any more think of performing the drudgery which he imposes upon his wife and daughters than a German or Norwegian. What is the use of having wives and children if they don't relieve us of our heavy work? In that respect we Americans are very much behind the times. We pay such absurd devotion to the weakness of woman that they rule us with a despotism unknown in any other country. Their smiles are threats, and their tears are despotic manifestoes, against which the bravest of us dare not rebel. It is absolutely horrible to think of the condition of servitude in which we are placed by the extraordinary powers vested in, and so relentlessly exercised by, the women of America. I, for one, am in favor of a revival of the old laws of Nuremberg, by which female tyranny was punished. By a decree of the famous Council of Eight, any woman convicted of beating her husband or otherwise maltreating him was forced to wear a dragon's head for the period of three days; and if she did not, at the expiration of that date, ask his pardon, she was compelled to undergo a regimen of bread and water for the space of three weeks, or until effectually reduced to submission. Something must be done, or we shall be compelled sooner or later to adopt a clause in the Constitution prohibiting from admission the State of Matrimony. What would the ladies do then? I think that would bring them to their senses.

Not only in the matter of domestic discipline, but of business and pleasure, are the people of Europe infinitely ahead of us. In France many of the railway stations are attended by female clerks, and in Germany the beer-saloons are ornamented by pretty girls, who carry around the foaming schoppens, having a spare smile and a joke for every customer. Of opera-singers, dancers, and female fiddlers, the most famous are produced in Europe. The wheeling girls of Hamburg, who roll after the omnibuses in circus fashion, are the only specimens in the line of popular attractions that I have not yet seen in the streets or public resorts of New York.

What would be thought of half a dozen of these street

WHEELING GIRLS.

acrobats rolling down Broadway or the Fifth Avenue? Doubtless they would attract considerable attention, and probably turn many a good penny. I fancy the Bowery boys would enjoy this sort of thing. A pretty girl of sixteen or seventeen, with her crinoline securely bundled up between her ankles, wheeling merrily along after an omnibus at the rate of five miles an hour, would be an attractive as well as extraordinary spectacle. For my part, I would greatly prefer it to our best female lectures on phrenology or physiology. I think a girl who can roll in that way must be possessed of uncommon genius. The wheeling boys of London are but a clumsy spectacle compared with this. No man of sensibility can witness such a sight without regarding it as the very poetry of motion.

But this digression has led me a little out of the way. I was on the road to Djerkin. A sharp pull of half a mile up the hill brought me to the door of the station, where I was kindly greeted by the family. Descending from my cariole a little stiff after the last long stage, I entered the general sitting-room, where there was a goodly assemblage of customers smoking and drinking, and otherwise enjoying themselves. The landlady, however, would not permit me to stop in such rude quarters, but hurried me at once into the fine room of the establishment. While she was preparing a venison steak and some coffee, I took a survey of the room, which was certainly ornamented in a very artistical manner. The sofa was covered with little scraps of white net-work; the bureau was dotted all over with little angels made of gauze, highly-colored pin-cushions, and fanciful paper boxes and card-stands. The walls were decorated with paintings of cows, stags, rocks, waterfalls, and other animals, and gems of Norwegian scenery, the productions of the genius of the family—the oldest son, a Justice of the Peace for the District, now absent on business at Christiania. They were very tolerably executed. The old lady was so proud of them that she took care to call my attention to their merits immediately upon entering the room, informing me, with much warmth of manner, that her son was a highly respectable man, of wonderful talents, who had held the honorable position of Justice of the Peace for the past ten years, and that there was something in my face that reminded her of her dear boy. In fact, she thought our features bore a striking resemblance—only Hansen had rather a more melancholy expression, his wife having unfortunately died about three years ago (here the poor old lady heaved a profound sigh). But I could judge for myself. There was his portrait, painted by a German artist who spent some months at this place last summer. I looked at the portrait with some curiosity. It was that of a man about forty years of age, with a black skull-cap on his head, a long queue behind, and a pair of spectacles on his nose —his face very thin and of a cadaverous expression; just such a man as you would expect to find upon a justice's bench of a country district in Norway. Was it possible I bore any resemblance to this learned man?

JUSTICE OF THE PEACE.

The very idea was so startling, not to say flattering, that I could hardly preserve my composure. I mumbled over something to the effect that it was a good face—for scenic purposes; but every time I tried to acknowledge the likeness to myself the words stuck in my throat. Finally, I was forced to ask the landlady if she would be so kind as to bring me a glass of brandy-wine, for I was afraid she would discover the internal convulsions which threatened every moment to rend my ribs asunder. While she was looking after the brandy-wine I made a hasty copy of the portrait, and I now leave it to the impartial reader to decide upon the supposed resemblance. It may be like me, but I confess the fact never would have impressed itself upon my mind from any personal observation of my own countenance taken in front of a looking-glass.

There was something so genial and cozy about the inn at Djerkin that I partially resolved to stop all night. At dinner-time the landlord made his appearance steaming hot from the kitchen. I no longer hesitated about staying. I am a great believer in the physiognomy of inns as well as of landlords. Traveling through a wild country like Norway, where there is little beyond the scenery to attract attention, the unpretending stations by the wayside assume a degree of importance equaled only by the largest cities in other countries. The approach, the aspect of the place, the physiognomy of the house, become matters of the deepest interest to the solitary wayfarer, who clings to these episodes in the day's journey as the connecting links that bind him to the great family of man. I claim to be able to tell from the general expression of an inn, commencing at the chimney-top and ending at the steps of the front door, exactly what sort of cheer is to be had within—whether the family are happily bound together in bonds of affection; how often the landlord indulges in a bout of hard drinking; and the state of control under which he is kept by the female head of the establishment; nay, I can almost guess, from the general aspect of the house, the exact weight and digestive capacity of mine host; for if the inn promise well for the creature comforts, so will the inn-keeper. And what can be more cheering to a tired wayfarer than to be met at the door by a jolly red-faced old fellow—

"His fair round belly with fat capon lined"—

beef-steaks in the expression of his eye; his bald pate the
fac-simile of a rump of mutton; plum-puddings and ap-
ple-dumplings in every curve of his chin; his body the

MODEL LANDLORD.

living embodiment of a cask of beer supported by two
pipes of generous wine; the whole man overflowing with
rich juices and essences, gravies, and strong drinks—a

breathing incarnation of all the good things of life, whom to look upon is to feel good-natured and happy in the present, and hopeful for the future; such a man, in short, as mine host of the Golden Crown, whose portrait I have endeavored to present.

If there be any likeness between myself and the son, it certainly does not extend to the father. He carries in his hands a steaming hot plum-pudding; he is a model landlord, and delights in feeding his customers. His voice is greasy like his face. When he laughs it is from his capacious stomach the sounds come. His best jokes are based upon his digestive organs. He gets a little boozy toward evening, but that is merely a hospitable habit of his to prove that his liquors are good. You commit yourself at once to his keeping with a delightful consciousness that in his hands you are safe. He is not a man to suffer an honest customer to starve. Nature, in her prodigality, formed him upon a generous pattern. Whatever does other people good likewise does him good. May he live a thousand years—mine host of the Golden Crown!—and may his shadow never be less!

CHAPTER XXXIV.

DOWN THE DRIVSDAL.

THE next morning I proceeded on my way, resolved, if ever I came this route again, to spend a week at Djerkin. A withered old man accompanied me on the back of the cariole. After half an hour's hard climbing up a very steep hill we reached the highest point of the Dovre Fjeld, 4594 feet above the level of the sea. From this point the view is exceedingly weird and desolate. Owing to the weather, however, which was dark and threatening, I did not stop long to enjoy the view of the barren wastes that lay behind, but was soon dashing at a slapping pace down into the valley of the Drivsdal—one of the most rugged and picturesque in Norway.

My journey down the valley of the Drivsdal was both
pleasant and interesting. A beautiful new road commences at Kongsvold, the last station on the Dovre Fjeld,

after passing Djerkin, and follows the winding of the river through the narrow gorges of the mountains all the
Q 2

way to Ny Orne. On each side towering and pine-covered mountains rear their rugged crests, sometimes approaching so close to the river as to overhang the road, which for miles on a stretch is hewn from the solid rock.

The innumerable clefts and fissures that mark the rugged fronts of the cliffs; the overhanging trees and shrubbery; the toppling boulders of granite, balanced in mid-air; the rushing torrents that dash from the moss-covered rocks; the seething and foaming waters of the Driv, whirling through the narrow gorges hundreds of feet below the road; the bright blue sky overhead, and the fitful gleams of sunshine darting through the masses of pine and circling into innumerable rainbows in the spray of the river, all combine to form a scene of incomparable beauty and grandeur such as I have rarely seen equaled in any part of the world, and only surpassed by the Siskiyou Mountains in the northern part of California.

About midway down the valley, after passing the settlement of Rise, I stopped to examine a curious passage of the river in the neighborhood of the Drivstuklere, where it dashes down between two solid walls of rocks, which at this point approach so as to form a passage of not more than fifteen feet in width. Securing my cariole horse to a tree by the side of the road, I descended a steep bank under the guidance of my skydskaarl, a bright little fellow about ten years of age, who first called my attention to this remarkable phenomenon. I was soon compelled to follow his example, and crawl over the rocks like a caterpillar to avoid falling into the frightful abyss below. For a distance of fifty or sixty yards, the river, compressed within a limit of fifteen feet, dashes with fearful velocity through its rugged and tortuous boundaries, filling the air with spray, and making an angry moan, as if threatening momentarily to tear the rokes from their solid beds, and sweep them into the broad and sullen pool below.

The trembling of the massive boulder upon which I lay outstretched peering into the raging abyss, the fierce

PASSAGE ON THE DRIV.

surging of the waters, the whirling clouds of spray, and gorgeous prismatic colors that flashed through them, created an impression that the whole was some wild, mad freak of the elements, gotten up to furnish the traveler with a startling idea of the wonders and beauties of Norwegian scenery.

CHAPTER XXXV.

A NORWEGIAN HORSE-JOCKEY.

LATE one evening I arrived at a lonely little station by the wayside, not far beyond the valley of the Drivs-dal. I was cold and hungry, and well disposed to enjoy whatever good cheer the honest people who kept the inn might have in store for me. The house and outbuild-ings were such as belong to an ordinary farming estab-lishment, and did not promise much in the way of enter-tainment. Upon entering the rustic doorway I was kind-ly greeted by the host—a simple, good-natured looking man—who, as usual, showed me into the best room. Now I am not aware of any thing in my appearance that entitles me to this distinction, but it has generally been my fate, in this sort of travel, to be set apart and isola-ted from the common herd in the fancy room of the es-tablishment, which I have always found to be corre-spondingly the coldest and most uncomfortable. It is a great annoyance in Norway to be treated as a gentle-man. The commonest lout can enjoy the cozy glow and social gossip of the kitchen or ordinary sitting-room, but the traveler whom these good people would honor must sit shivering and alone in some great barn of a room be-cause it contains a sofa, a bureau, a looking-glass, a few mantle-piece ornaments, and an occasional picture of the king or some member of the royal family. I have walk-ed up and down these dismal chambers for hours at a time, staring at the daubs on the walls, and picking up little odds and ends of ornaments, and gazing vacantly at them, till I felt a numbness steal all over me, accom-panied by a vague presentiment that I was imprisoned for life. The progress of time is a matter of no import-ance in Norway. To an American, accustomed to see

every thing done with energy and promptness, it is absolutely astounding—the indifference of these people to
the waste of hours. They seem to be forever asleep, or
doing something that bears no possible reference to their
ostensible business. If you are hungry and want something to eat in a few minutes, the probability is you will
be left alone in the fine room for several hours, at the
expiration of which you discover that the innkeeper is
out in the stable feeding his horses, his wife in the back
yard looking after the chickens, and his children sitting
at a table in the kitchen devouring a dish of porridge.
Upon expressing your astonishment that nothing is
ready, the good man of the house says "Ja! it will be
ready directly, min Herr!" and if you are lucky it comes
in another hour—a cup of coffee and some bread perhaps, which you could just as well have had in ten minutes. Patience may be a virtue in other countries, but
it is an absolute necessity in Norway. I believe, after
the few weeks' experience I had on the road to Trondhjem, I could without difficulty sit upon a monument
and smile at grief.

Perceiving through the cracks of the door that there
was a good fire in the kitchen, and hearing the cheerful
voices of the man and his wife, varied by the merry whistle of my skydskaarl, I made bold to go in and ask leave
to stand by the fire. The good people seemed a little
astonished at first that a person of quality like myself
should prefer the kitchen to the fine room with the sofa
and bureau, the mantle-piece ornaments and pictures of
the royal family; but, by dint of good-humored gossip
about the horses, and an extravagant compliment thrown
in about the beauty of the landlady's children—for which
I hope to be pardoned—I secured a comfortable seat by
the fire, and was soon quite at home. The great open
fireplace, the blazing pine logs, the well-smoked hobs, the
simmering pots and steaming kettles, had something in-
describably cheerful about them; and lighting my pipe,
I puffed away cozily during the pauses in the conversa-

tion, having a delightful consciousness that nature had peculiarly adapted me for the vulgar enjoyments of life, and that every thing approaching the refinements of civilization was a great bore. It was doubtless this taint of the savage in my disposition that made me look with such horror upon neat rooms and civilized furniture, and fall back with such zest upon the primitive comforts of savage life. When I told the people of the house that I was all the way from California—that I had come expressly to see their country—there was no end to the interest and excitement. "Dear me!" they cried, "and you have traveled a long way! You must be very tired! And you must be very rich to travel so far! Ah Gott—how wonderful!" "Did you come all the way in a cariole?" inquired the simple-minded host. "No; I came part of the way by sea, in a great ship." "How wonderful!" "And what sort of horses had they in California?" I told some tough stories about the mustang horses, in which the landlord was profoundly interested, for I soon discovered that horses were his great hobby. Whatever we talked of, he invariably came back to horse-flesh. His head was overrunning with horses. I praised his cariole horses, and he was enchanted. He gave me the pedigree of every horse in his stable, scarcely a word of which I understood, and then wound up by telling me he was considered the best judge of horses in all Norway. I did not think there was much in his appearance indicative of the shrewd horse-jockey, but was soon convinced of his shrewdness, for he informed me confidentially he had drawn the great prize at the last annual horse-fair at Christiania, and if I didn't believe it he would show it to me! I tried to make him understand that I had no doubt at all what he said was strictly true; but, not satisfied at this expression of faith in his word, he went to a big wooden chest in the corner and took out a bag of money, which he placed upon the middle of the table with a proud smile of triumph. "That," said he, "is the prize! A hundred and fifty silver dollars—*sil-*

ver, mind you—all SILVER!" But perhaps I didn't believe it was a prize? Well, he would convince me of
that. So he left the bag of money on the table and went

THE PRIZE.

into a back room to get the certificate of the society, in
which it was all duly written out, with his name in large
letters, the paper being neatly framed in a carved frame,

the work of his own hands. There it was; I could read
for myself! I tried to read it to oblige him, and as I
blundered over the words he took it into his head that I
was still incredulous. "Nai! nai!" said he, "you shall
see the money! You shall count it for yourself!" In
vain I strove to convince him that I was entirely satisfied on the subject—that he must not go to so much
trouble on my account. "Nai! nai!" cried the enthusiastic dealer in horse-flesh, "it is no trouble. You shall
see the money WITH YOUR OWN EYES!" And forthwith
he untied the string of the bag, and poured out the shining dollars in a pile on the middle of the table. His good
wife stood by, professing to smile, but I suspected, from
the watchful expression of her eye, that she did not feel
quite at ease. The skydskaarl leaned over with a general expression of the most profound astonishment and admiration. "See!" cried the old man; "this is the prize
—every dollar of it. But you must count it—I'll help
you—so!" As there was no getting over the task imposed upon me without hurting his feelings, I had to sit
down and help to count the money—no very pleasant
job for a hungry man. After summing up our respective piles, there appeared to be only a hundred and for-
ty-nine dollars—just a dollar short. "Lieb Gott!" cried
the man, "there must be a mistake! Let us count it
again!" I felt that there was a necessity for counting
it very carefully this time, for the landlady's eye was on
me with a very searching expression. "Een, to, tre, five,
fem, sex," and so on for nearly half an hour, when we
summed up our counts again. This time it was only a
hundred and forty-eight dollars—just two dollars short!
The old man scratched his head and looked bewildered.
The landlady moved about nervously, and stared very
hard at me. It was getting to be rather an embarrassing
affair. I blamed myself for being so foolishly drawn into
it. Wishing to know if there really was a mistake, I
begged my host to let me count it alone, which I did by
making fifteen piles of ten dollars each, carefully count-

ing every pile. It was all right; the whole amount was there, a hundred and fifty dollars. "All right!" said I, much relieved; "don't you see, every pile is exactly the same height!" "Ja! Ja!" said the man; "but I don't understand it. Here, wife, you and I must count it!" So the wife sat down, and they both began counting the money, varying every time they compared notes from two to ten dollars. Once they had it a hundred and sixty dollars. "The devil is in the money!" exclaimed the horse-dealer; "I'm certain I counted right." "And so am I!" said the woman; "I can not be mistaken. It is you who have made the mistake. You always were a stupid old fool about money!" This she said with some degree of asperity, for she was evidently displeased at the whole proceeding. "A fool, eh? A fool!" muttered the old man; "you do well to call me a fool before strangers!" "Ja, that's the way! I always told you so!" screamed the woman, in rising tones of anger; "you'll lose all your money yet!" "Lose it!" retorted the man; "don't you see I have made ten dollars by counting it to-night! There! count it yourself, and hold your peace, woman!" Here the wife, suppressing her wrath, made a careful and deliberate count, which resulted in the exact sum of a hundred and fifty dollars! I was much relieved; but by this time the old man, unable to bear the torrent of reproaches heaped upon him by his good wife for his stupidity, swore she must have made a mistake. He was sure he had counted a hundred and sixty; therefore he would count it again, all alone, which he proceeded to do, very slowly and cautiously. This time the result was a hundred and fifty-five dollars. "The devil's in it!" cried the astonished dealer; "there's some magic about it! I don't understand it. I must count it again!" The woman, however, being satisfied that it was all right, I now thought it best to return to my seat by the fire, where she soon began to busy herself preparing the supper, turning round now and then of course to let off a broadside at her old man. She took occasion to inform me, during the progress of her culinary labors, that he was a very good sort of man, but was somewhat addicted to brandy-wine, of which he had partaken a little too freely on the present occasion. I must excuse him. She would send him to bed presently. And now, if I pleased, supper was ready.

I could not help thinking, as I lay in bed that night, how lucky it was for these simple-minded people that they lived in the interior of Norway. Even in California, where public and private integrity is the prevailing trait of the people, it would hardly be considered safe to pull out a bag of money at a wayside inn and show it to every passing stranger. I have known men there in high public positions whom I would scarcely like to tempt in that way, especially if there was money enough in the bag to make robbery respectable.

All along the route during the next day the scenery was a continued feast of enjoyment. In looking back over it now, however, after the lapse of of several months, it would be difficult to recall any thing beyond its general features—pine-covered mountains, green valleys, dark rocky glens, foaming torrents of water, and groups of farm-houses by the wayside. At Bjerkager I reached the first of the " slow-stations ;" that is to say, the established post-houses, where a margin of three hours is allowed for a change of horses. I had supposed that in a country, and on a public route, where during the summer there must be considerable travel, it would hardly be possible that so long a delay could take place; but in this I was mistaken. The slow-stations are emphatically slow; the keepers are slow, the horses are slow, the whole concern is slow. From Bjerkager to Garlid, and from Garlid to Hov, including all delays, a distance of three hours and a half ordinary time, it took me all day. No entreaties, no offers of extra compensation, no expressions of impatience produced the slightest effect. The people at these places were not to be hurried. Kind and good-natured as they were in appearance and expression, I found them the most bull-headed and intract-able race of beings on the face of the earth.

I was particularly struck with the depressing lethargy that hung over a wretched little place called Soknaes, which I made out to reach the next morning. A dead silence reigned over the miserable huddle of buildings by the roadside. The houses looked green and mildew-ed. A few forlorn chickens in the stable-yard, and a half-starved dog crouching under the door-steps, too poor to bark and too lazy to move, were the only signs of life that greeted me as I approached. I knocked at the door, but no answer was made to the summons. Not a living soul was to be seen around the place. I attempted to whistle and shout. Still the terrible silence remained unbroken save by the dismal echoes of my own melan-choly music. At length I went to a rickety shed under which some carts were drawn up for shelter from the weather. In one of the carts, half-covered in a bundle of straw, was a bundle of clothes. It moved as I drew near; it thrust a boot out over the tail-board; it shook itself; it emitted a curious sound between a grunt and a yawn; it raised itself up and shook off a portion of the straw; it thrust a red night-cap out of the mass of shape-less rubbish; the night-cap contained a head and a mat-ted shock of hair; there was a withered, old-fashioned little face on the front part of the head, underneath the shock of hair, which opened its mouth and eyes, and gazed at me vacantly; it was an old man or a boy, I could not tell which till it spoke, when I discovered that it was something between the two, and was the skydskaarl or hostler of this remarkable establishment. He rubbed his eyes and stared again. "Hello!" said I. He grunted out something. "Heste og Cariole!" said I. "Ja! Ja!" grunted the hostler, and then he began to get out of the cart. I suppose he creaked, though I do not pretend that the sounds were audible. First one leg came out; slowly it was followed by the other. When they both got to the ground, he pushed his body gradually over the tail-board, and in about five minutes was standing before me.

"A horse and cariole," said I; "let me have them quick!"

"Ja! Ja!"

"*Strax!*" [directly!] said I.

"Ja! Ja!"

"How long will it be?"

"Ach!"—here he yawned.

"An hour?"

"Ja! Ja!"

"Two hours?"

"Ja! Ja!"

"Three hours?"

"Ja! Ja!"

"Sacramento! I can't stand that. I must have one STRAX—directly—forstöede?"

"Ja! Ja!" and the fellow rubbed his eyes and yawned again.

"Look here! my friend," said I, "if you'll get me a horse and cariole in half an hour, I'll give you two marks extra—forstöe?"

"Ja! Ja! twa mark" (still yawning).

"Half an hour, mind you!"

"*Tre time*—three hours!" grunted the incorrigible dunderhead.

"Then good-by—I must travel on foot!" and, with rage and indignation depicted in every feature, I flung my knapsack over my shoulder and made a feint to start.

"Adieu! farvel!" said the sleepy lout, good-naturedly holding out his hand to give me a parting shake. "Farvel, min Herr! May your journey be pleasant! God take care of you!"

The perfect sincerity of the fellow completely dissipated my rage, and, giving him a friendly shake, I proceeded on my way. As I turned the corner of the main building and struck into the road, I cast a look back. He was still standing by the cart, yawning and rubbing his eyes as before. That man would make money in California—if money could be made by a bet on laziness. He is lazier than the old Dutch skipper who was too lazy to go below, and gave orders to the man at the helm to follow the sun so as to keep him in the shade of the main-sail, by reason of which he sailed round the horizon till his tobacco gave out, and he had to return home for a fresh supply. I call that a strong case of laziness, but scarcely stronger than the traveler meets with every day in Norway.

CHAPTER XXXVI.

OUT OF MONEY.

I now began to enjoy the real pleasures of Norwegian travel. No longer compelled to endure the vexatious delays to which I had lately been subject, I bowled along the road, with my knapsack on my back, at the rate of four miles an hour, whistling merrily from sheer exuberance of health and lack of thought. The weather was charming. A bright sun shed its warm rays over hill and dale; the air was fresh and invigorating; the richest tints adorned the whole face of the country, which from Soknaes to Trondhjem gradually increases in fertility and breadth of outline, till it becomes almost unrivaled in the profusion of its pastoral beauties. Nothing can surpass the gorgeous splendor of the autumnal sunsets in this part of Norway. At an earlier period of the year there is perpetual daylight for several weeks, and for three days the sun does not descend below the horizon. The light, however, is too strong during that period to produce the rich and glowing tints which cover the sky and mountain-tops at a later season of the year. I was fortunate in being just in time to enjoy the full measure of its beauties, and surely it is not too much to say that such an experience is of itself worth a trip to Norway. I shall not attempt a description of Norwe-

TRAVELING ON FOOT.

gian skies, however, after the glowing picture of the North Cape at midnight drawn by the pen of my friend Bayard Taylor, the most faithful and enthusiastic of all the travelers who have given their experience of this interesting region.

Keeping along the banks of the Gula, the road winds around the sides of the hills, sometimes crossing open valleys, and occasionally penetrating the shady recesses of the pine forests, till it diverges from the river at Meelhus. Soon after leaving this station the views from the higher points over which the road passes are of great beauty and extent, embracing a glimpse, from time to time, of the great Trondhjem Fjord.

Night overtook me at the pretty little station of Esp. Next morning I was up bright and early, and, after a cup of coffee and some rolls, shouldered my knapsack and pushed on to Trondhjem.

Finding my purse growing lighter every day, I was compelled at this point to cut short my intended journey to the North Cape, and take the first steamer down the coast for Christiansund and Hamburg.

Arrived once more at the family head-quarters in Frankfort-on-the-Main, I spent a few months writing up the loose material I had thus gathered, and making foot-tours through the Odenwald, the Spessart, and the Schwartzwald. But I was not satisfied with what I had seen of the North. There was still a wild region, far beyond any explorations I had yet made, which constantly loomed up in my imagination—the chaotic land of frost and fire, where dwelt in ancient times the mighty Thor, the mystic deity of the Scandinavians.

CHAPTER XXXVII.

ICELANDIC TRAVEL.

Not many years have passed since it was considered something of an achievement to visit Iceland. The traveler who had the hardihood to penetrate the chilly fogs of the North, and journey by the compass through a region of everlasting snows and desolating fires, could well afford to stay at home during the remainder of his life, satisfied with the reputation generally accorded him by his fellow-men. It was something to have plunged into rivers of unknown depth, and traversed treacherous bogs and desert fjelds of lava—something to be able to speak knowingly of the learned Sagas, and verify the wonders of the Burned Njal.

An isolated spot of earth, bordering on the Arctic Circle, and cut off by icebergs and frozen seas from all intercourse with the civilized world during half the year, once the seat of an enlightened republic, and still inhabited by the descendants of men who had worshiped Odin and Thor, must surely have presented rare attractions to the enterprising traveler before it became a beaten track for modern tourists. A simple narrative of facts was then sufficient to enlist attention. Even the unlearned adventurer could obtain a reputation by an unvarnished recital of what he saw and heard. He could describe the Lögberg upon which the republican Parliament held its sittings, and attest from personal observation that this was the exact spot where judgments were pronounced by the *Thing.* He could speak familiarly of heathen gods and vikings after a brief intercourse with the inhabitants, who are still tinctured with the spirit of their early civilization. He could tell of frightful volcanoes, that fill the air with clouds of ashes, and desolate the earth with burning floods of lava, and of scalding hot water shot up out of subterranean boilers, and gaping fissures that emit sulphurous vapors, and strange sounds heard beneath the earth's surface, and all the marvelous experiences of Icelandic travel, including ghosts and hobgoblins that ramble over the icy wastes by night, and hide themselves in gloomy caverns by day—these he could dwell upon in earnest and homely language with the pleasing certainty of an appreciative audience. But times have sadly changed within the past few years. A trip to Iceland nowadays is little more than a pleasant summer excursion, brought within the capacity of every tyro in travel through the leveling agency of steam. When a Parisian lady of rank visits Spitzbergen, and makes the overland journey from the North Cape to the Gulf of Bothnia, of what avail is it for any gentleman of elegant leisure to leave his comfortable fireside? We tourists who are ambitious to see the world in an easy way need but sit in our cushioned chair, cozily smoking our cigar, while some enterprising lady puts a girdle round about the earth; for we may depend upon it she will reappear ere leviathan can swim a league, and present us with a

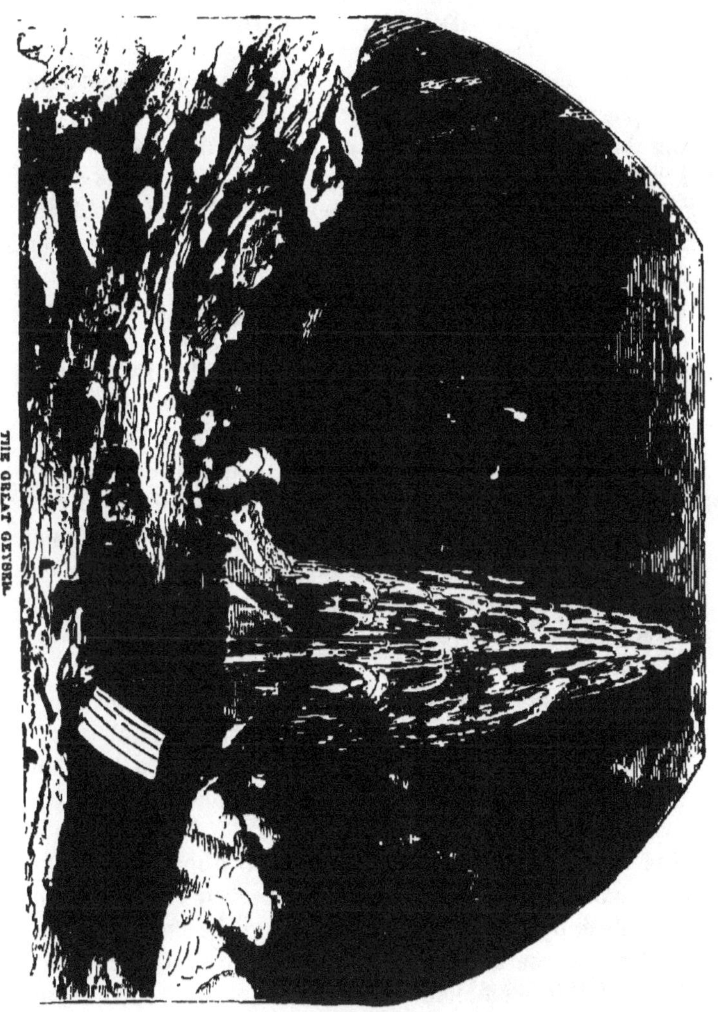

THE GREAT GEYSER.

bouquet of wonderful experiences, neatly pressed between the pages of an entertaining volume. The icebergs of the Arctic, the bananas of the tropics, the camels of the East, the buffaloes of the West, and the cannibals of the South, are equally at our service. We can hold the mountains, rivers, seas, and human races between our finger and thumb, and thus, as we gently dally with care, we may see the wonders of the world as in a pleasant dream. Thus may we enjoy the perils and hardships of travel at a very small sacrifice of personal comfort.

It was somewhat in this style that I reasoned when the idea occurred to me of making a trip to Iceland. From all accounts it was a very uncomfortable country, deficient in roads, destitute of hotels, and subject to various eccentricities of climate. Neither fame nor money was to be gained by such a trip—unless, indeed, I succeeded in catching the great auk, for which, it is said, the directors of the British Museum have offered a reward of a hundred pounds. This was a chance, to be sure. I might possibly be able to get hold of the auk, and thereby secure money enough to pay expenses, and make certain a niche in the temple of fame. It would be something to rank with the great men who had devoted their lives to the pursuit of the dodo and the roc. But there was a deplorable lack of information about the haunts and habits of the auk. I was not even satisfied of its existence, by the fact that two Englishmen visited Iceland a few years ago for the purpose of securing a specimen of this wonderful bird, and, after six weeks of unavailing search, wrote a book to prove that there was still reason to hope for success.

Upon the whole, I thought it would not do to depend upon the auk. There was but one opening left—to visit Iceland, sketch-book in hand, and faithfully do what others had left undone—make accurate sketches of the mountains, rivers, lava-fjelds, geysers, people, and costumes. In nothing is Iceland so deficient as in pictorial representation. It has been very minutely surveyed by the Danes, and Olsen has left nothing to wish for in the way of topographical delineation, but artists do not seem to have found it an attractive field for the exercise of their talent. At least I could obtain no good pictures of Iceland in Copenhagen. The few indifferent sketches published there, and in the journals of late English and German tourists, afford no adequate idea of the country. I have seen nothing of the kind any where that impressed my mind with the slightest notion of that land of fire, or the spirit and genius of Icelandic life. It would therefore be some gain to the cause of knowledge if I could present to five hundred thousand of my fellow-citizens, who do their traveling through these illuminated pages, a reasonably fair delineation of the country and the people, with such simple record of my own experiences as would render the sketches generally intelligible.

So one fine morning in May I shouldered my knapsack, and bade a temporary adieu to my friends in Frankfort. By night I was in Hamburg. The next day was agreeably spent in rambling about the gardens across the Alster Basin, and at 5 P.M. I left Altona for Kiel, a journey of three hours by rail across a flat and not very interesting tract of country within the limits of Schleswig-Holstein. From Kiel a steamer leaves for Korsör, on the island of Zealand, the terminus of the Copenhagen Railway. This is the most direct route between Hamburg and Copenhagen, though the trip may be very pleasantly varied by taking a steamer to Taars, and passing by diligence through the islands of Lalland, Falster, and Möen.

CHAPTER XXXVIII.

HANS CHRISTIAN ANDERSEN.

A FEW days after my arrival in Copenhagen I had the pleasure of making the acquaintance of Professor Andersen, of the Scandinavian Museum, a native Icelander, who very kindly showed me the chief objects of curiosity obtained from the Danish possessions in the North, consisting mostly of fish and geological specimens. The Minister of the Judiciary obligingly gave me a letter to the governor and principal amtmen of Iceland, and many other gentlemen of influence manifested the most friendly interest in my proposed undertaking. I was especially indebted to Captain Södring, late owner of the *Fox*, of Arctic celebrity, for much valuable information respecting the Northern seas, as well as for his cordial hospitalie and indefatigable efforts to make my sojourn in Copenhagen both agreeable and profitable. Indeed, I was delighted with the place and the people. The Danes are exceedingly genial in their manners, distinguished alike for their simplicity and intelligence. There is no trouble to which they will not put themselves to oblige a stranger. In my rambles through the public libraries and museums I was always accompanied by some professor attached to the institution, who took the greatest pains to explain every thing, and impress me with a favorable idea of the value of the collection. This was not a mere formal matter of duty; many of them spent hours and even days in the performance of their friendly labors, omitting nothing that might contribute to my enjoyment as a stranger. The visitor who can not spend his time agreeably in such society, surrounded by such institutions as Thorwaldsen's Museum and the National Collection of Scandinavian Antiquities, must be difficult to please indeed. The Tivoli or the Dyrhave, an evening at Fredericksberg, or a trip to "Hamlet's Grave" at Elsineur, would surely fill the measure of his contentment. Whether in the way of beautiful gardens, public amusements, charming excursions, or agreeable and intelligent society, I know of no European capital that can surpass Copenhagen. Our excellent minister, Mr. Wood, with whom I had the pleasure of spending an evening at Elsineur, speaks in the most complimentary terms of the Danes and their customs, and expresses some surprise, considering the general increase of European travel from our country, that so few American tourists visit Denmark.

I could not do myself the injustice to leave Copenhagen without forming the personal acquaintance of a man to whom a debt of gratitude is due by the young and the old in all countries—the ramblers in fairy-land, the lovers of romance, and the friends of humanity—all who can feel the divine influence of genius, and learn, through the teachings of a kindly heart, that the inhabitants of earth are

"Kindred by one holy tie"—

the quaint, pathetic, genial Hans Christian Andersen. Not wishing to impose any obligation of courtesy on him by a letter of introduction or the obliging services of my Danish friends, I called at his house unattended, and merely sent in my name and address. Unfortunately he was out taking his morning walk, and would not be back till the afternoon. By calling at three o'clock, the servant said, I would be very likely to find him at home. I then added to my card the simple fact that I was an American traveler on my way to Iceland for the purpose of making some sketches of the country, and would take the liberty of calling at the appointed hour. It may be a matter of interest to an American reader to have some idea of the peculiar neighborhood and style of house in which a great Danish author has chosen to take up his abode. The city of Copenhagen, it should be borne in mind, is intersected by canals which, during the summer months, are crowded with small trading vessels from Sweden and Jutland, and fishing-smacks from the neighboring islands and coast of Norway. The wharves bordering on these canals present an exceedingly animated appearance. Peasants, sailors, traders, and fishermen, in every variety of costume, are gathered in groups, enjoying a social gossip, or interchanging their various products and wares, and strawberries from Amak and fish from the Skager-Rack mingle their odors. In the second story of a dingy and dilapidated house, fronting one of these unsavory canals, a confused pile of dirty, shambling old tenements in the rear, and a curious medley of fish and fishermen, sloops and schooners, mud-scows and skiffs in front, lives the world-renowned author, Hans Christian Andersen. I say he lives there, but, properly speaking, he only lodges. It seems to be a peculiarity of his nature to move about from time to time into all the queer and uninviting places possible to be discovered within the limits of Copenhagen—not where

> "The mantling vine
> Lays forth her grape and gently creeps
> Luxuriant,"

but where the roughest, noisiest, busiest, and fishiest of an amphibious population is to be found. Here it is, apparently amid the most incongruous elements, that he draws from all around him the most delicate traits of human nature, and matures for the great outer world the most exquisite creations of his fancy. It is purely a labor of love in which he spends his life. The products of his pen have furnished him with ample means to live in elegant style, surrounded by all the allurements of rank and fashion, but he prefers the obscurity of a plain lodging amid the haunts of those classes whose lives and pursuits he so well portrays. Here he cordially receives all who call upon him, and they are not few. Pilgrims of every condition in life and from all nations do homage to his genius, yet, valuable as his time is, he finds enough to spare for the kindly reception of his visitors. His only household companions appear to be two old peasant women, whom he employs as domestics; weather-beaten and decrepit old creatures, with faces and forms very much like a pair of antiquated nut-crackers. He occupies only two or three rooms plainly furnished, and apparently lives in the simplest and most abstemious style.

When I called according to directions, one of the ancient nut-crackers merely pointed to the door, and said she thought Herr Andersen was in, but didn't know. I could knock there and try; so I knocked. Presently I heard a rapid step, and the door was thrown open. Before me stood the tall, thin, shambling, raw-boned figure of a man a little beyond the prime of life, but not yet old, with a pair of dancing gray eyes and a hatchet-face, all alive with twists, and wrinkles, and muscles; a long, lean face, upon which stood out prominently a great nose, diverted by a freak of nature a little to one side, and flanked by a tremendous pair of cheek-bones, with great hollows underneath. Innumerable ridges and furrows swept semicircularly downward around the corners of a great mouth—a broad, deep, rugged fissure across the face, that might have been mistaken for the dreadful child-trap of an ogre but for the sunny beams of benevolence that lurked around the lips, and the genial humanity that glimmered from every nook and turn. Neither mustache nor beard obscured the strong individuality of this remarkable face, which for the most part was of a dull granite color, a little mixed with limestone and spotted with patches of porphyry. A dented gutta-percha forehead, very prominent about the brows, and somewhat resembling in its general topography a raised map of Switzerland, sloped upward and backward to the top of the head; not a very large head, but wonderfully bumped and battered by the operations of the brain, and partially covered by a mop of dark wavy hair, a little thin in front and somewhat grizzled behind; a long, bony pair of arms, with long hands on them; a long, lank body, with a long black coat on it; a long, loose pair of legs, with long boots on the feet, all in motion at the same time—all shining, and wriggling, and working with an indescribable vitality; a voice bubbling up from the vast depths below with cheery, spasmodic, and unintelligible words of welcome—this was the wonderful man that stood before me, the great Danish improvisator, the lover of little children, the gentle Caliban who dwells among fairies and holds sweet converse with fishes, and frogs, and beetles! I would have picked him out from among a thousand men at the first glance as a candidate for

Congress, or the proprietor of a tavern, if I had met him any where in the United States. But the resemblance was only momentary. In the quaint awkwardness of his gestures and the simplicity of his speech there was a certain refinement not usually found among men of that class. Something in the spontaneous and almost child-like cordiality of his greeting; the unworldly impulsiveness of his nature, as he grasped both my hands in his, patted me affectionately on the shoulder, and bade me welcome, convinced me in a moment that this was no other, and could be no other, than Hans Christian Andersen.

"Come in! come in!" he said, in a gush of broken English; "come in and sit down. You are very welcome. Thank you—thank you very much. I am very glad to see you. It is a rare thing to meet a traveler all the way from California—quite a surprise. Sit down! Thank you!"

And then followed a variety of friendly compliments and remarks about the Americans. He liked them; he was sorry they were so unfortunate as to be engaged in a civil war, but hoped it would soon be over. Did I speak French? he asked, after a pause. Not very well. Or German? Still worse, was my answer. "What a pity!" he exclaimed; "it must trouble you to understand my English, I speak it so badly. It is only within a few years that I have learned to speak it at all." Of course I complimented him upon his English, which was really better than I had been led to expect. "Can you understand it?" he asked, looking earnestly in my face. "Certainly," I answered, "almost every word." "Oh, thank you—thank you. You are very good," he cried, grasping me by the hand. "I am very much obliged to you for understanding me." I naturally thanked him for being obliged to me, and we shook hands cordially, and mutually thanked one another over again for being so amiable. The conversation, if such it could be called, flew from subject to subject with a rapidity that almost took my breath away. The great improvisator dashed recklessly into every thing that he thought would be interesting to an American traveler, but with the difficulty of his utterance in English, and the absence of any knowledge on his part of my name or history, it was evident he was a little embarrassed in what way to oblige me most; and the trouble on my side was, that I was too busy listening to find time for talking.

"Dear! dear! And you are going to Iceland!" he continued. "A long way from California! I would like to visit America, but it is very dangerous to travel by sea. A vessel was burned up not long since, and many of my friends were lost. It was a dreadful affair."

From this he diverged to a trip he then had in contemplation through Switzerland and Spain. He was sitting for his statuette, which he desired to leave as a memento to his friends prior to his departure. A young Danish sculptor was making it. Would I like to see it? and forthwith I was introduced to the young Danish sculptor. The likeness was very good, and my comments upon it elicited many additional thanks and several squeezes of the hand—it was so kind of me to be pleased with it! "He is a young student," said Andersen, approvingly; "a very good young man. I want to encourage him. He will be a great artist some day or other."

Talking of likenesses reminded me of a photograph which I had purchased a few days before, and to which I now asked the addition of an autograph.

"Oh, you have a libel on me here!" cried the poet, laughing joyously—"a very bad likeness. Wait! I have several much better; here they are—" And he rushed into the next room, tumbled over a lot of papers, and ransacked a number of drawers till he found the desired package—"here's a dozen of them; take your choice; help yourself—as many as you please!" While looking over the collection, I said the likeness of one who had done so much to promote the happiness of some little

friends I had at home would be valued beyond measure; that I knew at least half a dozen youngsters who were as well acquainted with the "Little Match Girl," and the "Ugly Duck," and the "Poor Idiot Boy," as he was himself, and his name was as familiar in California as it was in Denmark. At this he grasped both my hands, and looking straight in my face with a kind of ecstatic expression, said, "Oh, is it possible? Do they really read my books in California? so far away! Oh! I thank you very much. Some of my stories, I am aware, have been published in New York, but I did not think they had found their way to the Pacific Coast. Dear me! Thank you! thank you! Have you seen my last—the—what do you call it in English?—a little animal—"

"Mouse," I suggested.

"No, not a mouse; a little animal with wings."

"Oh, a bat!"

"Nay, nay, a little animal with wings and many legs. Dear me! I forget the name in English, but you certainly know it in America—a very small animal!"

In vain I tried to make a selection from all the little animals of my acquaintance with wings and many legs. The case was getting both embarrassing and vexatious. At length a light broke upon me.

"A musquito!" I exclaimed, triumphantly.

"Nay, nay!" cried the bothered poet; "a little animal with a hard skin on its back. Dear me, I can't remember the name!"

"Oh, I have it now," said I, really desirous of relieving his mind—"a flea!"

At this the great improvisator scratched his head,

 looked at the ceiling and then at the floor, after which he took several rapid strides up and down the room, and struck himself repeatedly on the forehead. Suddenly grasping up a pen, he exclaimed, somewhat energetically, "Here! I'll draw it for you;" and forthwith he drew on a scrap of paper a diagram, of which the accompanying engraving is a fac-simile.

"A tumble-bug!" I shouted, astonished at my former stupidity.

The poet looked puzzled and distressed. Evidently I had not yet succeeded. What could it be?

"A beetle!" I next ventured to suggest, rather disappointed at the result of my previous guess.

"A beetle! A beetle!—that's it; now I remember —a beetle!" and the delighted author of "The Beetle" patted me approvingly on the back, and chuckled gleefully at his own adroit method of explanation. "I'll give you 'The Beetle,'" he said; "you shall have the only copy in my possession. But you don't read Danish! What are we to do? There is a partial translation in French—a mere notice."

"No matter," I answered. "A specimen of the Danish language will be very acceptable, and the book will be a pleasant souvenir of my visit."

He then darted into the next room, tumbled over a dozen piles of books, then out again, ransacked the desks, and drawers, and heaps of old papers and rubbish, talking all the time in his joyous, cheery way about his books and his travels in Jutland, and his visit to Charles Dickens, and his intended journey through Spain, and his delight at meeting a traveler all the way from California, and whatever else came into his head—all in such mixed-up broken English that the meaning must have been utterly lost but for the wonderful expressiveness of his face and the striking oddity of his motions. It came to me mesmerically. He seemed like one who glowed all over with bright and happy thoughts, which permeated all around him with a new intelligence. His presence shed a light upon others like the rays that beamed from the eyes of "Little Sunshine." The book was found at last, and when he had written his name in it, with a friendly inscription, and pressed both my hands on the gift, and patted me once more on the shoulder, and promised to call at Frankfort on his return from Switzerland to see his little friends who knew all about the "Ugly Duck" and the "Little Match Girl," I took my leave, more delighted, if possible, with the author than I had ever before been with his books. Such a man, the brightest, happiest, simplest, most genial of human beings, is Hans Christian Andersen.

The steamer *Arcturus* was advertised to sail for Reykjavik on the 4th of June, so it behooved me to be laying in some sort of an outfit for the voyage during the few days that intervened. A knapsack, containing a change of linen and my sketching materials, was all I possessed. This would have been sufficient but for the probability of rain and cold weather. I wanted a sailor's monkey-jacket and an overall. My friend Captain Södring would not hear of my buying any thing in that way. He had enough on hand from his old whaling voyages, he said, to fit out a dozen men of my pattern. Just come up to the house and take a look at them, and if there wasn't too much oil on them, I was welcome to the whole lot; but the oil, he thought, would be an advantage—it would keep out the water. In vain I protested—it was no use —the captain was an old whaler, and so was I, and when two old whalers met, it was a pity if they couldn't act like shipmates on the voyage of life. There was no re-sisting this appeal, so I agreed to accept the old clothes. When we arrived at the captain's house he disappeared in the garret, but presently returned bearing a terrific pile of rubbish on his shoulders, and accompanied by a stout servant-girl also heavily laden with marine curiosi-ties. There were sou'westers, and tarpaulins, and skull-caps; frieze jackets, and overalls, and hickory shirts; tar-paulin coats, and heavy sea-boots, and duck blouses with old bunches of oakum sticking out of the pockets; there were coils of rope-yarn well tarred, and jack-knives in leather cases, still black with whale-gurry; and a few telescopes and log-glasses. "Take 'em all," said the cap-tain. "They smell a little fishy, but no matter. It's all the better for a voyage to Iceland. You'll be used to the smell before you get to Reykjavik; and it's whole-some—very wholesome! Nothing makes a man so fat." I made a small selection—a rough jacket and a few oth-er essential articles. "Nonsense, man!" roared the cap-tain, "take 'em all! You'll find them useful; and if you don't, you can heave them overboard or give them to the sailors." And thus was I fitted out for the voyage.

CHAPTER XXXIX.

VOYAGE TO SCOTLAND.

THE *Arcturus* is a small screw steamer owned by Messrs. Koch and Henderson, and now some six years on the route between Copenhagen and Reykjavik. The Danish government pays them an annual sum for carrying the mails, and they control a considerable trade in fish and wool. This vessel makes six trips every year, touching at a port in Scotland both on the outer and return voyage. At first she made Leith her stopping-place; but, owing to superior facilities for her business at Grangemouth, she now stops at that port. The cost of passage is extremely moderate—only 45 Danish dollars, about $28 American, living on board 75 cents a day, and a small fee to the steward, making for the voyage out or back, which usually occupies about eleven days, inclusive of stoppages, something less than $40. I mention this for the benefit of my friends at home, who may think proper to make a very interesting trip at a very small expense; though, as will hereafter appear, the most considerable part of the expenditure occurs in Iceland. Captain Andersen (they are all Andersens, or Jonasens, or Hansens, or Petersens in Denmark), a very active and obliging little Dane, commands the *Arcturus*. He speaks English fluently, and is an experienced seaman; and if the tourist is not unusually fastidious about accommodations, there will be no difficulty in making an agreeable voyage. I found every thing on board excellent; the fare abundant and wholesome, and the sleeping-quarters not more like coffins than they usually are on board small steamers. A few inches cut off the passengers' legs or added to the length of the berths, and a few extra hand-spikes in the lee scuppers to steady the vessel, would be an improvement; but then one can't have every thing to suit him. Some grumbling took place, to be sure, after our departure from Scotland. A young Scotchman wanted a berth for a big dog in the same cabin with the rest of his friends, which the captain would not permit; an Englishman was disgusted with the "beastly fare;" and an old Danish merchant would persist in shaving himself at the public table every day—all of which caused an under-current of dissatisfaction during the early part of the voyage. Sea-sickness, however, put an end to it before long, and things went on all right after that.

But I must not anticipate my narrative. The scene upon leaving the wharf at Copenhagen was amusing and characteristic. For some hours before our departure the decks were crowded with the friends of the passengers. Every person had to kiss and hug every other person, and shake hands, and laugh and cry a little, and then hug and kiss again, without regard to age and not much distinction of sex. Some natural tears, of course, must always be shed on occasions of this kind. It was rather a melancholy reflection, as I stood aloof looking on at all these demonstrations of affection, that there was nobody present to grieve over my departure—not even a lap-dog to bestow upon me a parting kiss. Waving of hand-kerchiefs, messages to friends in Iceland, and parting benedictions, took place long before we left the wharf. At length the last bells were rung, the lingering loved ones were handed ashore, and the inexorable voice of the captain was heard ordering the sailors to cast loose the ropes. We were fairly off for Iceland!

In a few hours we passed, near Elsineur, the fine old Castle of Kronberg, built in the time of Tycho Brahe, once the prison of the unfortunate Caroline Matilda, queen of Christian VII., and in the great vaults of which it is said the Danish Roland, Holger Dansk, still lives, his long white beard grown fast to a stone table. We were soon out of the Sound, plowing our way toward the famous Skager-Rack. The weather had been showery and threatening for some time. It now began to rain and blow in good earnest.

We had on board only thirteen passengers, chiefly Danes and Icelanders. Among them was a newly-appointed amtman for the district of Reykjaness, with a very accomplished young wife. He was going to spend the honey-moon amid the glaciers and lava-fjelds of Iceland. It seemed a dreary prospect for so young and tender a bride, but she was cheerful and happy, except when the inevitable hour of sea-sickness came. Love, I suppose, can make the wilderness blossom as the rose, and shed a warmth over ice-covered mountains and a pleasant verdure over deserts of lava. A very agreeable and intelligent young man, Mr. Jonasen, son of the governor, was also on board. I saw but little of him during the passage—only his head over the side of his berth; but I heard from him frequently after the weather became rough. If there was any inside left in that young man by the time we arrived at Reykjavik, it must have been badly strained. As a son of Iona he completely reversed the scriptural order of things; for, instead of being swallowed by a great fish, and remaining in the belly thereof three days and nights, he swallowed numerous sprats and sardines himself, yet would never allow them internal accommodations for the space of three minutes. My room-mate was a young Icelandic student, who had been to the college at Copenhagen, and was now returning to his native land to die. There was something very sad in his case. He had left home a few years before with the brightest prospects of success. Ambitious and talented, he had devoted himself with unwearied assiduity to his studies, but the activity of his mind was too much for a naturally feeble constitution. Consumption set its seal upon him. Given up by the physicians in Copenhagen, he was returning to breathe his last in the arms of a loving mother.

On the second morning after leaving the Sound we passed close along the Downs of Jutland, a barren shore,

singularly diversified by great mounds of sand. The
wind sweeping in from the ocean casts up the loose sands
that lie upon this low peninsula, and drifts them against
some bush or other obstacle sufficiently firm to form a
nucleus. In the course of a few years, by constant accu-
mulations, this becomes a vast mound, sometimes over a
hundred feet high. Nearly the whole of Northern Jutland is diversified with sand-plains, heaths, and ever-
changing mounds, among which wandering bands of gipsies still roam. The shores along the Skagen are surrounded by dangerous reefs of quicksand, stretching for
many miles out into the ocean. Navigation at this point
is very difficult, especially during the winter, when terrific gales prevail from the northwest. The numerous
stakes, buoys, and other water-marks by which the channel is designated, the frequency of light-houses and signal telegraphs, and the wrecks that lie strewn along the
beach, over which the surging foam breaks like a perpetual dirge, afford striking indication of the dangers to
which mariners are subject in this wild region. Hans
Christian Andersen, in one of his most delightful works,
has thrown a romantic interest over the scenery of Jutland, giving a charm to its very desolation, and investing
with all the beauty of a genial humanity the rude lives
of the gipsies and fishermen who inhabit this wild region
of drifting sands and wintry tempests. Steen Blicher
has also cast over it the spell of his poetic genius; and
Von Buch, in his graphic narrative, has given a memora-
ble interest to its sea-girt shores, where " masts and skel-
etons of vessels stand like a range of palisades."

During our passage through the Skager-Rack we passed innumerable fleets of fishing-smacks, and often encountered the diminutive skiffs of the fishermen, with
two or three amphibious occupants, buffeting about
among the waves many miles from the shore. The weather had been steadily growing worse ever since our departure from Copenhagen. As we entered the North
Sea it began to blow fiercer than ever, and for two days

we experienced all the discomforts of chopping seas that drenched our decks fore and aft, and chilling gales mingled with fogs and heavy rains. It was cold enough for mid-winter, yet here we were on the verge of mid-summer. Our little craft was rendered somewhat unmanageable by a deck-load of coal and a heavy cargo of freight, and there were periods when I would have thought myself fortunate in being once more off Cape Horn in the good ship *Pacific.* The amtman and his young bride spent this portion of their honey-moon performing a kind of duet that reminded me of my friend Ross Wallace's lines in " Perdita:"

> " Like two sweet tunes that wandering met,
>   And so harmoniously they run,
>   The hearer deems they are but one."

At least the harmony was perfect, whatever might be thought of the music in other respects. Young Jonasen swallowed a few more sardines about this period of the voyage, which he vainly attempted to secure by sudden and violent contractions of the diaphragm. In short, there were but two persons in the cabin besides Captain Andersen and myself who had the temerity to appear at table—one an old Danish merchant, who generally received advices, midway through the meal, requiring his immediate presence on deck; and the other a gentleman from Holstein, who always lost his appetite after the soup, and had to jump up and run to his state-room for exercise.

In due time we sighted the shores of Scotland. A pilot came on board inside the Frith of Forth, and, as we steamed rapidly on our course, all the passengers forgot their afflictions, and gazed with delight on the sloping sward and woodland, the picturesque villages, and romantic old castles that decorate the shores of this magnificent sheet of water.

Our destination was Grangemouth, where we arrived early on Sunday morning. A few sailors belonging to some vessels in the docks, a custom-house inspector, and

three small boys, comprised the entire visible population
of the place. Judging by the manner in which the Sabbath is kept in Scotland, the Scotch must be a profoundly moral people. The towns are like grave-yards, and
the inhabitants bear a striking resemblance to sextons,
or men who spend much of their lives in burying the
dead.

I was very anxious to get a newspaper containing the
latest intelligence from America, but was informed that
none could be had on Sunday. I wanted to go up to
Edinburg: it was not possible on Sunday. I asked a
man where could I get some cigars? he didna ken; it
was Sunday. The depressed expression of the few people I met began to prey like a nightmare on my spirits.
Doubtless it is a very good thing to pay a decent regard
to the Sabbath, but can any body tell me where we are
commanded to look gloomy? The contrast was certainly very striking between the Scotch and the Danes. Of
course there is no such thing as drunkenness in Scotland,
no assaults and batteries, no robberies and murders, no
divorces, no cheating among the merchants of Glasgow
or the bankers of Edinburg, no sympathizing with rebellion and the institution of slavery—for the Scotch are a
sober and righteous people, much given to sackcloth and
ashes, manufactures of iron, and societies for the insu-
rance of property against fire.

The *Arcturus* was detained several days discharging
and taking in freight. I availed myself of the first train
to visit Edinburg. A day there, and an excursion to
Glasgow and Loch Lomond, agreeably occupied the time.
I must confess the scenery—beautiful as it is, and fraught
with all the interest that history and genius can throw
over it—disappointed me. It was not what I expected.
It was a damp, moist, uncomfortable reality, as Mantalini
would say—not very grand or striking in any respect.
A subsequent excursion to the Trosachs, Loch Katrine,
Loch Long, and the Clyde, afforded me a better opportunity of judging, yet it all seemed tame and common-

place compared with the scenery of California and Norway. If I enjoyed a fair specimen of the climate—rain, wind, and fog, varied by sickly gleams of sunshine—it strikes me it would be a congenial country for snails and frogs to reside in. The Highlands are like all other wild places within the limits of Europe, very gentle in their wildness compared with the rugged slopes of the Sierra Nevada. The Lady of the Lake must have possessed an uncommonly strong constitution if she made her nocturnal excursions on Loch Katrine in a thin white robe without suffering any bad consequences, for I found a stout overcoat insufficient to keep the chilling mists of that region from seeking in my bones a suitable location for rheumatism.

CHAPTER XL.

THE JOLLY BLOODS.

I WAS quietly sitting in my state-room, awaiting the departure of the steamer, when a tremendous racket on the cabin steps, followed by a rush of feet up and down the saloon, startled me out of a pleasant home-dream.

"Hello! What the devil! I say! Where's every body! Stoord!" Blast the fellow! Here, Bowser! What'r ye abeaout! Ho there! Where the dooce are our berths? By Jove! Ha! ha! This is jolly!"

Other voices joined in, with a general chorus of complaints and exclamations—"Egad! it's a *do!* No berths, no state-rooms! Ho, Stoord! Where's my trunk? I say, Stoord, where's my fishing-rod? Hey! hey! did you 'appen to see my overalls? I've lost my gun! 'Pon my word, this is a pretty do! Let's go see the Agent?" "Come on! Certainly!" "Oh, hang it, no!" "Oh yes!" "Here, Bowser! What the devil! Where's Bowser? Gone ashore, by Jove! A pretty kettle of fish!" Here there was a sudden and general stampede, and amid loud exclamations of "Beastly!" and "Disgusting!" the party left the cabin. I barely had time to see that it consisted of some four or five fashionable tourists—spirited young bloods of sporting proclivities, who had taken passage for Iceland. The prospect of having some company was pleasant enough, and from the specimen I had seen there could be no doubt it would be lively and entertaining.

Once more during the night I was aroused by a repetition of the noises and exclamations already described. The steamer was moving off. The passengers were all on board. We were battering our way through the canal. Soon the heaving waters of the ocean began to subdue the enthusiasm of the sportsmen, and before morning my ears were saluted by sounds and observations of a very different character.

I shall only add at present, in reference to this lively party of young "Britishers," that I found them very good fellows in their way—a little boisterous and inexperienced, but well-educated and intelligent. The young chap with the dog was what we would call in America a "regular bird." He and his dog afforded us infinite diversion during the whole passage—racing up and down the decks, into and out of the cabin, and all over each other. There was something so fresh and sprightly about the fellow, something so good-natured, that I could readily excuse his roughness of manner. One of the others, a quiet, scholastic-looking person, who did not really belong to the party, having only met them on board, was a young collegian well versed in Icelandic literature. He was going to Iceland to perfect himself in the language of the country, and make some translations of the learned Sagas.

A favorable wind enabled us to sight the Orkneys on the afternoon following our departure from the Frith of Forth. Next day we passed the Shetlands, of which we had a good view. The rocky shores of these islands, all rugged and surf-beaten, with myriads of wild-fowl darkening the air around them, presented a most tempting

A DANDY TOURIST.

field of exploration. I longed to take a ramble in the footsteps of Dr. Johnson ; but to see the Shetlands would be to lose Iceland, and of the two I preferred seeing the latter. After a pleasant passage of two days and a half from Grangemouth we made the Faroe Islands, and had the good fortune to secure, without the usual loss of time occasioned by fogs, an anchorage in the harbor of Thorshavn.

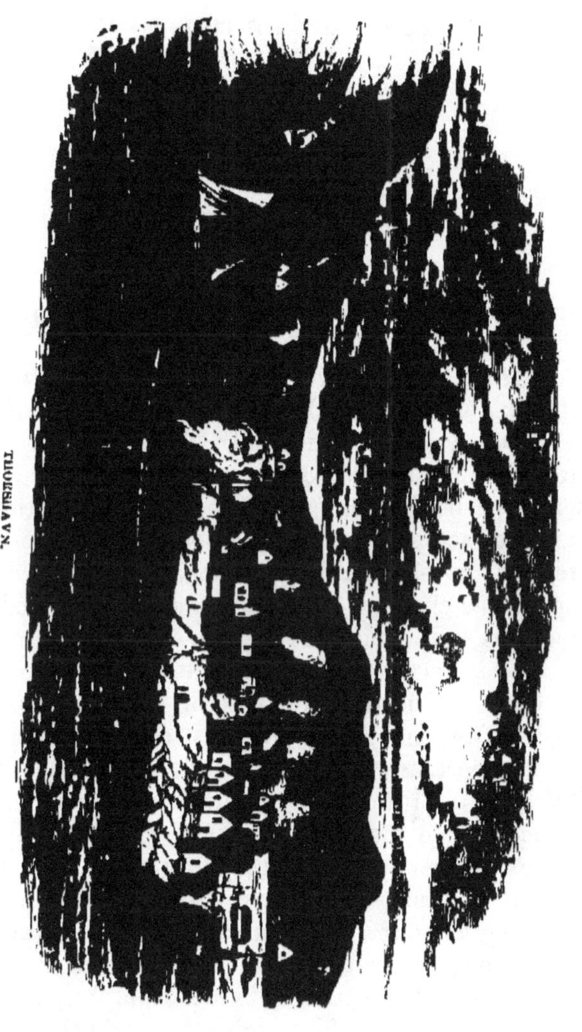

THORSHAVN.

CHAPTER XLI.

THE FAROE ISLANDS.

THE Faroe Islands lie about midway between Scotland and Iceland, and belong to Denmark. The whole
group consists of thirty-five small islands, some of which
are little more than naked rocks jutting up out of the
sea. About twenty are inhabited. The rest are too barren and precipitous to afford a suitable place of abode
even for the hardy Faroese. The entire population is
estimated at something over six thousand, of which the
greater part are shepherds, fishermen, and bird-catchers.
Owing to the situation of these islands, surrounded by
the open sea and within the influence of the Gulf Stream,
the climate is very mild, although they lie in the sixty-
second degree of north latitude. The winters are never
severe, and frost and snow rarely last over two months.
They are subject, however, at that season to frequent and
terrible gales from the north, and during the summer are
often inaccessible for days and even weeks, owing to
dense fogs. The humidity of the climate is favorable to
the growth of grass, which covers the hills with a brilliant coating of green wherever there is the least approach to soil; and where there is no soil, as in many
places along the shores, the rocks are beautifully draped
with moss and lichens. The highest point in the group
is 2800 feet above the level of the sea, and the general
aspect of them all is wild and rugged in the extreme.
Prodigious cliffs, a thousand feet high, stand like a wall
out of the sea on the southern side of the Stromoe. The
Mygenaes-holm, a solitary rock, guards, like a sentinel,
one of the passages, and forms a terrific precipice of 1500
feet on one side, against which the waves break with an
everlasting roar. Here the solan-goose, the eider-duck,

VIEW IN FAROE ISLANDS.

and innumerable varieties of gulls and other sea-fowl, build their nests and breed.

At certain seasons of the year the intrepid bird-hunters suspend themselves from the cliffs by means of ropes, and feather their own nests by robbing the nests of their neighbors. Enormous quantities of eggs are taken in this way. The eider-down, of which the nests of the eider-duck are composed, is one of the most profitable articles of Faroese traffic. The mode of life to which these men devote themselves, and their habitual contact with danger, render them reckless, and many perish every year by falling from the rocks. Widows and orphans are numerous throughout the islands.

The few scattering farms to be seen on the slopes of the hills and in the arable valleys are conducted on the most primitive principles. A small patch of potatoes and vegetables, and in certain exposures a few acres of grain, comprise the extent of their agricultural operations. Sheep-raising is the most profitable of their pursuits. The climate appears to be more congenial to the growth of wool than of cereal productions. The Faroese sheep are noted for the fineness and luxuriance of their fleece, and it always commands a high price in market. A considerable portion of it is manufactured by the inhabitants, who are quite skillful in weaving and knitting. They make a kind of thick woolen shirt, something like that known as the Guernsey, which for durability and warmth is unsurpassed. Sailors and fishermen all over the Northern seas consider themselves fortunate if they can get possession of a Faroese shirt. The costume of the men, which is chiefly home-made, consists of a rough, thick jacket of brown wool; a coarse woolen shirt; a knitted bag-shaped cap on the head; a pair of knee-breeches of the same material as the coat; a pair of thick woolen stockings, and sheep-skin shoes, generally covered with mud—all of the same brown or rather burnt-umber color. Exposure to the weather gives their skins, naturally of a leathery texture, something of the same dull and dingy aspect, so that a genuine Faroese enjoys one advantage—he can never look much more dirty at one time than another.

The women wear dresses of the same material, without much attempt at shape or ornament. A colored handkerchief tied around the head, a silver breast-pin, and a pair of ear-rings of domestic manufacture, comprise their only personal decorations. As in all countries where the burden of heavy labor is thrown upon the women, they lose their comely looks at an early age, and become withered, ill-shaped, and hard-featured long before they reach the prime of life. The Faroese women doubtless make excellent wives for lazy men; they do all the labors of the house, and share largely in those of the field. I do not know that they are more prolific than good and loving wives in other parts of the world, but they certainly enjoy the possession of as many little cotton-heads with dirty faces, turned up noses, ragged elbows, and tattered frocks, as one usually meets in the course of his travels. Two fair specimens of the rising generation, a little boy and girl, made an excellent speculation on the occasion of my visit to Thorshavn. Knowing by instinct, if not by my dress, that I was a stranger, they followed me about wherever I rambled, looking curiously and cautiously into my face, and mutually commenting upon the oddity of my appearance—which, by-the-way, would have been slightly odd even in the streets of New York, wrapped, as I was, in the voluminous folds of Captain Södring's old whaling coat, with a sketch-book in my hand and a pair of spectacles on my nose. However, no man likes to be regarded as an object of curiosity even by two small ragamuffins belonging to a strange race, so I just held up suddenly, and requested these children of Faroe to state explicitly the grounds of their interest in my behalf. What they said in reply it would be impossible for me to translate, since the Faroese language is quite as impenetrable as the Icelandic. They looked so startled and alarmed withal that a gleam of pity must have manifested its appearance in the corner of my eyes. The next moment their faces broke into a broad grin, and each held out a hand auda-

FAROESE CHILDREN.

ciously, as much as to say, "My dear sir, if you'll put a small copper in this small hand, we'll retract all injurious criticisms, and ever after regard you as a gentleman of extraordinary personal beauty!" Somehow my hand slipped unconsciously into my pocket, but, before handing them the desired change, it occurred to me to secure their likenesses for publication as a warning to the children of all nations not to undertake a similar experiment with any hope of success.

Thorshavn, so named after the old god Thor, is a small town of some five or six hundred inhabitants, situated on the southeastern side of the island of Stromoe. In front lies a harbor, indifferently protected by a small island and two rocky points. The anchorage is insecure at all times, especially during the prevalence of southerly and easterly gales, when it often becomes necessary to heave up and put to sea; and the dense fogs by which the approach to land is generally obscured render navigation about these islands extremely perilous. Of the town of Thorshavn little need be said. Its chief interest lies in the almost primeval construction of the houses and the rustic simplicity of its inhabitants. The few streets that run between the straggling lines of sheds and sod-covered huts scattered over the rocks are narrow and tortuous, winding up steep, stony precipices, and into deep, boggy hollows; around rugged points, and over scraggy mounds of gravel and grit. The public edifices, consisting of two or three small churches and the amtman's residence, are little better than martin-boxes. For some reason best known to the people in these Northern climes, they paint their houses black, except where the roofs are covered with sod, which nature paints green. I think it must be from some notion that it gives them a cheerful aspect, though the darkness of the paint and the chilly luxuriance of the green did not strike me with joyous impressions. If Scotland can claim some advantages as a place of residence for snails, Thorshavn must surely be a paradise for toads accustomed to feed upon the vapors of a dungeon. The wharves—loose masses of rock at the boat-landing—are singularly luxuriant in the

FAROESE ISLANDERS.

article of fish. Prodigious piles of fish lie about in every direction. The shambling old store-houses are crammed with fish, and the heads of fish and the back-bones of fish lie bleaching on the rocks. The gravelly patches of beach are slimy with the entrails of fresh fish, and the air is foul with the odor of decayed fish. The boatmen that lounge about waiting for a job are saturated with fish inside and out—like their boats. The cats, crows, and ravens mingle in social harmony over the dreadful carnival of fish. In fine, the impression produced upon the stranger who lands for the first time is that he has accidentally turned up in some piscatorial hell, where the tortures of skinning, drying, and disemboweling are performed by the unrelenting hands of man.

In addition to the standing population of Thorshavn, the fortifications—an abandoned mud-bank, a flag-staff, and a board shanty—are subject, in times of great public peril, to be defended by a standing army and navy of twenty-four soldiers, one small boat, one corporal, and the governor of the islands, who takes the field himself at the head of this bloody phalanx of Danes still reeking with the gore of slaughtered fish. Upon the occasion of the arrival of the *Arcturus*—the only steamer that ever touches here — the principal amtman, upon perceiving the vessel in the distance, immediately proceeds to organize the army and navy for a grand display. First he shaves and puts on his uniform; then calling together the troops, who are also sailors, he carefully inspects them, and selecting from the number the darkest, dirtiest, and most bloody-looking, he causes them to buckle on their swords. This done, he delivers a brief address, recommending them to abstain from the use of schnapps and other intoxicating beverages till the departure of the steamer. The dignity of official position requires that he should remain on shore for the space of one hour after the dropping of the anchor. He then musters his forces, marches them down to his war-skiff, from the stern of which waves the Danish flag, and, placing an oar in the hands of each man, he gives the order to advance and board the steamer. On his arrival alongside he touches his cap to the passengers in a grave and dignified manner, and expresses a desire to see our commander, Captain Andersen, who, during this period of the ceremony, is down below, busily occupied in arranging the brandy and crackers. The appearance of Captain Andersen on deck is politely acknowledged by the amtman, who thereupon orders his men to pull alongside, when the two cabin-boys and the cook kindly assist him over the gangway. Descending into the cabin, he carefully examines the ship's papers, pronounces them all right, and joins Captain Andersen in a social "smile." Then, having delivered himself of the latest intelligence on the subject of wool and codfish, he returns to his boat and proceeds to his quarters on shore. All this is done with a quiet and dignified formality both pleasing and impressive.

As an illustration of the severity of the laws that govern the Faroe Islands, and the upright and inexorable character of the governor and principal amtman, I must relate an incident that occurred under my own observation.

Shortly after the *Arcturus* had cast anchor, the party of British sportsmen already mentioned went ashore with their dogs and guns, and began an indiscriminate slaughter of all the game within two miles of Thorshavn, consisting of three plovers, a snipe, and some half a dozen sparrows. The captain had warned them that such a proceeding was contrary to law, and a citizen of Thorshavn had gently remonstrated with them as they passed through the town. When the slaughter commenced, the proprietors of the bog, in which the game abounded, rushed to the doors of their cabins to see what was going on, and perceiving that it was a party of Englishmen engaged in the destructive pastime of firing shotguns about and among the flocks of sheep that browsed on the premises, they straightway laid a complaint before the governor. The independent sons of Britain were not to be baffled of their sport in this manner. They cracked away as long as they pleased, by-Joved and blawsted the island for not having more game, and then came aboard. The steamer hove up anchor and sailed that night. Nothing farther took place to admonish us of the consequences of the trespass till our return from Iceland, when the principal amtman came on board with a formidable placard, neatly written, and translated into the three court languages of the place—Danish, French, and English. The contents of this document were as follows: that whereas, in the year 1763, a law had been passed for the protection of game on the Faroe Islands, which law had not since been rescinded; and whereas a subsequent law of 1786 had been passed for the protection of sheep and other stock ranging at large on the said islands, which law had not since been rescinded; and whereas it had been represented to the governor of the said islands that certain persons, supposed to be Englishmen, had lately come on shore, armed with shotguns, and, in violation of the said laws of the country, had shot at, maimed, and killed several birds, and caused serious apprehensions of injury to the flocks of sheep which were peaceably grazing on their respective ranges; now, therefore, this was earnestly to request that all such persons would reflect upon the penalties that would attach to similar acts in their own country, and be thus enabled to perceive the impropriety of pursuing such a course in other countries. Should they fail to observe the aforesaid laws after this warning, they would only have themselves to blame for the unpleasant consequences that must assuredly ensue, etc., etc. [Officially signed and sealed.]

Great formality was observed in carrying this important document on board. It was neatly folded and carefully done up, with various seals and blue ribbons, in a package about six inches wide by eighteen in length, and was guarded by the select half of the Faroese army and navy, being exactly twelve men, and delivered by the amtman of the island with a few appropriate and impressive remarks, after which it was hung up over the cabin gangway by the captain as a solemn warning to all future passengers. There can be no doubt that it produced the most salutary effects upon the sporting gentlemen. I was really glad the affair had taken place, as it evidently afforded his excellency a favorable opportunity of promulgating a most excellent state paper, cautiously conceived and judiciously worded. The preparation of it must have occupied his time advantageously to himself and his country during the entire period of our absence.

I must now turn back a little to say that, while my comrades were engaged in their unlawful work of killing the sparrows and frightening the sheep, I deemed it a matter of personal safety to keep out of range of their guns. Apart from the danger of arrest, the probable loss of an eye or disfigurement of some ornamental feature was a sufficient consideration to satisfy me of the policy of this course.

Taking a path across the rugged desert of rocks and bogs, extending for some miles back of Thorshavn, I quickly began to ascend a barren range of hills, abounding in greenstone traprock and zoolites, from the summit of which there is a magnificent view of the whole surrounding country, with glimpses of the cloud-capped summits of the neighboring islands. Beautiful little valleys, dotted with the sod-covered huts of the shepherds and fishermen, sweep down to the water's edge a thousand feet below; weird black bogs, and fields of scoria and burned earth, lie on the slopes of the distant hills to the right; and to the left are rugged cliffs, jutting out of the sea like huge castles, around which myriads of birds continually hover, piercing the air with their wild screams. The wind blew in such fierce gusts over the bleak and desolate range of crags on which I stood that I was glad enough to seek shelter down on the leeside.

It now occurred to me to go in search of a ruined church of which I had read in some traveler's journal said to be within four or five miles of Thorshavn. Some artificial piles of stones, near the ledge upon which I had descended, indicated the existence of a trail. On my way down, a legion of birds, about the size of puffins, began to gather around, with fierce cries and warning motions, as if determined to dispute my progress. They flew backward and forward within a few feet of my head, flapping their wings furiously, and uttering the most terrific cries of rage and alarm, so that I was sorely puzzled to know what was the matter. It was not long before I came upon some of their nests, which of course explained the difficulty. Having no immediate use for eggs or feathers, I left the nests unmolested and proceeded on my way. In about an hour I came suddenly upon a small green valley that lay some five hundred feet below, directly on the water's edge. By some mischance I had lost the trail, and, in order to descend, was obliged to slide and scramble down the cliffs—an experiment that I presently discovered would probably cost me a broken neck if persisted in; for when there seemed to be no farther obstruction, I came all at once upon a precipice at least sixty feet deep, without a single foothold or other means of descent than a clear jump to the bottom. Not disposed to follow the example of Sam Patch on dry land, I reluctantly turned back. By dint of scrambling and climbing, and slipping down various cliffs and slopes, I at length reached a point from which I had a view of some ruins and farm-houses still some distance below. Following the line of the regular trail till it struck into the cliffs, I had no farther difficulty in reaching the valley.

The good people at the farm-house—a family by the name of Petersen—received me in the kindest manner, with many expressions of wonder at the risk I had run in crossing the mountain without a guide. It was with considerable difficulty we made ourselves understood:

None of the family spoke any language except their own. The son, indeed, a fine young man of twenty, understood a few words of English, but that was all.   There is something, nevertheless, in genuine kindness and hospitality that makes itself intelligible without the aid of language.   I was immediately invited into the house, and while young Petersen entertained me with old prints and Faroese books, his mother prepared an excellent lunch.   Tired and worried after my trip, I could offer no objection.   Never shall I forget the coffee and cream, and the butter and bread, and delicate fruit-tarts placed on the nice white table-cloth by the good Mrs. Petersen. I ate and drank, and glowed all over with a childlike relish of the good things, while the whole family gathered round and tried to make me understand that they had a relative in California, who lived in the mines at a place called Six-mile-bar, and that they were glad to see a Californian, and wanted to know all about California. It is wonderful with how few words we can communicate our ideas when necessity compels us to depend upon our ingenuity.   Before I had parted from that family the whole matter was perfectly explained; the history of their absent relative was quite clear to me, and they had a very fair conception of the kind of country in which he lived.   Upon no consideration would they receive compensation for the lunch, and they even seemed offended when I endeavored to press it upon them. This, from people whom I had never seen before—a plain country family living in a wilderness where such luxuries as sugar and coffee could only be had at considerable expense—was absolutely refreshing.   For the first time since my arrival in Europe, after having traversed the whole Continent, I had encountered a specimen of the human race capable of refusing money.   Subsequently I learned that this was the common practice in the Faroe Islands.   The poorest shepherd freely offers to the stranger the hospitality of his hut; and it is a creed among these worthy people not to accept pay for coffee

KIRK GÖÜÖZ.

and bread, or indeed any thing else they may have to offer in the way of entertainment. My fellow-passengers were similarly treated in Thorshavn, where visitors are more frequent and the customs of the country less primitive.

The great object of interest at Kirk Göboe is the ancient church, from which the place derives its name; a long, low stone building, whitewashed and covered with a sod roof, but, owing to repeated repairs, now presenting no particular traces of antiquity, although reported to have been built in the eighth century. I have no data in reference to this interesting relic, and am not aware that antiquarians have ever attempted to trace out its origin. The probability is that it was built by some of those Culdee anchorites of whom Dasent speaks as the first settlers of Iceland.

The interior of the church contains an altar, and some wooden carvings on the head-boards of the pews, evidently of great antiquity. It is impossible to conjecture from their appearance whether they are five hundred or a thousand years old—at least without more research than a casual tourist can bestow upon them.

There is also within a few steps of the farm-house a much larger and more picturesque ruin of a church, built in a later style of architecture. The only information I could get about this ruin was that it dates back as far as the fifteenth century. The walls are of rough stone well put together, and now stand roofless and moss-covered, inhabited only by crows and swallows. The doors and windows are in the Gothic style. A sketch made from the door of the old church first mentioned, embracing the residence of the Petersen family, with a glimpse of the cliffs and rugged ledges behind upon which their flocks graze, will give the best idea of the whole premises.

Having thus pleasantly occupied a few hours at Kirk Göboe, I bade adieu to the worthy family who had so hospitably entertained me, and was about to set out for

FARM-HOUSE AND RUINS.

Thorshavn, when young Petersen, not content with the directions he had given me, announced his intention of seeing me safe over the mountain. In vain I assured him that, however pleasant his company would be, I had no apprehension of losing the way this time. Go he would, and go he did; and when we parted on the top of the mountain, in plain sight of Thorshavn, he cordially shook me by the hand, and said many kind words, which I could only interpret to mean that he and all his kith and kin wished me a pleasant voyage to Iceland, and many years of health and happiness.

When I now recall the fine, intelligent face of this young man, his bright dark eyes, healthy complexion, and strong, well-knit frame, the latent energy in all his movements, the genial simplicity of his manners, and his evident thirst for knowledge, I can not help feeling something akin to regret that so much good material should be wasted in the obscurity of a shepherd's life. So gifted by nature, what might not such a youth achieve in an appropriate sphere of action? And yet, perhaps, it is better for him that he should spend his life among the barren cliffs of Stromoe, with no more companions than his dog and his sheep, than jostle among men in the great outer world, to learn at last the bitter lesson that the eye is not satisfied with riches, nor the understanding with knowledge.

On the way down to the Valley of Thorshavn I met a man mounted on a shaggy little monster, which in almost any other country would have been mistaken for a species of sheep. As this was a fair specimen of a Faroese horse and his rider, I sat down on a rock after they had passed and took the best view of them I could get.

Late in the afternoon the scattered passengers were gathered together, and the good people of Thorshavn came down to the wharf to bid us farewell. In half an hour more we were all on board. "Up anchor!" was the order, and once more we went steaming on our way.

Short as our sojourn had been among these primitive

FAROESE ON HORSEBACK.

people, it furnished us with many pleasant reminiscences.
Their genial hospitality and simple good-nature, together
with their utter ignorance of the outer world, formed the
theme of various amusing anecdotes during the remainder of the passage.   Favored by a southerly wind and a
stock of good coal, we made the southeastern point of
Iceland in a little over two days from Thorshavn.

CHAPTER XLII.

FIRST IMPRESSIONS OF ICELAND.

It would be difficult to conceive any thing more impressive than this first view of the land of snow and fire. A low stretch of black boggy coast to the right; dark cliffs of lava in front; far in the background, range after range of bleak, snow-capped mountains, the fiery Jokuls dimly visible through drifting masses of fog; to the left a broken wall of red, black, and blue rocks, weird and surf-beaten, stretching as far as the eye could reach— this was Iceland! All along the grim rifted coast the dread marks of fire, and flood, and desolation were visible. Detached masses of lava, gnarled and scraggy like huge clinkers, seemed tossed out into the sea; towers, buttresses, and battlements, shaped by the very elements of destruction, reared their stern crests against the waves; glaciers lay glittering upon the blackened slopes behind; and foaming torrents of snow-water burst through the rifted crags in front, and mingled their rage with the wild rage of the surf—all was battle, and ruin, and desolation.

As we approached the point called Portland, a colossal bridge opened into view, so symmetrical in its outline that it was difficult to believe it was not of artificial construction. The arch is about fifty feet high by thirty in width, and affords shelter to innumerable flocks of birds, whose nests are built in the crevices underneath. Solangeese, eider-ducks, and sea-gulls cover the dizzy heights overhead, and whales have been known to pass through the passage below. Great numbers of blackfish and porpoises abound in this vicinity. From time to time, as we swept along on our way, we could discern a lonesome hut high up on the shore, with a few sheep and cat-

NATURAL BRIDGE.

tle on the slopes of the adjacent hills, but for the most part the coast was barren and desolate.

Early on the following morning the sun-capped peaks of Mount Hecla were visible. There has been no eruption from this mountain since 1845. The principal crater lies 5210 feet above the level of the sea, and is distant fifteen miles from the shore.

Toward noon we made the Westmann Isles, a small rocky group some ten miles distant from the main island. A fishing and trading establishment, owned by a company of Danes, is located on one of these islands. The *Arcturus* touches twice a year to deliver and receive a mail. On the occasion of our visit, a boat came out with a hardy-looking crew of Danes to receive the mail-bag. It was doubtless a matter of great rejoicing to them to obtain news from home. I had barely time to make a rough outline of the islands as we lay off the settlement.

The chief interest attached to the Westmann group is, that it is supposed to have been visited by Columbus in 1477, fifteen years prior to his voyage of discovery to the shores of America. It is now generally conceded that the Icelanders were the original discoverers of the American continent. Recent antiquarian researches tend to establish the fact that they had advanced as far to the southward as Massachusetts in the tenth century. They held colonies on the coasts of Greenland and Labrador, and must have had frequent intercourse with the Indians farther south. Columbus in all probability obtained some valuable data from these hardy adventurers. The date of his visit to Iceland is well authenticated by Beamish, Rafn, and other eminent writers on the early discoveries of the Northmen.

Nothing could surpass the desolate grandeur of the coast as we approached the point of Reykjaness. It was of an almost infernal blackness. The whole country seemed uptorn, rifted, shattered, and scattered about in a vast chaos of ruin. Huge cliffs of lava split down to their bases toppled over the surf. Rocks of every con-

COAST OF ICELAND.

ceivable shape, scorched and blasted with fire, wrested from the main and hurled into the sea, battled with the waves, their black scraggy points piercing the mist like giant hands upthrown to smite or sink in a fierce death-struggle. The wild havoc wrought in the conflict of elements was appalling. Birds screamed over the fearful wreck of matter. The surf from the inrolling waves broke against the charred and shattered desert of ruin with a terrific roar. Columns of spray shot up over the blackened fragments of lava, while in every opening the lashed waters, discolored by the collision, seethed and surged as in a huge caldron. Verily there is One whose "fury is poured out like fire; the rocks are thrown down by him; the mountains quake, and the hills melt, and the earth is burned at his presence."

Passing a singular rock standing alone some twenty miles off the land, called the *Meal-sack*, we soon changed

THE MEAL-SACK.

our course and bore up for the harbor of Reykjavik. By the time we reached the anchorage our voyage from Thorshavn had occupied exactly three days and six hours.

Trusting that the reader will pardon me for the fre-

quent delays to which I have subjected him since we
joined our fortunes at Copenhagen, I shall now proceed
to the important labors of the enterprise with this solemn understanding—that the journey before us is pretty
rough, and the prospect is strong that, in our random
dash at the wonders of Iceland, we will encounter some
perilous adventures by flood and field; but if I don't carry him safely and satisfactorily through them all, he must
console himself by the reflection that many a good man
has been sacrificed in the pursuit of knowledge, and that
he will suffer in excellent company.

CHAPTER XLIII.

REYKJAVIK, THE CAPITAL OF ICELAND.

My first view of the capital of Iceland was through a
chilling rain. A more desolate-looking place I had rarely if ever seen, though, like Don Quixote's market-woman
on the ass, it was susceptible of improvement under the
influence of an ardent imagination. As a subject for the
pencil of an artist, it was at least peculiar, if not picturesque. A tourist whose glowing fancies had not been
nipped in the bud by the rigors of an extended experience might have been able to invest it with certain weird
charms, but to me it was only the fag-end of civilization,
abounding in horrible odors of decayed polypi and dried
fish. A cutting wind from the distant Jokuls and a
searching rain did not tend to soften the natural asperities of its features. In no point of view did it impress
me as a cheerful place of residence except for wild ducks
and sea-gulls. The whole country for miles around is a
black desert of bogs and lava. Scarcely an arable spot
is to be seen save on the tops of the fishermen's huts,
where the sod produces an abundance of grass and weeds.
A dark gravelly slope in front of the town, dotted with
boats, oars, nets, and piles of fish; a long row of shambling old store-houses built of wood, and painted a dismal

REYKJAVIK, THE CAPITAL OF ICELAND.

black, varied by patches of dirty yellow; a general hodge-
podge of frame shanties behind, constructed of old boards
and patched up with drift-wood; a few straggling streets,
paved with broken lava and reeking with offal from the
doors of the houses; some dozens of idle citizens and
drunken boatmen lounging about the grog-shops; a gang
of women, brawny and weather-beaten, carrying loads
of codfish down to the landing; a drove of shaggy little
ponies, each tied to the tail of the pony in front; a pack
of mangy dogs prowling about in dirty places looking
for something to eat, and fighting when they got it—
this was all I could see of Reykjavik, the famous Icelandic capital.

The town lies on a strip of land between the harbor
and a lagoon in the rear. It is said to contain a population of two thousand, and if the dogs and fleas be taken
into consideration, I have no doubt it does. Where two
thousand human beings can stow themselves in a place
containing but one hotel, and that a very poor one, is a
matter of wonder to the stranger. The houses generally are but one story high, and seldom contain more than
two or three rooms. Some half a dozen stores, it is true,
of better appearance than the average, have been built
by the Danish merchants within the past few years; and
the residence of the governor and the public University
are not without some pretensions to style.

The only stone building in Reykjavik of any importance is the "Cathedral;" so called, perhaps, more in
honor of its great antiquity than any thing imposing
about its style or dimensions. At present it shows no
indications of age, having been patched, plastered, and
painted into quite a neat little church of modern appearance.

At each end of the town is a small gathering of sod-
covered huts, where the fishermen and their families live
like rabbits in a burrow. That these poor people are
not all devoured by snails or crippled with rheumatism
is a marvel to any stranger who takes a peep into their

T

GOVERNOR'S RESIDENCE, REYKJAVIK.

ICELANDIC HOUSES

CHURCH AT REYKJAVIK.

filthy and cheerless little cabins. The oozy slime of fish
and smoke mingles with the green mould of the rocks;
barnacles cover the walls, and puddles make a soft carpeting for the floors. The earth is overhead, and their
heads are under the earth, and the light of day has no
light job of it to get in edgewise through the windows.
The beaver-huts and badger-holes of California, taking

into consideration the difference of climate, are palatial residences compared with the dismal hovels of these Icelandic fishermen. At a short distance they look for all the world like mounds in a grave-yard. The inhabitants, worse off than the dead, are buried alive. No gardens, no cultivated patches, no attempt at any thing ornamental relieves the dreary monotony of the premises. Dark patches of lava, all littered with the heads and entrails of fish; a pile of turf from some neighboring bog; a rickety shed in which the fish are hung up to dry; a gang of wolfish-looking curs, horribly lean and voracious; a few prowling cats, and possibly a chicken deeply depressed in spirits—these are the most prominent objects visible in the vicinity. Sloth and filth go hand in hand.

The women are really the only class of inhabitants, except the fleas, who possess any vitality. Rude, slatternly, and ignorant as they are, they still evince some sign of life and energy compared with the men. Overtaxed by domestic cares, they go down upon the wharves when a vessel comes in, and by hard labor earn enough to purchase a few rags of clothing for their children. The men are too lazy even to carry the fish out of their own boats. At home they lie about the doors, smoking and gossiping, and too often drunk. Some are too lazy to get drunk, and go to sleep over the effort. In truth, the prevailing indolence among all classes is so striking that one can almost imagine himself in a Southern clime. There is much about Reykjavik to remind a Californian traveler of San Diego. The drunken fellows about the stores, and the racing of horses up and down the streets, under the stimulus of liquor rather than natural energy, sometimes made me feel quite at home.

On the morning after my arrival I called to see my young friend Jonasen, the governor's son, and was most hospitably entertained by the family. I had a letter of introduction to the governor from the Minister of the Judiciary at Copenhagen, but thought it unnecessary to present it. His excellency is a good specimen of the

ICELANDERS AT WORK

better class of Icelanders—simple, kind-hearted, and polite. My casual acquaintance with his son was sufficient to enlist his warmest sympathies. I thought he would destroy his equilibrium as well as my own by repeatedly drinking my health and wishing me a hearty welcome to Iceland. He said he had never seen a Californian before, and seemed astonished to find that they had noses, mouths, ears, and skins like other people. In one respect he paid me a practical compliment that I have rarely enjoyed in the course of my travels—he spoke nearly as bad French as I did. Now I take it that a man who speaks bad French, after years of travel on the Continent of Europe, is worthy of some consideration. He is at least entitled to the distinction of having well preserved his nationality; and when any foreigner tries to speak it worse, but doesn't succeed, I can not but regard it as a tribute of respect.

Young Jonasen, I was glad to see, had gotten over his struggle with the sardines, and was now in a fair way to enjoy life. His sister, Miss Jonasen, is a very charming young lady, well educated and intelligent. She speaks English quite fluently, and does the honors of the executive mansion with an easy grace scarcely to be expected in this remote part of the world. Both are natives of Iceland.

I should be sorry to be understood as intimating, in my brief sketch of Reykjavik, that it is destitute of refined society. There are families of as cultivated manners here as in any other part of the world; and on the occasion of a ball or party, a stranger would be surprised at the display of beauty and style. The University and public library attract students from all parts of the island, and several of the professors and literary men have obtained a European reputation. Two semi-monthly newspapers are published at Reykjavik, in the Icelandic language. They are well printed, and said to be edited with ability. I looked over them very carefully from begining to end, and could see nothing to object to in any portion of the contents.

CHAPTER XLIV.

GEIR ZÖEGA.

WISHING to see as much of the island as possible during the short time at my disposal, I made application to young Jonasen for information in regard to a guide, and through his friendly aid secured the services of Geir Zöega, a man of excellent reputation.

A grave, dignified man is Geir Zöega, large of frame and strong of limb; a light-haired, blue-eyed, fresh, honest-faced native, warm of heart and trusty of hand; a jewel of a guide, who knows every rock, bog, and mud-puddle between Reykjavik and the Geysers; a gentleman by nature, born in all probability of an iceberg and a volcano; a believer in ghosts and ghouls, and a devout member of the Church. All hail to thee, Geir Zöega! I have traveled many a rough mile with thee, used up thy brandy and smoked thy cigars, covered my chilled body with thy coat, listened to thy words of comfort pronounced in broken English, received thy last kind wishes at parting, and now I say, in heartfelt sincerity, all hail to thee, Geir Zöega! A better man never lived, or if he did, he could be better spared at Reykjavik.

To my great discontent, I found it indispensable to have five horses, although I proposed making the trip entirely without baggage. It seemed that two were necessary for myself, two for the guide, and one to carry the provisions and tent, without which it would be very difficult to travel, since there are no hotels in any part of the interior. Lodgings may be had at the huts of the peasants, and such rude fare as they can furnish; but the tourist had better rely upon his own tent and provisions, unless he has a craving to be fed on black bread and curds, and to be buried alive under a dismal pile of sods.

GEIR ZOEGA.

The reason why so many horses are required is plain enough. At this time of the year (June) they are still very poor after their winter's starvation, the pasturage is not yet good, and, in order to make a rapid journey of any considerable length, frequent changes are necessary. Philosophy and humanity combined to satisfy me that the trip could not well be made with a smaller number. I was a little inquisitive on that point, partly on the score of expense, and partly on account of the delay

T 2

and trouble that might arise in taking care of so many animals.

If there is any one trait common among all the nations of the earth, it is a natural sharpness in the traffic of horse-flesh. My experience has been wonderfully uniform in this respect wherever it has been my fortune to travel. I have had the misfortune to be the victim of horse-jockeys in Syria, Africa, Russia, Norway, and even California, where the people are proverbially honest. I have weighed the horse-jockeys of the four continents in the balance, and never found them wanting in natural shrewdness. It is a mistake, however, to call them unprincipled. They are men of most astonishing tenacity of principle, but unfortunately they have but one governing principle in life—to get good prices for bad horses.

On the arrival of the steamer at Reykjavik the competition among the horse-traders is really the only lively feature in the place. Immediately after the passengers get ashore they are beset by offers of accommodation in the line of horse-flesh. Vagabonds and idlers of every kind, if they possess nothing else in the world, are at least directly or indirectly interested in this species of property. The roughest specimens of humanity begin to gather in from the country around the corners of the streets near the hotel, with all the worn-out, lame, halt, blind, and spavined horses that can be raked up by hook or crook in the neighborhood. Such a medley was never seen in any other country. Barnum's woolly horse was nothing to these shaggy, stunted, raw-backed, bow-legged, knock-kneed little monsters, offered to the astonished traveler with unintelligible pedigrees in the Icelandic, which, if literally translated, must surely mean that they are a mixed product of codfish and brushwood. The size has but little to do with the age, and all rules applicable as a test in other parts of the world fail here. I judged some of them to be about four months old, and was not at all astonished when informed by disinterested spectators that they ranged from twelve to fifteen years.

ICELANDIC HORSES.

Nothing, in fact, could astonish me after learning that the horses in Iceland are fed during the winter on dried fish. This is a literal fact. Owing to the absence of grain and the scarcity of grass, it becomes necessary to keep life in the poor animals during the severest months of the season by giving them the refuse of the fisheries; and, what is very surprising, they relish it in preference to any other species of food. Shade of Ceres! what an article of diet for horses! Only think of it—riding on the back of a horse partly constructed of fish! No wonder some of them blow like whales.

In one respect the traveler can not be cheated to any great extent; he can not well lose more than twelve specie dollars on any one horse, that being the average price. To do the animals justice, they are like singed cats—a great deal better than they look. If they are not much for beauty, they are at least hardy, docile, and faithful; and, what is better, in a country where forage is sometimes difficult to find, will eat any thing on the face of the earth short of very hard lava or very indigestible trap-rock. Many of them, in consequence of these valuable qualities, are exported every year to Scotland and Copenhagen for breeding purposes. Two vessels were taking in cargoes of them during our stay at Reykjavik.

I was saved the trouble of bargaining for my animals by Geir Zöega, who agreed to furnish me with the necessary number at five Danish dollars apiece the round trip; that is, about two dollars and a half American, which was not at all unreasonable. For his own services he only charged a dollar a day, with whatever *buono mano* I might choose to give him. These items I mention for the benefit of my friends at home who may take a notion to make the trip.

I was anxious to get off at once, but the horses were in the country and had to be brought up. Two days were lost in consequence of the heavy rains, and the trail was said to be in very bad condition. On the morning

of the third day all was to be ready; and having purchased a few pounds of crackers, half a pound of tea, some
sugar and cheese, I was prepared to encounter the perils
of the wilderness. This was all the provision I took. Of
other baggage I had none, save my overcoat and sketch-
book, which, for a journey of five days, did not seem unreasonable. Zöega promised me any amount of suffering; but I told him Californians rather enjoyed that sort
of thing than otherwise.

CHAPTER XLV.

THE ENGLISH TOURISTS.

My English friends were so well provided with funds
and equipments that they found it impossible to get
ready. They had patent tents, sheets, bedsteads, mat-
tresses, and medicine-boxes. They had guns, too, in handsome gun-cases; and compasses, and chronometers, and
pocket editions of the poets. They had portable kitch-
ens packed in tin boxes, which they emptied out, but
never could get in again, comprising a general assortment of pots, pans, kettles, skillets, frying-pans, knives
and forks, and pepper-castors. They had demijohns of
brandy and kegs of Port wine; baskets of bottled porter and a dozen of Champagne; vinegar by the gallon
and French mustard in patent pots; likewise collodium
for healing bruises, and musquito-nets for keeping out
snakes. They had improved oil-lamps to assist the daylight which prevails in this latitude during the twenty-
four hours, and shaving apparatus and nail-brushes, and
cold cream for cracked lips, and dentifrice for the teeth,
and patent preparations for the removal of dandruff from
the hair; likewise lint and splints for mending broken
legs. One of them carried a theodolite for drawing inaccessible mountains within a reasonable distance; another a photographic apparatus for taking likenesses of
the natives and securing fac-similes of the wild beasts;

while a third was provided with a brass thief-defender for running under doors and keeping them shut against persons of evil character. They had bags, boxes, and bales of crackers, preserved meats, vegetables, and pickles; jellies and sweet-cake; concentrated coffee, and a small apparatus for the manufacture of ice-cream. In addition to all these, they had patent overcoats and undercoats, patent hats and patent boots, gum-elastic bed-covers, and portable gutta-percha floors for tents; ropes, cords, horse-shoes, bits, saddles and bridles, bags of oats, fancy packs for horses, and locomotive pegs for hanging guns on, besides many other articles commonly deemed useful in foreign countries by gentlemen of the British Islands who go abroad to rough it. This was roughing it with a vengeance! It would surely be rough work for me, an uncivilized Californian, to travel in Iceland or any other country under such a dreadful complication of conveniences.

When all these things were unpacked and scattered over the beds and floors of the hotel, nothing could excel the enthusiasm of the whole party—including myself, for I really had seen nothing in the course of my travels half so amusing. As an old stager in the camping business, I was repeatedly appealed to for advice and assistance, which of course I gave with the natural politeness belonging to all Californians, suggesting many additions. Warming-pans for the sheets, pads of cider-down to wear on the saddles, and bathing-tubs to sit in after a hard ride, would, I thought, be an improvement; but as such things were difficult to be had in Reykjavik, the hope of obtaining them was abandoned after some consideration. "In fact," said they, "we are merely roughing it, and, by Jove, a fellow must put up with some inconveniences in a country like this!"

To carry all these burdens, which, when tied up in packs, occupied an extra room, required exactly eighteen horses, inclusive of the riders, and to bargain for eighteen horses was no small job. The last I saw of the En-

ENGLISH PARTY AT REYKJAVIK.

glishmen they were standing in the street surrounded by a large portion of the population of Reykjavik, who had every possible variety of horses to sell—horses shaggy and horses shaved, horses small and horses smaller, into the mouths of which the sagacious travelers were intently peering in search of teeth—occasionally punching the poor creatures on the ribs, probing their backs, pulling them up by the legs, or tickling them under the tail to ascertain if they kicked.

At the appointed hour, 6 A.M., Zöega was ready at the door of the hotel with his shaggy cavalcade, which surely was the most extraordinary spectacle I had ever witnessed. The horned horses of Africa would have been commonplace objects in comparison with these remarkable animals destined to carry me to the Geysers of Iceland. Each one of them looked at me through a stack of mane containing hair enough to have stuffed half a dozen chairs; and as for their tails, they hung about the poor creatures like huge bunches of wool. Some of them were piebald and had white eyes—others had no eyes at all. Seeing me look at them rather apprehensively, Zöega remarked,

"Oh, sir, you needn't be afraid. They are perfectly gentle!"

"Don't they bite?" said I.

"Oh no, sir, not at all."

"Nor kick?"

"No, sir, never."

"Nor lie down on the way?"

"No, sir, not at all."

"Answer me one more question, Zöega, and I'm done." [This I said with great earnestness.] "Do these horses ever eat cats or porcupines, or swallow heavy brooms with crooked handles?"

"Oh no, sir!" answered my guide, with a look of some surprise; "they are too well trained for that."

"Then I suppose they subsist on train-oil as well as codfish?"

" Yes, sir, when they can get it. They are very fond of oil."

I thought to myself, No wonder they are so poor and small. Horses addicted to the use of oil must expect to be of light construction. But it was time to be off.

A cup of excellent coffee and a few biscuit were amply sufficient to prepare me for the journey. Our pack-horse carried two boxes and a small tent—all we required. Before starting Zöega performed the Icelandic ceremony of tying the horses in a row, each one's head to the tail of the horse in front. This, he said, was the general practice. If it were not done they would scatter outside of town, and it would probably take two hours to catch them again. I had some fear that if one of the number should tumble over a precipice he would carry several of his comrades with him, or their heads and tails.

CHAPTER XLVI.

THE ROAD TO THINGVALLA.

It was a gray, gloomy morning when we sallied forth from the silent streets of Reykjavik. A chilly fog covered the country, and little more was to be seen than the jagged outline of the lava-hills, and the boggy sinks and morasses on either side of the trail. The weird, fire-blasted, and flood-scourged wilderness on all sides was as silent as death, save when we approached some dark lagoon, and startled up the flocks of water-fowl that dwelt in its sedgy borders. Then the air was pierced with wild screams and strange cries, and the rocks resounded to the flapping of many wings. To me there was a peculiar charm in all this. It was different from any thing I had recently experienced. The roughness of the trail, the absence of cultivated fields, the entire exemption from the restraints of civilization, were perfectly delightful after a dreary residence of nearly a year in Germany. Here, at least, there were no passport bureaus, no meddlesome police, no conceited and disagreeable habitués of public places with fierce dogs running at their heels, no *Verbotener Wegs* staring one in the face at every turn. Here all ways possible to be traveled were open to the public; here was plenty of fresh air and no lack of elbow-room; here an unsophisticated American could travel without being persecuted every ten minutes by applications from distinguished officers in livery for six kreutzers; here an honest Californian could chew tobacco when he felt disposed, and relieve his mind by an occasional oath when he considered it essential to a vigorous expression of his thoughts.

It seemed very strange to be traveling in Iceland, actually plodding my way over deserts of lava, and breathing blasts of air fresh from the summit of Mount Hecla! I was at last in the land of the Sagas—the land of fire, and brimstone, and boiling fountains!—the land which, as a child, I had been accustomed to look upon as the *ultima Thule*, where men, and fish, and fire, and water were pitted against each other in everlasting strife. How often had the fascinating vision of Icelandic travel crossed my mind; and how often had I dismissed it with a sigh as too much happiness to hope for in this world! And now it was all realized. Was I any the happier? Was it what I expected? Well, we won't probe these questions too far. It was a very strange reality, at all events.

For the first eight miles the weather was thick and rainy; after that the sun began to dissipate the gloom, and we had a very pleasant journey. Though a little chilly in consequence of the moisture, the air was not really cold. As well as I could judge, the thermometer ranged about 54° Fahrenheit. It frequently rises to 70° at Thingvalla during the months of July and August; and at the Geysers, and in some of the adjacent valleys, the heat is said to be quite oppressive.

Notwithstanding the roughness of the trail, which in many places passed for miles over rugged fields of lava,

A ROUGH ROAD.

full of sharp, jagged points and dangerous fissures, we traveled with considerable speed, seldom slackening from a lope. Zöega untied the horses from each other's tails soon after passing the road to Hafuarfiord, as there was no farther danger of their separating, and then, with many flourishes of his whip and strange cries, well understood by our animals, led the way. I must confess that, in spite of some pretty hard experience of bad roads in the coast range of California, there were times during our mad career over the lava-beds when visions of maimed limbs and a mutilated head crossed my mind. Should my horse stumble on a stray spike of lava, what possible chance of escape would there be? Falling head foremost on harrows and rakes would be fun to a fall here, where all the instruments capable of human destruction, from razors, saws, and meat-axes down to spike-nails and punches, were duly represented.

In the course of our journey we frequently overtook pack-trains laden with dried fish from the sea-shore. The main dependence of the people throughout the country, during the winter, is upon the fish caught during the summer. When dried it is done up in packs and fastened on each side of the horse, something in the Mexican style; and each train is attended by three or four men, and sometimes by women. About the month of June the farmers and shepherds go down to Reykjavik, or some other convenient fishing-station on the sea-shore, and lay in their supplies of fish and groceries, which they purchase from the traders by exchanges of wool, butter, and other domestic products. After a few days of novelty and excitement they go back to their quiet homes, where they live in an almost dormant state until the next season, rarely receiving any news from the great outer world, or troubling their heads about the affairs which concern the rest of mankind. Those whom we met had in all probability not seen a stranger for a year. They are an honest, primitive people, decently but very coarsely clad in rough woolen garments manufactured

by themselves, and shaped much in the European style.
On their feet they wear moccasins made of sheepskin.
Whenever we met these pack-trains in any convenient
place, the drivers stopped to have a talk with Zöega,
often riding back a mile or two to enjoy the novelty of
his conversation. Being fresh from the capital, he naturally abounded in stirring news about the price of codfish, and the value of lard and butter, wool, stockings,
mittens, etc., and such other articles of traffic as they felt
interested in. He could also give them the latest intelligence by the steamer, which always astonished them,
no matter whether it concerned the throwing overboard
of three ponies on the last voyage, or the possible re-
sumption of operations on the Icelandic telegraph. In
every way Zöega was kind and obliging, and, being well
known every where, was highly appreciated as a man
possessed of a remarkable fund of information. At parting they generally stopped to kiss hands and take a pinch
of snuff.

The first time I witnessed the favorite ceremony of
snuff-taking I was at a loss to understand what it meant.
A man with a small horn flask, which it was reasonable
to suppose was filled with powder and only used for load-
ing guns or pistols, drew the plug from it, and, stopping
quite still in the middle of the road, threw his head back
and applied the tube to his nose. Surely the fellow was
not trying to blow his brains out with the powder-flask!
Two or three times he repeated this strange proceeding,
snorting all the time as if in the agonies of suffocation.
The gravity of his countenance was extraordinary. I
could not believe my eyes.

"What an absurd way of committing suicide!" I remarked to Zöega.

"Oh, sir, he is only taking snuff!" was the reply.

"But if he stops up both nostrils, how is he going to
breathe?" was my natural inquiry.

Zöega kindly explained that when the man's nose was
full he would naturally open his mouth, and as the snuff

was very fine and strong it would eventually cause him to sneeze. In this way it was quite practicable to blow out the load.

"But don't they ever hang fire and burst their heads?" I asked, with some concern.

"Why no, sir, I've never heard of a case," answered Zöega, in his usual grave manner; "in this country every body takes snuff, but I never knew it to burst any body's head."

It was really refreshing the matter-of-fact manner in which my guide regarded all the affairs of life. He took every thing in a literal sense, and was of so obliging a disposition that he would spend hours in the vain endeavor to satisfy my curiosity on any doubtful point.

"Why, Zöega," said I, "this is a monstrous practice. I never saw any thing like it. Are you quite sure that fellow won't kick when he tries to blow his nose?"

"Yes, sir, they never kick."

"Tell me, Zöega, are their breeches strong?"

"Oh yes, sir."

"That's lucky." I was thinking of an accident that once occurred to a young man of my acquaintance. Owing to a defect in the breech of his gun, the whole load entered his head and killed him instantaneously.

The gravity of these good people in their forms of politeness is one of the most striking features in their social intercourse. The commonest peasant takes off his cap to another when they meet, and shaking hands and snuff-taking are conducted on the most ceremonious principles. They do not, however, wholly confine themselves to stimulants for the nose. As soon as they get down to Reykjavik and finish their business, they are very apt to indulge in what we call in California "a bender;" that is to say, they drink a little too much whisky, and hang around the stores and streets for a day or two in a state of intoxication. At other times their habits are temperate, and they pass the greater part of their lives among their flocks, free from excitement, and as happy as people can be with such limited means of comfort. The uniformity of their lives would of course be painful to a people possessed of more energy and a higher order of intelligence; but the Icelanders are well satisfied if they can keep warm during the dreary winters, and obtain their usual supplies during the summer. Sometimes a plague sets in among their sheep and reduces them to great distress. Fire, pestilence, and famine have from time to time devastated the island. Still, where their wants are so few, they can bear with great patience the calamities inflicted upon them by an all-wise Providence. Owing perhaps to their isolated mode of life, they are a grave and pious people, simple in their manners, superstitious, and credulous. They attend church regularly, and are much devoted to religious books and evening prayers. No family goes to bed without joining in thanksgiving for all the benefits conferred upon them during the day. Living as they do amid the grandest phenomena of nature, and tinctured with the wild traditions of the old Norsemen, it is not surprising that they should implicitly believe in wandering spirits of fire and flood, and clothe the desolate wastes of lava with a poetic imagery peculiarly their own. Every rock, and river, and bog is invested with a legend or story, to the truth of which they can bear personal witness. Here a ghost was overtaken by the light of the moon and turned to stone; there voices were heard crying for help, and because no help came a farmer's house was burned the next day; here a certain man saw a wild woman, with long hair, who lived in a cave, and never came out to seek for food save in the midst of a storm, when she was seen chasing the birds; there a great many sheep disappeared one night, and it was thought they were killed and devoured by a prodigious animal with two heads—and so on, without end. Nothing is too marvelous for their credulity. One of my most pleasant experiences was to talk with these good people, through the aid of my guide, and hear them tell of the wonderful sights they had seen with their own eyes. Nor do I believe that they had the remotest intention of stretching the truth. Doubtless they imagined the reality of whatever they said. It was very strange to one who had lived so long among a sharp and rather incredulous race of men to hear full-grown people talk with the simplicity of little children.

About half way on our journey toward Thingvalla it was necessary to cross a bog, which is never a very agreeable undertaking in Iceland, especially after heavy rains. This was not the worst specimen of its kind, though; we afterward passed through others that would be difficult to improve upon without entirely removing the bottom. A considerable portion of Iceland is intersected by these treacherous stretches of land and water, through which

the traveler must make his way or relinquish his journey.
Often it becomes a much more difficult matter to find
the way out than to get in. Along the sea-coast, to the
southward and eastward, some of these vast bogs are
quite impassable without the assistance of a guide thoroughly acquainted with every spot capable of bearing a
horse. On the route to the Geysers we generally contrived to avoid the worst places by making a detour
around the edges of the hills, but this is not always practicable. In many places the hills themselves abound in
boggy ground.

The formation of the Icelandic bog is peculiar. I have
seen something similar on the Pacific coast near Cape
Mendocino, but by no means so extensive and well-defined. In Iceland it consists of innumerable tufts of earth
from two to three feet high, interwoven with vegetable
fibres which render them elastic when pressed by the
foot. These tufts stand out in relief from the main
ground at intervals of a few feet from each other, and
frequently cover a large extent of country. The tops
are covered with grass of a very fine texture, furnishing
a good pasture for sheep and other stock. So regular
and apparently artificial is the appearance of these grassy
tufts, that I was at first inclined to think they must be
the remains of cultivated fields—probably potato-hills, or
places where corn had grown in former times. Nor was
it altogether unreasonable to suppose that groves of wood
might once have covered these singular patches of country, and that they had been uprooted and destroyed by
some of those violent convulsions of nature which from
time to time have devastated the island. Dr. Dasent
produces ample testimony to show that, in old times, not
only corn grew in Iceland, but wood sufficiently large to
be used in building vessels. Now it is with great difficulty that a few potatoes can be raised in some of the
warmest spots, and there is not a single tree to be found
on the entire island. The largest bushes I saw were only
six or eight feet high.

U

A singular fact connected with the bog-formation is that it is often found in dry places—on the slopes of mountains, for example, in certain localities where the water never settles and where the ground is perpetually dry. I was greatly puzzled by this, and was scarcely satisfied by the explanation given by Zöega, my guide, who said it was caused by the action of the frost. In proof of the fact that they are not of artificial formation, and that the process by which they are developed is always going on, he stated that in many places where they had been leveled down for sheep-corrals or some such purpose, a similar formation of tufted hillocks had grown up in the course of a few years.

I was continually troubled by the circuits made by Zöega to avoid certain tracts of this kind which to me did not look at all impracticable. Once I thought it would be a good joke to show him that a Californian could find his way through a strange country even better than a native; and watching a chance when he was not on the look-out—for I suspected what his objection would be—I suddenly turned my horse toward the bog, and urged him to take the short cut. It was such a capital idea, that of beating my own guide about two miles in a journey of little more than half a mile! But, strange to say, the horse was of Zöega's opinion respecting roads through Iceland. He would not budge into the bog till I inflicted some rather strong arguments upon him, and then he went in with great reluctance. Before we had proceeded a dozen yards he sank up to his belly in the mire, and left me perched up on two matted tufts about four feet apart. Any disinterested spectator would have supposed at once that I was attempting to favor my guide with a representation of the colossal statue at Rhodes, or the Natural Bridge in Virginia. Zöega, however, was too warmly interested in my behalf to take it in this way. As soon as he missed me he turned about, and, perceiving my critical position, shouted at the top of his voice,

AN ICELANDIC BOG.

"Sir, you can't go that way!"

"No," said I, in rather a desponding tone, "I see I can't."

"Don't try it, sir!" cried Zöega; "you'll certainly sink if you do!"

"I'll promise you that, Zöega," I answered, looking gloomily toward the dry land, toward which my horse was now headed, plunging frantically in a labyrinth of tufts, his head just above the ground.

"Sir, it's very dangerous!" shouted Zöega.

"Any sharks in it?" I asked.

"No, sir; but I don't see your horse!"

"Neither do I, Zöega. Just sing out when he blows!"

But the honest Icelander saw a better method than that, which was to dismount from his own horse, and jump from tuft to tuft until he got hold of my bridle. With it of course came the poor animal, which by hard pulling my trusty guide soon succeeded in getting on dry land. Meantime I discovered a way of getting out myself by a complicated system of jumps, and presently we all stood in a group, Zöega scraping the mud off the sides of my trembling steed, while I ventured to remark that it was "a little boggy in that direction."

"Yes, sir," said Zöega; "that was the reason I was going round."

And a very sensible reason it was too, as I now cheerfully admitted. After a medicinal pull at the brandy we once more proceeded on our way.

I mentioned the fact that there are dry bog-formations on the sides of some of the hills. It should also be noted that the wet bogs are not always in the lowest places. Frequently they are found on elevated grounds, and even high up in the mountains. Approaching a region of this kind, when the tufts are nearly on a level with the eye, the effect is very peculiar. It looks as if an army of grim old Norsemen, on their march through the wilderness, had suddenly sunk to their necks in the treacherous earth, and still stood in that position with their shaggy heads bared to the tempests. Often the traveler detects something like features, and it would not be at all difficult, of a moonlight night, to mistake them for ghostly warriors struggling to get out on dry land. Indeed, the simple-minded peasants, with their accustomed fertility of imagination, have invested them with life, and relate many wonderful stories about their pranks of dark and stormy nights, when it is said they are seen plunging about in the water. Hoarse cries are heard through the gusts of the tempest; and solitary travelers on their journey retreat in dismay, lest they should be dragged into the treacherous abode of these ghostly old Norsemen.

Not long after our unpleasant adventure we ascended an eminence or dividing ridge of lava, from which we had a fine view of the Lake of Thingvalla. Descending by a series of narrow defiles, we reached a sandy cañon winding for several miles nearly parallel with the shores of the lake. The sides of the hills now began to exhibit a scanty vegetation, and sometimes we crossed a moist patch of pasture covered with a fine grass of most brilliant and beautiful green. A few huts, with sod walls or fences around the arable patches in the vicinity, were to be seen from time to time, but in general the country was very thinly populated. Flocks of sheep, and occasionally a few horses, grazed on the hill-sides.

The great trouble of our lives in the neighborhood of these settlements was a little dog belonging to my guide. Brusa was his name, and the management of our loose horses was his legitimate occupation. A bright, lively, officious little fellow was Brusa, very much like a wolf in appearance, and not unlike a human being in certain traits of his character. Montaigne says that great fault was found with him, when he was mayor of his native town, because he was always satisfied to let things go along smoothly; and though the citizens admitted that they had never been so free from trouble, they could not see the use of a mayor who never issued any ordinances or created any public commotions. Our little dog was of precisely the same way of thinking. He could see no use in holding office in our train without doing something, whether necessary or not. So, when the horses were going along all right, he felt it incumbent upon him to give chase to the sheep. Stealing away quietly, so that Zöega might not see him at the start, he would suddenly dart off after the poor animals, with his shaggy hair all erect, and never stop barking, snapping, and biting at their legs till they were scattered over miles of territory. He was particularly severe upon the cowardly ewes and lambs, actually driving them frantic with terror; but the old rams that stood to make fight he always passed with quiet disdain. It was in vain Zöega would hold up, and utter the most fearful cries and threats of punishment: "Hur-r-r-r! Brusa! B-r-r-r-usa!! you B-r-r-usa!!!" Never a bit could Brusa be stopped once he got fairly under way. Up hill, and down hill, and over the wild gorges he would fly till entirely out of sight. In about half an hour he generally joined the train again, looking, to say the least of it, very sheepish. I have already spoken of the gravity and dignity of Zöega's manner. On occasions of this kind it assumed a parental severity truly impressive. Slowly dismounting from his horse, as if a great duty devolved upon him, he would unlock one of the boxes on the pack-horse, take therefrom a piece of bread, deliberately grease the same with butter, and then holding it forth, more in sorrow than in anger, invite Brusa to refresh himself after his fatiguing chase of the sheep. The struggle between a guilty conscience and a sharp appetite would now become painfully perceptible on the countenance of Brusa as well as in the relaxation of his tail. As he approached the tempting morsel nothing could be more abject than his manner—stealing furtive glances at the eyes of his master, and trying to conciliate him by wagging the downcast tail between his legs. Alas, poor Brusa! I suspected it from the beginning. What do you think of yourself now? Grabbed by the back of the neck in the power-

GEIR ZÖEGA AND BRUSA.

ful hands of Geir Zöega!   Not a particle of use for you
to whine, and yelp, and try to beg off.   You have been
a very bad fellow, and must suffer the consequences.
With dreadful deliberation Zöega draws forth his whip,
which has been carefully hidden in the folds of his coat
all this time, and, holding the victim of his displeasure in
mid-air, thus, as I take it, apostrophizes him in his native
language: "O Brusa! have I not fed thee and cherished
thee with parental care?   (Whack! yelp! and whack
again.)   Have I not been to thee tender and true?
(Whack! whack! accompanied by heart-rending yelps
and cries.)   And this is thy ingratitude!   This is thy
return for all my kindness!   O how sharper than a ser-

pent's tooth is the sting of ingratitude! (Whack.) I warned thee about those sheep—those harmless and tender little lambs! I begged thee with tears in my eyes not to run after them; but thou wert stubborn in thine iniquity; and now what can I do but—(whack)—but punish thee according to my promise? Wilt thou ever do it again? O say, Brusa, wilt thou ever again be guilty of this disreputable conduct? (A melancholy howl.) It pains me to do it (whack), but it is (whack) for thine own good! Now hear and repent, and henceforth let thy ways be the ways of the virtuous and the just!" It was absolutely delightful to witness the joy of Brusa when the whipping was over. Without one word of comment Zöega would throw him the bread, and then gravely mount his horse and ride on. For hours after the victim of his displeasure would run, and jump, and bark, and caper with excess of delight. I really thought it was a kindness to whip him, he enjoyed it so much afterward.

Whenever our loose horses got off the trail or lagged behind, the services of our dog were invaluable. Zöega had a particular way of directing his attention to the errant animal. "Hur-r-r-r!—(a roll of the tongue)—Hur-r-r-r Brusa!" and off Brusa would dash, his hair on end with rage, till within a few feet of the horse, when he would commence a series of terrific demonstrations, barking and snapping at the heels of the vagrant. Backing of ears to frighten him, or kicks at his head, had no terrors for him; he was altogether too sagacious to be caught within reach of dangerous weapons.

I know of nothing to equal the sagacity of these Icelandic dogs save that of the sheep-dogs of France and Germany. They are often sent out in the pastures to gather up the horses, and will remain by them and keep them within bounds for days at a time. They are also much used in the management of sheep. Unlike the regular shepherd-dog of Europe, however, they are sometimes thievish and treacherous, owing to their wolfish origin. I do not think we could have made ten miles a day without Brusa. In the driving of pack-trains a good dog is indispensable. I always gave the poor fellow something to eat when we stopped in consideration of his services.

CHAPTER XLVII.

THE ALMANNAJAU.

WE rode for some time along an elevated plateau of very barren aspect till something like a break in the outline became visible a few hundred yards ahead. I had a kind of feeling that we were approaching a crisis in our journey, but said nothing. Neither did Zöega, for he was not a man to waste words. He always answered my questions politely, but seldom volunteered a remark. Presently we entered a great gap between two enormous cliffs of lava.

"What's this, Zöega?" I asked.

"Oh, this is the Almannajau?"

"What! the great Almannajau, where the Icelandic Parliament used to camp!"

"Yes, sir; you see the exact spot down there below."

And, in good truth, there it was, some hundreds of feet below, in a beautiful little green valley that lay at the bottom of the gap. Never had my eyes witnessed so strange and wild a sight. A great fissure in the earth nearly a hundred feet deep, walled up with prodigious fragments of lava, dark and perpendicular, the bases strewn with molten masses, scattered about in the strangest disorder; a valley of the brightest green, over a hundred feet wide, stretching like a river between the fire-blasted cliffs; the trail winding through it in snake-like undulation—all now silent as death under the grim leaden sky, yet eloquent of terrible convulsions in by-gone centuries and of the voices of men long since mingled with the dust. Upon entering the gorge between the

ENTRANCE TO THE ALMANNAJAU.

shattered walls of lava on either side, the trail makes a
rapid descent of a few hundred yards till it strikes into
the valley. I waited till my guide had descended with
the horses, and then took a position a little below the
entrance, so as to command a view out through the
gorge and up the entire range of the Almannajau.

The appended sketch, imperfect as it is, will convey

THE ALMANNAJAU.

some idea of the scene; yet to comprise within the brief compass of a sheet of paper the varied wonders of this terrible gap, the wild disorder of the fragments cast loose over the earth, the utter desolation of the whole place, would be simply impossible. No artist has ever yet done justice to the scene, and certainly no mere amateur can hope to attain better success.

Looking up the range of the fissure, it resembles an immense walled alley, high on one side, and low, broken, and irregular on the other. The main or left side forms a fearful precipice of more than eighty feet, and runs in a direct line toward the mountains, a distance of four or five miles. On the right, toward the plain of Thingvalla, the inferior side forms nearly a parallel line of rifted and irregular masses of lava, perpendicular in front and receding behind. The greater wall presents a dark, rugged face, composed of immense pillars and blocks of lava, defined by horizontal and vertical fissures, strangely irregular in detail, but showing a dark, compact, and solid front. In places it is not unlike a vast library of books, shaken into the wildest confusion by some resistless power. Whole ranges of ink-colored blocks are wrenched from their places, and scattered about between the ledges. Well may they represent the law-books of the old Icelandic Sagas and judges, who held their councils near this fearful gorge! Corresponding in face, but less regular and of inferior height, is the opposite wall. In its molten state the whole once formed a burning flood, of such vast extent and depth that it is estimated by geologists nearly half a century must have elapsed before it became cool. The bottom of this tremendous crack in the sea of lava is almost a dead level, and forms a valley of about a hundred feet in width, which extends, with occasional breaks and irregularities, entirely up to the base of the mountain. This valley is for the most part covered with a beautiful carpeting of fine green grass, but is sometimes diversified by fragments of lava shivered off and cast down from the walls on either side.

The gorge by which we entered must have been impracticable for horses in its original state. Huge masses of lava, which doubtless once jammed· up the way, must have been hurled over into the gaping fissures at each side, and something like a road-way cleared out from the chaos of ruin. Pavements and side-stones are still visible, where it is more than probable the old Icelanders did many a hard day's work. Eight or nine centuries have not yet obliterated the traces of the hammer and chisel; and there were stones cast a little on one side that still bear the marks of horses' hoofs—the very horses in all probability ridden by old Sagas and lawgivers. Through this wild gorge they made their way into the sheltered solitudes of the Almannajau, where they pitched their tents and held their feasts previous to their councils on the Lögberg. Here passed the members of the Althing; here the victims of the Lögberg never repassed again.

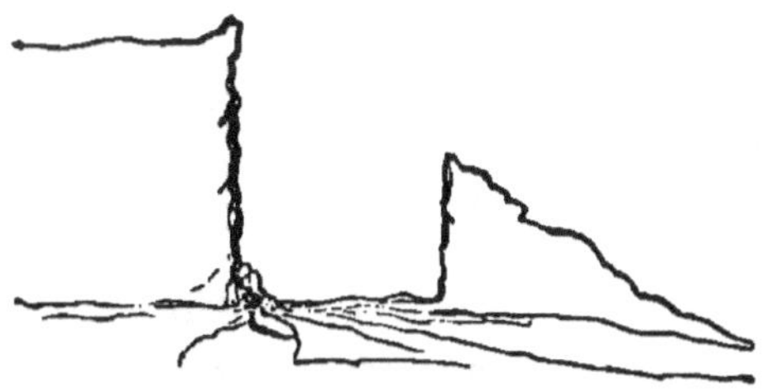

SKELETON VIEW OF THE ALMANNAJAU.

There are various theories concerning the original formation of this wonderful fissure. It is supposed by some that the flood of lava by which Thingvalla was desolated in times of which history presents no record must have cooled irregularly, owing to the variation of thickness in different parts of the valley; that at this point, where its depth was great, the contracting mass separated, and the inferior portion gradually settled downward toward the point of greatest depression.

Others, again, hold the theory that there was a liquid drain of the molten lava underneath toward the lake, by means of which a great subterranean cavity was formed as far back as the mountain; that the crust on top, being of insufficient strength to bear its own great weight, must have fallen in as the whole mass cooled, and thus created this vast crack in the earth.

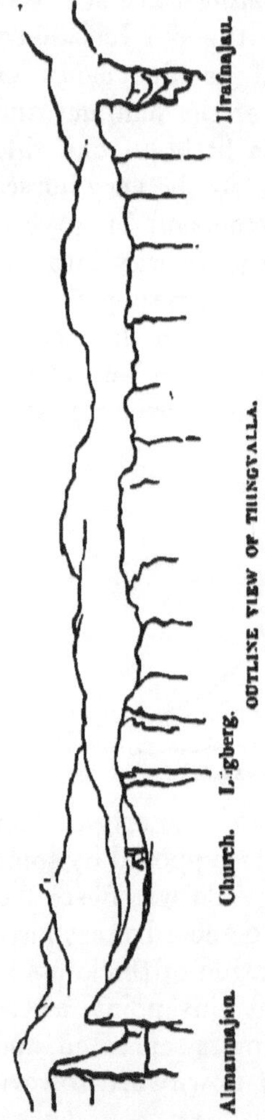

I incline to the first of these theories myself, as the most conformable to the contractile laws of heat. There is also something like practical evidence to sustain it. A careful examination of the elevations and depressions on each wall of the gap satisfied me that they bear at least a very striking analogy. Points on one side are frequently represented by hollows on the other, and even complicated figures occasionally find a counterpart, the configuration being always relatively convex or concave. This would seem to indicate very clearly that the mass had been forcibly rent asunder, either by the contractile process of heat, or a convulsion of the earth. The most difficult point to determine is why the bottom should be so flat and regular, and what kept the great mass on each side so far intact as to form one clearly-defined fissure a hundred feet wide and nearly five miles in length? This, however, is not for an unlearned tourist like myself to go into very deeply.

How many centuries have passed away since all this happened the first man who "gazed through the rent of ruin" has failed to leave on record—if he ever knew it. The great walls of the fissure stood grim and black before the old Icelandic Sagas, just as they now stand before the astonished eyes of the tourist. History records no material change in its aspect. It may be older than the Pyramids of Egypt; yet it looks as if the eruption by which it was caused might have happened within a lifetime, so little is there to indicate the progress of ages. I could not but experience the strangest sensations in being carried so far back toward the beginning of the world.

At the distance of about a mile up the "Jau" a river tumbles over the upper wall of lava, and rushes down the main fissure for a few hundred yards, when it suddenly diverges and breaks through a gap in the inferior wall, and comes down the valley on the outside toward the lake.

During my stay at Thingvalla I walked up to this part of the Almannajau, and made a rough sketch of the waterfall.

From the point of rocks upon which I stood the effect was peculiar. The course of the river, which lies behind the Jau, on the opposite side, is entirely hidden by the great wall in front, and nothing of it is visible till the whole river bursts over the dark precipice, and tumbles, foaming and roaring, into the tremendous depths below, where it dashes down wildly among the shattered fragments of lava till it reaches the outlet into the main valley. A mist rises up from the falling water, and whirls around the base of the cataract in clouds, forming in the rays of the sun a series of beautiful rainbows. The grim, jagged rocks, blackened and rifted with fire, make a strange contrast with the delicate prismatic colors of the rainbows, and their sharp and rugged outline with the soft, ever-changing clouds of spray.

The flocks of the good pastor of Thingvalla were quietly browsing among the rugged declivities where I stood. Here were violence and peace in striking contrast; the tremendous concussion of the falling water; the fearful marks of convulsion on the one hand, and on the other

FALL OF THE ALMANAJAU.

"The gentle flocks that play upon the green."

As I put away my imperfect sketch, and sauntered
back toward the hospitable cabin of the pastor, a figure

ICELANDIC SHEPHERD-GIRL.

emerged from the rocks, and I stood face to face with an
Icelandic shepherdess.

Well, it is no use to grow poetical over this matter.
To be sure, we were alone in a great wilderness, and she

was very pretty, and looked uncommonly coquettish with her tasseled cap, neat blue bodice, and short petticoats, to say nothing of a well-turned pair of ankles; but then, you see, I couldn't speak a word of Icelandic, and if I could, what had I, a responsible man, to say to a pretty young shepherdess? At most I could only tell her she was extremely captivating, and looked for all the world like a flower in the desert, born to blush unseen, etc. As she skipped shyly away from me over the rocks I was struck with admiration at the graceful sprightliness of her movements, and wondered why so much beauty should be wasted upon silly sheep, when the world is so full of stout, brave young fellows who would fall dead in love with her at the first sight. But I had better drop the subject. There is a young man of my acquaintance already gone up to Norway to look for the post-girl that drove me over the road to Trondhjem, and at least two of my friends are now on the way to Hamburg for the express purpose of witnessing the gyrations of the celebrated wheeling girls. All I hope is, that when they meet with those enterprising damsels they will follow my example, and behave with honor and discretion.

Standing upon an eminence overlooking the valley, I was struck with wonder at the vast field of lava outspread before me. Here is an area at least eight miles square, all covered with a stony crust, varying from fifty to a hundred feet in thickness, rent into gaping fissures and tossed about in tremendous fragments; once a burning flood, covering the earth with ruin and desolation wherever it flowed; now a cold, weird desert, whose gloomy monotony is only relieved by stunted patches of brushwood and dark pools of water—all wrapped in a death-like silence. Where could this terrible flood have come from? The mountains in the distance look·so peaceful in their snowy robes, so incapable of the rage from which all this desolation must have sprung, that I could scarcely reconcile such terrible results with an origin so apparently inadequate.

I questioned Zöega on this point, but not with much success. How was it possible, I asked, that millions and billions of tons of lava could be vomited forth from the crater of any mountain within sight? Here was a solid bed of lava spread over the valley, and many miles beyond, which, if piled up, shrunken and dried as it was, would of itself make a mountain larger than the Skjaldbraid Jokul, from which it is supposed to have been ejected.

"Now, Zöega," said I, "how do you make it out that this came from the Skjaldbraid Jokul?"

"Well, sir, I don't know, but I think it came from the inside of the world."

"Why, Zöega, the world is only a shell—a mere egg-shell in Iceland I should fancy—filled with fiery gases."

"Is that possible, sir?" cried Zöega, in undisguised astonishment.

"Yes, quite possible—a mere egg-shell!"

"Dear me, I didn't know that! It is a wonderful world, sir."

"Very—especially in Iceland."

"Then, sir, I don't know how this could have happened, unless it was done by spirits that live in the ground. Some people say they are great monsters, and live on burnt stones."

"Do you believe in spirits, Zöega?"

"Oh yes, sir; and don't you? I've seen them many a time. I once saw a spirit nearly as large as the Skjaldbraid. It came up out of the earth directly before me where I was traveling, and shook its head as if warning me to go back. I was badly frightened, and turned my horse around and went back. Then I heard that my best friend was dying. When he was dead I married his wife. She's a very good woman, sir, and, if you please, I'll get her to make you some coffee when we get back to Reykjavik."

So goes the world, thought I, from the Skjaldbraid Jokul to a cup of coffee! Why bother our heads about these troublesome questions, which can only result in proving us all equally ignorant. The wisest has learned nothing save his own ignorance. He "meets with darkness in the daytime, and gropes in the noonday as in the night."

CHAPTER XLVIII.

THINGVALLA.

THE extensive valley called Thingvalla, or the Valley of the "Thing," lies at the head of a lake of the same name, some fifteen miles in length by six or seven in width. The waters of this lake are beautifully clear, and the scenery around it is of the wildest and most picturesque character. Rugged mountains rise from its shores in various directions, and islands reflect their varied outlines in its glassy surface. Cranes, wild ducks, plovers, and occasionally swans, abound in the lagoons that open into it from Thingvalla. The bed of this fine sheet of water corresponds in its configuration with the surrounding country. It is of volcanic formation throughout, and the rifts and fissures in the lava can be traced as far as it is practicable to see through the water.

On passing out of the Almannajau near the lower fall, where the river breaks out into the main valley, the view toward the lake is extensive and imposing. Along the course of the river is a succession of beautiful little green flats, upon which the horses and cattle of the good pastor graze; and farther down, on the left, lies the church and farm-house. Still beyond are vast plains of lava, gradually merging into the waters of the lake; and in the far distance mountain upon mountain, till the view is lost in the snowy Jokuls of the far interior.

Descending into this valley we soon crossed the river, which is fordable at this season, and in a few minutes entered a lane between the low stone walls that surround the station.

CHURCH AT THINGVALLA.

The church is of modern construction, and, like all I saw in the interior, is made of wood, painted a dark color, and roofed with boards covered with sheets of tarred canvas. It is a very primitive little affair, only one story high, and not more than fifteen by twenty feet in dimensions. From the date on the weather-cock it appears to have been built in 1858.

The congregation is supplied by the few sheep-ranches in the neighborhood, consisting at most of half a dozen families. These unpretending little churches are to be seen in the vicinity of every settlement throughout the whole island. Simple and homely as they are, they speak well for the pious character of the people.

The pastor of Thingvalla and his family reside in a group of sod-covered huts close by the church. These cheerless little hovels are really a curiosity, none of them being over ten or fifteen feet high, and all huddled together without the slightest regard to latitude or longitude, like a parcel of sheep in a storm. Some have windows in the roof, and some have chimneys; grass and weeds grow all over them, and crooked by-ways and dark alleys run among them and through them. At the base they are walled up with big lumps of lava, and two of them have board fronts, painted black, while the remainder are patched up with turf and rubbish of all sorts, very much in the style of a stork's nest. A low stone wall encircles the premises, but seems to be of little use as a barrier against the encroachments of live-stock, being broken up in gaps every few yards. In front of the group some attempt has been made at a pavement, which, however, must have been abandoned soon after the work was commenced. It is now littered all over with old tubs, pots, dish-cloths, and other articles of domestic use.

The interior of this strange abode is even more complicated than one would be led to expect from the exterior. Passing through a dilapidated doorway in one of the smaller cabins, which you would hardly suppose to

THE PASTOR'S HOUSE.

be the main entrance, you find yourself in a long dark passage-way, built of rough stone, and roofed with wooden rafters and brushwood covered with sod. The sides are ornamented with pegs stuck in the crevices between the stones, upon which hang saddles, bridles, horse-shoes, bunches of herbs, dried fish, and various articles of cast-off clothing, including old shoes and sheepskins. Wide or narrow, straight or crooked, to suit the sinuosities of the different cabins into which it forms the entrance, it seems to have been originally located upon the track of a blind boa-constrictor, though Bishop Hatton denies the existence of snakes in Iceland. The best room, or rather house—for every room is a house—is set apart for the accommodation of travelers. Another cabin is occupied by some members of the pastor's family, who bundle about like a lot of rabbits. The kitchen is also the dog-kennel, and occasionally the sheep-house. A pile of stones in one corner of it, upon which a few twigs or scraps of sheep-manure serve to make the fire, constitute the cooking department. The beams overhead are decorated with pots and kettles, dried fish, stockings, petticoats, and the remains of a pair of boots that probably belonged to the pastor in his younger days. The dark turf walls are pleasantly diversified with bags of oil hung on pegs, scraps of meat, old bottles and jars, and divers rusty-looking instruments for shearing sheep and cleaning their hoofs. The floor consists of the original lava-bed, and artificial puddles composed of slops and offal of divers unctuous kinds. Smoke fills all the cavities in the air not already occupied by foul odors, and the beams, and posts, and rickety old bits of furniture are dyed to the core with the dense and variegated atmosphere around them. This is a fair specimen of the whole establishment, with the exception of the travelers' room. The beds in these cabins are the chief articles of luxury. Feathers being abundant, they are sewed up in prodigious ticks, which are tumbled topsy-turvy into big boxes on legs that serve for bedsteads, and then covered over with piles of all the loose blankets, petticoats, and cast-off rags possible to be gathered up about the premises. Into these comfortable nests the sleepers dive every night, and, whether in summer or winter, cover themselves up under the odorous mountain of rags, and snooze away till morning. During the long winter nights they spend on an average about sixteen hours out of the twenty-four in this agreeable manner. When it is borne in mind that every crevice in the house is carefully stopped up in order to keep out the cold air, and that whole families frequently occupy a single apartment not over ten by twelve, the idea of being able to cut through the atmosphere with a cleaver seems perfectly preposterous. A night's respiration in such a hole is quite sufficient to saturate the whole family with the substance of all the fish and sheepskins in the vicinity; and the marvel of it is that they don't come out next day wagging their fins or bleating like sheep. I wonder they ever have any occasion to eat. Absorption must supply them with a large amount of nutriment; but I suppose what is gained in that way is lost in the fattening of certain other members of the household. Warmth seems to be the principal object, and certainly it is no small consideration in a country where fuel is so scarce.

I can not conceive of more wretched abodes for human beings. They are, indeed, very little better than fox-holes —certainly not much sweeter. Yet in such rude habitations as these the priests of Iceland study the classical languages, and perfect themselves in the early literature of their country. Many of them become learned, and devote much of their lives to the pursuits of science. In the northern part of the country the houses are said to be better and more capacious; but the example I have given is a fair average of what I saw.

The passionate devotion of the Icelanders to their homes is almost inconceivable. I have never seen any thing like it. The most favored nations of the earth can not furnish examples of such intense and all-absorbing

X

love of home and country. I traveled with a native of Reykjavik some weeks after my visit to Thingvalla, and had an opportunity of judging what his impressions were of other countries. He was a very intelligent man, well versed in Icelandic literature, and spoke English remarkably well. Both himself and wife were fellow-passengers on the *Arcturus* from Reykjavik to Grangemouth. I was curious to know what a well-educated man would think of a civilized country, and watched him very closely. He had never seen a railway, locomotive, or carriage of any kind, not even a tree or a good-sized house. We stopped at Leith, where we took passage by the train to Edinburg. As soon as the locomotive started he began to laugh heartily, and by the time we reached Edinburg he and his wife, though naturally grave people, were nearly in convulsions of laughter. I had no idea that the emotion of wonder would be manifested in that way by civilized beings. Of course I laughed to see them laugh, and altogether it was very funny. We took rooms at the same hotel, opposite to Sir Walter Scott's monument. Now it is needless to say that Edinburg is one of the most beautiful cities in the world. Even Constantinople can scarcely surpass it in picturesque beauty. The worthy Icelander, be it remembered, had never seen even a town, except Reykjavik, of which I have already attempted a description. It was night when we arrived at Edinburg, so that I had no opportunity of judging what his impressions would be at that time. Next morning I knocked at his room door. His wife opened it, looking very sad, as I thought. At the window, gazing out over the magnificent scene, embracing the Monument, the Castle, and many of the finest of the public buildings, stood her husband, the big tears coursing down his face.

"Well," said I, "what do you think of Edinburg?"

"Oh!" he cried, "oh, I am so home-sick! Oh, my dear, dear native land! Oh, my own beautiful Iceland! Oh that I were back in my beloved Reykjavik! Oh, I shall die in this desert of houses! Oh that I could once more breathe the pure fresh air of my own dear, dear island home!"

Such were literally his expressions. Not one word had he to say about the beauties of Edinburg! To him it was a hideous nightmare. The fishy little huts of Reykjavik, the bleak lava-deserts of the neighborhood, and the raw blasts from the Jokuls, were all he could realize of a Paradise upon earth. Yet he was a highly-cultivated and intelligent man, not destitute of refined tastes. Truly, I thought to myself,

> "The shuddering tenant of the frigid zone
> Boldly proclaims the happiest spot his own."

While I waited outside the pastor's house, enjoying the oddity of the scene, Zöega busied himself unsaddling the horses. I sat down on a pile of fagots, and, with some trouble and a little assistance from my guide, succeeded in getting off my overalls, which had been thoroughly drenched with rain and saturated with mud. The occasional duckings we had experienced in crossing the rivers did not add to my comfort. I was chilled and wet, and would have given a Danish dollar for the privilege of sitting at a fire. All this time there was no sign of life about the premises save the barking of an ill-favored little dog that was energetically disclaiming any acquaintance with Brusa. I regret to say that Brusa lost much of his bravado air in the presence of this insignificant cur, but it was quite natural; the cur was at home and Brusa wasn't. At first our dog seemed disposed to stand his ground, but upon the near approach of the house-dog he dropped his tail between his legs and ingloriously sneaked between the legs of the horses, which of course gave the gentleman of the house a high opinion of his own prowess—so much so, indeed, that the craven spirit of Brusa never before appeared in such a despicable light. He cringed and howled with terror, which so flattered the vanity of the other that a ferocious attack was the immediate consequence. Fortunately, a kick from one of the horses laid Brusa's aggress-

or yelping in the mud, an advantage of which Brusa promptly availed himself, and the pastor's dog would have fared badly in the issue but for the interference of Zöega, who separated the contending parties, and administered a grave rebuke to the party of our part respecting the impropriety of his conduct.

Though it occurred to me that I had seen the retreating figure of a man as we rode up, I was at a loss to understand why nobody appeared to ask us in or bid us welcome, and suggested to Zöega that I thought this rather an unfriendly reception. Now, upon this point of Icelandic hospitality Zöega was peculiarly sensitive. He always maintained that the people, though poor, are very hospitable—so much so that they made no complaint when a certain Englishman, whose name he could mention, stopped with them for days, ate up all their food and drank up all their coffee, and then went off without offering them even a small present. "No wonder," said Zöega, "this man told a great many lies about them, and laughed at them for refusing money, when the truth was he never offered them money or any thing else. It was certainly a very cheap way of traveling."

"But what about the pastor, Zöega? I'm certain I caught a glimpse of him as he darted behind the door."

"Oh, he'll be here directly; he always runs away when strangers come."

"What does he run away for?"

"Why, you see, sir, he is generally a little dirty, and must go wash himself and put on some decent clothes."

While we were talking the pastor made his appearance, looking somewhat damp about the face and hair, and rather embarrassed about the shape of his coat, which was much too large for him, and hung rather low about his heels. With an awkward shuffling gait he approached us, and, having shaken hands with Zöega, looked askant at me, and said something, which my guide interpreted as follows:

"He bids you welcome, sir, and says his house is at

your service. It is a very poor house, but it is the best he has. He wishes to know if you will take some coffee, and asks what part of the world you are from. I tell him you are from California, and he says it is a great way off, clear down on the other side of the world, and may God's blessing be upon you. Walk in, sir."

THE PASTOR OF THINGVALLA.

Pleased with these kind words, I stepped up to the good pastor and cordially shook him by the hand, at the same time desiring Zöega to say that I thanked him very much, and hoped he would make it convenient to call and see me some time or other in California, which, I regret to add, caused him to look both alarmed and embarrassed. A queer, shy man was this pastor—a sort of living mummy, dried up and bleached by Icelandic snows. His manner was singularly bashful. There was something of the recluse in it—a mixture of shyness, awkwardness, and intelligence, as if his life had been spent chiefly among sheep and books, which very likely was the case. All the time I was trying to say something agreeable he was looking about him as if he desired to make his escape into some Icelandic bog, and there hide himself during my stay. I followed him through the passage-way already mentioned into the travelers' room, where he beckoned me to take a seat, and then, awkwardly seating himself on the edge of a chair as far away as he could get without backing through the wall, addressed me in Danish. Finding me not very proficient in that tongue, he branched off into Latin, which he spoke as fluently as if it had been his native language. Here again I was at fault. I had gone as far as *Quosque tandem* when a boy, but the vicissitudes of time and travel had knocked it all out of my head. I tried him on the German, and there, to use a familiar phrase, had the "dead-wood on him." He couldn't understand a word of that euphonious language. However, a slight knowledge of the Spanish, picked up in Mexico and California, enabled me to guess at some of his Latin, and in this way we struggled into something of conversation. The effort, however, was too great for the timid recluse. After several pauses and lapses into long fits of silence, he got up and took his leave. Meantime Zöega was enjoying himself by the fire in the kitchen, surrounded by the female members of the family, who no doubt were eagerly listening to the latest news from Reykjavik. Whenever their voices became audible I strongly suspected that the ladies were asking whether the steamer had brought any crinoline from Copenhagen.

The pastor's family appeared to be composed entirely of females. Like all the Icelandic women I had seen, they do all the work of the establishment, attend to the cows, make the cheese, cut the hay, carry the heavy burdens, and perform the manual labor generally. This I found to be the case at all the farm-houses. Sometimes the men assist, but they prefer riding about the country or lying idle about the doors of their cabins. At Reykjavik, it is true, there is a population of Danish sailors and fishermen, and it would be scarcely fair to form an opinion from the lazy and thriftless habits of the people there. But I think the civilization of Iceland is very much like that of Germany in respect to women. They are not rated very high in the scale of humanity. Still, overworked and degraded as they are, the natural proclivities of the sex are not altogether obliterated. In former times their costume was picturesque and becoming, and some traces of the old style are yet to be seen throughout the pastoral districts; a close body, a jaunty little cap on the head, with a heavy tassel, ornamented with gold or silver bands, silver clasps to their belts, and filigree buttons down the front, give them a very pleasing appearance. Of late years, however, fashion has begun to assert her sway, even in this isolated part of the world, and the native costume is gradually becoming modernized.

The pastor having joined the more congenial circle of which Zöega was the admired centre, I was left alone in the chilly little room allotted to travelers to meditate upon the comforts of Icelandic life. It was rather a gloomy condition of affairs to be wet to the skin, shivering with cold, and not a soul at hand to sympathize with me in my misery. Then the everlasting day—when would it end? Already I had been awake and traveling some fourteen hours, and it was as broad daylight as ever. Nothing could be more wearying than the everlasting daylight that surrounded me—not bright and sunshiny, but dreary and lead-colored, showing scarcely any perceptible difference between morning, noon, and night.

The coffee soon came to my relief, and the pastor followed it to wish me a good appetite and ask if I wanted any thing else. I again renewed the attempt at conversation, but it was too much for his nervous temperament and shrinking modesty. He always managed, after a few words, to slip stealthily away up into the loft or out among the rocks to avoid the appearance of intrusion, or the labor of understanding what I said, or communicating his ideas—I could not tell which.

After a slight repast I walked out to take a look at the Lögberg, or Rock of Laws, which is situated about half a mile from the church. This is, perhaps, of all the objects of historical association in Iceland, the most interesting. It was here the judges tried criminals, pronounced judgments, and executed their stern decrees.

SKELETON VIEW OF THE LÖGBERG.

On a small plateau of lava, separated from the general mass by a profound abyss on every side, save a narrow neck barely wide enough for a foothold, the famous "Thing" assembled once a year, and, secured from intrusion in their deliberations by the terrible chasm around, passed laws for the weal or woe of the people. It was only necessary to guard the causeway by which they entered; all other sides were well protected by the encircling moat, which varies from thirty to forty feet in width, and is half filled with water. The total depth to the

X 2

bottom, which is distinctly visible through the crystal pool, must be sixty or seventy feet. Into this yawning abyss the unhappy criminals were cast, with stones around their necks, and many a long day did they lie beneath the water, a ghastly spectacle for the crowd that peered at them over the precipice.

All was now as silent as the grave. Eight centuries had passed, and yet the strange scenes that had taken place here were vividly before me. I could imagine the gathering crowds, the rising hum of voices; the pause, the shriek, and plunge; the low murmur of horror, and then the stern warning of the lawgivers and the gradual dispersing of the multitude.

The dimensions of the plateau are four or five hundred feet in length by an average of sixty or eighty in width. A diagram, taken from an elevated point beyond, will give some idea of its form. The surface is now covered with a fine coating of sod and grass, and furnishes good pasturage for the sheep belonging to the pastor.

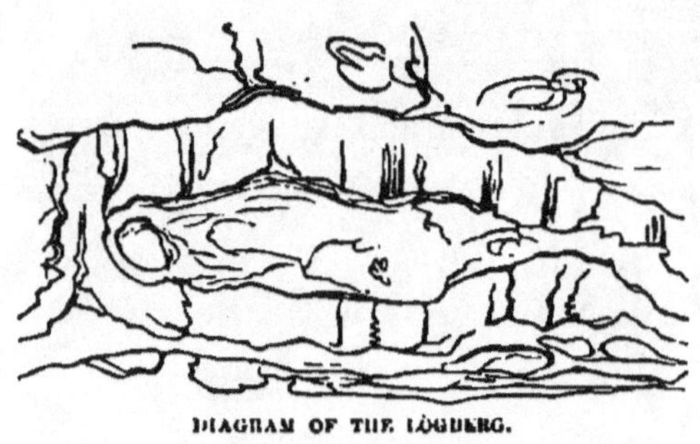

DIAGRAM OF THE LÖGBERG.

CHAPTER XLIX.

THE ROAD TO THE GEYSERS.

It was ten o'clock at night when I reached the parsonage. In addition to my rough ride from Reykjavik, and the various trying adventures on the way, I had walked over nearly the whole range of the Almannajau,

sketched the principal points of interest, visited the Lögberg, and made some sketches and diagrams of that, besides accomplishing a considerable amount of work about
the premises of the good pastor, all of which is now submitted to the kind indulgence of the reader. Surely if
there is a country upon earth abounding in obstacles to
the pursuit of the fine arts, it is Iceland. The climate
is the most variable in existence—warm and cold, wet
and dry by turns, seldom the same thing for half a day.
Such, at least, was my experience in June. Wild and
desolate scenery there is in abundance, and no lack of
interesting objects any where for the pencil of an artist;
but it is difficult to conceive the amount of physical dis-
comfort that must be endured by one who faithfully ad-
heres to his purpose. Only think of sitting down on a
jagged piece of lava, wet to the skin and shivering with
cold; a raw, drizzling rain running down your back and
dropping from the brim of your hat, making rivers on
your paper where none are intended to be; hints of
rheumatism shooting through your bones, and visions
of a solitary grave in the wilderness crossing your mind;
then, of a sudden, a wind that scatters your papers far
and wide, and sends your only hat whirling into an abyss
from which it is doubtful whether you will ever recover
it—think of these, ye summer tourists who wander,
sketch-book in hand, through the "warbling woodland"
and along "the resounding shore," and talk about being
enterprising followers of the fine arts! Try it in Iceland
a while, and see how long your inspiration will last!
Take my word for it, unless you be terribly in earnest,
you will postpone your labors till the next day, and then
the next, and so on to the day that never comes.

Not the least of my troubles was the difficulty of getting a good night's rest after the fatiguing adventures
of the day. There was no fault to be found with the
bed, save that it was made for somebody who had never
attained the average growth of an American; and one
might do without a night-cap, but how in the world

could any body be expected to sleep when there was no night? At twelve o'clock, when it ought to be midnight and the ghosts stirring about, I looked out, and it was broad day; at half past one I looked out again, and the sun was shining; at two I got up and tried to read some of the pastor's books, which were written in Icelandic, and therefore not very entertaining; at three I went to work and finished some of my sketches; and at

AN ARTIST AT HOME.

four I gave up all farther hope of sleeping, and sallied forth to take another look at the Almannajau.

On my return Zöega was saddling up the horses. A cup of coffee and a dry biscuit put me in traveling order, and we were soon on our way up the valley.

For the first few miles we followed the range of the "Jau," from which we then diverged across the great lava-beds of Thingvalla. It was not long before we struck into a region of such blasted and barren aspect that the imagination was bewildered with the dreary desolation of the scene. The whole country, as far as the eye could reach, was torn up and rent to pieces. Great masses of lava seemed to have been wrested forcibly from the original bed, and hurled at random over the face of the country. Prodigious fissures opened on every side, and for miles the trail wound through a maze of sharp points and brittle crusts of lava, with no indication of the course save at occasional intervals a pile of stones on some prominent point, erected by the peasants as a way-mark for travelers. Sometimes our hardy little horses climbed like goats up the rugged sides of a slope, where it seemed utterly impossible to find a foothold, so tortured and chaotic was the face of the earth; and not unfrequently we became involved in a labyrinth of fearful sinks, where the upper stratum had given way and fallen into the yawning depths below. Between these terrible traps the trail was often not over a few feet wide. It was no pleasant thing to contemplate the results of a probable slip or a misstep. The whole country bore the aspect of baffled rage—as if imbued with a demoniac spirit, it had received a crushing stroke from the Almighty hand that blasted and shivered it to fragments.

There were masses that looked as if they had turned cold while running in a fiery flood from the crater— wavy, serrated, frothy, like tar congealed or stiffened on a flat surface. One piece that I sketched was of the shape of a large leaf, upon which all the fibres were marked. It measured ten feet by four. Another bore a resemblance to a great conch-shell. Many were impressed with the roots of shrubs and the images of various sur-

LAVA-FJELDS.

rounding objects—snail-shells, pebbles, twigs, and the like.
On a larger scale, bubbling brooks, waterfalls, and whirl-
pools were represented—now no longer a burning flood,
but stiff, stark, and motionless. One sketch, which is re-
produced, bore a startling resemblance to some of the
marble effigies on the tombs of medieval knights.

The distant mountains were covered with their perpetual mantles of snow. Nearer, on the verge of the valley, were the red peaks of the foot-hills. To the right
lay the quiet waters of the lake glistening in the sunbeams. In front, a great black fissure stretched from the
shores of the lake to the base of the mountains, presenting to the eye an impassable barrier. This was the famous Hrafnajau—the uncouth and terrible twin-brother
of the Almannajau.

A toilsome ride of eight miles brought us to the edge
of the Pass, which in point of rugged grandeur far surpasses the Almannajau, though it lacks the extent and
symmetry which give the latter such a remarkable effect.
Here was a tremendous gap in the earth, over a hundred
feet deep, hacked and shivered into a thousand fantastic
shapes; the sides a succession of the wildest accidents;
the bottom a chaos of broken lava, all tossed about in
the most terrific confusion. It is not, however, the extraordinary desolation of the scene that constitutes its
principal interest. The resistless power which had rent
the great lava-bed asunder, as if touched with pity at the
ruin, had also flung from the tottering cliffs a causeway
across the gap, which now forms the only means of passing over the great Hrafnajau. No human hands could
have created such a colossal work as this; the imagination is lost in its massive grandeur; and when we reflect that miles of an almost impassable country would
otherwise have to be traversed in order to reach the opposite side of the gap, the conclusion is irresistible that
in the battle of the elements Nature still had a kindly
remembrance of man.

Five or six miles beyond the Hrafnajau, near the sum-

THE HRAFNAGJÁ.

mit of a dividing ridge, we came upon a very singular volcanic formation called the Tintron. It stands, a little to the right of the trail, on a rise of scoria and burned earth, from which it juts up in rugged relief to the height of twenty or thirty feet. This is, strictly speaking, a huge clinker not unlike what comes out of a grate—hard, glassy in spots, and scraggy all over. The top part is shaped like a shell; in the centre is a hole about three feet in diameter, which opens into a vast subterranean cavity of unknown depth. Whether the Tintron is an extinct crater, through which fires shot out of the earth in by-gone times, or an isolated mass of lava, whirled through the air out of some distant volcano, is a question that geologists must determine. The probability is that it is one of those natural curiosities so common in Iceland which defy research. The whole country is full of anomalies—bogs where one would expect to find dry land, and parched deserts where it would not seem strange to see bogs; fire where water ought to be, and water in the place of fire.

While the pack-train followed the trail, Zöega suggested that the Tintron had never been sketched, and if I felt disposed to "take it down"—as he expressed it—he would wait for me in the valley below; so I took it down.

During this day's journey we crossed many small rivers which had been much swollen by the recent rains. The fording-places, however, were generally good, and we got over them without being obliged to swim our horses. One river, the Brúará, gave me some uneasiness. When we arrived at the banks it presented a very formidable obstacle. At the only place where it was practicable to reach the water it was a raging torrent over fifty yards wide, dashing furiously over a bed of lava with a velocity and volume that bade apparent defiance to any attempt at crossing. In the middle was a great fissure running parallel with the course of the water, into which the current converged from each side, forming a series of cataracts that shook the earth, and made a loud reverberation from the depths below.

THE TINTRON LOCK.

I stopped on an elevated bank to survey the route before us. There seemed to be no possible way of getting over. It was all a wild roaring flood plunging madly down among the rocks. While I was thinking what was to be done, Zöega, with a crack of his whip, drove the animals into the water and made a bold dash after them. It then occurred to me that there was a good deal of prudence in the advice given by an Icelandic traveler: "*Never go into a river till your guide has tried it.*" Should Zöega be swept down over the cataract, as appeared quite probable, there would be no necessity for me to follow him. I had a genuine regard for the poor fellow, and it would pain me greatly to lose him; but then he was paid so much per day for risking his life, and how could I help it if he chose to pursue such a perilous career? Doubtless he had come near being drowned many a time before; he seemed to be used to it. All I could do for him in the present instance would be to break the melancholy intelligence to his wife as tenderly as possible. While thus philosophizing, Zöega plunged in deeper and deeper till he was surrounded by the raging torrent on the very verge of the great fissure. Was it possible he was going to force his horse into it? Surely the man must be crazy.

"Stop, Zöega! stop!" I shouted, at the top of my voice; "you'll be swept over the precipice. There's a great gap in the river just before you."

"All right, sir!" cried Zöega. "Come on, sir!"

Again and again I called to him to stop, but he seemed to lose my voice in the roar of the falling waters. Dashing about after the scattered animals, he whipped them all up to the brink of the precipice, and then quietly walked his own horse across on what looked to me like a streak of foam. The others followed, and in a few minutes they all stood safely on the opposite bank. I thought this was very strange. A remote suspicion flashed across my mind that Zöega was in league with some of those water-spirits which are said to infest the rivers of Iceland. Wondering what they would say to a live Californian, I plunged in and followed the route taken by my guide. Upon approaching the middle of the river I discovered that what appeared to be a streak of foam was in reality a wooden platform stretched across the chasm and covered by a thin sheet of water. It was pinned down to the rocks at each end, and was well braced with rafters underneath. From this the river derives its name —Brûará, or the Bridge.

The general aspect of the country differed but little from what I have already attempted to describe. Vast deserts of lava, snow-capped mountains in the distance, a few green spots here and there, and no apparent sign of habitation—these were its principal features. Below the falls the scene was peculiarly wild and characteristic. Tremendous masses of lava cast at random amid the roaring waters; great fissures splitting the earth asunder in all directions; every where marks of violent convulsion. In the following sketch I have endeavored to depict some of these salient points. When it is taken into consideration that the wind blew like a hurricane through the craggy ravines; that the rain and spray whirled over, and under, and almost through me; that it was difficult to stand on any elevated spot without danger of being blown over, I hope some allowance will be made for the imperfections of the performance.

About midway between Thingvalla and the Geysers we descended into a beautiful little valley, covered with a fine growth of grass, where we stopped to change horses and refresh ourselves with a lunch. While Zöega busied himself arranging the packs and saddles, our indefatigable little dog Brusa availed himself of the opportunity to give chase to a flock of sheep. Zöega shouted at him as usual, and as usual Brusa only barked the louder and ran the faster. The sheep scattered over the valley, Brusa pursuing all the loose members of the flock with a degree of energy and enthusiasm that would have done credit to a better cause. Upon the lambs he was

BRIDGE RIVER

particularly severe. Many of them must have been stunted in their growth for life by the fright they received; and it was not until he had tumbled half a dozen of them heels over head, and totally dispersed the remainder, that he saw fit to return to head-quarters. The excitement once over, he of course began to consider the consequences, and I must say he looked as mean as it was possible for an intelligent dog to look. Zöega took him by the nape of the neck with a relentless hand, and heaving a profound sigh, addressed a pathetic remonstrance to him in the Icelandic language, giving it weight and emphasis by a sharp cut of his whip after every sentence. This solemn duty performed to his satisfaction, and greatly to Brusa's satisfaction when it was over, we mounted our horses once more and proceeded on our journey.

A considerable portion of this day's ride was over a rolling country, somewhat resembling the foot-hills in certain parts of California. On the right was an extensive plain, generally barren, but showing occasional green patches; and on the left a rugged range of mountains, not very high, but strongly marked by volcanic signs. We passed several lonely little huts, the occupants of which rarely made their appearance. Sheep, goats, and sometimes horses, dotted the pasture-lands. There was not much vegetation of any kind save patches of grass and brushwood. A species of white moss covered the rocks in places, presenting the appearance of hoar-frost at a short distance.

CHAPTER L.

THE GEYSERS.

Upon turning the point of a hill where our trail was a little elevated above the great valley, Zöega called my attention to a column of vapor that seemed to rise out of the ground about ten miles distant. For all I could judge, it was smoke from some settler's cabin situated in a hollow of the slope.

"What's that, Zöega?" I asked.

"That's the Geysers, sir," he replied, as coolly as if it were the commonest thing in the world to see the famous Geysers of Iceland.

"The Geysers! That little thing the Geysers?"

"Yes, sir."

"Dear me! who would ever have thought it?"

I may as well confess at once that I was sadly disappointed. It was a pleasure, of course, to see what I had read of and pictured to my mind from early boyhood; but this contemptible little affair looked very much like a humbug. A vague idea had taken possession of my mind that I would see a whole district of country shooting up hot water and sulphurous vapors—a kind of hell upon earth; but that thing ahead of us—that little curl of smoke on the horizon looked so peaceful, so inadequate a result of great subterranean fires, that I could not but feel some resentment toward the travelers who had preceded me, and whose glowing accounts of the Geysers had deceived me. At this point of view it was not at all equal to the Geysers of California. I had a distinct recollection of the great cañon between Russian River Valley and Clear Lake, the magnificent hills on the route, the first glimpse of the infernal scene far down in the bed of the cañon, the boiling, hissing waters, and clouds of vapor whirling up among the rocks, the towering crags on the opposite side, and the noble forests of oak and pine that spread "a boundless contiguity of shade" over the wearied traveler, and I must say a patriotic pride took possession of my soul. We had beaten the world in the production of gold; our fruits were finer and our vegetables larger than any ever produced in other countries; our men taller and stronger, our women prettier and more prolific, our lawsuits more extensive, our fights the best ever gotten up, our towns the most rapidly built and rapidly burned—in short, every thing was on a grand, wide, broad, tall, fast, overwhelming scale, that bid defiance to competition, and now I was satisfied we could even beat old Iceland in the matters of Geysers. I really felt a contempt for that little streak of smoke. Perhaps something in the expression of my eye may have betrayed my thoughts, for Zöega, as if he felt a natural pride in the wonders of Iceland and wished them to be properly appreciated, hastily added, "But you must not judge of the Geysers by what you now see, sir! That is only the little Geyser. He don't blow up much. The others are behind the first rise of ground."

"That may be, Zöega. I have no doubt they are very fine, but it is not within the bounds of possibility that they should equal the Geysers of California."

"Indeed, sir! I didn't know you had Geysers there."

"Didn't know it! Never heard of the Geysers of California?"

"Never, sir."

"Well, Zöega, that is remarkable. Our Geysers are the finest, the bitterest, the smokiest, the noisest, the most infernal in the world; and as for mountains, our Shasta Bute would knock your Mount Hecla into a cocked hat!"

"Is it possible!"

"Of course it is."

"And have you great lava-beds covering whole valleys as we have here?"

"Certainly—only they are made of gold. We call them Placers—Gold Placers."

"A wonderful country, sir!"

"Would you like to go there, Zöega?"

"No, sir; I'd rather stay here."

And so we talked, Zöega and I, as we jogged along pleasantly on our way. Our ride, after we caught the first sight of the smoke, continued for some two hours over a series of low hills, with little green valleys lying between, till we came to an extensive bog that skirts the base of the Langarfjal, a volcanic bluff forming the background of the Geysers. It was now becoming interesting. Half an hour more would settle the matter conclusively between California and Iceland. Crossing the bog where it was not very wet, we soon came to a group of huts at the turning-point of the hill, where we were met

SHEPHERD AND FAMILY.

by a shepherd and his family. All turned out, big and little, to see the strangers. The man and his wife were fair specimens of Icelandic peasantry—broad-faced, blue-eyed, and good-natured, with yellowish hair, and a sort of mixed costume, between the civilized and the barbarous. The children, of which there must have been over a dozen, were of the usual cotton-head species found in all Northern countries, and wore any thing apparently they could get, from the cast-off rags of their parents to sheepskins and raw hide. Nothing could surpass the friendly interest of the old shepherd. He asked Zöega a thousand questions about the " gentleman," and begged that we would dismount and do him the honor to take a cup of coffee, which his wife would prepare for us in five minutes. Knowing by experience that five minutes in Iceland means any time within five hours, I was reluctantly obliged to decline the invitation. The poor fellow seemed much disappointed, and evidently was sincere in his offers of hospitality. To compromise the matter, we borrowed a spade from him, and requested him to send some milk down to our camp as soon as the cows were milked.

Although these worthy people lived not over half a mile from the Geysers, they could not tell us when the last eruption had taken place—a most important thing for us to know, as the success of the trip depended almost entirely upon the length of time which had elapsed since that event. The man said he never took notice of the eruptions. He saw the water shooting up every few days, but paid no particular attention to it. There might have been an eruption yesterday, or this morning, for all he knew; it was impossible for him to say positively. " In truth, good friend," said he to Zöega, " my head is filled with sheep, and they give me trouble enough." It was evidently filled with something, for he kept scratching it all the time he was talking.

Many travelers have been compelled to wait a week for an eruption of the Great Geyser, though the interval between the eruptions is not usually more than three days. A good deal depends upon the previous state of the weather, whether it has been wet or dry. Sometimes the eruptions take place within twenty-four hours, but not often. The Great Geyser is a very capricious old gentleman, take him as you will. He goes up or keeps quiet just to suit himself, and will not put himself the least out of the way to oblige any body. Even the Prince Napoleon, who visited this region a few years ago, spent two days trying to coax the grumbling old fellow to favor him with a performance, but all to no purpose. The prince was no more to a Great Geyser than the commonest shepherd—not so much, in fact, for his finest displays are said to be made when nobody but some poor shepherd of the neighborhood is about. In former times the eruptions were much more frequent than they are now, occurring at least every six hours, and often at periods of only three or four. Gradually they have been diminishing in force and frequency, and it is not improbable they will cease altogether before the lapse of another century. According to the measurements given by various travelers, among whom may be mentioned Dr. Henderson, Sir George Mackenzie, Forbes, Metcalfe, and Lord Dufferin, the height to which the water is ejected varies from eighty to two hundred feet. It is stated that these Geysers did not exist prior to the fifteenth century; and one eruption—that of 1772—is estimated by Olsen and Paulsen to have reached the extraordinary height of three hundred and sixty feet. All these measurements appear to me to be exaggerated.

Ascending a slope of dry incrusted earth of a red and yellowish color, we first came upon the Little Geyser, a small orifice in the ground, from which a column of steam arose. A bubbling sound as of boiling water issued from the depths below, but otherwise it presented no remarkable phenomena. In a few minutes more we stood in the middle of a sloping plateau of some half a mile in circuit, which declines into an extensive valley on the right. Within the limits of this area there are some forty springs and fissures which emit hot water and vapors. None of them are of any considerable size, except the Great Gey-

ser, the Strokhr, and the Little Geyser. The earth seems
to be a mere crust of sulphurous deposits, and burnt clay,
and rotten trap-rock, and is destitute of vegetation except in a few spots, where patches of grass and moss present a beautiful contrast to the surrounding barrenness.
In its quiescent state the scene was not so striking as I
had expected, though the whirling volumes of smoke
that filled the air, and the strange sounds that issued
from the ground in every direction, filled my mind with
strong premonitions of what might take place at any
moment. I did not yet relinquish my views in reference
to the superiority of the California Geysers; still, I began to feel some misgiving about it when I looked around
and saw the vastness of the scale upon which the fixtures
were arranged here for hydraulic entertainments. If we
could beat Iceland in the beauty of our scenery, it was
quite apparent that the advantage lay here in the breadth
and extent of the surrounding desolation—the great lava-
fields, the snow-capped Jokuls, and the distant peaks of
Mount Hecla.

We rode directly toward the Great Geyser, which we
approached within about fifty yards. Here was the
camping-ground—a pleasant little patch of green sod,
where the various travelers who had preceded us had
pitched their tents. Zöega knew every spot. He had
accompanied most of the distinguished gentlemen who
had honored the place with their presence, and had something to say in his grave, simple way about each of them.
Here stood Lord Dufferin's tent. A lively young gentleman he was; a very nice young man; told some queer
stories about the Icelanders; didn't see much of the
country, but made a very nice book about what he saw;
had a great time at the governor's, and drank every body
drunk under the table, etc. Here, close by, the Prince
Napoleon pitched his tent—a large tent, very handsomely decorated; room for all his officers; very fine gentleman the prince; had lots of money; drank plenty of
Champagne; a fat gentleman, not very tall; had black-

ish hair, and talked French; didn't see the Great Geyser go up, but saw the Strokhr, etc. Here was Mr. Metcalfe's tent; a queer gentleman, Mr. Metcalfe; rather rough in his dress; wrote a funny book about Iceland; told some hard things on the priests; they didn't like it at all; didn't know what to make of Mr. Metcalfe, etc. Here was Mr. Chambers's camp—a Scotch gentleman; very nice man, plain and sensible; wrote a pamphlet, etc. And here was an old tent-mark, almost rubbed out, where an American gentleman camped about ten years ago; thought his name was Mr. Miles. This traveler also wrote a book, and told some funny stories.

"Was it Pliny Miles?" I asked.

"Yes, sir, that was his name. I was with him all the time."

"Have you his book?"

"Yes, sir, I have his book at home. A very queer gentleman, Mr. Miles; saw a great many things that I didn't see; says he came near getting drowned in a river."

"And didn't he?"

"Well, sir, I don't know. I didn't see him when he was near being drowned. You crossed the river, sir, yourself, and know whether it is dangerous."

"Was it the Brúará?"

"No, sir; one of the other little rivers, about knee-deep."

Here was food for reflection. Zöega, with his matter-of-fact eyes, evidently saw things in an entirely different light from that in which they presented themselves to the enthusiastic tourists who accompanied him. Perhaps he would some time or other be pointing out my tent to some inquisitive visitor, and giving him a running criticism upon my journal of experiences in Iceland. I deemed it judicious, therefore, to explain to him that gentlemen who traveled all the way to Iceland were bound to see something and meet with some thrilling adventures. If they didn't tell of very remarkable things, nobody would care about reading their books. This was the great art of travel; it was not exactly lying, but putting on colors to give the picture effect.

"For my part, Zöega," said I, "having no great skill as an artist, and being a very plain, unimaginative man, as you know, I shall confine myself strictly to facts. Perhaps there will be novelty enough in telling the truth to attract attention."

"The truth is always the best, sir," replied Zöega, gravely and piously.

"Of course it is, Zöega. This country is sufficiently curious in itself. It does not require the aid of fiction to give it effect. Therefore, should you come across any thing in my narrative which may have escaped your notice, depend upon it I thought it was true—or ought to be."

"Yes, sir; I know you would never lie like some of these gentlemen."

"Never! never, Zöega! I scorn a lying traveler above all things on earth."

But these digressions, however amusing they were at the time, can scarcely be of much interest to the reader.

Even after the lapse of several years the marks around the camping-ground were quite fresh. The sod is of very fine texture, and the grass never grows very rank, so that wherever a trench is cut to let off the rain, it remains, with very little alteration, for a great length of time.

On the principle that a sovereign of the United States ought never to rank himself below a prince of any other country, I selected a spot a little above the camping-ground of his excellency the Prince Napoleon. By the aid of my guide I soon had the tent pitched. It was a small affair—only an upright pole, a few yards of canvas, and four wooden pins. The whole concern did not weigh twenty pounds, and only covered an area of ground about four feet by six. Zöega then took the horses to a pasture up the valley. I amused myself making a few sketches of the surrounding objects, and thinking how strange it was to be here all alone at the Geysers of Iceland. How many of my friends knew where I was? Not one, perhaps. And should all the Geysers blow up together and boil me on the spot, what would people generally think of it? Or suppose the ground were to give way and swallow me up, what difference would it make in the price of consols or the temperature of the ocean?

When Zöega came back, he said, if I pleased, we would now go to work and cut sods for the Strokhr. It was a favorable time "to see him heave up." The way to make him do that was to make him sick. Sods always made him sick. They didn't agree with his stomach. Every gentleman who came here made it a point to stir him up. He was called the Strokhr because he churned things that were thrown down his throat; and Strokhr means *churn*. I was very anxious to see the performance suggested by Zöega, and readily consented to assist him in getting the sods.

The Strokhr lay about a hundred yards from our tent, nearly in a line between the Great and Little Geysers. Externally it presents no very remarkable feature, being nothing more than a hole in the bed of rocks, about five feet in diameter, and slightly funnel-shaped at the orifice. Standing upon the edge, one can see the water boiling up and whirling over about twenty feet below. A hollow, growling noise is heard, varied by an occasional hiss and rush, as if the contents were struggling to get out. It emits hot vapors, and has a slight smell of sulphur; otherwise it maintains rather a peaceful aspect, considering the infernal temper it gets into when disturbed.

Zöega and I worked hard cutting and carrying the sods for nearly half an hour, by which time we had a large pile on the edge of the orifice. Zöega said there was enough. I insisted on getting more. "Let us give him a dose that he won't forget." "Oh, sir, nobody ever puts more than that in; it is quite enough." "No; I

mean to make him deadly sick. Come on, Zöega." And
at it we went again, cutting the sod, and carrying it over
and piling it up in a great heap by the hole. When we
had about a ton all ready, I said to Zöega, "Now, Zöega,
fire away, and I'll stand here and see how it works."
Then Zöega pushed it all over, and it went slapping and
dashing down into the steaming shaft. For a little while
it whirled about, and surged, and boiled, and tumbled
over and over in the depths of the churn with a hollow,
swashing noise terribly ominous of what was to come.
I peeped over the edge to try if I could detect the first
symptoms of the approaching eruption. Zöega walked
quietly away about twenty steps, saying he preferred not
to be too close. There was a sudden growl and a rum-
ble, a terrible plunging about and swashing of the sods
below, and fierce, whirling clouds of steam flew up, almost blinding me as they passed.

"Sir," said Zöega, gravely, "you had better stand
away. It comes up very suddenly when it once starts."

"Don't be afraid, Zöega; I'll keep a sharp look-out
for it. You may depend there's not a Geyser in Iceland
can catch me when I make a break." .

"Very well, sir; but I'd advise you to be careful."

Notwithstanding this good counsel, I could not resist
the fascination of looking in. There was another tremendous commotion going on—a roar, a whirling over
of the sods, and clouds of steam flying up. This time I
ran back a few steps. But it was a false alarm. Nothing came of it. The heaving mass seemed to be produ-
cing the desired effect, however. The Strokhr was evidently getting very sick. I looked over once more. All
below was a rumbling, tumbling black mass, dashing over
and over against the sides of the churn. Soon a threatening roar not to be mistaken startled me. "Look out,
sir!" shouted Zöega; "look out!" Unlike the Frenchman who looked out when he should have looked in, I
unconsciously looked in when I should have looked out.
With a suddenness that astonished me, up shot the seeth-

ing mass almost in my face. One galvanic jump—an involuntary shout of triumph—and I was rolling heels over head on the crust of earth about ten feet off, the hot water and clumps of sod tumbling down about me in every direction. Another scramble brought me to my feet, of which I made such good use that I was forty yards beyond Zöega before I knew distinctly what had happened. The poor fellow came running toward me in great consternation.

"Are you hurt, sir? I hope you're not hurt!" he cried, in accents of great concern.

"Hurt!" I answered. "Didn't you see me rolling over on the ground laughing at it? Why, Zöega, I never saw any thing so absurd as that in my life; any decent Geyser would have given at least an hour's notice. This miserable little wretch went off half cocked. I was just laughing to think how sick we made him all of a sudden!"

"Oh, that was it, sir! I thought you were badly hurt."

"Not a bit of it. You never saw a man who had suffered serious bodily injury run and jump with joy, and roll with laughter as I did."

"No, sir, never, now that I come to think of it."

Somehow it was always pleasant to talk with Zöega, his simplicity was so refreshing.

The display was really magnificent. An immense dark column shot into the air to the height of sixty or seventy feet, composed of innumerable jets of water and whirling masses of sod. It resembled a thousand fountains joined together, each with a separate source of expulsion. The hissing hot water, blackened by the boiled clay and turf, spurted up in countless revolving circlets, spreading out in every direction and falling in torrents over the earth, which was deluged for fifty feet around with the dark, steaming flood. This, again sweeping into the mouth of the funnel, fell in thick streams into the churn, carrying with it the sods that were scattered within its vortex, and once more heaved and surged about in the huge caldron below.

The eruption continued for about five minutes without any apparent diminution of force. It then subsided into fitful and convulsive jets, as if making a last effort, and finally disappeared with a deep growl of disappointment. All was now quiet save the gurgling of the murky water as it sought its way back. Zöega said it was not done yet—that this was only a beginning. I took my sketch-book and resolved to seize the next opportunity for a good view of the eruption, taking, in the mean time, a general outline of the locality, including a glimpse of the Langarfjal. Just as I had finished up to the orifice the same angry roar which had first startled me was repeated, and up shot the dark, boiling flood in grander style than ever. This time it was absolutely fearful. There could be no doubt the dose of sods we had tumbled into the stomach of the old gentleman was making him not only dreadfully sick, but furiously angry.

At this moment, as if the elements sympathized in his distress, fierce gusts of wind began to blow down from the Langarfjal. So sudden and violent were they that it was difficult to maintain a foothold in our exposed position; and the tall column of fountains, struck with the full violence of the wind, presented a splendid spectacle of strength and rage—surging, and swaying, and battling to maintain its erect position, and showing in every motion the irresistible power with which it was ejected. Steam, and water, and sods went whirling down into the valley; the very air was darkened with the shriven and scattered currents; and a black deluge fell to the leeward, hundreds of yards beyond the orifice. The weird and barren aspect of the surrounding scenery was never more impressive.

" What do you think of the Strokhr, sir ?" asked Zöega, with some pride. "Is it equal to the Geysers of California ?"

I was rather taken aback at the honest bluntness of

this question, and must admit that I felt a little crest-fallen when I came to compare the respective performances. Therefore I could only answer, in rather a casual way,

"Well, Zöega, to tell you the truth, ours don't get quite so sick as this, owing, no doubt, to the superior salubrity of our climate. You might throw sods into them all day, and they wouldn't make such a fuss about it as the Strokhr makes about a mere handful. Their digestion, you see, is a great deal stronger."

"Oh, but wait, sir, till you see the Great Geyser; that's much better than the Strokhr."

"Doubtless it is very fine, Zöega. Still I can't help but think our California Geysers are in a superior condition of health. It is true they smoke a good deal, but I don't think they impair their digestion by such stimulating food as the Geysers of Iceland. Judging by the eruptions of the Strokhr, I should say he feeds exclusively on fire and water, which would ruin the best stomach in the world."

Zöega looked troubled. He evidently did not comprehend my figurative style of speech. So the conversation dropped.

The column of water ejected from the Strokhr, unlike that of the Great Geyser, is tall and slender, and of almost inky blackness. In the case of the Great Geyser no artificial means interrupt its operations; in that of the Strokhr the pressure of foreign substances produces results not natural to it.

After the two eruptions which I have attempted to describe, the waters of the Strokhr again subsided into sobs and convulsive throes. Some half an hour now elapsed before any thing more took place. Then there was another series of growls, and a terrible swashing about down in the churn, as if all the demons under earth were trying to drown one another, and up shot the murky flood for the third time. Thus it continued at intervals more and more remote, till a late hour in the night, making desperate efforts to disgorge the sods that were swept back after every ejection, and to rid itself of the foul water that remained. These attempts gradually grow fainter and fainter, subsiding at last into mere grumblings. I looked into the orifice the next morning, and was surprised to find the water yet discolored. It was evident, from the uneasy manner in which it surged about, that the dose still produced unpleasant effects.

Having finished my sketch, I returned to the tent, in front of which Zöega had meantime spread a cloth, with some bread and cheese on it, and such other scraps of provisions as we had. A little boy from the neighboring sheep-ranch brought us down some milk and cream, and I thought if we only had a cup of tea now to warm us up after the chilly wind our supper would be luxurious.

"Just in time, sir," said Zöega; "I'll make the tea in a minute."

"Where's your fire."

"Oh, we don't need fire here—the hot water is always ready. There's the big boiler up yonder!"

I looked where Zöega pointed, and saw, about a hundred yards off, a boiling caldron. This was our grand tea-kettle. Upon a nearer inspection, I found that it consisted of two great holes in the rocks, close together, the larger of which was about thirty feet in circumference, and of great depth. The water was as clear as crystal. It was easy to trace the white stratum of rocks, of which the sides were formed, down to the neck of the great shaft through which the water was ejected. Flakes of steam floated off from the surface of the crystal pool, which was generally placid. Only at occasional intervals did it show any symptoms of internal commotion. By dipping my finger down a little way I found that it was boiling hot. Five minutes immersion would be sufficient to skin and boil an entire man.

Nature has bountifully put these boilers here for the use of travelers. Not a stick or twig of wood grows within a circuit of many miles, and without fuel of course it would be impossible to cook food. Here a leg of mutton submerged in a pot can be beautifully boiled; plum-puddings cooked; eggs, fish, or any thing you please, done to a nicety. All this I knew before, but I had no idea that the water was pure enough for drinking purposes. Such, however, is the fact. No better water ever came out of the earth—in a boiled condition. To make a pot of tea, you simply put your tea in your pot, hold on to the handle, dip the whole concern down into the water, keep it there a while to draw, and your tea is made.

I found it excellent, and did not, as I apprehended, discover any unpleasant flavor in the water. It may be slightly impregnated with sulphur, though that gives it rather a wholesome smack. To me, however, it tasted very much like any other hot water.

SIDE-SADDLE.

When I returned to the tent, and sat down to my frugal repast, and ate my bread and cheese, and quaffed the fragrant tea, Zöega sitting near by respectfully assisting me, something of the old California feeling came over me, and I enjoyed life once more after years of travel through the deserts of civilization in Europe. What a glorious thing it is to be a natural barbarian! This was luxury! this was joy! this was Paradise upon earth! Ah me! where is the country that can equal California? Brightest of the bright lands of sunshine; richest, rarest, loveliest of earth's beauties! like Phædra to the mistress of his soul, I love you by day and by night, behave in the company of others as if I were absent; want you; dream of you; think of you; wish for you; delight in you—in short, I am wholly yours, body and soul! If ever I leave you again on a wild-goose chase through Europe, may the Elector of Hesse-Cassel appoint me his prime minister, or the Duke of Baden his principal butler!

Very little indication of the time was apparent in the sky. The sun still shone brightly, although it was nearly ten o'clock. I did not feel much inclined to sleep, with so many objects of interest around. Apart from that, there was something in this everlasting light that disturbed my nervous system. It becomes really terrible in the course of a few days. The whole order of nature seems reversed. Night has disappeared altogether. Nothing but day remains—dreary, monotonous, perpetual day. You crave the relief of darkness; your spirits, at first exuberant, go down, and still down, till they are below zero; the novelty wears away, and the very light becomes gloomy.

People must sleep, nevertheless. With me it was a duty I owed to an overtaxed body. Our tent was rather small for two, and Zöega asked permission to sleep with an acquaintance who lived in a cabin about two miles distant. This I readily granted. It was something of a novelty to be left in charge of two such distinguished characters as the Great Geyser and the Strokhr. Possibly they might favor me with some extraordinary freaks of humor, such as no other traveler had yet enjoyed. So, bidding Zöega a kindly farewell for the present, I closed the front of the tent, and tried to persuade myself that it was night.

With the light streaming in through the crevices of the tent, it was no easy matter to imagine that this was an appropriate time to "steep the senses in forgetfulness." I was badly provided with covering, and the weather, though not absolutely cold, was damp and chilly. In my hurry to get off, I had forgotten even the small outfit with which I originally thought of making the journey. All I now had in the way of bedding was a thin shawl, and an old overall belonging to Captain Andersen, of the steamer. I put one on the ground and the other over my body, and with a bag of hard bread under my head by way of a pillow, strove to banish the notion that it was at all uncomfortable. There was something in this method of sleeping to remind me of my California experience. To be sure there was a lack of blankets, and fire, and pleasant company, and balmy air, and many other luxuries; but the general principle was the same, except that it was impossible to sleep. The idea of being utterly alone, in such an outlandish part of the world, may have had something to do with the singular activity of my nervous system. It seemed to me that somebody was thrusting cambric needles into my skin in a sudden and violent manner, and at the most unexpected places; and strange sounds were continually buzzing in my ears. I began to reflect seriously upon the condition of affairs down underneath my bed. Doubtless it was a very fiery and restless region, or all these smokes and simmering pools would not disfigure the face of the country. How thick was the shell of the earth at this particular spot? It sounded very thin all over —a mere crust, through which one might break at any moment. Here was boiling water fizzing and gurgling all around, and the air was impregnated with strong odors of sulphur. Suppose the whole thing should burst up of a sudden? It was by no means impossible. What would become of my sketches of Iceland in the event of such a catastrophe as that? What sort of a notice would my editorial friends give of the curious manner in which

I had disappeared? And what would Zöega think in the morning, when he came down from the farm-house, and saw that his tent and provision-boxes were gone down in a great hole, and that an American gentleman, in whom he had the greatest confidence, had not only carried them with him, but failed to pay his liabilities before starting? Here, too, was the sun only slightly dipped below the horizon at midnight, and the moon shining overhead at the same time. Every thing was twisted inside out and turned upside down. It was truly a strange country.

Having tossed and tumbled about for an indefinite length of time, I must have fallen into an uneasy doze. During the day I had been thinking of the rebellion at home, and now gloomy visions disturbed my mind. I thought I saw moving crowds dressed in black, and heard wailing sounds. Funerals passed before me, and women and children wept for the dead. The scene changed, and I saw hosts of men on the battle-field, rushing upon each other and falling in deadly strife. A dreary horror came over me. It was like some dreadful play, in which the stake was human life. Blood was upon the faces of the dying and the dead. In the effort to disentangle the right from the wrong—to seek out a cause for the calamity which had fallen upon us—a racking anguish tortured me, and I vainly strove to regain my scattered senses. Then, in the midst of this confused dream, I heard the booming of cannon—at first far down in the earth, but gradually growing nearer, till, with a start, I awoke. Still the guns boomed! Surely the sounds were real. I could not be deceived. Starting to my feet, I listened. Splashing and surging waters, and dull, heavy reports, sounded in the air. I dashed aside the lining of the tent and looked out. Never shall I forget that sight—the Great Geyser in full eruption! A tremendous volume of water stood in bold relief against the sky, like a tall weeping willow in winter swaying before the wind, and shaking the white frost from its drooping branches. Whirling vapors and white wreaths floated off toward the valley. All was clear overhead. A spectral light, which was neither of day nor of night, shone upon the dark, lava-covered earth. The rush and plashing of the fountain and the booming of the subterranean guns fell with a startling distinctness upon the solitude. Streams of glittering white water swept the surface of the great basin on all sides, and dashed hissing and steaming into the encircling fissures. A feathery spray sparkled through the air. The earth trembled, and sudden gusts of wind whirled down with a moaning sound from the wild gorges of the Langarfjal.

It did not appear to me that the height of the fountain was so great as it is generally represented. So far as I could judge, the greatest altitude at any time from the commencement of the eruption was not over sixty feet. Its volume, however, greatly exceeded my expectations, and the beauty of its form surpassed all description. I had never before seen, and never again expect to see, any thing equal to it. This magnificent display lasted, altogether, about ten minutes. The eruption was somewhat spasmodic in its operation, increasing or diminishing in force at each moment, till, with a sudden dash, all the water that remained was ejected, and then, after a few gurgling throes, all was silent.

I no longer attempted to sleep. My mind was bewildered with the wonders of the scene I had just witnessed. All I could do was to make a cup of tea at the big boiler on the slope above my tent, and walk about, after drinking it, to keep my feet warm. Soon the sun's rays appeared upon the distant mountains. A strange time of the night for the sun to be getting up—only half past one—when people in most other parts of the world are snug in bed, and don't expect to see a streak of sunshine for at least four or five hours. How different from any thing I had ever before seen was the sunrise in Iceland! No crowing of the cock; no singing of the birds; no merry plow-boys whistling up the horses in the barn-yard; no cherry-checked milk-maids singing love-ditties as they tripped the green with their pails upon their heads. All was grim, silent, and death-like. And yet surely, for all that, the delicate tints of the snow-capped mountains, the peaks of which were now steeped in the rays of the rising sun, the broad valley slumbering in the shade, the clear, sparkling atmosphere, and the exquisite coloring of the Laugarfjal—the mighty crag that towers over the Geysers—were beauties enough to redeem the solitude and imbue the deserts with a celestial glory.

There are various theories concerning the cause of these eruptions of water in Iceland. That of Lyell, the geologist, seems the most reasonable. The earth, as it is well known, increases in heat at a certain ratio corresponding with the depth from the surface. There are cavities in many parts of it, arising from subterranean disturbances, into which the water percolates from the upper strata. In Iceland the probability is that these cavities are both numerous and extensive, owing to volcanic causes, and form large receivers for the water of the surrounding neighborhood. Wherever there is a natural outlet, as at the Geysers, this water, which is boiled by the heat of the earth, is forced to the surface by compression of steam, and remains at the mouth of the pipe, or shaft, until an accumulation of compressed steam drives it up in the form of a fountain. The periodical occurrence of these eruptions in some of the hot-springs and not in others may arise from a difference in the depth of the receiver, or more probably from the existence of several outlets for the escape of steam in some, and only one in others. A good illustration of this theory is presented in the boiling of an ordinary tea-kettle. When the compression of steam is great, the cover is lifted up and the water shoots from the spout, by which means the pressure is relieved and the water subsides. The same thing is repeated until the space within the kettle becomes sufficiently large to admit of a more rapid condensation of the steam. The action of the Strokhr, which, as I have shown, differs from that of the Great Geyser, may be accounted for on the same general principle.

GREAT GEYSER AND RECEIVER.

STROKR AND RECEIVER.

The foreign substances thrown in on top of the boiling water stops the escape of steam, which, under ordinary circumstances, is sufficiently great not to require the periodical relief of an eruption. An accumulation of compressed steam takes place in the reservoir below, and this continues until the obstruction is ejected.

This, I believe, is substantially Lyell's theory; though, having no books by me at present, I quote entirely from memory, and it is possible I may be mistaken in some of the details. The preceding diagrams will enable the reader to understand more clearly the whole process by which these eruptions are produced.

Six long hours remained till ordinary breakfast-time. What was to be done? It was getting terribly lonesome. I felt like one who had been to a theatre and seen all the performances. Zöega had promised to be back by eight o'clock; but eight o'clock in Iceland, on the 21st of June, is a late hour of the day. A treatise on trigonometry might be written between sunrise and that unapproachable hour. The only thing I could do was to make some more tea and eat a preliminary breakfast. When that was done nothing remained but to go to work in front of my little tent and finish up my rough sketches. This is a very absorbing business, as every body knows who has tried it, and I was deeply into it when Zöega made his appearance.

"Well, sir," said he, "what success? Did he erupt?"

"Of course he erupted, Zöega. You didn't suppose a Great Geyser would keep a gentleman all the way from California waiting here an entire night without showing him what he could do?"

"No, sir; but he sometimes disappoints travelers. How do you like it? Does he compare with your California Geysers?"

"Well, Zoega, he throws up more hot water, to be sure, because our Geysers don't erupt at all; but here is the grand difference. We Californians are a moral people; we don't live so near to (I pointed down below) as you do in Iceland."

"I don't understand you, sir," said Zöega, with a puzzled expression.

I called him over and whispered in his ear, "Zöega, I hope you're a good man. Do you say your prayers regularly?"

"Yes, sir."

"Then you are all right. Let us be going. I don't like this neighborhood."

"Whenever you wish, sir. The horses are all ready."

And Zöega proceeded to strike the tent and pack the animals, muttering to himself and shaking his head gravely, as if he thought the Californians were a very peculiar race of men, to say the least of them.

Another cup of tea and a few biscuits served to brace us up for the journey, and we mounted our horses and turned their heads homeward. Brusa was so delighted at the idea of being *en route* once more that he signalized our departure by giving chase to a flock of sheep, which he dispersed in a most miraculous manner, and then, of course, received the customary punishment.

CHAPTER LI.

THE ENGLISH SPORTS IN TROUBLE.

Our ride back to Thingvalla was over the same trail which we had traveled on the preceding day, with the exception of a short cut to the right of the Tintron rock. We made very good speed, and reached the Parsonage early in the afternoon.

During our absence a young Englishman had arrived from the North, where he had been living for a year. I found him in the travelers' room, surrounded by a confused medley of boxes, bags, books, and Icelandic curiosities, which he was endeavoring to reduce to some kind of order. Had I not been told he was an Englishman I should never have suspected it, either from his appearance or manner. When I entered the room he stood up and looked at me, and I must say, without intending him the slightest disrespect, that he was the most extraordi-

nary looking man I ever saw in all my life, not excepting
a tattooed African chief that I once met at Zanzibar.
Whether he was young or old it was impossible to say
—he might be twenty-five or just as likely fifty.   Dirty
and discolored with travel, his face was generally dark,
though it was somewhat relieved by spots of yellow.
His features were regular, and of almost feminine softness; his eyes were dark brown; and his hair, which
was nearly black, hung down over his shoulders in lank
straight locks, sunburnt or frostbitten at the ends.   On
his head he wore a tall, conical green wool hat, with a
broad brim, and a brown band tied in a true lover's knot
at one side.   The remainder of his costume consisted of
a black cloth roundabout, threadbare and dirty; a pair
of black casimere pantaloons, very tight about the legs
and burst open in several places; and a pair of moccasins on his feet, adorned with beads and patches of red
flannel.   If he wore a shirt it was not conspicuous for
whiteness, for I failed to discover it.   When he saw that
a stranger stood before him, he looked quite overwhelmed with astonishment, and gasped out some inarticulate
words, consisting principally of Icelandic interjections.

"How do you do, sir?" said I, in the usual California
style.   "I'm glad to meet an Englishman in this wild
country!"

"Ye'ow-w-w!" (a prolonged exclamation.)

"Just arrived, sir?"

"Nay-y-y!" (a prolonged negative.)

"You speak English, I believe, sir?"

"Oh-h-h!   Ya-a-a-s.   Are—you—an—Englishman?"

"No, sir.   An American, from California."

"De-e-e-a-r-r m-e-e!"

Here there was a pause, for I really did not know what
to make of the man.   He looked at the ceiling, and at
the floor, and out of the window, and started a remark
several times, but always stopped before he got under
way, or lost it in a prolonged "Oh-o-o-a!"   Again and
again he attempted to speak, never getting beyond a

word or two. It seemed as if some new idea were continually crossing his mind and depriving him of his breath ;
he labored under a chronic astonishment. At first I supposed it might be the natural result of a year's absence
in the interior of Iceland, but subsequent acquaintance
with him satisfied me that it was constitutional. He

Z

was astonished all the way from Reykjavik to Scotland. When it rained he opened his eyes as if they would burst; looked up in the sky, and cried "Oh-h-h!" When it blew he tumbled into his berth, covered himself up in the blankets, peeped out in the most profound amazement, and ejaculated "Ah-h-h! Oh-h-h! Hay-y-y! Ye'ow-w-w!" When the weather was fine he came up on deck, peered over the bulwarks, up at the rigging, down into the engine-room, and was perfectly astounded at each object, exclaiming alternately "Oh-h-o-o-a-a-h!" "Ah-ha!" "H-a-y!" and "Ye'ow-w-w-w!" At Thingvalla his main food was curds and black bread, yet he had an abundance of the best provisions. He was a thorough Icelandic scholar, and spoke the language with ease and grace, only when interrupted by the novel ideas that so often struck him in the head. With all his oddity, he was a gentleman by birth and education, and was very amiable in his disposition. He had evidently spent much of his life over books; his knowledge of the world scarcely equaled that of a child. From all that I could gather of his winter's experiences in North Iceland, the climate was not very severe, except at occasional intervals when there was a press of ice-fields along the coast. The mean temperature was quite moderate. He suffered no inconvenience at all from the weather. At times it was very pleasant. He had the misfortune to break his leg in climbing over some lava-bergs, which crippled him for some weeks, but he was now getting all right again. This account of his experiences, which I obtained from him during the evening, took many divergences into the "Ohs!" and "Ahs!" and was really both instructive and entertaining. When he came to the breaking of his leg, I expressed my astonishment at the equanimity with which he bore it, which so astonished him, when he came to think of it in that light, that he cried "Oh-h-a-a! ya-a-s! It—was—very—bad!" as if he had entirely forgotten how bad it was, and now made a new and most singular discovery.

As there was only the one small room we had to sleep at pretty close quarters, the Englishman on the sofa and I in the bed, which for some reason was awarded to me by the good pastor. Having no preference, I offered to exchange; but this only astonished my eccentric neighbor, and set him off into a labyrinth of interjections. Our heads were placed pretty close together, and it was some time before I could settle myself to sleep, owing to a variety of peculiar sounds he made in whispering to himself. He seemed to be telling himself some interminable story from one of the Sagas. Several times I dozed off, and was awakened by some extraordinary ejaculation.

"I beg your pardon," said I, at length, rising up, and looking in the face of my neighbor, who was lying on his back, with his eyes wide open, "I beg your pardon, sir; did you speak to me?"

"Oh-h-h-a!" shouted the Englishman, jumping up as if touched with a streak of electricity. "Dear me! ha —oh-o-o! How very odd!"

"Sir?"

"Eh?"

"Good-night, sir!" I said, and lay down again. The Englishman also composed himself to rest, but presently rose up, and, looking over at me, exclaimed "Ou-o-o-ah!"

This was all. Then we both composed ourselves to sleep. Tired as I was after my ride from the Geysers and the bad night I had passed there, it was no wonder I soon lost all consciousness of the proximity of my eccentric room-mate, and the probability is I would have gotten well through the night but for another singular and unexpected interruption.

"Hello! What the devil! Who's here? By Jove, this is jolly! I say! Where the dooce is our American friend? Down, Bowser! Down! Blawst the dog! Ho! ho! Look here, Tompkins! I say! Here's a go!"

There was a tramping of feet, a knocking about of loose things in the room, and a chorus of familiar voices in the adjoining passage. It is needless to say that the party of sporting Englishmen had arrived from Reykjavik.

"Oh-h-a! Ye-o-w!" exclaimed my room-mate, starting up, and gazing wildly at the lively young gentleman with the dog. "Oh-o-o! How very odd!"

The jolly sportsman looked at the apparition in perfect amazement. Both stared at each other for a moment, as if such an extraordinary sight had never been witnessed on either side before.

"By Jove! this is jolly!" muttered the lively gentleman, turning on his heel and walking out; "a devilish rum-looking chap, that!"

"Oh-o-o-o!" was all my astonished room-mate said, after which he turned over and composed himself to sleep. I had purposely refrained from manifesting any symptoms of wakefulness, well-knowing that there would be no farther rest that night if I once discovered myself to the traveling party.

At a seasonable hour in the morning, however, I got up, and looked about in search of my fellow-passengers, whom I really liked, and in whose progress I felt a considerable interest. They were camped close by the church, under the lee of the front door. Two canvas tents covered what was left of them. A general wreck of equipments lay scattered all around—broken poles, boxes, tinware, etc. It was plain enough they had encountered incredible hardships.

The usual greetings over, I inquired how they had enjoyed the trip from Reykjavik. In reply they gave me a detailed and melancholy history of their experiences. Riley's Narrative of Shipwreck, and subsequent hardships on the coast of Africa, was nothing to it. Of the twenty-five horses with which they left Reykjavik only thirteen were sound of wind, and of these more than half were afflicted with raw backs. The pack-animals, eighteen in number, were every one lame. Then the packs were badly done up, and broke to pieces on the way.

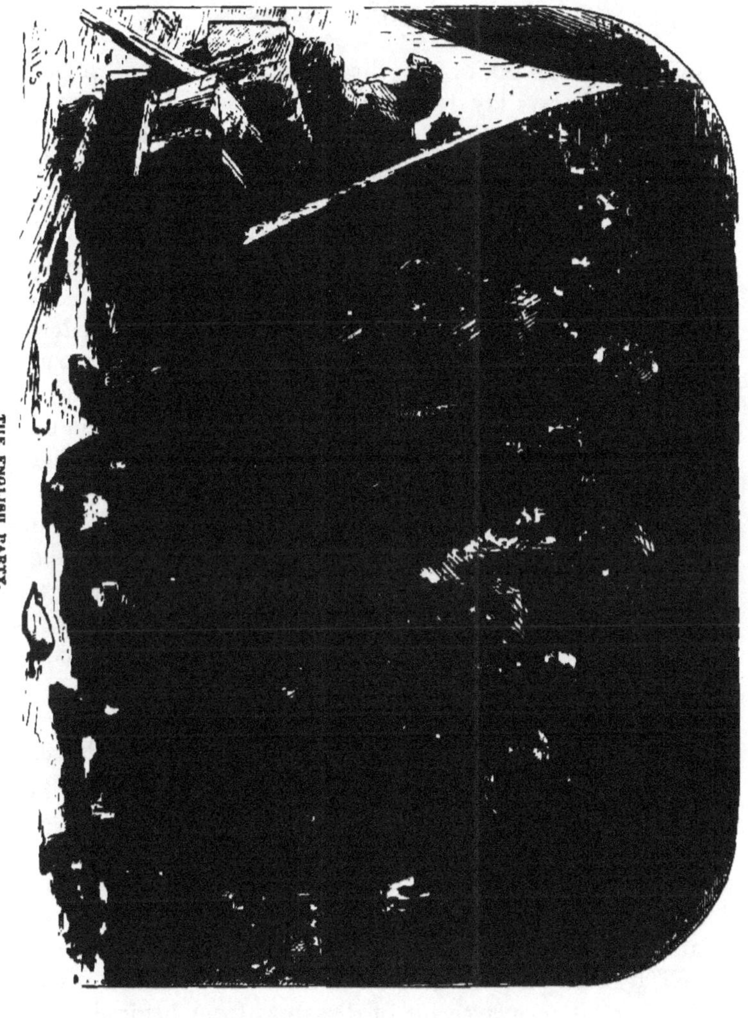

THE ENGLISH PARTY.

Sometimes the ropes cut the horses' backs, and sometimes the horses lay down on the road, and tried to travel with their feet in the air. Incredible difficulty was experienced in making twelve miles the first day. It rained all the time. The bread was soaked; the tea destroyed; the sugar melted; and the Champagne baskets smashed. When the packs were taken off it was discovered that some of them were quite empty, and the contents, consisting originally of hair-brushes, flea-powder, lip-salve, and cold-cream, were strewn along the road probably all the way from Reykjavik. The cot-fixtures were swelled and wouldn't fit; the tea-kettle was jammed into a cocked-hat; the tent-pins were lost, and the hatchet nowhere to be found. It was a perfect series of jams, smashes, and scatterings. Even the sheets were filled with mud, and wholly unfit for use until they could be washed and done up. One horse lay down on the portable kitchen, and flattened it into a general pancake; another attempted to take an impression of his own body on the photographic apparatus, and reduced it (the apparatus) to fragments; another, wishing perhaps to see his face as others saw him, raked off the looking-glasses against a point of lava, and walked on them; and, lastly, one stupid beast contrived in some way to get his nose into a mustard-case which had fallen from a pack in front, and, snuffing up the mustard, got his nostrils burnt and went perfectly crazy, kicking, plunging, and charging at all the other horses till he drove them all as crazy as himself, whereby a prodigious amount of damage was done. In short, it was a series of disasters from beginning to end; and here they were now but two days' journey from Reykjavik (I had made the whole distance easily in seven hours), and, by Jove, there was no telling how much longer it would be possible to keep the guide. They had already quarreled with him several times, and threatened to discharge him. He was a stupid dunce, and a rascal and a cheat into the bargain. On the whole, it was a "rum" sort of a country to travel in. No game,

no roads, no shops, no accommodations for man or beast!
And who ever saw such houses for people to live in?
Mere sheep-pens! Disgustingly filthy! A beastly set
of ragamuffins! By Jove, sir, if it wasn't for the name
of the thing, a fellow might as well be in the infernal
regions at once! In truth, I must acknowledge that the
interior of an Icelandic hut does not present a very attractive spectacle to a stranger.

I deeply sympathized with my friends, and urged them
to leave the remainder of their baggage. If there was
any medicine left, a dose of quinine all around might do
them good and prevent any ill effects from the rain; but,
on the whole, I thought they would get along better with
less baggage.

"Less baggage!" cried all together. "Why, hang it,
our baggage is scattered along the trail clear back to
Reykjavik! It has been growing less ever since we
started. By the time we reach the Geysers it is questionable if we'll have as much as a fine-tooth comb left!"

"Then," said I, "you can travel. Sell a dozen of your
horses on the way, and you'll be rid of another trouble!"

"Sell them; they wouldn't bring a farthing. They're
not worth a groat."

"Then turn them loose."

"That's a jolly idea," said the lively sportsman; "how
the deuce are we to travel without pack-horses?"

"Oh, nothing easier. You don't need pack-horses
when you have no packs."

"By Jove, there's something in that!" said the jolly
gentleman. "Our American friend ought to know. He's
seen the elephant before."

This proposition gave rise to an animated discussion,
during which I wished them a prosperous tour, and took
my leave. Of their subsequent career I have heard nothing, save that they arrived safely in England, and published various letters in the newspapers giving glowing
accounts of their Icelandic experience.

Nothing of importance occurred on the way back to

INTERIOR OF ICELANDIC HUT.

Reykjavik. I arrived there early in the afternoon safe and sound, and greatly benefited by the trip. Like the beatings received by Brusa, the experience was delightful when it was over. I paid off my excellent guide Geir Zöega, and made him a present of the few articles that remained from the expedition. It is a great pleasure to be able to recommend a guide heartily and conscientiously. A worthier man than Geir Zöega does not exist, and I hereby certify that he afforded me entire satisfaction. No traveler who desires an honest, intelligent, and conscientious guide can do better than secure his services. Long life and happiness to you, Geir Zöega! May your shadow never be less; and may your invaluable little dog Brusa live to profit by your wise counsel and judicious administration of the rod.

CHAPTER LII.

A FRIGHTFUL ADVENTURE.

THE *Arcturus* had been delayed in discharging freight by a series of storms which prevailed at the bay, and was now down at Haparanda Fjord taking in ballast. The probability was that she would not leave for several days. Meantime I was extremely anxious to see a little more of domestic life in Iceland, and made several foot-expeditions to the farm-houses in the neighborhood of Reykjavik.

At one of these I passed a night. In giving the details of an awkward adventure that befell me on that occasion, it is only necessary for me to say of the house that it was built in the usual primitive style, already described at some length. The people were farmers, and the family consisted of an old man and his wife, three or four stout sons, and a buxom daughter some twenty years of age. A few words of Danish enabled me to make them understand that I wished for a cup of coffee, some bread, and lodgings for the night. They were ex-

ceeding kind, and seemed greatly interested in the fact
that I was an American—probably the first they had
ever seen. The coffee was soon ready; a cloth was
spread upon the table, and a very good supper of bread,
cheese, and curds placed before me. I passed some hours
very sociably, giving them, as well as I could by means
of signs and diagrams, aided by a few words of Danish,
a general idea of California, its position on the globe, and
the enormous amount of gold which it yielded. Evidently they had heard some exaggerated rumors of the
country. The name was familiar to them, but they had
no idea where this El Dorado was, or whether there was
any truth in the statement that the mountains were made
of gold, and all the rocks in the valleys of pure silver.
My efforts to enlighten them on these points were rather
ludicrous. It was miraculous how far I made a few
words go, and how quick they were to guess at my meaning.

About eleven o'clock the old people began to manifest symptoms of drowsiness, and gave me to understand
that whenever I felt disposed to go to bed the girl would
show me my room. A walk of ten or twelve miles over
the lava-bergs rendered this suggestion quite acceptable,
so I bade the family a friendly good-night, and followed
the girl to another part of the house. She took me into
a small room with a bed in one corner. By a motion of
her hand she intimated that I could rest there for the
night. I sat down on the edge of the bed and said it
was very good—that I was much obliged to her. She
still lingered in the room, however, as if waiting to see
if she could be of any farther assistance. I could not be
insensible to the fact that she was a very florid and good-
natured looking young woman; but, of course, that was
none of my business. All I could do with propriety was
to thank her again, and signify by taking off my overcoat that I was about to go to bed. Still she lingered,
apparently disposed to be as friendly as circumstances
would permit. It was somewhat awkward being alone

in a strange room with a person of the opposite sex, young and rather pretty, without saying any thing particular. Her silence, as well as my own, was getting embarrassing. I attempted to carry on a conversation in Danish, of which I soon discovered she knew even less than I did myself. She answered my remarks, however, in her native tongue, with a very sweet voice, and in such a sociable way that I felt sure she meant to be kind and hospitable. In vain I waited for her to leave. It was getting late, and her parents might feel anxious about her. Still she manifested no disposition to go away. What could the girl mean? was a question that now began to enter my head. Probably I had taken possession of her room, and she had no other place to sleep. If so, it was not my fault. Nobody could hold me responsible for such a peculiar family arrangement. Seeing no alternative but to test the point, I gradually began to take off my coat. So far from being abashed at the movement, she seized hold of the sleeves and helped me off with it. I did the same with my vest, and still with the same result. Then I pulled off my boots, but with no better prospect of relief from my embarrassing dilemma. Finally I came to my pantaloons, at which I naturally hesitated. It was about time for the young woman to leave, if she had any regard for my feelings. I thanked her very cordially; but she showed no symptoms of leaving. It was plain that she meant to help me through with the business. I sat for some time longer before I could bring myself to this last trying ordeal. There was something so pure and innocent in the expression of the young woman's face—such an utter unconsciousness of any impropriety in our relative positions, that I scarcely knew what to do or think. "She wants to help me off with my pantaloons—that's plain!" said I to myself. "Perhaps it is the custom in Iceland; but it is very awkward, nevertheless." The fact is, you see, I was not quite old enough to be the girl's father, nor yet quite young enough to be put to bed like her

AN AWKWARD PREDICAMENT.

youngest brother. Between the two extremes of the case I was considerably troubled. To reject her kind offers of service might be deemed rude, and nothing was farther from my intention than to offend this amiable young person. Allowing a reasonable time to elapse, I saw there was no getting over the difficulty, and began to remove the last article of my daily apparel. Doubtless she had long foreseen that it would eventually come to that. In a very accommodating manner, she took a position directly in front, and beckoned to me to elevate one of my legs, an order which I naturally obeyed. Then she seized hold of the pendent casimere and dragged away with a hearty good-will. I was quickly reduced to my natural state with the exception of a pair of drawers, which, to my horror, I discovered were in a very ragged condition, owing to the roughness of my travels in this wild region. However, by an adroit movement I whirled into bed, and the young woman covered me up and wished me a good night's sleep. I thanked her very cordially, and so ended this strange and rather awkward adventure.

Such primitive scenes are to be found only in the interior. In the towns the women are in dress and manners very like their sisters elsewhere. Hoops and crinoline are frequently to be seen not only among the Danes, who, as a matter of course, import them from Copenhagen, but among the native women, who can see no good reason why they should not be as much like pyramids or Jokuls as others of their sex. Bonnets and inverted pudding-bowls are common on the heads of the Reykjavik ladies, though as yet they have not found their way into the interior. All who can afford it indulge in a profusion of jewelry—silver clasps, breast-pins, tassel-bands, etc., and various articles of filigree made by native artists. These feminine traits I had not expected to find so fully developed in so out-of-the-way a country. But where is it that lovely woman will not make herself still more captivating? I once saw in Madagascar a belle of the first rank, as black as the ace of spades, and greased all over with cocoa-nut oil, commit great havoc among her admirers by a necklace of shark's teeth and a pair of brass anklets, and nothing else. The rest of her costume, with a trifling exception, was purely imaginary; yet she was as vain of her superior style, and put on as many fine airs, as the most fashionable lady in any civilized country. After all, what is the difference between a finely-dressed savage and a finely-dressed Parisian? None at all that I can see, save in the color of the skin and the amount of labor performed by the manufacturer, the milliner, the tailor, or the schoolmaster. Intrinsically the constitution of the mind is identically the same. I speak now of men as well as women, for the most affected creatures I have seen in Europe are of the male sex. So pardon me, fair ladies, for any reflection upon your crinoline, and accept as my apology this candid avowal—that while you are naturally angelic, and always beautiful beyond comparison, in spite of what you do to disfigure your lovely persons, we men are naturally savages, and are driven to the barbarous expedient of adorning and beautifying our ugly bodies with gewgaws, tinsel, and jimcrackery, in order that they may be acceptable in your eyes.

On my return to Reykjavik I found that the steamer was to sail next day. I was very anxious to visit Mount Hecla, but my time and means were limited, and would not permit of a farther sojourn in this interesting land. It was a great satisfaction to have seen any thing of it at all; and if I have given the reader even a slight glimpse of its wonders, my trip has not been entirely unsuccessful.

THE END.

LIBRARY OF THE UNIVERSITY OF

VALUABLE STANDARD WORKS

FOR PUBLIC AND PRIVATE LIBRARIES,

PUBLISHED BY HARPER & BROTHERS, NEW YORK.

☞ *For a full List of Books suitable for Libraries, see HARPER & BROTHERS'
TRADE-LIST and CATALOGUE, which may be had gratuitously on application
to the Publishers personally, or by letter enclosing Five Cents.*

☞ *HARPER & BROTHERS will send any of the following works by mail, postage
prepaid, to any part of the United States, on receipt of the price.*

MOTLEY'S DUTCH REPUBLIC. The Rise of the Dutch Republic. By
JOHN LOTHROP MOTLEY, LL.D., D.C.L. With a Portrait of William of
Orange. 3 vols., 8vo, Cloth, $10 50.

MOTLEY'S UNITED NETHERLANDS. History of the United Netherlands: from the Death of William the Silent to the Twelve Years' Truce
—1609. With a full View of the English-Dutch Struggle against Spain,
and of the Origin and Destruction of the Spanish Armada. By JOHN
LOTHROP MOTLEY, LL.D., D.C.L. Portraits. 4 vols., 8vo, Cloth, $14 00.

NAPOLEON'S LIFE OF CÆSAR. The History of Julius Cæsar. By His
Imperial Majesty NAPOLEON III. Two Volumes ready. Library Edition,
8vo, Cloth, $3 50 per vol.
  Maps to Vols. I. and II. sold separately. Price $1 50 each, NET.

HAYDN'S DICTIONARY OF DATES, relating to all Ages and Nations.
For Universal Reference. Edited by BENJAMIN VINCENT, Assistant Secretary and Keeper of the Library of the Royal Institution of Great Britain;
and Revised for the Use of American Readers. 8vo, Cloth, $5 00; Sheep,
$6 00.

HARTWIG'S POLAR WORLD. The Polar World: a Popular Description
of Man and Nature in the Arctic and Antarctic Regions of the Globe. By
Dr. G. HARTWIG, Author of "The Sea and its Living Wonders," "The
Harmonies of Nature," and "The Tropical World." With Additional
Chapters and 163 Illustrations. 8vo, Cloth, Beveled Edges, $3 75.

WALLACE'S MALAY ARCHIPELAGO. The Malay Archipelago: the Land
of the Orang-Utan and the Bird of Paradise. A Narrative of Travel, 1854–
1862. With Studies of Man and Nature. By ALFRED RUSSEL WALLACE.
With Ten Maps and Fifty-one Elegant Illustrations. Crown 8vo, Cloth,
$3 50.

WHYMPER'S ALASKA. Travel and Adventure in the Territory of Alaska,
formerly Russian America—now Ceded to the United States—and in various other parts of the North Pacific. By FREDERICK WHYMPER. With
Map and Illustrations. Crown 8vo, Cloth, $2 50.

ORTON'S ANDES AND THE AMAZON. The Andes and the Amazon:
or, Across the Continent of South America. By JAMES ORTON, M.A.,
Professor of Natural History in Vassar College, Poughkeepsie, N. Y., and
Corresponding Member of the Academy of Natural Sciences, Philadelphia.
With a New Map of Equatorial America and numerous Illustrations.
Crown 8vo, Cloth, $2 00.

LOSSING'S FIELD-BOOK OF THE REVOLUTION. Pictorial Field-Book of the Revolution; or, Illustrations, by Pen and Pencil, of the History, Biography, Scenery, Relics, and Traditions of the War for Independence. By Benson J. Lossing. 2 vols., 8vo, Cloth, $14 00; Sheep, $15 00; Half Calf, $18 00; Full Turkey Morocco, $22 00.

LOSSING'S FIELD-BOOK OF THE WAR OF 1812. Pictorial Field-Book of the War of 1812; or, Illustrations, by Pen and Pencil, of the History, Biography, Scenery, Relics, and Traditions of the Last War for American Independence. By Benson J. Lossing. With several hundred Engravings on Wood, by Lossing and Barritt, chiefly from Original Sketches by the Author. 1088 pages, 8vo, Cloth, $7 00; Sheep, $8 50; Half Calf, $10 00.

WINCHELL'S SKETCHES OF CREATION. Sketches of Creation: a Popular View of some of the Grand Conclusions of the Sciences in reference to the History of Matter and of Life. Together with a Statement of the Intimations of Science respecting the Primordial Condition and the Ultimate Destiny of the Earth and the Solar System. By Alexander Winchell, LL.D., Professor of Geology, Zoology, and Botany in the University of Michigan, and Director of the State Geological Survey. With Illustrations. 12mo, Cloth, $2 00.

WHITE'S MASSACRE OF ST. BARTHOLOMEW. The Massacre of St. Bartholomew: Preceded by a History of the Religious Wars in the Reign of Charles IX. By Henry White, M.A. With Illustrations. 8vo, Cloth, $1 75.

ALFORD'S GREEK TESTAMENT. The Greek Testament: with a critically-revised Text; a Digest of Various Readings; Marginal References to Verbal and Idiomatic Usage; Prolegomena; and a Critical and Exegetical Commentary. For the Use of Theological Students and Ministers. By Henry Alford, D.D., Dean of Canterbury. Vol. I., containing the Four Gospels. 944 pages, 8vo, Cloth, $6 00; Sheep, $6 50.

ABBOTT'S HISTORY OF THE FRENCH REVOLUTION. The French Revolution of 1789, as viewed in the Light of Republican Institutions. By John S. C. Abbott. With 100 Engravings. 8vo, Cloth, $5 00.

ABBOTT'S NAPOLEON BONAPARTE. The History of Napoleon Bonaparte. By John S. C. Abbott. With Maps, Woodcuts, and Portraits on Steel. 2 vols., 8vo, Cloth, $10 00.

ABBOTT'S NAPOLEON AT ST. HELENA; or, Interesting Anecdotes and Remarkable Conversations of the Emperor during the Five and a Half Years of his Captivity. Collected from the Memorials of Las Casas, O'Meara, Montholon, Antommarchi, and others. By John S. C. Abbott. With Illustrations. 8vo, Cloth, $5 00.

ADDISON'S COMPLETE WORKS. The Works of Joseph Addison, embracing the whole of the "Spectator." Complete in 3 vols., 8vo, Cloth, $6 00.

ALCOCK'S JAPAN. The Capital of the Tycoon: a Narrative of a Three Years' Residence in Japan. By Sir Rutherford Alcock, K.C.B., Her Majesty's Envoy Extraordinary and Minister Plenipotentiary in Japan. With Maps and Engravings. 2 vols., 12mo, Cloth, $3 50.

ALISON'S HISTORY OF EUROPE. First Series: From the Commencement of the French Revolution, in 1789, to the Restoration of the Bourbons, in 1815. [In addition to the Notes on Chapter LXXVI., which correct the errors of the original work concerning the United States, a copious Analytical Index has been appended to this American edition.] Second Series: From the Fall of Napoleon, in 1815, to the Accession of Louis Napoleon, in 1852. 8 vols., 8vo, Cloth, $16 00.

BANCROFT'S MISCELLANIES. Literary and Historical Miscellanies. By George Bancroft. 8vo, Cloth, $3 00.

BALDWIN'S PRE-HISTORIC NATIONS. Pre-Historic Nations; or, Inquiries concerning some of the Great Peoples and Civilizations of Antiquity, and their Probable Relation to a still Older Civilization of the Ethiopians or Cushites of Arabia. By JOHN D. BALDWIN, Member of the American Oriental Society. 12mo, Cloth, $1 75.

BARTH'S NORTH AND CENTRAL AFRICA. Travels and Discoveries in North and Central Africa: being a Journal of an Expedition undertaken under the Auspices of H. B. M.'s Government, in the Years 1849–1855. By HENRY BARTH, Ph.D., D.C.L. Illustrated. 3 vols., 8vo, Cloth, $12 00.

HENRY WARD BEECHER'S SERMONS. Sermons by HENRY WARD BEECHER, Plymouth Church, Brooklyn. Selected from Published and Unpublished Discourses, and Revised by their Author. With Steel Portrait. Complete in 2 vols., 8vo, Cloth, $5 00.

LYMAN BEECHER'S AUTOBIOGRAPHY, &c. Autobiography, Correspondence, &c., of Lyman Beecher, D.D. Edited by his Son, CHARLES BEECHER. With Three Steel Portraits, and Engravings on Wood. In 2 vols., 12mo, Cloth, $5 00.

BELLOWS'S OLD WORLD. The Old World in its New Face: Impressions of Europe in 1867–1868. By HENRY W. BELLOWS. 2 vols., 12mo, Cloth, $3 50.

BOSWELL'S JOHNSON. The Life of Samuel Johnson, LL.D. Including a Journey to the Hebrides. By JAMES BOSWELL, Esq. A New Edition, with numerous Additions and Notes. By JOHN WILSON CROKER, LL.D., F.R.S. Portrait of Boswell. 2 vols., 8vo, Cloth, $4 00.

BRODHEAD'S HISTORY OF NEW YORK. History of the State of New York. By JOHN ROMEYN BRODHEAD. First Period, 1609–1664. 8vo, Cloth, $3 00.

BULWER'S PROSE WORKS. Miscellaneous Prose Works of Edward Bulwer, Lord Lytton. 2 vols., 12mo, Cloth, $3 50.

BURNS'S LIFE AND WORKS. The Life and Works of Robert Burns. Edited by ROBERT CHAMBERS. 4 vols., 12mo, Cloth, $6 00.

CARLYLE'S FREDERICK THE GREAT. History of Friedrich II., called Frederick the Great. By THOMAS CARLYLE. Portraits, Maps, Plans, &c. 6 vols., 12mo, Cloth, $12 00.

CARLYLE'S FRENCH REVOLUTION. History of the French Revolution. Newly Revised by the Author, with Index, &c. 2 vols., 12mo, Cloth, $3 50.

CARLYLE'S OLIVER CROMWELL. Letters and Speeches of Oliver Cromwell. With Elucidations and Connecting Narrative. 2 vols., 12mo, Cloth, $3 50.

CHALMERS'S POSTHUMOUS WORKS. The Posthumous Works of Dr. Chalmers. Edited by his Son-in-Law, Rev. WILLIAM HANNA, LL.D. Complete in 9 vols., 12mo, Cloth, $13 50.

COLERIDGE'S COMPLETE WORKS. The Complete Works of Samuel Taylor Coleridge. With an Introductory Essay upon his Philosophical and Theological Opinions. Edited by Professor SHEDD. Complete in Seven Vols. With a fine Portrait. Small 8vo, Cloth, $10 50.

CURTIS'S HISTORY OF THE CONSTITUTION. History of the Origin, Formation, and Adoption of the Constitution of the United States. By GEORGE TICKNOR CURTIS. 2 vols., 8vo, Cloth, $6 00.

DAVIS'S CARTHAGE. Carthage and her Remains: being an Account of the Excavations and Researches on the Site of the Phœnician Metropolis in Africa and other adjacent Places. Conducted under the Auspices of Her Majesty's Government. By Dr. DAVIS, F.R.G.S. Profusely Illustrated with Maps, Woodcuts, Chromo-Lithographs, &c. 8vo, Cloth, $4 00.

DRAPER'S CIVIL WAR. History of the American Civil War. By John W. Draper, M.D., LL.D., Professor of Chemistry and Physiology in the University of New York. In Three Vols. 8vo, Cloth, $3 50 per vol.

DRAPER'S INTELLECTUAL DEVELOPMENT OF EUROPE. A History of the Intellectual Development of Europe. By John W. Draper, M.D., LL.D., Professor of Chemistry and Physiology in the University of New York. 8vo, Cloth, $5 00.

DRAPER'S AMERICAN CIVIL POLICY. Thoughts on the Future Civil Policy of America. By John W. Draper, M.D., LL.D., Professor of Chemistry and Physiology in the University of New York. Crown 8vo, Cloth, $2 50.

DU CHAILLU'S AFRICA. Explorations and Adventures in Equatorial Africa: with Accounts of the Manners and Customs of the People, and of the Chase of the Gorilla, the Crocodile, Leopard, Elephant, Hippopotamus, and other Animals. By Paul B. Du Chaillu. Numerous Illustrations. 8vo, Cloth, $5 00.

DU CHAILLU'S ASHANGO LAND. A Journey to Ashango Land: and Further Penetration into Equatorial Africa. By Paul B. Du Chaillu. New Edition. Handsomely Illustrated. 8vo, Cloth, $5 00.

DOOLITTLE'S CHINA. Social Life of the Chinese: with some Account of their Religious, Governmental, Educational, and Business Customs and Opinions. With special but not exclusive Reference to Fuhchau. By Rev. Justus Doolittle, Fourteen Years Member of the Fuhchau Mission of the American Board. Illustrated with more than 150 characteristic Engravings on Wood. 2 vols., 12mo, Cloth, $5 00.

EDGEWORTH'S (Miss) NOVELS. With Engravings. 10 vols., 12mo, Cloth, $15 00.

GIBBON'S ROME. History of the Decline and Fall of the Roman Empire. By Edward Gibbon. With Notes by Rev. H. H. Milman and M. Guizot. A new cheap Edition. To which is added a complete Index of the whole Work, and a Portrait of the Author. 6 vols., 12mo, Cloth, $9 00.

GROTE'S HISTORY OF GREECE. 12 vols., 12mo, Cloth, $18 00.

HALE'S (Mrs.) WOMAN'S RECORD. Woman's Record: or, Biographical Sketches of all Distinguished Women, from the Creation to the Present Time. Arranged in Four Eras, with Selections from Female Writers of each Era. By Mrs. Sarah Josepha Hale. Illustrated with more than 200 Portraits. 8vo, Cloth, $5 00.

HALL'S ARCTIC RESEARCHES. Arctic Researches and Life among the Esquimaux: being the Narrative of an Expedition in Search of Sir John Franklin, in the Years 1860, 1861, and 1862. By Charles Francis Hall. With Maps and 100 Illustrations. The Illustrations are from Original Drawings by Charles Parsons, Henry L. Stephens, Solomon Eytinge, W. S. L. Jewett, and Granville Perkins, after Sketches by Captain Hall. 8vo, Cloth, $5 00.

HALLAM'S CONSTITUTIONAL HISTORY OF ENGLAND, from the Accession of Henry VII. to the Death of George II. 8vo, Cloth, $2 00.

HALLAM'S LITERATURE. Introduction to the Literature of Europe during the Fifteenth, Sixteenth, and Seventeenth Centuries. By Henry Hallam. 2 vols., 8vo, Cloth, $4 00.

HALLAM'S MIDDLE AGES. State of Europe during the Middle Ages. By Henry Hallam. 8vo, Cloth, $2 00.

HILDRETH'S HISTORY of THE UNITED STATES First Series: From the First Settlement of the Country to the Adoption of the Federal Constitution. Second Series: From the Adoption of the Federal Constitution to the End of the Sixteenth Congress. 6 vols., 8vo, Cloth, $18 00.

HARPER'S PICTORIAL HISTORY OF THE REBELLION. Harper's Pictorial History of the Great Rebellion in the United States. With nearly 1000 Illustrations. In Two Vols., 4to. Price $6 00 per vol.

HARPER'S NEW CLASSICAL LIBRARY. Literal Translations. The following Volumes are now ready. Portraits. 12mo, Cloth, $1 50 each.

CÆSAR.—VIRGIL.—SALLUST.—HORACE.—CICERO'S ORATIONS—CICERO'S OFFICES, &c.—CICERO ON ORATORY AND ORATORS.—TACITUS (2 vols.). —TERENCE.—SOPHOCLES.—JUVENAL—XENOPHON.—HOMER'S ILIAD.— HOMER'S ODYSSEY.—HERODOTUS.—DEMOSTHENES.—THUCYDIDES.— ÆSCHYLUS.—EURIPIDES (2 vols.).

HELPS'S SPANISH CONQUEST. The Spanish Conquest in America, and its Relation to the History of Slavery and to the Government of Colonies. By ARTHUR HELPS. 4 vols., 12mo, Cloth, $6 00.

HUME'S HISTORY OF ENGLAND. History of England, from the Invasion of Julius Cæsar to the Abdication of James II., 1688. By DAVID HUME. A new Edition, with the Author's last Corrections and Improvements. To which is Prefixed a short Account of his Life, written by Himself. With a Portrait of the Author. 6 vols., 12mo, Cloth, $9 00.

JAY'S WORKS. Complete Works of Rev. William Jay: comprising his Sermons, Family Discourses, Morning and Evening Exercises for every Day in the Year, Family Prayers, &c. Author's enlarged Edition, revised. 3 vols., 8vo, Cloth, $6 00.

JOHNSON'S COMPLETE WORKS. The Works of Samuel Johnson, LL.D. With an Essay on his Life and Genius, by ARTHUR MURPHY, Esq. Portrait of Johnson. 2 vols., 8vo, Cloth, $4 00.

KINGLAKE'S CRIMEAN WAR. The Invasion of the Crimea, and an Account of its Progress down to the Death of Lord Raglan. By ALEXANDER WILLIAM KINGLAKE. With Maps and Plans. Two Vols. ready. 12mo, Cloth, $2 00 per vol.

KRUMMACHER'S DAVID, KING OF ISRAEL. David, the King of Israel: a Portrait drawn from Bible History and the Book of Psalms. By FREDERICK WILLIAM KRUMMACHER, D.D., Author of "Elijah the Tishbite," &c. Translated under the express Sanction of the Author by the Rev. M. G. EASTON, M.A. With a Letter from Dr. Krummacher to his American Readers, and a Portrait. 12mo, Cloth, $1 75.

LAMB'S COMPLETE WORKS. The Works of Charles Lamb. Comprising his Letters, Poems, Essays of Elia, Essays upon Shakspeare, Hogarth, &c., and a Sketch of his Life, with the Final Memorials, by T. NOON TALFOURD. Portrait. 2 vols., 12mo, Cloth, $3 00.

LIVINGSTONE'S SOUTH AFRICA. Missionary Travels and Researches in South Africa; including a Sketch of Sixteen Years' Residence in the Interior of Africa, and a Journey from the Cape of Good Hope to Loando on the West Coast; thence across the Continent, down the River Zambesi, to the Eastern Ocean. By DAVID LIVINGSTONE, LL.D., D.C.L. With Portrait, Maps by Arrowsmith, and numerous Illustrations. 8vo, Cloth, $4 50.

LIVINGSTONE'S ZAMBESI. Narrative of an Expedition to the Zambesi and its Tributaries, and of the Discovery of the Lakes Shirwa and Nyassa. 1858-1864. By DAVID and CHARLES LIVINGSTONE. With Map and Illustrations. 8vo, Cloth, $5 00.

MARCY'S ARMY LIFE ON THE BORDER. Thirty Years of Army Life on the Border. Comprising Descriptions of the Indian Nomads of the Plains; Explorations of New Territory; a Trip across the Rocky Mountains in the Winter; Descriptions of the Habits of Different Animals found in the West, and the Methods of Hunting them; with Incidents in the Life of Different Frontier Men, &c., &c. By Brevet Brigadier-General R. B. MARCY, U.S.A., Author of "The Prairie Traveller." With numerous Illustrations. 8vo, Cloth, Beveled Edges, $3 00.

M'CLINTOCK & STRONG'S CYCLOPÆDIA. Cyclopædia of Biblical, Theological, and Ecclesiastical Literature. Prepared by the Rev. John M'Clintock, D.D., and James Strong, S.T.D. 3 *vols. now ready.* Royal 8vo. Price per vol., Cloth, $5 00; Sheep, $6 00; Half Morocco, $8 00.

MACAULAY'S HISTORY OF ENGLAND. The History of England from the Accession of James II. By Thomas Babington Macaulay. With an Original Portrait of the Author. 5 vols., 8vo, Cloth, $10 00; 12mo, Cloth, $7 50.

MOSHEIM'S ECCLESIASTICAL HISTORY, Ancient and Modern; in which the Rise, Progress, and Variation of Church Power are considered in their Connection with the State of Learning and Philosophy, and the Political History of Europe during that Period. Translated, with Notes, &c., by A. Maclaine, D.D. A new Edition, continued to 1826, by C. Coote, LL.D. 2 vols., 8vo, Cloth, $4 00.

NEVIUS'S CHINA. China and the Chinese: a General Description of the Country and its Inhabitants; its Civilization and Form of Government; its Religious and Social Institutions; its Intercourse with other Nations; and its Present Condition and Prospects. By the Rev. John L. Nevius, Ten Years a Missionary in China. With a Map and Illustrations. 12mo, Cloth, $1 75.

OLIN'S (Dr.) LIFE AND LETTERS. 2 vols., 12mo, Cloth, $3 00.

OLIN'S (Dr.) TRAVELS. Travels in Egypt, Arabia Petræa, and the Holy Land. Engravings. 2 vols., 8vo, Cloth, $3 00.

OLIN'S (Dr.) WORKS. The Works of Stephen Olin, D.D., late President of the Wesleyan University. 2 vols., 12mo, Cloth, $3 00.

OLIPHANT'S CHINA AND JAPAN. Narrative of the Earl of Elgin's Mission to China and Japan, in the Years 1857, '58, '59. By Laurence Oliphant, Private Secretary to Lord Elgin. Illustrations. 8vo, Cloth, $3 50.

OLIPHANT'S (Mrs.) LIFE OF EDWARD IRVING. The Life of Edward Irving, Minister of the National Scotch Church, London. Illustrated by his Journals and Correspondence. By Mrs. Oliphant. Portrait. 8vo, Cloth, $3 50.

PAGE'S LA PLATA. La Plata: the Argentine Confederation and Paraguay. Being a Narrative of the Exploration of the Tributaries of the River La Plata and Adjacent Countries, during the Years 1853, '54, '55, and '56, under the Orders of the United States Government. New Edition, containing Farther Explorations in La Plata, during 1859 and '60. By Thomas J. Page, U.S.N., Commander of the Expeditions. With Map and numerous Engravings. 8vo, Cloth, $5 00.

POETS OF THE NINETEENTH CENTURY. The Poets of the Nineteenth Century. Selected and Edited by the Rev. Robert Aris Willmott. With English and American Additions, arranged by Evert A. Duyckinck, Editor of "Cyclopædia of American Literature." Comprising Selections from the Greatest Authors of the Age. Superbly Illustrated with 132 Engravings from Designs by the most Eminent Artists. In elegant small 4to form, printed on Superfine Tinted Paper, richly bound in extra Cloth, Beveled, Gilt Edges, $6 00; Half Calf, $6 00; Full Turkey Morocco, $10 00.

PRIME'S COINS, MEDALS, AND SEALS. Coins, Medals, and Seals, Ancient and Modern. Illustrated and Described. With a Sketch of the History of Coins and Coinage, Instructions for Young Collectors, Tables of Comparative Rarity, Price-Lists of English and American Coins, Medals, and Tokens, &c., &c. Edited by W. C. Prime, Author of "Boat Life in Egypt and Nubia," "Tent Life in the Holy Land," &c., &c. 8vo, Cloth, $3 50.

SPRING'S SERMONS. Pulpit Ministrations; or, Sabbath Readings. A Series of Discourses on Christian Doctrine and Duty. By Rev. Gardiner Spring, D.D., Pastor of the Brick Presbyterian Church in the City of New York. Portrait on Steel. 2 vols., 8vo, Cloth, $6 00.

SHAKSPEARE. The Dramatic Works of William Shakspeare, with the Corrections and Illustrations of Dr. JOHNSON, G. STEEVENS, and others. Revised by ISAAC REED. Engravings. 6 vols., Royal 12mo, Cloth, $9 00.

SMILES'S LIFE OF THE STEPHENSONS. The Life of George Stephenson, and of his Son, Robert Stephenson; comprising, also, a History of the Invention and Introduction of the Railway Locomotive. By SAMUEL SMILES, Author of "Self-Help," &c. With Steel Portraits and numerous Illustrations. 8vo, Cloth, $3 00.

SMILES'S HISTORY OF THE HUGUENOTS. The Huguenots: their Settlements, Churches, and Industries in England and Ireland. By SAMUEL SMILES. With an Appendix relating to the Huguenots in America. Crown 8vo, Cloth, Beveled, $1 75.

SMILES'S SELF-HELP. Self-Help; with Illustrations of Character, Conduct, and Perseverance. By SAMUEL SMILES. New Edition, Revised and Enlarged. 12mo, Cloth.

SPEKE'S AFRICA. Journal of the Discovery of the Source of the Nile. By Captain JOHN HANNING SPEKE, Captain H. M. Indian Army, Fellow and Gold Medalist of the Royal Geographical Society, Hon. Corresponding Member and Gold Medalist of the French Geographical Society, &c. With Maps and Portraits and numerous Illustrations, chiefly from Drawings by Captain GRANT. 8vo, Cloth, uniform with Livingstone, Barth, Burton, &c., $4 00.

STRICKLAND'S (Miss) QUEENS OF SCOTLAND. Lives of the Queens of Scotland and English Princesses connected with the Regal Succession of Great Britain. By AGNES STRICKLAND. 8 vols., 12mo, Cloth, $12 00.

THE STUDENT'S HISTORIES.
    France. Engravings. 12mo, Cloth, $2 00.
    Gibbon. Engravings. 12mo, Cloth, $2 00.
    Greece. Engravings. 12mo, Cloth, $2 00.
    Hume. Engravings. 12mo, Cloth, $2 00.
    Rome. By Liddell. Engravings. 12mo, Cloth, $2 00.
    Old Testament History. Engravings. 12mo, Cloth, $2 00.
    New Testament History. Engravings. 12mo, Cloth, $2 00.
    Strickland's Queens of England. Abridged. Engravings. 12mo, Cloth, $2 00.

TENNYSON'S COMPLETE POEMS. The Complete Poems of Alfred Tennyson, Poet Laureate. With numerous Illustrations by Eminent Artists, and Three Characteristic Portraits. 8vo, Paper, 50 cts.; Cloth, $1 00.

THOMSON'S LAND AND THE BOOK. The Land and the Book; or, Biblical Illustrations drawn from the Manners and Customs, the Scenes and the Scenery of the Holy Land. By W. M. THOMSON, D.D., Twenty-five Years a Missionary of the A.B.C.F.M. in Syria and Palestine. With two elaborate Maps of Palestine, an accurate Plan of Jerusalem, and several hundred Engravings, representing the Scenery, Topography, and Productions of the Holy Land, and the Costumes, Manners, and Habits of the People. 2 large 12mo vols., Cloth, $5 00.

TICKNOR'S HISTORY OF SPANISH LITERATURE. With Criticisms on the particular Works, and Biographical Notices of Prominent Writers. 3 vols., 8vo, Cloth, $5 00.

VÁMBÉRY'S CENTRAL ASIA. Travels in Central Asia. Being the Account of a Journey from Teheran across the Turkoman Desert, on the Eastern Shore of the Caspian, to Khiva, Bokhara, and Samarcand, performed in the Year 1863. By ARMINIUS VÁMBÉRY, Member of the Hungarian Academy of Pesth, by whom he was sent on this Scientific Mission. With Map and Woodcuts. 8vo, Cloth, $4 50.

ENGLISHMAN'S GREEK CONCORDANCE. The Englishman's Greek Concordance of the New Testament: being an Attempt at a Verbal Connection between the Greek and the English Texts; including a Concordance to the Proper Names, with Indexes, Greek-English and English-Greek. 8vo, Cloth, $5 00.

WOOD'S HOMES WITHOUT HANDS. Homes Without Hands: being a Description of the Habitations of Animals, classed according to their Principle of Construction. By J. G. WOOD, M.A., F.L.S., Author of "Illustrated Natural History." With about 140 Illustrations, engraved by G. Pearson, from Original Designs made by F. W. Keyl and E. A. Smith, under the Author's Superintendence. 8vo, Cloth, Beveled Edges, $4 50.

WILKINSON'S ANCIENT EGYPTIANS. A Popular Account of their Manners and Customs, condensed from his larger Work, with some New Matter. Illustrated with 500 Woodcuts. 2 vols., 12mo, Cloth, $3 50.

MAURY'S (M. F.) PHYSICAL GEOGRAPHY OF THE SEA. The Physical Geography of the Sea, and Its Meteorology. By M. F. MAURY, LL.D., late U.S.N. The Eighth Edition, Revised and greatly Enlarged. 8vo, Cloth, $4 00.

ANTHON'S SMITH'S DICTIONARY OF ANTIQUITIES. A Dictionary of Greek and Roman Antiquities. Edited by WILLIAM SMITH, LL.D., and Illustrated by numerous Engravings on Wood. Third American Edition, carefully Revised, and containing, also, numerous additional Articles relative to the Botany, Mineralogy, and Zoology of the Ancients. By CHARLES ANTHON, LL.D. Royal 8vo, Sheep extra, $6 00.

ANTHON'S CLASSICAL DICTIONARY. Containing an Account of the principal Proper Names mentioned in Ancient Authors, and intended to elucidate all the Important Points connected with the Geography, History, Biography, Mythology, and Fine Arts of the Greeks and Romans; together with an Account of the Coins, Weights, and Measures of the Ancients, with Tabular Values of the same. Royal 8vo, Sheep extra, $6 00.

DWIGHT'S (REV. DR.) THEOLOGY. Theology Explained and Defended, In a Series of Sermons. By TIMOTHY DWIGHT, S.T.D., LL.D. With a Memoir of the Life of the Author. Portrait. 4 vols., 8vo, Cloth, $8 00.

FOWLER'S ENGLISH LANGUAGE. The English Language in Its Elements and Forms. With a History of Its Origin and Development, and a full Grammar. Designed for Use In Colleges and Schools. Revised and Enlarged. By WILLIAM C FOWLER, LL.D., late Professor in Amherst College. 8vo, Cloth, $2 50.

GIESELER'S ECCLESIASTICAL HISTORY. A Text-Book of Church History. By Dr. JOHN C. L. GIESELER. Translated from the Fourth Revised German Edition by SAMUEL DAVIDSON, LL.D., and Rev. JOHN WINSTANLEY HULL, M.A. A New American Edition, Revised and Edited by Rev. HENRY B. SMITH, D.D., Professor in the Union Theological Seminary, New York. Four Volumes ready. (*Vol. V. in Press.*) 8vo, Cloth, $2 25 per vol.

GODWIN'S (PARKE) HISTORY OF FRANCE. The History of France. From the Earliest Times to the French Revolution of 1789. By PARKE GODWIN. Vol. I. (Ancient Gaul). 8vo, Cloth, $3 00.

HALL'S (ROBERT) WORKS. The Complete Works of Robert Hall; with a brief Memoir of his Life, by Dr. GREGORY, and Observations on his Character as a Preacher, by Rev. JOHN FOSTER. Edited by OLINTHUS GREGORY, LL.D., and Rev. JOSEPH BELCHER. Portrait. 4 vols., 8vo, Cloth, $8 00.

HAMILTON'S (SIR WILLIAM) WORKS. Discussions on Philosophy and Literature, Education and University Reform. Chiefly from the *Edinburgh Review.* Corrected, Vindicated, and Enlarged, in Notes and Appendices. By Sir WILLIAM HAMILTON, Bart. With an Introductory Essay, by Rev. ROBERT TURNBULL, D.D. 8vo, Cloth, $3 00.

HUMBOLDT'S COSMOS. Cosmos: a Sketch of a Physical Description of the Universe. By ALEXANDER VON HUMBOLDT. Translated from the German, by E. C. OTTÉ. 5 vols., 12mo, Cloth, $6 25.

ROBINSON'S GREEK LEXICON OF THE TESTAMENT. A Greek and English Lexicon of the New Testament. By EDWARD ROBINSON, D.D., LL.D., late Professor of Biblical Literature in the Union Theological Seminary, New York. A New Edition, Revised, and in great part Rewritten. Royal 8vo, Cloth, $6 00.

www.ingramcontent.com/pod-product-compliance
Lightning Source LLC
Chambersburg PA
CBHW021939110726
47901CB00003B/900